THE LIGHT BRINGER

THE DRAGON GATE SERIES
VOLUME II

RANDY ELLEFSON

Evermore Press
GAITHERSBURG, MARYLAND

Evermore Press, LLC
Gaithersburg, Maryland
www.evermorepress.org

Publisher's Note: This book includes fictional passages. All names, characters, locations, and incidents are products of the author's imagination, or have been used fictitiously. Any semblance to actual persons living or dead, locales, or events is coincidental and not intended by the author.

The Light Bringer / Randy Ellefson. -- 1st ed.
ISBN 978-1-946995-55-1 (paperback)
ISBN 978-1-946995-56-8 (hardcover)

Contents

ACKNOWLEDGEMENTS

Special thanks to Kristi-Lee Landrey, Sandra Chiwike, and
Erica Thajeb

Maps by Randy Ellefson

Cover design by Miblart

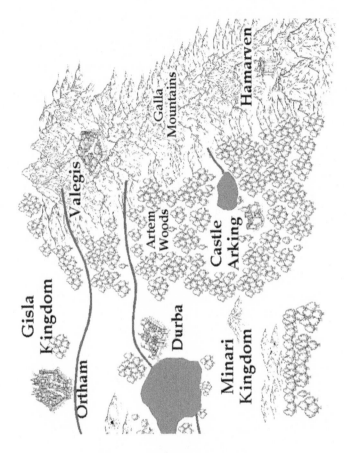

Map of Minari Kingdom, on Rovell
Color map: http://bit.ly/DGS2Map1

TO QUEST OR NOT TO QUEST

A vortex of multi-colored, changing lights, swirling wind, and a thunderous whooshing noise surrounded Anna. Powerless to stop what was happening, she noticed a knot of dread and worry replace the tingling in her stomach. Her eyes darted down, seeking the surface that she felt her feet standing on, its invisibility adding to her disorientation. Across from her stood Ryan, with Matt and Eric to the right and left, all facing each other in a circle, their shocked expressions likely matching hers. Eric mouthed "shit" at the shared realization that, just as they had feared, they were being summoned from Earth for another quest they could not refuse, and which could get them killed.

Barely in time, she remembered to put one arm across her breasts and the other over her privates as her Earth clothes vanished and she stood nude a moment. Then a long white robe covered her, matching boots on her feet, an amulet that showed one person healing another replacing the usual pendant she wore around her neck, her long blonde hair in a tight braid. She was once again to be the priestess Eriana of Coreth, the Light Bringer. Her gray eyes went to the others, seeing Ryan in his golden armor and helmet for his role as a knight, a large sword on one hip.

Eric wore dark leather, a bandoleer of knives across his chest, and a shorter sword hanging from his belt, where a rope had was tied around his waist. And Matt stood in a black wizard's robe, a bag of spell books slung over one shoulder, a staff in one hand.

In the week since the planet Honyn had summoned the "Ellorian Champions," as they'd been called, to save them from dragons. The episode had already started to feel like none of it had really happened, a feeling that had grown when they told their friend Jack minutes ago, his face registering disbelief on hearing about their quest with elves, dwarves, dragons, ogres, gods, magic, and supernatural healing all being real—at least on another planet. But he had just seen them vanish from Anna's Maryland apartment. And there was no denying that a quest was happening again right now.

As the summoning spell ended, Anna simultaneously noticed the circle of fading blue light surrounding them and a thunderous banging on wood to one side, the cacophony reverberating in a large, dark, enclosed space she could not make out. A sense of immediate danger filled the air. Her white robe caught the light and made her feel like a target, a feeling that worsened when an arrow struck nearby and bounced to her feet with a clatter. She thought it seemed poorly made for reasons she had no time to ponder.

Words etched blue fire faded from the gray stone beneath her boots. Around them stood the rest of the Quest Ring that had summoned them, chest-high pillars of stone also covered in fading, glowing runes. Beyond them stood a red-robed wizard in his twenties, his long black hair disheveled, intense, wide eyes moving from one of them to the next. No one else seemed nearby except for whoever—or whatever—was violently pounding on doors somewhere beyond the wizard. Then Anna saw torchlight through a wide crack in a splintering door as intruders came closer to breaking it down. From the racket, several other doors were nearby and nearly breached.

"Ellorians!" said the wizard, stepping toward them.

"What is happening?" Eric raised a throwing knife he'd yanked from his black leather, seeming as in command of what to do as ever. Anna trusted his judgement and martial arts skilled more than the other two. If anyone could get them out of whatever was happening, Eric could. Hearing his matter-of-fact approach provided the first sense that they would get the chaos around them under control.

"We are under attack," the wizard replied, stopping his advance.

"By what?" Anna asked, backing away. As the blue light faded, her eyes adjusted and to see that a large, dilapidated hall of grey limestone stretched from left to right before them, scattered oak furniture casting shadows, torn but unfaded tapestries hanging askew from the walls. They appeared to be standing in an alcove set aside for the Quest Ring, with no exits from the big hall except those that had something bashing in the barred doors.

As if noticing what she had, Eric asked a better question. "Is there a way out of here?"

The wizard answered Anna instead. "Ogres. Goblins. They found me before I could summon you. I am surprised I made it this far."

"The exit?" Ryan demanded, sword in hand. Was he more willing to use it now? He had hesitated to fight so much on the last quest that Anna wasn't sure he could be trusted to help. But she saw only alarm and determination on his handsome face. An aggressive posture, instead of a cringing one, further reassured her. Maybe he had changed after all.

The wizard who summoned them shook his head. Anna noticed he looked exhausted and beaten, his robe stained with mud. "You will have to kill them. I have spent my energy getting here and casting the spell to summon you."

As he said it, he pitched forward to crack his head on one of the pillars, an arrow protruding from his back. Eric jumped forward faster than Anna and helped drag him inside the Quest Ring, which had now gone dark.

"Enurarki," said Matt, and the crystal atop his staff shone with light that surrounded them. "Still works," he said, sounded as relieved as Anna felt. Only now did she fully realize her fears that few of them would be capable of playing their unwanted roles again. Matt could cast some spells, but the most fearsome he did came from the staff.

"Good," said Eric. "Ryan, stand in front. Your armor can shield us. Matt, can you do something to make them back off?"

"Let me think," replied Matt. Ryan took up a position in front of them.

The injured man looked up with painfilled eyes and clutched Eric's leather sleeve. "The quest. I must tell you why you're here."

"In a minute."

Anna knelt, wondering how to heal this man. She didn't know the gods of this world and said as much when Eric asked her to do it. How could she call on a god to send healing power through her into this man? "Wait," she said, looking at his hand, where a silver ring with three diamonds curled around one finger, indicating how many healing spells were still in it. "The Trinity Ring."

"Good call," said Eric. "Hold on. Gotta pull the arrow out or it won't do much good." He made an apologetic face at the injured wizard and then pulled the arrow from his chest amid a cry of pain, which mixed with the hoarse bellows of the attackers and a shattering of more wood. He spoke a word and a soft glow spread from his hand over the man. Both the arrow wound and the gash on his head vanished. He sat up, looking grateful and relieved. Another arrow struck nearby.

"Matt?" Anna eyed the intruders as they open more of the door. She saw greenish skin, half naked bodies, and hideous faces with extended jaws, two large teeth jutting up like on a wild boar, bulbous noses, and random tufts of unkempt black hair over thick, menacing brows. Equally crude cudgels, maces, and swords threatened maiming and death.

"I'm trying to think of a good spell." Matt fumbled with the bag and pulled out a thick spell book with black leather binding and gold lettering on it.

"Try faster," said Eric, rising to join Ryan. Anna saw herself and their summoner in the line of fire and backed away so that Ryan's body shielded hers. She gestured for the man to join her, but he spoke from where he was instead.

"The quest," began the wizard, "you must succeed to restore peace. You are to—" An arrow struck him in the eye and flung him on his back.

Anna gasped. "Eric!" The rogue looked back and came over to drag the man to her. Sightless eyes stared at the ceiling. "The ring. Use the most powerful spell." All but her wore an identical Trinity Ring.

"Yeah," he said, yanking the arrow from the wizard's skull with a grimace and then spoke the word. The same soft glow lit the wounds, but no healing occurred. He swore.

"What?" Ryan asked, not looking back an arrow bounced off his golden armor.

"Ring didn't work. He's dead."

"Most powerful of the spells?" Ryan asked, as the ring was named for having three of them, each of different strengths, a specific command for each.

"Yeah."

"What does that mean about the quest?" Anna asked. "He didn't tell us what we need to do."

Eric met her gaze. "Then I don't think we're bound by it."

"We can go home?" Ryan asked over one shoulder.

"I think so. Only one way to know. There's no one else here to tell us."

Anna wondered if he was right. If no one told them the quest, they obviously couldn't do it and were not trapped here by the summoning spell until it was complete like usual. She remembered something about there being a time limit in that they needed to be told the quest shortly after being summoned, but she thought it was an hour or more. They didn't have that much time. As if to prove her point, a loud crashed heralded the arrivals of the goblins, bellowing as they charged, several eight-foot-tall ogres with two small horns and mottled red skin among them.

"Matt!" Eric yelled. He rose and quickly threw small knives that flew into the darkness to disappear. The only indication of success was a body, then another, falling face down on the floor to be trampled by the mob coming to kill them.

"Going with the shield instead!" Matt yelled.

Anna wished he had done it sooner, but the shield would only prevent them from being reached. Whatever spell he had been thinking of before may have offered a chance to repel the attackers and a chance to escape this place. Now they were about to be trapped within a shield, but it was better than nothing.

White light sprang from the top of Matt's staff, outward, and then cascaded down around them just outside the circle of pillars to touch the floor, giving them ten feet of protection. The shield was transparent save for the soft white glow. They didn't have to wait long to see if it was working. Two arrows bounced harmlessly off, then another. A second door shattered open and more foes arrived, charging. A third door would soon break down. They were not getting out of here easily. The goblins and ogres, and a few other creatures Anna couldn't identify, slowed as they neared, coming to a standstill. The four Earth friends backed up to the center of the ring. Anna stared at the disgusting attackers and shuddered, looking away from one creepy killer to the next. Assuming the remaining door held an equal number at bay, she guessed a hundred were here.

As they silently stood, the last door crashed open and the crowd deepened, nearly filling the hall. The room grew brighter for the additional torches, which allowed her to see the mob parting as someone pushed forward from the rear. The individual finally stopped before them, taut black skin under the black chainmail with silver engravings on it, a long bow over one shoulder, a sleek narrow blade on one hip. Haughty, red, slanted eyes stared coldly at them in a face that was as sinister as it was beautiful, long white hair pulled back into a ponytail that let the sharply pointed ears be visible. He bore a long scar on one cheek. No one had to say it out loud, for they all recognized a dark elf from their last quest.

The dark elf's eyes jolted Anna on meeting her gaze, as he appraised first one of them and then another. He nodded in apparent satisfaction while looking at the dead wizard behind them. Then his eyes alertly scanned the perimeter of Matt's spell and Anna went cold. He was planning something, she knew, and it didn't take long to learn what. With a gesture, he indicated they were to be surrounded. The goblins squeezed themselves around the Quest Ring, which stood only a few feet from the walls on three sides. The ogres were too big to fit and instead came up beside the dark elf. Anna looked at Matt. The wizard was the only way they would survive this.

"What now?" Anna whispered to Eric, who had proven himself a more efficient planner than the rest of them.

"Attack," said the dark elf in elven, which they all understood thanks to a spell cast on them on their last quest. Those surrounding them began slamming their weapons into the shield, which showed no signs of failing. The elf silently watched, not taking part, a grim smile of anticipation growing. He withdrew the sword from its sheath.

"All those blows are weakening me," observed Matt, his arm shuddered.

Eric nodded. "I think that's what they're counting on."

"They're not intending to capture us," Ryan remarked, speaking loud over the dull thudding of weapons hitting the shield.

Anna knew he was right. Would they just kill her or do something worse than death first? She trembled again.

"Matt," began Eric, fingering a throwing knife, "do we think things can get out through the shield but not in?"

"I'm not sure."

Ryan met Eric's gaze and said, "You know, you and I could easily stab every single the ones on these three sides, especially, because there's no room for them to back up. That would make them stop."

"Wait," said Anna. She had noticed something. "The Quest Ring can send us back if Matt sticks the top of the staff into the hole in one pillar. I just saw it. There." She pointed to a hole with a shape matching the prongs and crystal. The pillar was the one at the back, opposite where the dark elf stood. This didn't surprise her. While the Quest Rings appeared similar, minor variations were apparent, but what they all had in common was a tallest pillar at the rear, opposite the opening they usually arrived facing. They had seen this hole before on the last Quest Ring but never tried it.

"Okay," said Matt, wincing as the blows continued, "but I'm not sure what happens to this shield when I move the staff to do that. It kind of reminds me of an umbrella right now, and if I tilt the staff to do this, maybe one side lifts up? What if it doesn't stop them anymore and they get to us before I can send us back?"

Eric spoke confidently. "It's our only chance. But I have an idea. Matt, get ready to put the staff in the hole. Anna, help and stay in the middle. Both of you. Ryan and I will protect both of you. Ryan, time to test whether we can strike them, but they can't strike us. If it works, we need to attack all the ones back near the hole first."

"Got it," the knight said.

"Hurry," said Matt, voice strained.

"Hold on," said Eric. "Need to demoralize." Anna watched him flick the throwing knife with one hand. It passed through the shield and struck the dark elf in the chest. The elf took a step back, wobbled, and then fell back. Eric pulled out his short sword.

"Wait, start at the front corner," said Ryan. He didn't wait for agreement and thrust his sword between two pillars into the belly of a goblin, which squealed in pain and fell back. Eric began doing the same on the other side. Anna saw the wisdom of the knight's suggestion. The dead bodies would keep those farther back from escaping over them. The two made quick work of it, twenty goblin bodies now surrounding them just outside the Quest Ring, some dead or about to be. Knight and rogue then moved to the front of the alcove and began stabbing at ogres that came within reach.

"Now!" yelled Eric.

Matt began tilting the staff and Anna grabbed hold of the end. She cast one frantic look back and then guided the staff head into the rearmost pillar's hole with both hands, resulting in an audible click. The words of blue fire abruptly ignited, causing the ogres to step back.

"Stay on guard!" Eric yelled to Ryan as he stabbed forward again. "We don't know how fast we're safe from–"

The room disappeared, the now-familiar vortex pulling them into some unknown space between worlds. Anna covered her body with her hands again, since the robe would soon vanish, leaving her nude before her Earth clothes replaced it. Her eyes studiously stayed on Eric's so they didn't wander, especially as the rogue made no attempt to cover himself, not for the first time, and unlike everyone else. She saw looks of relief and something on their faces, maybe satisfaction that they handled it well enough to survive. Time seemed to pass quicker on the return, and she sensed she was sitting down as a final flash of light momentarily blinding her.

CHAPTER TWO

MASTERY

Jack jumped to his feet and stepped back twice, brown eyes darting between the four new arrivals, then around as if to make sure no one else was present. He cut an athletic figure, his brown hair short enough to not move with his activity. A paper towel in one hand, wet and red, dripped onto the hard floor. "You guys scared the crap out of me."

Matt blinked to clear his eyes, noticing that they had returned to Anna's Gaithersburg, Maryland apartment as expected. Everyone was back in the exact spot they'd been in before the summoning. He still sat on the edge of the couch, a laptop before him on the table and still open to the webpage he'd been perusing. Ryan sat on the couch's other side, one hand in the bag of ChexMix he'd been munching on. Eric was back to spinning around in an office chair, though he was stopping himself. Jack had apparently been kneeling beside the dining room chair that Anna now sat in, the glass of red Zinfandel she had been drinking broken on the floor, the red liquid half cleaned up. All of them now wore the same clothes as they had been before disappearing. They were breathing harder, which made him realize he was doing the same.

Adrenaline drove him to his feet. Ryan and Eric rose, too, the former beginning to pace. And yet Anna stayed down, lifting one foot like a cat that had stepped in something. Matt saw spilled wine soaking one white sock, shards of glass in a pile nearby. The symbolism of it struck him. Had their lives become just as fragile?

"Jesus," said Eric, dark eyes assessing them one by one. "Glad that worked."

"Language," Ryan admonished him absently, blue eyes far away as he ran a hand over his face and through his blond hair. He didn't look as big without the golden armor, but he still intimidated. Matt let Ryan's comment about taking the name of the Lord in vain pass. Ryan could have his faith in God if it helped him deal with what they were facing. Besides, maybe everything they'd heard about their entire lives was real after all, including God.

"Everyone okay?" he asked.

Anna sighed and removed the wet sock. "Physically? Yeah. Not sure about the rest of me."

"Yeah," agreed Matt. "That was messed up in so many ways, from the guy getting killed in front of us, to that creepy dark elf. This wasn't anything like the first time. Could you imagine if that had been that way?"

"What happened?" Jack asked, coming to help Anna step away from the broken glass. Before anyone could answer, Ryan stepped up to the kitchen table and grabbed the beer, drinking a little too much. Jack started, "Hey that was—never mind."

Ryan lowered the bottle and flashed an apologetic glance. "Sorry. I need it more than you."

"You guys weren't gone more than five minutes."

Eric filled him in, concluding by observing, "We never even got the name of the wizard who summoned us."

"We don't even know what planet we were on," added Anna, sitting on the couch.

"It could have been Honyn," Matt began, "like the first quest, just to another kingdom or continent. But there's no way to know."

"Mostly," began Ryan, "I'm just glad we're back again, but I feel like we let down whoever needed us. Besides the wizard, I mean. Even though it's not our job to do this stuff. Or it's not supposed to be."

Matt didn't agree out loud because he knew he didn't have to. The real Ellorian Champions were missing, except the wizard Soliander, who he was pretending to be, and who had attacked them on Honyn. They never found out why and might never know. It topped their list of unanswered questions, such as where the real champions were, how he and the others became unwilling substitutes, and what they could do to stop the quests. He had thought about this many times and knew no answers were coming anytime soon. Maybe if they told everyone the truth, they would be left alone.

Eric sat, brow furrowed. "It's been a week since we returned from Honyn, and we've been wondering if that was a one-time quest. I think we have our answer."

Ryan said, "I didn't want to say it out loud."

Matt did. "We've been permanently substituted for the Ellorian Champions and will continuously be summoned in their place, for quests we don't want, can't refuse, and are likely to get killed doing."

He felt bad for saying it out load, as an awful silence descended on the room. He sensed he was the only one who wasn't all that upset by the idea. His life was okay. All of theirs were, too, but none had the potential that he did. The elf Lorian had tested his affinity for magic on the last quest and revealed how naturally talented Matt was. He had never felt powerful before. Of course, he'd never been terrified either. Not like that. He'd been bullied and beaten up a few times growing up, just like Eric, but while his friend had become a martial artist who could now kick seemingly anyone's ass, whether on Earth or not, Matt was no such thing. Thin, wiry, not exactly strong like Ryan, Matt had only intelligence as a natural asset. And it led to him getting beaten up.

He sat and began furiously typing on his laptop.

"What are you writing?" Anna asked, peeking over his shoulder.

"The spells I just looked up, before I forget."

"Not sure it will do you any good here."

"You never know, and I hope you're wrong."

Ryan said, "I hope you won't need them."

"Me, too, but I need to start memorizing spells on these quests and writing them down once here. Honestly, you guys should, too. I wish those spell books would come back with me."

Eric said, "I'll wait until it matters, like after magic works on Earth."

Matt shook his head. "We already know it does because we wouldn't get summoned without it."

"True, but it appears to not be quite the same thing. Someone is casting it elsewhere, and the Quest Rings are pulling us or sending us back. Maybe it's only one-way."

"That would suck," Matt blurted out. "I mean, how am I supposed to get better at it if I can't practice? As we just saw, there may be no chance on a quest."

Jack had put the wet paper towel in the trash and now asked, "What if you could stop people from telling you what the quest is? Then you could send yourselves home without having to do it. I mean, I realize it makes you look bad, but you're not the real champions anyway. Why do you have to maintain their reputations? It's not your problem. In fact, why not just admit you aren't them?"

Eric sighed. "You have a point, but I'm not sure it would be wise to say we're imposters. It raises questions we can't answer. During the Dragon Gate quest, everyone was clearly impressed and gave us a lot of respect, maybe even leeway. I think we might end up in danger if we confess. I mean, these guys have a fearsome reputation that might keep some people from messing with us, if they thought to try."

"It didn't stop Cirion," Anna remarked.

Matt agreed with her. The dashing rogue had led a band of mercenaries to Castle Darlonon to try closing the Dragon Gate before they could do it, causing problems for them. While Eric was right, there would always be people who weren't intimidated by the Ellorians. He said as much.

"Fair enough," admitted Eric, "and I agree it might not be our job to maintain their reputation. I just think it's safer right now. Maybe I'm wrong."

"Maybe Jack is right," Ryan suggested. "Let's think this through. What would happen if we refused the quest by not letting them tell us about it?"

Jack offered, "Run out the clock? How long do they have to tell you? Do they know? Do you?"

"Not really," Matt admitted. "We didn't exactly get an instruction manual. I don't think Lorian said much about this did he?"

Eric pursed his lips. "I thought he said something like an hour. I would imagine it gets awkward keeping us from knowing so most people might tell us immediately. This guy certainly tried. Just wasn't fast enough. But not knowing this makes it harder to stall after we arrive without seeming weird about it. It's also likely that everyone who does a summons knows this and it's only us that do not. They would likely be in a hurry to bind us to the quest by telling us what it's for."

Anna remarked, "That wizard who just died seemed urgent."

"Not urgent enough," said Ryan. "Could you imagine if he'd said it? We would have been stuck there with all of those... what were they? I recognized ogres, and the dark elf. I'm not sure we would have gotten out of there."

Matt smiled without humor. There was no way Ryan was ever forgetting what an ogre looked like after their encounter on Honyn.

"I thought the other things might be goblins," Eric said, and images suddenly flashed in Matt's head.

"Yeah, they were goblins," he asserted.

Jack asked, "How can you be so sure?"

Though Jack hadn't been there, they had told him about the Honyn quest, but Matt reminded him, "Remember, when Soliander attacked me, he did that mind meld spell on me and I ended up with a bunch of his memories. Most of the time I have no idea what's in my head from that, but sometimes when we're talking, images, scenes, and info pop up. Those were goblins. Now that I think about it, there was actually an orc or two in the back, but they never got close enough for me to really see them."

"A motley group of monsters," muttered Anna, shuddering.

"Let's go back to this idea of refusing a quest," said Jack, sitting at the dining room table and ignoring the mess he had been cleaning. "Maybe you can tell them that something urgent is going on back home and you really need to return."

Eric said, "They would just summon us again and the excuse would be unlikely to work a second time. Besides, they have their own urgency that brought us there."

Anna said, "Lorian made it clear that the worlds interact with each other, so if we do this, everyone will hear about it soon and they'll know we're lying."

Matt nodded, more memories surfacing as he pictured the real champions arriving on one world after another, some of them saying they had heard about a quest on another planet. It was common knowledge that some traveling between the worlds happened. "I can confirm this is true. The worlds interact."

Jack suggested, "Tell them not to say anything."

Eric shook his head. "Wouldn't work for long. I mean, we could try it a few times, but I don't think it's a long-term solution."

Matt had to agree. It would make them look bad. Protecting the reputation of the real champions was one thing, but now they were it and would give themselves a reputation. They were benefiting from the real reputation now and would create a new one that would do more harm to themselves than anyone else. The risk wasn't worth it. Not yet, anyway.

"What *is* a long-term solution?" Anna asked.

"Getting out of the quest cycle," said Ryan. "We just don't know how they did it." He looked at Matt. "Anything pop into your mind when I said that?"

The techie searched his thoughts and impressions. "No. I don't know how we were substituted."

"In the meantime," began Eric, "I think we need to prepare as much as we can. After we returned to Stonehenge, we only had so much time to quiet everything down here, and we weren't sure we'd be summoned a second time. Now we know this is ongoing. We have to train for whatever comes up. There isn't much we can do about magic or healing, but we can all learn swordsmanship, martial arts, how to handle a knife, and just basic self-defense. How to use a bow."

"And ride a horse," added Ryan. "I've been riding for a decade, and all the stuff I do at the Renaissance Festival acting like a knight made me even better. But you guys only have basic skills. No offense. If we're fleeing at a gallop or have to jump over even something small like a fallen tree, you're probably falling off and getting hurt or killed."

"Maybe I have a spell for that," Matt joked, and they all laughed, which felt like a welcome relief from the tension. Sometimes it didn't seem like they had much to laugh about anymore, and if this continued, which was likely, that might just get worse. He wasn't catching up on things like TV shows he was missing episodes of, not that this was important, but that was the point to him. When were they supposed to have down time and just relax, get some escapism?

"Well," Anna began, "I've always wanted to ride, so I'm game. I'm not sure I can afford it, though."

Ryan shook his head. "No, look, I'm paying for everything we need, lessons, gear, whatever. We can't let money get in the way. You know I've never used my parent's money for much, but that's changing. They don't check my credit cards anyway. They may never even notice."

"I agree," Eric said, always practical. "We don't have time to care about anyone's feelings about Ryan picking up the tab, okay? We need each other and we all have to take this stuff seriously."

Everyone agreed aloud. Like the others, Matt had never asked for anything from Ryan, whose parents were rich, but he'd never turned down something either. He wasn't going to start now. Eric was right. He usually was.

Ryan said, "I need somewhere to send things we order online, which is probably most of it. Anna?"

Her eyebrows rose in question before falling. "Of course. Send it here. Not a lot of room, but we'll think of something."

"A storage unit. I'll get on that."

"There's an archery range at Lake Needwood," offered Jack. "I pass it all the time. I don't know if they do lessons, but I can look into stuff like this, especially while you guys are gone."

"Great. What else might we need?" Matt asked. "Gear doesn't matter because we can't take it with us, so it's only stuff we can use to train ourselves."

Eric, who worked as martial arts instructor, said, "I can teach everyone hand-to-hand fighting and self-defense. That's an easy one."

Matt asked, "Can you teach us at your job?"

"Good question. I think so, but that would require Ryan paying for it when that isn't necessary. The owner wouldn't let me teach people who aren't paying."

"We'll think of something," said Ryan. "I could teach a lot of the horseback riding, but I probably can't unless I have my own horses and a ring. I do have a horse, just the one, but it's stabled elsewhere, and I doubt they would let me teach there with going through some sort of approval process that we don't have time for. Besides, it would be a job, and I would just keep disappearing, getting myself fired, so it doesn't make any sense. I want each of you to have one-on-one lessons, but if we do lessons every day, it might also raise questions."

"Every day?" Anna asked.

"The faster the better."

"Okay, I can't disagree with that. It's just a lot."

Matt agreed. Maybe they were getting carried away. How were they supposed to live their lives and keep jobs? And starting all of that physical training wasn't something he was going to handle well, but he didn't want to admit it. He had complained about physical exertion enough times to them that he felt like Eric was smirking at him even though he wasn't.

He said, "I think we have to pace ourselves. Some of us aren't exactly in good shape. I guess we need to change that."

"Physical conditioning," began Eric with a straight face. "Strength training, at least a little. I can handle some of that. We might need gym memberships or something."

"Adding to my list," said Ryan, typing on his phone. "There are some great gyms in the area."

Anna suggested, "The fitness training classes I took means I can help with conditioning. We might want to start a jogging routine, for example. Get our cardio better. We will never be in control of whether we have horses or something. We might have to do a lot of walking, even running at times."

Eric observed. "I think we need to be prepared for anything, as much as we can be."

"You know," began Ryan, "on the first quest, Eric and Matt knowing sign language seemed pretty useful for communicating when we needed to be quiet. How hard would it be to teach us?"

Matt nodded. He had learned it from his deaf mother and taught a curious Eric years ago. That hadn't gone smoothly, but they'd had time, unlike now. There was no real crash course in it. They would have to work on it often. "Not hard, but it may take a long time to get good at it, and there's no spell for it, I don't think, like when Lorian cast one to teach us all a bunch of languages at once. We should definitely get started for at least the basics."

Anna admitted, "I'm feeling a little overwhelmed, guys. How will we have the time for all of this?"

Matt liked his career as a software developer, but maybe it needed to wait. He was only a few years into it anyway. "Yeah, I was thinking the same thing. Ryan doesn't need a job. We aren't so lucky."

"Do you think you should quit?" Ryan asked. "I can pay bills and other stuff."

Seeing dubious expressions, Eric shook his head. "I don't know. I think it's premature. I mean, someone has now summoned us twice, and we have every reason to believe we will be again, but what if it's a week? Or a month?"

"My gut tells me it won't be," Anna said.

Eric sighed. "I know. But we can't quit yet. That might cause scrutiny we want to avoid. That said, we could request some time off, as if we're bothered by some of what happened when we disappeared from Stonehenge. The world knows about that one, but not this one tonight, and they never will. But you know something? None of us would handle more than a few hours of something like horseback riding at first anyway. Our bodies have to get used to it over this first week, especially. It was rough when we were on Honyn. I think we're fine for now, and we have at least a couple days of making arrangements to do. I think we need to get started and not go overboard too fast."

Matt agreed and kept some of his worries to himself. Except for Eric pretending to be Andier of Roir, the Silver-Tongued Rogue, each of the others had struggled with their roles on the Honyn. Andier's ability to smooth talk people, read situations, and use his street smarts to his advantage had fit Eric's past as a juvenile delinquent, when he broke into places, stole for food and money, and lived by his wits until being jailed. It made him believable as Andier, a man skilled at disarming traps, picking locks, and scaling walls. Eric's rock climbing, parkour skills, martial arts aptitude, and knife throwing ability—honed at RenFest—had made him almost oddly suited for the role of Andier, but the others hadn't been so lucky.

On the first quest to Honyn, Ryan had nearly gotten Eric killed over his own issues. An expert horseman who played a knight at RenFest every summer, Ryan gave the appearance of being suited to play a knight. Muscular and tall, he knew how to don armor, swing a sword, use a lance, and speak in a commanding voice meant to impress. But it was all a show. Now he had to be a real knight on their unwanted quests, playing the role of Lord Orrin of Andor, the Dragon Slayer.

Aside from knowing nothing of real swordsmanship and tactics, Ryan had been afraid of actual violence or hurting anyone since they had known him, but they had never understood why—until the ogre battle. His fear that he had nearly killed one ogre in self-defense led him to heal it with the Trinity Ring on one hand. It had risen and almost killed Eric. Only in the aftermath did he finally admit that he was the one who had paralyzed his brother Daniel when goofing around as children, the guilt haunting him ever since—and causing his attitude.

He had gotten past that as that quest continued, finally killing the dragon who posed the greatest threat to them, but Matt still wondered if the big guy had really conquered his phobia. On this second quest just now, Matt had felt relieved to see Ryan stabbing the goblins threatening them, so maybe they didn't have to worry about Ryan's conscious putting them at risk anymore.

Anna was another problem that might have been resolved, but he couldn't be sure. An atheist, she had been visibly annoyed to discover her own role – the Priestess Eriana of Coreth, the Light Bringer, a healer who channeled the power of gods to save the dying. How could a woman who didn't believe in such things change her heart so fully that a god chose her as a vessel for their power? Her transformation had been slow and nearly as deadly in its delays as Ryan's, but Matt was the one she had finally healed at the end, so he knew she could do it. But every time they arrived on a planet, she had to reach a god she had never heard of to make contact. Someone had given her a scroll of information and help with this the first time. Just now, that wizard who summoned them had died partly because Anna had no idea what gods to ask for help from. Without these Trinity Rings all but she wore, this could be a serious problem.

And Matt wasn't fine in his role as the Majestic Magus, Soliander of Aranor, one of the most powerful wizards on any world. He hadn't known a thing about magic. Only training from the elf Lorian had made it possible to summon power using Soliander's staff. Matt had relied on it right up until the end when it had been knocked from his hand and failure to cast a spell had meant death. Not having the staff on Earth had hindered his ability to perform magic here. How was he supposed to practice? Did he need to be terrified to do anything without it? Was magic even working here? He sighed and tried to ignore his worries.

For the rest of the night, they sat together, often not speaking, each with an agreed upon aspect of training to develop on behalf of them all. While Matt had taught sign language informally and leisurely to Eric, they needed something faster, and he soon used Ryan's credit card to purchase a number of manuals for him as a teacher and the others as students. Jack researched archery locations, instructors, gear that matched the medieval or Renaissance periods, and ordered more supplies, including practice targets of their own. Eric planned a curriculum of karate and other disciplines to teach them, then purchased some training equipment they could use away from his job as needed. Ryan researched horses he could buy, for the "school horses" typically available were not good enough and would not compare to the battle trained mounts he would expect them to be given. Anna looked into physical conditioning and strength, including endurance, running speed, and flexibility, which Eric's training would help with.

She finally asked, "Where are we going to do some of this, guys?"

They sat in silence for a minute, and then Ryan said, "I have an idea."

———— ● · ● ————

Ryan pursed his lips, waiting for Eric's response. They stood inside the partially empty guest house at the estate of Ryan's parents in Potomac, Maryland, where mostly rich people lived. Outside, tall trees loomed in nearly every direction, just far enough away from the house to prevent falling leaves from clogging gutters. The shade they cast moved with the breeze so that sunlight danced across the hardwood floors inside, never staying constant. There were no curtains or hardware to hang them, or furniture. His parents had renovated the place years ago, having all the walls painted, new cabinets added, the whole bit, but then they stopped short of finishing it when Ryan had paralyzed Daniel so long ago. The thought made him sigh, for the building was frozen in time back to that period and it always brought unpleasant memories back. Even so, it seemed the best option for what he and his friends needed.

"I think this will work," Eric admitted, looking around.

Ryan felt a little relieved at the reaction. He admired Eric even before this business with being champions arose, but his friend's critical thinking skill wasn't something he'd really noticed before. Eric would find the flaw in just about anything. While the others had good ideas, no one picked them apart like his former juvenile delinquent friend.

Sometimes he wondered if that past was where Eric got the skill from. Had breaking into places, stealing, and making his way by his wits made him not just street smart, but savvy? Eric thought things through with a speed and precision that would have made Ryan jealous if he really cared about being that way himself. In his mind, Eric was their leader, though Ryan was supposed to act like it on arriving for a quest, or any other time they needed to impress on people how important and powerful they supposedly were as the Ellorian Champions. He was the most imposing for his height and muscular physique, the golden and gilded armor of Lord Korrin of Andor an impressive sight.

More people wanted to talk to him, too, for Eric was supposed to be Andier of Roir, the Silver-Tongue Rogue, with a reputation for swindling people or tricking them into revealing too much. Matt as the Majestic Magus Soliander of Aranor just scared everyone. And Anna as the Light Bringer Eriana of Coreth, who saved countless lives by channeling a god's healing power through her, inspired reverence, respect, and awe, much of it causing people to be very polite and keep some distance.

All of this left Ryan to receive the exuberance of desperate people grateful for their arrival to save them. He was the showman, too, having played a knight for years at the local Renaissance Festival for fun, so beyond knowing how to don armor and swing a sword (just not for real), he was best suited to the apparent-leader role. That Eric held that position behind the scenes was fine with him. They just had to stay on the same page.

And so Ryan sighed in relief on hearing Eric accept the use of the guest house as a training area. On the same property where his parents and he lived with his brother, the building stood two stories and had its own three-car garage, driveway, and gate with unmanned security. An acre of land, with a line of thick pine trees, separated it from the main house. As long as they kept quiet, everything but the horseback riding could be done here without his family even knowing they were using it. The property had some empty acres where archery could happen, too.

Looking at some old Persian rugs the family was storing stacked atop each other in the living room, Ryan said, "I think we have to clean it up a little. Use the dining room for storage due to the chandelier being in the way anyway. Can't swing anything in there. We can move some of the other unused furniture there, create the spaces we need."

"Is there a basement?" Eric asked.

"Yeah. And it's got some big open space, depending on what's been put down there."

"Let's have a look."

They soon decided the first floor would have minimal equipment in case anyone happened by, like the gardeners and others who maintained the property. They didn't want suspicions forming. Gym mats and exercise gear would occupy the basement that would be kept dark when not in use. They realized that, if anyone did catch their cars here, that maybe they should pretend they were using it as a place to hang out, and they would need somewhere to sit anyway. Some couches, tables, and an entertainment system would help convince anyone they weren't up to anything weird. Matt, being a techie, could set up a security camera to alert them to anyone dropping by if they were downstairs. The need for such a ploy became apparent sooner than expected.

The front door opened with a bang and Ryan's younger brother rolled his wheelchair over the threshold and into the foyer, then the living room, from where he smirked at them as they sat on the pile of Persian rugs in the adjacent dining room. His long black hair lay in a ponytail over one shoulder, tattoos visible on his arms, one of which he had full use of. He was a quadriplegic thanks to the accident Ryan had caused when they were kids, but he never seemed to bear his older brother ill will. If anything, Ryan was the affected one, his guilt a frequent shadow on him, except that now that they knew supernatural healing existed, Ryan was determined to help Anna figure out how to do it on Earth and heal his brother.

"I can't imagine what you two are doing in here," he said, using the wheelchair's controls to position himself to see them better.

"Daniel," said Eric by way of greeting.

"Hiding from you," Ryan said. "How did you know we were here?"

Rolling toward them, his brother replied, "I was playing with my drone just now and the camera picked up the cars out front."

Ryan silently cursed. He hadn't planned on using the garage but now they would need to. That might require more cleaning out depending on what was in there. He wasn't even sure they had working garage door openers. Part of him wanted to tell Daniel the truth, but so far only Jack knew. No one else had been discussed and Ryan hadn't raised the possibility. It might be better, really, since Daniel could keep their parents and anyone else from prying while they were gone. But how do you tell your younger brother that you are being magically summoned to other worlds full of magic and fantastic creatures? Having been an avid *Dungeons and Dragons* and Tolkien fan, Daniel would have loved it and been supremely jealous. But he also wouldn't have believed a word of it and thought Ryan was making fun of him.

"What *are* you doing in here?" Daniel persisted.

"Checking out the place," said Eric, and Ryan realized his friend was a better liar and should do the talking. "The press has been a pain, so I was thinking to move. Ryan suggested here."

"Not seriously though," said Ryan, not sure he liked that lie. Daniel would invite himself too often. "Just showing him around. The media will die down."

Daniel looked skeptical. "Yeah, maybe. Did you see that report today of someone being healed in Argentina somewhere? With new stories of weird shit cropping up all the times now, you guys and the Stonehenge thing should be forgotten before long. All you did was vanish for three weeks without explanation." He paused. "Still waiting for you to tell me what really happened."

Eric and Ryan exchanged a look, and on a sudden instinct, Ryan told the truth as if he was lying. "Someone summoned us to another world for a quest to save the planet from a horde of dragons. I fought off some ogres, too."

"Me, too," added Eric, sounding flippant. "Matt and Anna tagged along but were only so much help. It was really us."

"Yeah, and then I killed this dragon. It was freakin' huge. Breathing fire and everything, but my armor was fireproof."

"Well, *mostly* fireproof," Eric corrected with a grin.

"Yeah. It doesn't work so well against dragon fire, just other kinds. And 'almost' only counts in horseshoes and hand grenades."

Daniel smirked. "Did you get to deflower a virgin while you were at it?"

Ryan pretended to consider. "Come to think of it, no."

"I think we got screwed," Eric suggested.

Daniel's shrewd eyes appraised them. "You know something? Reports of weird shit going on around the world started right about the time you guys went missing. You probably missed a few of them, and it took a while for them to really start catching on in the news, like about two weeks, which was a couple weeks ago. Be straight with me. What the fuck happened out there?"

Eric opened his mouth, but Ryan knew he was going to joke and adopted a more serious tone. "Seriously, we don't know. It surprised us when everyone said we had been gone three weeks."

The martial artist added, "That *did* explain why the SUV we'd driven there was gone. We were wondering where the hell it went because we would've thought we'd hear someone driving off with it."

Daniel rolled closer on the hardwood floor. "So, are you suggesting it was some sort of time dilation shit? I mean, that only happens in sci-fi."

"Yeah, but all this other stuff is supposedly happening in the real world," said Ryan, "so maybe we were just the first of these incidents." He looked at Eric because he hadn't thought of this before, but now was no time for discussing it. *Had* they been the first?

"Do you guys feel any different after?"

They exchanged a look and shrugged. "Like what?"

"I don't know, like the ability to do magic or heal people like some are saying? I assume you would tell me *that* at least."

"Come on, man," started Ryan, "Of course, I would tell you if that was going on. Besides, the first thing I would do if I could heal people would be get you out of that chair I put you in."

Daniel frowned. "What makes you think I *want* out of this chair?"

That brought Ryan up short. He had never thought of that. He had just assumed Daniel wanted to be healed, which he wanted Anna to do the moment she was able. This was the first time he'd broached the subject because there hadn't been a way to do so before without being weird about it.

"Why would you not want to?" he asked. "Don't you want to walk again? Run? Go swimming?"

"Yeah, sure, those are all fine. Why not? Ryan, just because people are talking about being healed lately doesn't mean it's not a bunch of bullshit. I accepted being in this chair for the rest of my life a long time ago. Don't get your hopes up about this crap. That's all it is."

"Yeah, okay. I didn't mean it like that. I just thought that if you had the chance, you would take it." He hesitated to ask. "Would you?"

Daniel turned around and started rolling out. "Ask me when it's possible and you know a cute girl who can do it."

———— ❖ · ❖ ————

Anna breathed a sigh of relief and started her white Kia Optima, driving away from her apartment complex. It had been a long few days. Her thighs and butt still hurt from the first hour-long horseback lesson she'd shared with the boys, with another scheduled in a few days when they recovered. Eric had given them all some initial karate lessons that hadn't been so bad. Matt's sign language work was less painful, at least. She was a little sore from her first jog as well, but things were coming along. She just needed a break from it all.

A girl's night out was just what she needed. She had avoided her girlfriends a bit since the reappearance at Stonehenge, partly because everyone had so many questions and fending them off was the opposite of relaxing. She expected a few more queries tonight, but felt more comfortable dodging them now. As much as she enjoyed the boys, she had to get away from everything involving them now. She had spent all of her free time on preparing for their new reality. The worst part was the pressure—the feeling that every minute counted because someone could summon them without warning. They needed years of expertise but had no time to gain it. And they felt lucky to not have already been taken again. The stress was getting to her.

She put it from her mind with an effort. Five minutes later, she picked up her dance instructor friend Jade, an Asian woman who wore her jet-black hair in an asymmetrical bob, the front past her chin on one side, a dash of green through it. Ten minutes after and they met roommates Heather and Raven, who piled into the back. Ann headed for the highway, a night of dinner, dancing, and drinking with them ahead of her.

"So girl," began Raven from the backseat, "Anna, what's up with you hanging with these boys all the time? You doing a foursome and not inviting us?"

Anna blushed as they all laughed. "I don't have that much stamina."

"I do!" said Raven. She lifted up her phone and started videotaping their conversation, as she liked to do, sometimes posting it online with faces blurred out. She had a decent online following.

"I would go for Ryan," said Heather, pushing blush on her white cheeks. "I like my men big."

"Who doesn't?" Raven asked, cackling.

"I think average is just fine," said Jade from the front seat.

Raven said, "That Eric is supposed to be a karate guy or something? That's hot. I like flexible men."

Laughing and already feeling her stress melt away, Anna asked, "Is there anything you *don't* like in men?"

"What about Matt?" Jade asked, turning to look in the backseat, which is when Anna realized her friend hadn't put on a seat belt and told her to, but didn't get a reaction as Jade added, "I think he's cute. I like smart guys."

"That's because you're Asian," began Raven. "Your boys all got big brains."

"Seriously, though," started Heather, "first you disappeared with those guys in England for three weeks and now you're hanging out with them all the time. Come on, what's going on?"

Anna sighed, noticing Raven's camera recording. She'd ask her not to post anything about what Heather just said, or her response, because it would reveal her identity.

"We've just been hiding out from the press. They were driving us crazy and the only people who understood what it was like was them. I didn't have to explain anything to them, or answers questions I can't answer."

"You really don't know where you were all that time?" Jade asked.

Anna repeated the agreed upon lie that Ryan had told Daniel.

"I don't know where we were during those three weeks," Anna concluded. By now, her car had reached the highway and they were doing 70 mph in a big block of vehicles, heading south on I-270 against rush hour traffic toward Rockville.

"Maybe you need one of those healers that people keep talking about," began Jade, still not wearing her seatbelt. She was making Anna nervous. "They could get your memories back or figure out how three weeks of time went away for you."

That was just what Anna needed, someone poking around and forcing her to make up more lies. She felt stressed by it, but she knew they were just making small talk and would likely drop it soon.

"I think you mean a hypnotist," Heather corrected.

"No. I don't. We could find one of these people and they could answer the mystery."

"That shit ain't real, girl," said Raven, still taping on her phone. "Come on. And you know Anna don't believe in that."

"Yeah, but they showed that one on video," said Jade. "The guy's leg was mangled and it just went back to normal."

That surprised Anna. She hadn't heard of that story, but then she'd been too busy and not really catching up on these stories as much as she should, especially when it sort of concerned her. She would get on that tomorrow. "Seriously, Jade, please put your seatbelt on."

"Come on, that video was fake, like the moon landing." Raven let out a cackle, since she wasn't serious.

"Would you let someone heal you?" Jade asked Anna, putting her seatbelt on with an eye-roll.

Seeing that, Anna relaxed. "If it actually worked? Yeah, sure."

"See?" Raven asked. "She had to qualify that."

"I would want a hunky doctor type to heal me," began Heather, "and then I could show him my gratitude."

They erupted in laughter and Anna said, "I've really missed you guys."

Her face hurt from the grin, and then she felt a tingling in her stomach. A moment passed before an awful realization struck. Her wide eyes went to Jade beside her, then the cars hurtling along around them. A glance in the rearview mirrored showed a freight truck a little too close behind. White light blinded her, but it wasn't coming from the headlights there, just around her body. She frantically looked to the left to plow through the HOV lane to the median and stop, but cars blocked her way. She began screaming "no" as her foot plunged for the brake pedal and passed through air, her hands no longer around a steering wheel. The faces of Ryan, Matt, and Eric appeared before her, their resigned expressions turning to alarm on seeing her screaming.

CHAPTER THREE

UNEXPECTED COMPANY

Soliander of Aranor felt nervous. Some would have been surprised that a man of such power could feel that way, or that he would admit it to himself, but he was no fool. Refusing to acknowledge it could lead to death, and worse. He had summoned sentient forces to do his bidding many times, and some of them could detect such a feeling and exploit it. That would lead to first one mistake and then another. All but one of his apprentices over the years had resisted acknowledging their feelings and potential impact, so he usually made the most prideful summon a demon, inevitably lose control of it, and have it take them away to eternal damnation while the other candidates watched, aghast. He smiled. Either their willingness to heed his advice soared or they left his tutelage for good.

That lone standout apprentice had always been the most promising. Soliander had been trying to find him for years, but the former student knew it and was in hiding. Far worse than being a demon's slave awaited Everon for betraying Soliander. Tracking his whereabouts had been especially difficult during Soliander's years as one of the Ellorian Champions. Any pursuit was doomed to fail when you could disappear from the trail without warning. His spies had turned up little, and in the years since breaking free of the quest cycle, Soliander still hadn't found Everon, though he'd come close.

His eyes went to a window, beyond which lay the darkness of night and a tower, golden light twinkling from its windows. A prisoner occupied the top room, guarded by the supernatural and dark elves. Diara's capture had been fortuitous. She had refused to give up her lover Everon's location, but the *Mind Trust* spell had solved that problem. All ethical wizards respected that forbidden magic and wouldn't use it. But it had its uses.

Magically sifting through her memories had yielded much, including Everon's hide-out, but Soliander had acted in haste and cost himself his quarry. He should have taken time to plan an ambush, rather than immediately arriving via magic portal and laying waste to everything in his path. Everon was not there. If Soliander's vast network of spies asking questions about Everon had not made it clear that someone dangerous was after him, the destruction Soliander wrought on his home had. He knew from Diara's memories that Everon was unsure if Soliander was behind the inquiries. After all, everyone thought Soliander was missing, just like the rest of the Ellorian Champions, and yet dark elves with bluish-steel blades had often done the asking.

Only two people knew how to create such items made from the soclarin ore. And Everon only knew because he'd stolen the secret from Soliander. Those items were how they were inadvertently tipping each other off as to their activities, whereabouts, or both. One of Soliander's spies had captured a man with such a blade, which Soliander knew he hadn't created. The *Mind Trust* spell on the man led to Diara, and then to the home she shared with Everon. Since Soliander's attack, Everon abandoned every place he'd been with Diara, who he was sure to notice had gone missing. The degree of abandonment—and the fear it revealed—told Soliander that Everon knew it was him, even if the former apprentice did not understand how that was possible. Setting traps might be the only way to get him now.

It was one reason Soliander had opened the Dragon Gate on Honyn. Not only had he needed more of the ore, but he wasn't sure if Everon knew the gate led to the only place to get it. Had the apprentice run out of what he'd stolen from Soliander's stash? If he knew where to get it, learning that the gate was open would lure him there, Soliander's *Detect Presence* spell triggering an alarm that would bring them together once more at last. These betrayals about the ore were minor except for how they had enabled the betrayal that really mattered, the one for which Everon was to pay for eternity once Soliander got him. It was all arranged. He just needed his victim.

But now another mystery beyond Everon's whereabouts had Soliander's attention. Somehow his life had become all about finding people. First Everon. Now Ryan, Anna, Eric, and Matt. And maybe Korrin, Andier, and Eriana. He didn't know where his fellow Ellorian Champions were any more than anyone else did. He had assumed they were dead or trapped on Earth. But he hadn't been able to find Earth with any locator spell since he had returned from there years ago, and last seen the champions. He had never heard of Earth or seen it before someone summoned all four of them there, or since. It was as if Earth had never existed.

But now the locator spell found Earth on the first try. And second. And third. Even his apprentice Darron could find it. Soliander knew why, even how. Magic had returned to working on Earth, rendering the planet detectable. And the pendant being returned to Stonehenge had triggered this. He knew this even without the images in his head from the brief *Mind Trust* connection with Matt. Stonehenge looked about the same as when he'd last seen it in person, but the stones appeared considerably weathered, far more so than a few years would have suggested. This wasn't the only sign that the world had transformed. When he had been there, it hadn't been noticeably different from any other world he'd been to, but the images in Matt's memories were startling.

Vast buildings and cities of glass, steel, and precisely carved stone. Little boxes with moving images and sound. Enclosed, moving wagons of metal. Portable, long range communication devices. Handheld devices that fired deadly projectiles. An enormous mushroom cloud that obliterated an entire city. And more. So much more. He knew the names of these from Matt's thoughts. Computers. TVs. Phones. Guns. Nuclear explosions.

All of them revealed a world far different from the one he'd visited years ago with his friends. The images of Stonehenge had included a flashlight, a phone, an SUV, and a visitor's center that certainly hadn't been there before. Someone could have added it since, of course, but the technology apparent in it suggested that only a few years having passed was highly unlikely. A suspicion had formed and seemed the obvious explanation, but he had to go there to find out.

There were two names he would have expected to find in Matt's memories of important people, but there had been no trace of them. Maybe it wasn't surprising and meant nothing. Everything he had learned was unusually disjointed due to the way the *Mind Trust* spell had been abruptly broken. That had apparently scattered the retained information, and the thought made him feel lucky. Sometimes it isn't the memories gained that are scattered, but the caster's mind, leaving the wizard infantilized, a useless, drooling idiot. This was another reason the spell was forbidden. He had dodged a bullet, to use an Earth expression he now knew. Matt had nearly destroyed both of them when he escaped the *Mind Trust* spell.

It gave more reason to visit Earth. He needed to understand what was happening there. That he might find some sign of his lost friends compelled him to go, even if nothing else would have. He certainly wanted answers to the mystery of why Matt and the others had impersonated him and the real champions. He sensed from Matt's memories that there was little they really knew. There were no images of Korrin, Eriana, or Andier. But he'd seen Lorian, the elf who had shouted Soliander's name at him in the ruins of Castle Darlonon. He had been considering grabbing the elf for information, but Lorian was less important. What really mattered now was this visit to Earth.

He needed to know so many things, including who truly controlled the nuclear warheads. Only he and a few others held such power, and he had purposely destroyed most of the others. That wasn't a power any mortal should have, only the gods. As far as he knew, only he could do it now, but he sensed from the spell Lorian had done on Matt that the latter was unusually strong in magic. Perhaps he had the power, if not the skill. Matt was no wizard, he knew. Not really. And yet he had taken control of the staff in Soliander's hand and burned him with it. He was caught between grudging admiration and irritation about that, but vengeance on Matt wasn't a priority, not that he wouldn't take the chance if it arose. But he had more pressing concerns. He wanted to know who controlled these warheads.

But even that paled compared to understanding the changes on Earth and what had happened since his departure from there. The latter had been eating away at him for years. And now he could finally learn a great many truths, not the least of which might have been where his former friends were, and where they went. The fate of Korrin and Andier concerned him, but not like that of Eriana, the Lady

Hope, her disappearance crushing any hope—or even goodness—left in him. Had she seen the look of fear and awful realization in his eyes the last time they were together? He was certain she had, as their eyes met one final time before they disappeared in a flash of light.

His eyes again went to the window and the tower where Diara sat in chains. What would Eriana think of him having imprisoned her younger sister? He wanted to laugh. If Eriana still lived, she would likely be furious. But she would also understand. After all, if it hadn't been for Diara, Everon could not have betrayed them all. While Soliander was certain the Lady Hope was dead, he could never fully resign himself to the idea. And it was the primary reason he hadn't killed Diara. Eriana might understand imprisoning her sister, especially to gain information on his former apprentice, but she would never forgive killing her, even if Diara had it coming. If Soliander ever found Eriana alive, he would have some explaining to do, but stating why he'd locked up her sister was a lot of less troubling than why he'd killed her.

And so Diara lived, and in good health, at that. He had made no secret to his prisoner that Eriana was the only reason he kept her alive. Besides, he didn't need her cooperation when the *Mind Trust* spell bypassed all of that, so telling her the truth affected nothing. He had long since learned everything he needed to know and had not visited her in some time. Maybe he would after his trip to Earth, depending on what he learned of Eriana's whereabouts.

The possibility that she still lived caused his heart to pound. And he knew that this was why he was nervous. Never mind the strange visions of Earth, and what Matt and his friends might know, or that magic had resumed working there once more, possibility heralding an extraordinarily dangerous situation, made all the worse by the existence of nuclear warheads, among other inventions.

No, what threatened his self-control was whether or not Eriana was alive. He calmed himself and summoned his current apprentice, Darron, a dark-skinned dark elf who would excel at the excursion now planned. The black hair would hide the pointed ears, but something would have to be done about the red eyes.

The apprentice wizard entered his chambers wearing clothes neither had seen anyone wearing before, except in Soliander's memories from Matt. Blue jeans, a t-shirt, and sneakers covered his lithe form. He carried a black backpack in one hand. It had taken implanting the idea in someone's head to get her to create these replicas, which would have to do for now. Darron fidgeted quietly, as if tying to get used to the attire.

"Must I really wear this, Master Zoran?" Darron asked, tugging at the tight jeans and using the false name Soliander had been using since even before the Ellorian Champions had vanished. No one knew that Zoran the Devastator was really Soliander of Aranor, the Majestic Magus, hero wizard from among the missing Ellorian Champions.

"Yes," Soliander replied. "It is the fashion there. You must fit in, as will I if I can join you. You will carry your wizard's robes and other items in that bag."

The apprentice lifted it awkwardly. "Its design is strange, but I must admit the many pockets seem quite functional."

"What I have seen of this world is strange. You must not gawk upon arrival."

"Yes, master. What is it you want me to do?"

"You will arrive near the home of the man named Matt. It will be night. You will ensure no one is watching. I need you to act nonchalant while finding a quiet place to contact me via the orb, while no one can observe you. You must avoid suspicion."

"Of course."

"This world does not know magic, from what I understand. Once you can contact me, I will ask you to perform a simple spell while I watch via the orb. If the spell works, I will join you."

"And if the spell does not work?"

You will be trapped there forever instead of me, Soliander thought. "We will deal with that at the time. You may have trouble getting the orb to work as well, but keep trying."

He didn't get into what would happen next. The apprentice would likely find fitting in difficult and would get stranded or apprehended on a strange world without magic to help him. Soliander didn't much care. If that befell the apprentice, they'd never see each other again. He didn't think it likely, however. Matt and the others could not have been summoned from Earth unless magic was working on Earth again. Even the spell Soliander was about to cast to send Darron there would fail if the planet was still locked, but he had to be sure. If the spell worked and the orb functioned on Earth, and the apprentice performed magic while Soliander watched, then and only then would he feel comfortable casting himself there personally.

He sighed. The time had come. He rose from behind the stone table with its spell books, scrolls, and magic runes carved into its surface. Along the way, he stopped at a table to place a soft, black cloth over a golden orb that had been glowing softly, various images fleeting across its surface. Then he went to stand before Darron. The apprentice didn't seem as nervous as Soliander felt, but then he had little idea how important this moment was. That inspired Soliander to calm himself and place one hand on Darron's shoulder. Words of magic slithered from his mouth as the power began to course through him, enveloping the apprentice, who seemed remarkably trusting as Soliander made him vanish from before him. Strange how the disappearance of someone so unimportant to him might lead to the reappearance of those who mattered so very much.

———— ❖ • ❖ ————

Erin Jennings tightened the top of the white thermos she'd brought from Florida, a comfort from home just like the tea itself. She seldom went for designer flavors or even coffee, just regular tea, mostly because the taste was a holdover from a life long gone but never forgotten. How could anyone forget such a life? The only equivalent in this world were fictionalized stories. Sometimes it all seemed like a dream, but she knew better. And everything she had done since helped her prepare for today.

Twenty years had passed since it ended abruptly in what she had surmised was an explosion, but she didn't really know. One moment she'd been standing with her dearest friends and the next she stood in a rural field somewhere by herself, a little dazed, very confused, and apparently not at all dressed for the fashions of the day, as she learned when she went to the nearest home for help. The style of the house had been as strange to Erin as her clothing to the occupants, who had initially assumed she was taking part in a nearby festival.

Erin had learned to be quick thinking from many moments of being thrust into new, unexpected situations. At those times, she had sometimes counted on her reputation to get by. People were often too intimidated to cross her or her companions, but this time no one seemed to recognize her. Taking her cue, she had played along, having mastered the art of asking questions to control the conversation's flow, as one of her friends, who was infinitely wilier, had taught her. And so she came to understand that this place was different from any other she had visited.

Those elderly homeowners had been a stroke of good luck, she now knew. It was late afternoon when she knocked on their door and she accepted their invitation to dinner. Seeing an opportunity as the night wore on and she professed to not knowing who to contact to come get her, she had asked for a room and been given one.

Her hosts were forgetful but kind, and a little clueless about modern technology. They had a missing, and presumed dead, granddaughter Erin's age, and whom she reminded them of. The result was treating her like family and doting on her, especially on learning that she was lost. They didn't ask too many questions, to which they sometimes didn't remember her awkward answers anyway, and that had allowed her to give a better response when they asked again. They didn't begrudge the ignorance she struggled to hide, for there were so many things so alien to her, from the TV to phones, computers, and the internet, that pretending she had familiarity challenged her. With wide eyes had Erin taken it all in.

And so her month-long stay with them had begun, as she discreetly pumped them for information, gorged on TV news programs, and used the internet on their old computer once she figured out how from watching them struggle to do so themselves. Hour after hour had she immersed herself, slowly learning one important idea after another.

She was on the south island of New Zealand. She needed a passport to get on a plane to England to find Stonehenge, which was still standing since she'd last seen it. It had changed since then, but then it seemed like everything had and this place was no longer recognizable, not that she had seen much anyway. While people believed in a lone god, there were no confirmed reports of Him answering anyone. Magic didn't seem to work, and no one believed in it. An internet search of her friend's names turned up nothing, but two other names brought up a lot, and yet all of it was considered a myth from a thousand years past. Had she been flung into the future? All signs pointed to it. Ever since, a kind of grief had lurked in the back of her mind, that everyone and everything she had ever known was just gone.

Eventually she left behind the elderly couple who had given her a wad of cash and a suitcase of old clothes and other knickknacks as she set off for Christchurch, a nearby city with international flights. She promised to repay them, but they told her not to worry about, as they weren't using any of it anyway. Getting the documentation she needed for international travel would have been impossible were it not for their missing granddaughter, whom they had been raising after their own daughter died. She bore just enough resemblance for Erin to get a nerdy young man she flirted with to issue her a new driver's license in the girl's name, which she adopted, becoming Erin Jennings. Similar machinations finally got her the passport, credit cards, and a new identity, all of it helped by those sweet grandparents having done little to formalize the girl's death. They hadn't had the heart to go through that again and hoped they might find the real Erin one day, but it had been years and they seemed resigned that it wouldn't happen.

She finally stood before Stonehenge, which had weathered considerably since she last saw it a month earlier. A nearby visitor center looked decades old but hadn't been here before. Something was clearly amiss. She stayed in Britain for a year, working as a server and making new friends to avoid suspicion, hoping for a sign of her true friends, but it never came. When it became apparent that she was in this brave new land for the rest of her life, she moved to America and married someone a few years older and with a promising future. Nearly twenty years had passed.

She spent those years preparing for today, acquiring supposed magic items from around the world, a few of which were upstairs in her hotel room. None had worked, but she had heard reports of random people being able to do one thing or another. And the Stonehenge disappearance could never have happened without magic. Some people could also heal others. Most dismissed that as nonsense, but Erin knew it had been possible in her old life, which was about to collide with her new one. She felt nervous. So much depended on this conversation with the Stonehenge Four. It was important to have this talk in person. Their expressions would tell her more than words ever could.

As she sipped her tea in a hotel dining area in Gaithersburg, Maryland, the loud, excited voices of two approaching teenage girls broke her thoughts. The first words she could make out got her undivided attention.

"The guy vanished right on camera!" said the blonde one as they swept into the dining area, moving around the small tables and chairs, the afternoon sun streaming across the floor.

The brunette asked, "Do you think that's what happened at Stonehenge, but no one was there to see it?"

"Could be. Damn, the TV isn't on. Where's the remote?"

Erin's eyes went to it on the counter, from where one girl grabbed the TV control and furiously pushed buttons to no avail. "Damn thing is busted!"

"Grab a cookie and let's go. Come on!"

They ran from the room and Erin strode right behind them, her long skirt snapping as she marched to the nearest stairs. She ascended three flights, taking two steps at a time. She finally burst into the hall and swiftly unlocked her room door, then headed straight for the TV, which came on, already set to the news from her viewing it earlier today. Words gushed from an excited black reporter as Erin read the chryon across the screen's button, "Man Magically Vanishes on Camera."

"Lisa," the reporter continued, addressing a news anchor on the split screen, "as you can see from the footage, I was right in the middle of our interview when he disappeared."

Lisa replied, "I know some people are speculating that this is just a special effect, added afterward."

"Yeah, and I'm here to tell you this is absolutely not the truth. I saw it right in front of me and there are a dozen witnesses to this, some of whom caught it on their cellphones."

As the two women talked, a silent replay of the moment began repeating, sometimes in slow motion. The techie, Matt, stood shyly talking into the microphone held toward him, green eyes on the reporter as he only rarely glanced at the camera as if uncomfortable before it. A light breeze touched his shoulder-length, wavy brown hair. And suddenly the smile left his face as he stopped talking midsentence, one hand going to his stomach, those eyes widening in a clear look of alarm, and a soft white glow surrounding him. A murmur slowly began from those near, and the camera tilted a moment as if the holder was startled out of position before recovering just in time. A glow enveloped Matt and then disappeared along with him.

The anchor interrupted the reporter, "Hey listen, we're going to have to switch to another story, possibly related, that is just coming in. There are reports of a very serious, multi-car accident on I-270 near Gaithersburg. Initial reports suggest that a bright flash of light, similar to the one that occurred nearby during the interview of Matt Sorenson, happened just moments before the collision, which has involved several cars, one of which has overturned. We currently don't know if this is related to Matt

Sorenson's previous disappearance with Anna Sumner, Ryan LaRue, and Eric Foster."

The screen switched from showing Lisa to a helicopter view of wrecked cars along a four-lane highway, traffic snarled in both directions. Several people outside vehicles were frantically trying to help one person thrown from a car and others who appeared trapped inside. A white sheet covered a body that lay a considerable distance from the wreckage.

The anchor added, "There are initial reports of serious injuries and one fatality. All lanes of I-270 south are blocked. Police and ambulances are approaching the scene now and we will keep you updated on this breaking story."

Erin hit the mute button and flopped heavily on the bed's edge, an awful realization going through her. She had been wondering if it was possible for a week and now had her answer. Anna, Matt, Ryan, and Eric had somehow become a kind of new Ellorian Champions, replacing the real ones. The stakes had risen. Questions swirled. She had to help them.

Now it was absolutely critical that she find them the moment they returned.

—— • • • ——

Daniel knew something wasn't right, but then it didn't take a genius. It wasn't easy to control a drone with one hand, but he did well enough. He just had to give up performing elaborate tricks. And tricks were on his mind when the display camera showed his brother's car in front of the guest house, the trunk and passenger door open. He had first felt relieved and buzzed around the building for signs of what Ryan was doing, but there was no sight of him, so Daniel landed out of the way with the camera aimed at the house and the motion sensor on. He'd see when his brother reappeared. If he did.

The police had shown up last night, looking for him. Neither Daniel nor his parents had been surprised, having seen footage of Matt vanishing on camera and confirmed reports about Anna's car on I-270. Those first moments with the cops had been awful. Daniel wasn't the only one who had feared the worst, his mother nearly collapsing at the possibility that the police had arrived to tell them their oldest son was dead. But the fatality had been a female, as were the other passengers, though no one had been publicly identified, pending the families being informed. They hadn't even been willing to say whether the bodies came from Anna's car or the dozen other vehicles involved.

They had been calling Ryan all night and trying to track his phone with no luck, which didn't surprise Daniel. Their parents had installed GPS trackers on Ryan's car and phone after the Stonehenge Four had returned from three weeks of being missing. It had led to some arguments with Ryan complaining that he felt like a prisoner. He had finally disabled them.

Daniel had assumed that his brother was gone, like Matt and Anna. Eric hadn't been found either, his last known whereabouts being his job, where he had finished for the day and was apparently planning to leave, according to his boss. And then suddenly he was gone, with no sign of actually walking out. His disappearance had not been witnessed or reported until the police noticed that two of the Stonehenge Four had gone missing and they tried tracking down the other two, leading to Ryan and Eric. The police found the latter's car at work, his boss showing the officers the abandoned belongings, as Eric had just finished teaching a class in his karate clothes and not changed yet. He was now presumed missing. So was Ryan.

Now Daniel called to his nurse, Susan, a young brunette he enjoyed flirting with. He wanted help and a witness for their excursion down to the guest house. It was time to see what his brother was up to down there. He hadn't believed anything Ryan and Eric had said the other day due to their joking tone. His older brother was hiding something but had never lied to him. Or he didn't think so anyway. The big guy could be irritating like any sibling, but Daniel trusted him. He wasn't hard to get a read on, really, unlike Eric.

"What do you need, hon?" Susan asked as she arrived from another room. He never grew tired of the East Baltimore accent and predilection for calling him that.

"Keep this between us, but I just found Ryan's car at the guest house. We need to head down there."

"Um. Okay. Are we expecting trouble of any kind?"

They had discussed the situation. "Pretty sure no. I don't think he's there, but I want to see what's going on and I can only get to the first floor."

"Sure. I'll get my purse, by which I mean gun."

"I love it when you're sexy," he called as she walked away.

Within minutes, they were beside Ryan's black Dodge Charger, where his car and house keys lay on the pavement beside it. Exchanging a wary look with the nurse, Daniel had her tell him what was inside the backseat. He could already see that the trunk was empty.

"Just a couple boxes." She pulled a long, rectangular one out. On the side were pictured arrows with red fletching.

"What the hell does he need with those?"

"Taking up archery?"

Daniel put his hands on the drone's remote and made it start up again, piloting it into the open front door of the guest house. That Ryan had not meant to leave was clear, but Daniel still didn't expect foul play. Even so, sending in the drone with its camera was better than going in personally. He saw more boxes inside but no people, including the second floor as he moved it around everywhere but the basement, as the door was closed. He landed the drone there.

"Okay, let's go in."

He had wondered if he'd been seeing right through the camera, but there was no denying it now. Someone had stacked books on medieval customs and warfare on a table. A dozen swords of varying lengths lay atop the Persian rugs. Several round and rectangular steel or wooden shields leaned against a wall. Three Western-style horseback riding saddles were in one corner where helmets, crops, horse blankets and more were stacked. Four boxes held what looked like long bows, and another four were crossbows, each of slightly different styles and none of them looking modern. That contrasted with a big screen TV hanging on the wall, a make-shift entertainment center filled with electronics that weren't plugged in, the boxes everything had come in still here. The tables for a living room set were haphazardly placed, possibly because they were waiting on missing couches.

"Is this all for RenFest?" Susan asked, picking up a sword by the hilt.

Scowling, Daniel replied, "I doubt it. I mean, he's been doing it for years and never needed all of this stuff here."

"What's with the TV? It's like he's setting up to hang out here or something. Is he moving down here?"

"No. I don't think so. He didn't say anything. And I doubt he would start with all of this these things. I mean you don't furnish a house with weapons, then go furniture shopping."

"True, but your brother is weird."

Daniel saw light from under the basement door. "Can you open it? I'll send the drone."

Wordlessly, Susan did, and he piloted the device down the stairs to the wide cellar. His first priority was again verifying that no one was here, which he did. He was dying to go down himself but had her go without him, as she confirmed what the camera showed him. A punching bag hung in one corner, as did another, maybe for kicking. They had set two treadmills and a stair climber up. Several gym mats were stacked in one corner, but nearly half the floor had been covered with them. Someone had stacked several archery targets along with their stands. The biggest surprise was two armor stands, one holding the suit of plate mail that Ryan wore at the Renaissance Festival, the other empty.

Now Daniel knew his brother was lying. The last 24 hours had proven it, but he'd been certain all along that they weren't telling the truth about what happened at Stonehenge. "We don't remember" is such a lame excuse and exactly what he might have said if something odd had happened. But what he really wanted to know now was why it looked like they were preparing to train in using these weapons? Where had they gone? And why?

He couldn't help saying it aloud as Susan returned to his side. "What the hell are they doing?"

CHAPTER FOUR

THE ORBS
OF DOMINION

Thoughts rushed through Anna's head with the same chaotic intensity as the roaring of sound and light that accompanied a summoning. Her friends. The car. The highway. Speed. And no one at the helm. She still clenched her hands before her on a steering wheel that wasn't there anymore. Her right foot wasn't placed against an accelerator, but beneath her as she stood, yelling "no" over and over. The concerned faces of Eric, Ryan, and Matt before her made another round of thoughts tear through her. A quest. Danger. People watching. Their expectations. The ruse of being the Ellorian Champions. Their startled reaction to her arriving screaming. She stopped herself just as the summoning ended.

Her breath came hard, eyes darting around for peril like the last time. The Quest Ring stood with its light fading. A dozen calm people outside it. No weapons drawn. A gray partly cloudy sky above, the sun nearly overhead. A castle in the distance. Mountains behind it, dramatic hills and a river between. A hill beneath their feet. No more people. No creatures. No danger. Not yet.

Anna twisted her back to those who had summoned them, trying to slow her breathing, calm her face, and wipe the panic from her eyes. Eric came around to her, one firm hand on her arm through the now familiar white robe of Eriana.

"What happened?" he whispered.

"I was driving."

"What?"

"70 miles an hour, the highway." She heard Ryan step closer in the golden armor, his boot scraping the smooth stones beneath their feet.

"Were you alone?"

She shook her head, too afraid of what was happening back on Earth to say it aloud.

"Oh shit," muttered Ryan.

"Okay," started Eric, "we can talk about that in a minute. There are people looking at us. We need to act like heroes and–"

"I can't," she said, shaking her head.

"You don't have to say anything. Ryan."

"Right." The big guy turned away, his voice regal and cheerful as he said, "I apologize. We needed a moment to discuss something urgent that was happening before your summons."

A gravelly voice replied, "Of course. We understand that we have pulled you from your lives and you may time to adjust. We are deeply sorry for any inconvenience, but our matter is most urgent."

"The quests always are!" Ryan said heartily, and Anna thought his time playing a knight at the Renaissance Festival had prepared him well for what he was doing. He sounded convincing. The thought made her pull herself together, and she turned to face their summoners, forcing a smile. There was nothing she could do about her friends now anyway, but she felt sick. Only now did she notice Ryan didn't have Lord 's lance with him, so at least they wouldn't be facing dragons. From what they knew, the

Quest Rings supplied them with likely weapons from whatever stash of them the real Ellorian Champions had somewhere, presumably on their own world of Elloria.

Gesturing toward one side, away from the river valley below, the speaker said, "If you are ready, lords and lady, it is important that we quickly get out of sight."

"Are we in danger?" Eric asked, scanning around them.

"Not precisely. All will become clear in a moment. Please follow us."

Ryan and Eric went first, leaving Anna beside Matt, whose concerned eyes were on her. She hooked one arm with his as they followed.

Amid the summoning spell, they were always facing each other so far these three times, and sometimes they arrived in that position, but once they had been turned in the same direction so that they faced what she thought of as the opening of a Quest Ring. This is where they went now, and she noticed this ring was once again different from the others in various details. It reminded her of Greek architecture, with white pillars of equal height all around, each one standing on a stone wall and supporting a matching, circular top that was open to the sky. Three steps at the front led them to a marble path. The way continued straight, where the castle waited in the distance, a town before it, but they turned away and followed a branching path into the trees. Twenty paces away awaited a two-story stone building, vegetation partially overgrowing it.

No one spoke on the way, giving Anna time to assess their companions. Her eyes went to a tall, regal, striking woman in tight-fitting red leather that matched her wavy, red hair. She oozed intelligence, sophistication, and strength as she strode ahead of them. Two similarly dressed men trailed her. One wore deep blue, his hair stark white. The other man wore dark green and had brown hair.

They seemed to defer to the woman. None of them carried anything, and yet Anna sensed they were very dangerous. She was certain they were magical in some way they would likely reveal.

The wizard who had summoned them had a gravelly voice, a balding head of graying black hair, and walked with a slight limp, but she couldn't tell much else from behind. His brown wooden staff thumped on the marble as he went, a purple robe brushing the stone.

A slender but muscled man in silver plate mail sauntered beside him, a sword at one hip, a dagger on the other. A helmet with a white plume of feather had been tied to one waist. Short brown hair and a close beard framed a rugged face with sharp eyes. Anna sensed he held a high rank compared to the dozen, less ostentatiously dressed warriors behind her and Matt. No one else was present, including anyone who seemed like royalty. Due to this and the attempt at getting them out of the castle's line of sight, she questioned whether someone did not approve of their summoning.

As they approached the building, Anna saw several very large saddles on the ground, similar to ones for horses but so large—the size of a compact car—that she wondered what enormous creatures they could be for. The leather-clad trio entered first without a sense of danger, followed by the wizard and the silver-armored knight, the four Earth friends, and finally most of the other warriors, two remaining outside and guarding the doors, which were left open.

The building's interior seemed comprised of a single principal room, two open doors leading to smaller ones not much bigger than a closet. A staircase ascended to the upper level, old tapestries flying from the walls, no other decorations in sight. The room was functional and from the proximity of the Quest Ring, she wondered if it had been designed specially for them, and whether they had ever summoned the real Ellorian Champions before. No one seemed to second guess their identities, so maybe not.

They remained on the first floor, where a broad, rectangular table with cushion-less wooden chairs around it filled the center. Everyone stayed standing but the champions, wizard, and silver-armored warrior, who spoke first.

"I am Novir, Commander of the King's Guard," he began, voice confident until he added with a frown, "or what's left of it. The wizard is Derin. You stand in the Kingdom of Minari, on the planet Rovell, near Castle Arking."

Ryan said, "I assume you know us, but I am Lord Korrin." He then introduced the others and asked, "What happened to the King's Guard? How many of you are left?"

Novir answered, "The rest of the guard still live, we think, but their minds are not their own anymore. More will become plain as we tell you what has led up to your summoning. Those you see with us here are not the King's Guard, but the most trusted men from among our other forces."

The wizard Derin spoke up. "First, I must apologize for our haste in leaving the Quest Ring. The king has not been informed of your summons and would not be pleased, but we have done the right thing and he cannot see it, with good reason."

"Is his mind also not his own now?" Eric asked.

"Yes. The Orbs of Dominion have enthralled him."

Anna grew alarmed. Would they find themselves similarly enthralled, whatever that meant? They had already lost control of their physical lives, but now their minds might be taken over, too?

"We are not familiar with these Orbs of Dominion," Ryan said. "Please tell us more."

Derin nodded. "Of course. No one is certain who invented the orbs, but there are believed to be two, a master orb and a slave. Legend says that the creator, a wizard, kept the master for himself and sent his apprentice to ensnare rulers with the slave orb, which was mounted atop a staff. This allowed it to enthrall individuals or large groups if it was raised high enough for them to see. Somehow, both the wizard and his apprentice came to ruin, and the orbs passed through various hands before disappearing. Today, it is unknown who has the master, but it has clearly been activated. We know where the slave orb is, and this is what you are here to retrieve and deactivate, by destroying it if possible."

"How do they work?" Matt asked, leaning forward, green eyes intent.

"The master orb is like a communication orb, allowing the one controlling it to interact visually and verbally across great distances. But it only works with the slave orb, which is called this because anyone looking into the slave can have their mind taken over by the one who controls the master."

Matt asked, "Does this control continue after the slave orb is removed from their presence or deactivated?"

"Yes. It is permanent or can be until the master orb releases the individual. This happens if the one controlling the orbs dies or relinquishes control somehow."

Eric observed, "And the Minarin King has looked into the slave orb and is now under someone's control."

"Yes."

"And you do not know who controls him?"

"We do not. But your quest does not include determining this, though it would be helpful to know."

Eric asked, "How did this happen?"

The warrior Novir answered, "The slave orb was being kept in the nearby dwarven Kingdom of Hamarven, deep beneath the mountains. Only a few dwarves knew this. It was among various rare, precious, or dangerous items under heavy guard. We do not know how long this has been true, and there has been so little mention of the orbs for centuries that many do not believe they are real. Many have never heard of them.

"According to the dwarves, the slave orb suddenly turned on after so many years of inactivity. The dwarves guarding it were so surprised that they mistakenly stepped closer and became ensnared. Whoever took control convinced them to bring other guards nearer, and one by one, those under its control grew in number so that they could walk out of where the dwarves kept it, carrying it before them, ensnaring more as they went."

Anna inwardly groaned at how easily more people could be affected. It was brilliant and awful. "I can see why these are so dangerous."

Novir nodded. "Yes. They brought it before the queen and captured her mind. The king passed years ago. We do not know how many among the dwarves the orb enslaved, and there is some question as to how many people can be controlled. It is unknown how the orbs really affect someone, but we suspect that the enslaved just become willing to take orders. We aren't sure how much they are aware of."

"Maybe it's like the orb hypnotizes them," mused Matt.

Novir didn't seem to understand the remark and continued as if Matt hadn't said it. "Before long, the dwarves arrived in our kingdom with the orb. We are not sure what their intent was, whether they came to ensnare our king or if they only did so on their way north. The result is the same."

"They succeeded." Eric surmised.

"Yes. We are on friendly terms with the dwarven kingdom, and so no one thought any harm would come from their request to meet with our king. Once the audience was granted, they unveiled the orb, and all were lost to it. I was not on duty or else I would have been among them. I had heard of the request and was en route to the throne room when I learned something was amiss. There are ways into that room, known to only a few, and I used one. I saw the thrall the orb had cast over everyone. I also heard a voice commanding King Orin and him obeying."

"What was the command?"

"To assist in the orb's travel further northwest to a place known as Bolin Hill, where the dwarves were to give the orb to someone else."

"Who?"

"It was not specified, but we now know, as you will see. The power of the slave orb allowed the dwarves to leave unmolested, due to the King's Guard members enforcing the king's orders. The orb did not enthrall all of my men, as not all were on duty. Regardless, in their departure, the dwarves ensnared anyone they encountered, leaving some behind, and taking others with them. Some who departed with them were our finest warriors. I sought Denir at once and on learning of my description of the orb and what occurred, he surmised we are dealing with the Orbs of Dominion."

Denir spoke up. "As you know, we must attempt to solve our own problems before attempting to summon yourselves, or the Quest Rings do not bring you."

"What do you mean?" Anna asked. She thought Lorian might have explained this, but she wasn't sure. So much had happened that she couldn't retain it all. Then she realized others expected to know and struggled to justify her question, making up something. "What I mean is that there are variations in the way the Quest Rings work. They are not all precisely the same. We prefer not to assume but get confirmation on how a specific one is performing, especially if we use it to return."

Denir looked intrigued. "I was unaware of this. Thank you. Quite interesting devices." He looked at Matt, who nodded as if to thank him. "I cast the summoning spell and answered the questions I was asked about the quest and what we had done to resolve the matter ourselves. Upon completion, the Quest Ring's oracle, I believe you call it?"

"Correct," said Matt, though the expression was news to Anna and likely him, too.

"The oracle agreed the quest was valid and brought you here moments later."

"I see," said Anna, wishing she could see this in action but suspecting she never would. "Thank you."

"Of course. As I was saying, we explained to the Quest Ring our previous attempts to resolve this. Our first attempt at securing the slave orb was as the dwarves fled, but this led to nothing but more enthralled warriors and we had to back away. We lost over two hundred good men and women to the orb. Our second attempt was another failure, but one that provided insight into how dire the circumstances truly are."

"What happened?"

Novir said. "We sent a handful of men and one wizard to the rendezvous point, Bolin Hill. They arrived first because the dwarves and our captured men were on foot. It gave them time to see who they were meeting."

He exchanged a look with Denir, and Anna sensed they had debated whether to reveal something. "We need to know everything you can tell us," she said.

Denir sighed heavily. "We learned that the Orb of Dominion was bound for the Lords of Fear."

The Earth friends shared an inquisitive look, and Novir spoke up. "As you were, uh, missing for a few years, you may not have heard of them. They began making a name for themselves since then."

"Who are they?"

"An assassin, a necromancer, a sorcerer, and an undead knight."

Eric smirked. "Sounds like a charming group."

Anna knew he was kidding but had a terrible feeling about this. She had already encountered one undead knight on Honyn when it grabbed her and announced she would be its bride after death. Her skin prickled with goosebumps from the awful cold that had settled in her bones. The memory was one of many that sometimes kept her up at night. She brushed the thought aside with an effort, just as she kept trying to ignore her fears about what had happened to her friends when she vanished from the car. Focusing on the details of the impending quest helped her some. "Why are they called the Lords of Fear? Are they actual lords?"

The wizard said, "Yes. Or they were. Some have been stripped of their titles."

"Why?" she asked.

"Nothing good. They sometimes assassinate royalty or other prominent figures, or extort them. They have started wars between kingdoms. They have assisted others in achieving evil. And they go after powerful supernatural items like these orbs, so much so that people on various worlds have taken to hiding them from this threat."

"So they operate across worlds. Are they from this one?"

"They are not, and we believe that, now that they have what they came for, that they are attempting to leave with the orb. It cannot remain in their hands. It is dangerous regardless, but with the Lords of Fear using it, there is indeed much to fear. Their methods are nightmarish and true to their nickname. The assassin is not above poison, for example, whether this is given directly, in food or drink, or on her weapons. Should you fight her, you must be certain not to let a blade slice you."

"It's a woman?" Anna asked in surprise.

Denir said, "Yes, and she was the daughter of a countess, her father being an Earl who has since disowned her."

Eric leaned forward. "Do you know anything else that might help us understand her? We might be able to use the details to our advantage."

Novir spoke up. "She is known to love both men and women, but same-gender relations carry a penalty of death in Nysuun, even for royals. As teens, her and the princess she loved were condemned. After watching her love die by fire, Kori escaped the same fate and disappeared. There has been much speculation about her history since, but we know she joined a secretive group that trained her in hand-to-hand fighting, weapons, and other skills an assassin needs. But they would not let her seek revenge. It appears she was bound, perhaps supernaturally, by a pledge to them, but she freed herself from it and got her revenge. The organization tried to kill her for this, so she did the same to them, but whereas they failed, she was successful. The group is no more."

Anna couldn't hide her disbelief. "She killed *all* of them?"

"Yes. Kori of Nysuun is among the most ruthless women alive."

Anna tried to mute her intimidation. If the others were just as deadly, she and her friends might be in worse trouble with this quest than it seemed. Not sure she wanted to know, she asked, "Who are the others?"

"The sorcerer is Lord Garian of Ormund."

Ryan perked up. "Ormund? On Honyn?"

Novir turned to him. "Yes. We understand you closed the Dragon Gate there recently."

"We did. We met someone from Ormund along the way."

"Cirion," muttered Anna, remembering the dashing man who first tried to seduce her, then interfered with their quest to close the gate. He was trouble of more than one kind. "Hopefully, he won't appear. Who is Lord Garian?"

Novir answered, "He was the prince and heir to the throne, but no longer. His father stripped him of his peerage."

Anna cocked an eyebrow. "What did he do to cause *that*?"

Denir replied, "While magic is not quite forbidden in the kingdom, it is viewed with suspicion and not openly practiced. When Garian discovered he had the talent in his teens, he secretly sought training and received it, but his master had plans of his own."

A scowling Matt asked, "To control him?"

Novir answered, "He wanted power over Garian once the prince became king. I suspect the master treated Garian poorly, knowing the prince could tell no one."

Denir interjected, "Yes, and it is this, coupled with learning dark wizardry, that seemed to alter Lord Garian's heart. His personality was seen to change even before the truth of his secret life and talent was discovered. Having a member of the royal family practicing magic was not well received, and perhaps it was the impetuous nature of youth that led him to publicly flaunt his skills. We believe he did this to show that it was of no danger to anyone, but the king, his father, did not view it that way."

Matt finished, "And so they stripped him of his titles."

Denir nodded. "And banished. I expect he will one day return to claim the throne and abolish laws against magic."

Matt said, "I can't say I blame him. He doesn't sound like he's that bad of a guy."

Denir sighed. "He enjoys sympathy in some quarters, but his actions since then leave little doubt that he can only be a hero to unsavory people. He is very charming, as if the spell he weaves is one of seduction more than wizardry. You should know that you will not identify him by a sorcerer's attire, for he seeks to hide his talents and skills, I think more to surprise people than from shame, though perhaps his past inspires it. Do not look for a wizard's robe or staff, but a well-dressed man of royal refinement in a tunic and trousers, the ingredients for spells discreetly on his person. He keeps a wand up one sleeve should he need it. Beware the Dragon's Fire Wand, for it is powerful."

Eric observed, "You refer to him as a sorcerer, not a wizard."

"Yes, but there is no difference, though sorcerer has a connotation of using dark arts."

Anna wondered what he was willing to do. She recalled that Matt had two of Soliander's spell books in the bag he always arrived with. The techie had said one had seemingly more innocent or benevolent spells, while the other tended toward dangerous and possibly immoral. She thought of it every time her friend was looking in that one, wondering what he was learning. She had wanted to look through it herself, but Matt tended to find excuses for secrecy, which only made her more curious, but not quite concerned. Still, when he performed a spell, she sometimes wondered which book he got it from.

"Speaking of dark arts," she began, "who is the necromancer?"

Denir began, "Lord Areon the Soul Stealer was a priest who married into royalty, but lost his title when his wife was murdered. He was too late to heal her and began practicing necromancy to not only resurrect his wife, but to get revenge on her killers, as they were executed too mercifully for his tastes."

Grimacing, Anna asked, "Did he succeed?"

Denir looked unsure how to answer. "Stories conflict as to whether he was successful, but I believe he did not reanimate his love in satisfactory condition, and they remain apart."

Novir added, "They banished him for this. There is a bounty on his head. His god forsook him so that he cannot heal anymore."

"Did that push him further into necromancy, so he still had power?"

Denir looked at her approvingly. "Yes. He has since shown little regard for life, or death, and has become powerful in his quest to restore his love."

"That's tragic and very creepy," Anna remarked, shuddering. No one should love so deeply as to become corrupted throughout their being. Sometimes letting go was better, however painful. But then she had never known such love for another or herself. Could it really be so wonderful, then so awful? Part of her didn't want to know, but she was sort of curious. She supposed she couldn't really judge this lord, but if he was doing unholy things to others, that would be enough to condemn him in her eyes.

Breaking her thoughts, Matt asked, "What's sorts of things is he capable of? Raising the dead? Defying it himself? Controlling them?"

Denir replied, "All of that and more. Communication with the departed has given him vast knowledge found in no library. That may have been how they knew of the orb. That said, this communication is difficult to achieve, as not all deceased are accessed as easily as some. We will never know."

"Novir," began Ryan, "Do you have a mace or flail I can borrow? My sword may be of limited use against the undead, assuming he has a bunch with him."

"Of course." He gestured to one warrior, who had a spiked, black mace on one hip. They gave this to him.

"Thank you," said Ryan. "This may also be useful with the undead knight, as well. I don't suppose he became that way because of the necromancer?"

Denir fixed him with an appraising look before turning to Matt. "Indeed. And this story may be of special interest to Soliander."

Matt cocked an eyebrow. "Why is that?"

"The undead knight is technically King of Aranor now. That is your home kingdom, is it not?"

Matt nodded slowly. "Tell me."

"Lord Voth was an ambitious knight, second-in-command of the knights, in service to the king. Some in the knighthood believed the king had grown weak, spoiled, and uninterested in the greatness some wanted of their monarch. And so they staged a successful coup, killing the king and much of the royal family."

"That is a betrayal of their oath as knights," Ryan observed, frowning.

Novir smirked. "There was worse to come. Voth's commander assumed the throne, but not for long. Voth killed him and took his place."

Denir added, "Yes, but he miscalculated. The population had supported the coup due to the popularity of the commander he had just killed, and they were irate at his murder at the hands of Lord Voth.

"Good for them," Ryan said. "What happened?"

"They swarmed the castle, and when Lord Voth, now King of Aranor, ordered his knights to slay the mob, they refused, seeing him as a worse ruler than those they had executed. And so they opened the gates and let the mob have Lord Voth."

Eric laughed and held up one apologetic hand for his reaction. "No honor among thieves, we say on... we've heard said on another planet. Seems like he caused his own downfall."

"Yes," agreed Denir. "He does not elicit much sympathy, only terror. The royalty had access to an ice dragon, and so his punishment was to have it breathe on him, encasing him in ice and killing him. This resulted in one of his nicknames, the Ice King.

Matt asked, "And he somehow escaped from this?"

Novir nodded. "With help. He was on display in the throne room of Aranor by the new king. An unknown wizard and the necromancer Areon reincarnated him as undead. Lord Voth had his vengeance and reclaimed the throne, the room now perpetually covered in ice, the kingdom ruled by a prime minister because Lord Voth seems to have interests elsewhere."

Denir added, "All that he touches dies, for the power of the grave is the only thing flowing in his veins. Aranor is now called the Kingdom without a King, though it technically has one."

"Is he bound to the necromancer?"

"That is unknown. He appears to have his freedom and voluntarily works with the other Lords of Fear. Together for several years now, we saw them meddling in many kingdoms on quite a few worlds. Sometimes they work alone, in which case it can be harder to determine whether they cause something, but they are unmistakable when together."

Anna asked, "Who was the wizard who freed Lord Voth along with the necromancer?"

"There are many rumors about this, but no one is certain."

"Is it safe to believe that this person is the one who has the master Orb of Dominion?"

Denir replied, "No, though it may well be. We could find out if we let them succeed in their journey, but we cannot allow that."

Anna agreed but said nothing. These Lords of Fear sounded like the evil version of themselves, but without quests binding them. Did they always work for the same person, doing missions? Were they genuinely bound or only by a promise? The difference mattered because the latter can always be broken. Maybe these Lords of Fear weren't as well understood as the Ellorian Champions. Perhaps there was more to them. Now she was curious but doubted they would sit down and chat about it all. How could they get information directly from the lords?

"What is happening now?" she asked.

Denir answered, "Our second attempt at recovering the orb failed because our men recognized the Lords of Fear and knew they could not possibly beat them. When the dwarves and other enthralled arrived, they gave the orb to Lord Voth, then went with them. They and the rest of our captured forces are heading toward Ortham, a large city in the Kingdom of Gisla to the north. It has a portal to other worlds. We cannot be certain this is their goal, but we suspect it is."

Novir interjected, "Our contacts in the city have confirmed that the lords arrived on this planet via this gate some days prior to all of this. There was strong suspicion about it, but it only seemed known after we learned their identity at Bolin Hill."

"Wait," started Ryan, "how could an undead knight just walk through? Isn't either side guarded? Wouldn't someone see him and stop him? Or did people try to get killed?"

Denir answered, "We can easily identify most undead because of their appearance. However, Lord Voth does not look undead. Being frozen in ice killed and preserved him. Once raised from the dead, he does not decay, which is common of undead, as you know. Their bodies remain as they were at the moment of reanimation, likely by the design of the forces used to raise them. Otherwise, they would continue to fall apart and the problem of their existence would soon resolve itself as they become a pile of bones."

"Good point," admitted Ryan, then added apologetically, "Eriana and Soliander likely knew that, but I forget that sort of thing."

Cocking an eyebrow about that, Novir said, "They arrived and walked away, as the others give no casual observer reason to be concerned. But people noticed the cold from Lord Voth, and his startling blue eyes, rumored to be made of ice. Guards followed, and eventually he walked on grass that died under his feet. Between that and his healthy appearance, and the known description of the others, the Lords of Fear were identified even before we contacted Ortham to ask."

"Is it known in Ortham that they are returning to the city and have the orb?"

"Yes," Novir answered. "We consulted with them on this and agreed that the path from the city gates to the portal must be evacuated, but it is unknown how successful they will be. The population likely doesn't understand the danger. We must assume the lords intend to hold the orb aloft and ensnare anyone who sees it."

"The guy controlling the master orb has to be watching through it, though, right?"

"Yes. We are assuming he is keeping close watch on matters as they unfold."

Matt remarked, "I assume those in Ortham can close the gate."

Desir replied, "Yes, and they have left it open until the last moment, if needed. We are on friendly enough terms with Gisla Kingdom, at least on this front. Our plan is that all of you will arrive before then so that closing the portal is unnecessary. It takes some effort to reopen it, though perhaps less so if you will help, Soliander."

Matt said, "Of course. Is this the only portal they can use?"

"No, but it seems the likely one. As you know, travel between worlds requires more power than most can afford or wield, if they are wizards. We do not know if Lord Garian has such power, but maybe not. We expect they are attempting to leave the planet this way. They must be stopped, the orb taken away, preferably destroyed."

Novir said. "As the king knows nothing of your quest, you can expect no real help from the kingdom, sadly, as our king has issued orders to not interfere with the lords. And no one should be told who you are. Only those in this room know the truth."

"We understand," Ryan said, but Anna thought he said it unconvincingly. These men were risking their lives to free their king and kingdom, and their understanding of the gravity of the situation needed to be conveyed better. She was going to say something when the king's guardsman spoke first.

Novir added, "While we are doing the right thing, it would be treason until the king's mind is his own again."

Anna sensed the weight on him and wanted to reassure him. "He will see that it is good then. No one will learn our identities or purpose from us. We already have other names we can use, such as Anna for myself." Hiding the truth in plain sight seemed bold but obvious.

"Thank you, my lady." Denir placed four small bags on the table, each clinking. "We do not expect you will need to purchase supplies, but we know the unexpected happens. Please accept these coins and gems to satisfy any needs that may arise."

Ryan and Eric sat nearest him and took a pouch each for themselves, giving the others to Matt and Anna. She knew better to look inside, as did Ryan. She suspected Eric did too, but he did it anyway, and Matt dumping the contents on the table did not surprise her. She thought it was just boyish greed, but then he asked a smart question that made her feel sorry for doubting him.

He asked, "How much is this in these kingdoms? Is it enough to attract attention? Should we be careful showing this much?"

Denir said, "We thought of that. The coins are not platinum, which would be noticed at once except among royalty. There is only a little gold, one piece each, because they would also notice this in poor quarters. I recommend finer places if the need arises, which we do not expect. You should use the silvers and coppers."

"And the gems?"

"Emergency use only, and only in a city at a reputable trader. Use them out of sight, not in a main room where others would see the transaction."

Eric nodded. "Got it. I've been meaning to ask, how big are these orbs?"

"Half the size of a human head."

"How do we stop ourselves from being ensnared by them?"

Matt regarded him. "I think I might know a spell." He lifted the bag with Soliander's spell books in it and pulled out one in black leather with gold writing, the one Anna knew to have "nicer" spells in it, as opposed to the one with silver markings. Everyone waited quietly as he flipped through the pages. "Found it. It protects against any attempt to read the mind. I remembered if after what happened on Honyn, when I, uh, ran into that wizard who tried to do that. If I had cast this spell on myself beforehand, he may not have been able to learn anything."

Anna asked, "Can it be cast on more than one person?"

"One at a time." Matt's eyes scanned the page. "Wait, I can do it on a group."

Denir asked, "May I ask the name of this spell? I don't believe we have such a one on Rovell."

"*Mind Shield*," replied Matt. He let the wizard look at the spell and Anna wondered if sharing like that was a good idea or not, but then it wasn't an offensive one. Maybe they needed to talk over something like that, and establish some grounds rules before giving a dangerous spell to a world that didn't already have it. It might be like introducing an animal into an ecosystem that developed without it, destroying a delicate balance.

The wizard looked over the spell. "It says you need eyes from a blind fish, two eyes for each person. Do you have any with you?"

Matt shook his head. "I don't think so. I will have to check my supplies."

Denir said, "We have similar fish. This spell looks like it would work here on this planet. You are more experienced traveling between worlds than I, but most spells from other worlds work here as long as you have the needed materials, or can substitute them."

"The substitutions typically work?" Eric asked.

"Yes."

"Where could we get these fish eyes? I don't suppose someone sells them?"

"No. They are not commonly needed. There is an underwater lake to the southeast in the mountains, from where you could get them, but it is in the opposite direction from where the Lords of Fear have gone. I'm afraid that puts us under great pressure, but it might be needed."

Novir spoke up. "I know of another place north of Valegis, a mountain town. It is on the way, less of a detour, but it is more dangerous."

"How so?"

"The Kirii Cave not only has the large, batlike Kirii in it, but there is a leviathan in the waters, which is why I have heard of the place, as have most. We would have to be careful to not disturb any of kirii, but I think it is worth the risk. Four champions of your power could easily defeat anything we awaken. It lies within another dwarven kingdom, in a valley of the Galla Mountains."

"How do we get the fish?" Anna asked, imagining the famous Ellorian Champions standing around with fishing poles, the idea almost making her smile despite all of her worries. "Is there something faster than a net?"

Derin responded and turned to Matt, "A simple cantrip can round them up with little trouble. You know of it?"

Matt appeared to think for a moment and shook his head. "Perhaps you can show me."

"It would honor me to teach the great Soliander the merest of spells."

Eric said, "Okay, so given time being an issue, how do we get to this cave and then the city quickly?"

Novir gestured to the three leather clad companions, who had remained silent as they leaned against a wall listening to all of this. "The dragons will take us."

CHAPTER FIVE

THE KIRII CAVE

Ryan arched an eyebrow and turned to look at the humans that were apparently shape-shifting dragons, just like the ones on Honyn, except that none of those had been civil, just murderous toward any that were not their kind. The male in blue smirked at him, the one in green looked bored, and the female in red sauntered toward him, her intense gaze locked onto his. She seemed fiery and sexy, powerful and sleek and dangerous. He had only seen two dragons before, both golden, and each had tried to kill him. She had no obvious weapons with her, but he doubted this would matter. Only the calm with which Novir revealed their nature kept him sitting still instead of rising to face a potential threat.

She stopped before him in an aggressive yet alluring stance that made the word "vixen" pop into his mind. "Fear not, Dragon Slayer," she said in a rich alto. "We know your reputation, but we also know you only kill the ones who deserve it. And there are none such here." She leaned over and ran a finger along his jaw, leaving a trail of heat as the scent of roasted embers filling his nostrils. "We're not even offended by your nickname."

Clearing his throat uncomfortably and amazed that a dragon was hitting on him, Ryan said, "I have others, like the Pride of Andor."

"And do you feel pride, Lord Korrin?"

"To be talking to you? Absolutely."

She smiled then, all the way to her stunning eyes, and he felt certain that, by some miracle, he had just flattered a dragon. A freakin' dragon.

She added, "You will ride me, Pride of Andor." Hearing Eric quietly laugh, Ryan shot him an amused yet stern look to keep his mouth shut. "One other can accompany you, as we each can take two."

"Eriana, if it pleases you."

The dragon looked at her and nodded. "It does."

Denir said, "The dragons rarely involve themselves in the affairs of others on Rovell, but they recognize the threat that the orbs pose for all, including them. Three have agreed to assist us."

The red dragon strode to the head of the table as the other two came to flank her. She rested one arm around the neck of the one in blue leather. "I am Jolian. My brother Brazin here will carry Novir. The others will ride with our green friend, Sebast. We should leave now. I am curious to see this leviathan up close and see how she compares to us."

Eric caught Ryan's eye and said, "We would like a moment alone to discuss our plans."

Denir nodded. "Of course. We will step outside and prepare the saddles and what supplies you may need. Please join us when ready."

"Thank you."

Everyone filed out, Jolian the last to go with a last look at Ryan before closing the doors. They waited a moment for the voices to move farther away, and within a minute, the sound of enormous wings snapping in the air reached them, the ground shaking slightly from the steps of dragons.

Anna smirked at Ryan. "I think she likes you."

He tried to put her on the defensive instead of himself. "Jealous?"

She chuckled. "I can't compete with that."

They all laughed a moment before turning serious, with Eric, as usual, being the one to get down to business.

"Anna," he said, coming over to her, "how are you doing?"

Ryan thought she looked like she didn't want the reminder of what had happened on Earth as she pursed her lips. He shared her concern. The car had almost certainly crashed. The only question was how hurt her friends were. It might also cause another round of attention from the media, as if they needed more of that.

"Worried," she admitted. "There's nothing I can do. It's already too late."

Ryan came around to her, wanting to make her feel better. "Try to have faith. I know we've argued about God and all, and I'm sorry about that. You don't need faith in Him so much. I know it takes an effort, to just trust that everything may have worked out fine, nothing but minor bruises and scrapes. We can't know and letting our minds go to the worst possible outcomes... well, it won't help us all get back to find out the good news that everyone is fine."

She smiled, putting a hand on his arm. "Thank you, Ryan. You're right. I need to focus on our own problems right now."

"Yeah. Just, if you need anything about all of this, we're all here. You'd do the same, helping us if it had been us instead of you, so don't think you're being a burden or something. We're all family now."

"Yes," said Eric, "just physically protecting each other isn't enough. There's a lot more going on with all of us. Fear, uncertainty, not knowing what the hell we're doing."

"I hear you."

— • • —

Eric turned to the table and gestured for them to come over. "Memorize the map in case we get separated. Keep your own money bag, too."

They studied the map, noting roads and the compass direction, anything that might be useful should they be on their own to find their way back to the Quest Ring. The importance of not becoming lost or separated hung in the air.

To the east loomed the Galla Mountains that they had seen outside, the dwarven Kingdom of Hamarven toward its southern end and directly east of their position. Most of the Minari Kingdom lay west, but they'd never see it. To the northeast, past the Artem Woods, more of the mountains awaited with the town of Valegis nestled between the peaks. And nearly due west from there, outside the peaks on a plain, lay their ultimate destination of Ortham just over the border with Gisla Kingdom. If they got lost, it looked like all they had to do was walk south, parallel to the mountains. They had three options for that. Walking along the foothills risked attack from anything in them. Walking through Artem Woods to the west of the peaks offered the same. But still further west, miles from the trees, lay a road all the way from Ortham down to Castle Arking and the Quest Ring. As long as the mountains were on their left, they were heading south when coming back.

With the map memorized, Eric asked Matt, "Are you certain you can cast this *Mind Shield* spell?"

"Yeah, it doesn't look hard. Getting the fish eyes will be the issue."

"Without it," began Anna, folding her arms, "this Orb of Dominion really worries me. This may be our only protection against it."

Ryan had tried not to think what would happen if they became enthralled because the idea gave him the creeps, so he changed the subject. "Even with the spell, this sounds pretty difficult. I don't like the sound of these Lords of Fear at all."

Eric sighed. "Yeah, we should think about this on the way to this Kirii Cave. We need ideas, plans. The mace was a good idea, Ryan, but don't discount that soclarin sword you have. There's no telling what advantages the real Soliander gave it for fighting undead."

"True. I'll keep the mace as backup."

Eric asked, "Matt, Anna, what do we know about curing poisons? This assassin woman, Kori, sounds like serious trouble with poisoned blades."

Anna said, "In theory, I can heal that. I need to spend some time trying to communicate with a god. I must ask Novir and the others before we leave, if they have any choices for me, so I can try while we travel. I wish there was a way to do that as soon as I arrive on a quest. It's a lot of pressure to quickly know a god and reach out to one, get an answer."

"Yeah," agreed Matt. "At least the spells I remember will still work. My ability to shield us may be crucial. I suggest we stick together when we encounter these guys. They make me nervous already."

"Good idea. On the plus side, they don't know we're coming or that we have dragons with us. Oh, I just had an idea. When we get near the orb, we should pretend that we're enthralled by it and are under their control. This would gain their trust that we aren't a threat and maybe allow us to get close before they realize the truth."

Ryan clapped a hand on his shoulder. "That's brilliant. Love this idea."

"Do we need anything else before we get going?" Matt asked, as another thud shook the building.

Ryan smirked. "Yeah, dragon flying lessons. I think we should ask when we get out there, you know, like we usually do, as if like we're just confirming how things are on this world."

"That's good," Eric agreed. "They're intelligent, so it's not like we have to give commands from reins or something. Let's check that. Everyone ready?"

Ryan let the others go ahead of him as they left the room behind. He was undoubtedly the one to take on this Lord Voth, but the undead knight didn't concern him as much as the assassin and her poisoned blades. He imagined her targeting Anna or Matt. Maybe he and Eric needed to get Lord Voth and the assassin away from the other two as a tactic. He sighed, not sure what to do. The Lords of Fear had worked as a team, doing whatever they were up to for far longer than him and his friends. The dragons might be crucial, and after they finished at the Kirii Cave, they needed to discuss what options they provided. Surely they would do more than fly them around. They could affect the success of this quest.

The truth of this became apparent after they stepped from the building and followed a warrior around the corner, away from the Quest Ring. They walked onto the grass, a light autumn breeze stirring the pine trees. The season was the same as on Earth right now.

Behind the structure was an open field, shielded from the distant castle's view by trees, and it was here that the three dragons awaited in their natural forms. Rays of sun broke through the overcast sky, and Ryan saw that a sheer cliff drop awaited anyone foolish enough to venture too far to one side. A wide crevasse ran perpendicular and away from Castle Arking, a rushing river audible below, or perhaps it was a waterfall out of sight. Mist rose from the cliff, and in the distance, the thick Artem Woods stretched for miles, the leaves turning red, gold, and brown.

He turned to gaze at the dragons, the sheer size and mass of them as intimidating as the wicked talons, white teeth taller than him, and powerful wings. Not counting the necks, heads, and tails, each was bigger than a two-story, single-family home. He'd once seen a video of a jet engine flipping a car upside and hurling it away. The impression that the air blast from one stroke of a wing could send him off the cliff made him uneasy. Just one dragon could more than level the playing field against the Lords of Fear. He also wondered how a brother and sister dragon were different colors, and whether anything else about them was unique, but there was no time to ask.

The blue dragon stood nearest and was ready, silver eyes cold and indifferent as he gazed down at Ryan. Maybe he was imagining it, but he felt some disdain. Brazin's sister had been flirting with him. Was he irritated about it? Did dragons even fool around with humans? Was it possible? Or was the idea just insulting to one such as Brazin? Ryan wasn't sure but didn't feel comfortable with him and was glad to not be riding him.

Past him, Jolian rose to her feet and stretched her wings, a saddle now affixed to her, the warriors who had assisted with it stepping away toward the green dragon beyond. Jolian was noticeably larger than the other two, red scales gleaming as a ray of sun broke through the overcast sky to touch her. She took a deeper breath, the saddle girth expanding and contracting snugly as she did so, before a small burst of flames erupted from her nostrils, smoke curling up from them after it was over. She seemed satisfied and rested on her hindquarters, massive head turning to regard the Ellorian Champions. Her red eyes seemingly met Ryan's. It was hard to tell, given that they were bigger than a horse. But he saw kindness in them, which Brazin's baleful gaze made easier to recognize.

Warriors were now saddling the green dragon, Sebast, as he crouched to make it simpler for them. Ryan tried to watch in case he needed to do the same thing, but he couldn't see much from here. Was saddling a dragon noticeably different from a horse? It almost had to be.

Approaching Novir, who stood beside Denir, Ryan said, "So we've ridden dragons before, of course. It's just different across worlds."

Novir smiled. "Say no more." He led him toward Brazin, who cooperated by crouching and moving the nearer blue wing back. "You see the saddle is before the wings, of course. These may differ from others, but unlike a horse, dragons can at least tell you how to saddle them, if you must. They know where we are going and will largely take care of direction, but if you must, you can use the four straps to control the flight path. One each left, right, top, bottom. Use two at once as needed and flying straight and level means pulling on the top and bottom at together."

"Got it."

"I will lead the way, but they know where the Kirii Cave is, generally."

"Generally?" That was hardly good enough. What if something happened to Novir?

Novir winked and used a small rope ladder to climb the side of Brazin, settling into the seat and strapping himself into the saddle with a wide belt that he hooked to it once before and behind him. As he started pulling up the ladder, he yelled down. "Of course, I don't need to tell you to always strap yourself in first in case they decide to take flight. Things like a rope can wait!"

"I just wanted to see if *you* knew that!" Ryan joked. He wondered what other "obvious" tips he would not think of and learn the hard way. If he fell off a dragon high in the air, would it realize and be able to catch him? Finding out wasn't appealing.

As Anna went to get a scroll with information about gods from Denir, Ryan walked to Jolian. Was he supposed to pass in front of or behind Brazin? With horses, you avoided going behind unless you put a hand on their rump to let them know you were there. A startled horse had been known to kick and badly wound or even kill a fool. Would a dragon do it by accident, or would Brazin do it to Ryan on purpose? He wasn't sure what would happen as he neared the giant head, but the blue giant suddenly rose and let them pass under his neck.

"I think you need to go up first," Ryan said to Anna when she joined him. He took her hand to the rope ladder. "I can be in front for control, if I need it. I'm more used to, well, horses anyway."

"Yeah," she muttered, looking apprehensive. But she climbed the ladder and clambered into her seat behind his. Ryan followed, grinning. He hadn't been this close to a dragon before, except after he'd killed it. The expanding and contracting dragon body as she breathed him feel like he was dreaming, and despite the danger awaiting them, for the moment he didn't need to face it and marveled at what he was doing.

At the top, he found Anna trying to adjust the straps and so he briefly helped her, figuring it out. A wide belt opened on one side and had to be tightly cinched around the waist. Then two hooks fastened it to the saddle. She had already gotten her feet into two stirrups that were unlike those on a horse in that it firmly attached them to the saddle. This meant no trying to control the dragon with the feet. The stirrups seemed more like another way to brace yourself.

Keeping his weapons out of the way, he soon had himself situated and tested his own security of position, feeling reasonably satisfied, trying to ignore the forty-foot drop to the ground. It being so much worse than falling off a horse made him chuckle nervously. He thought that if he was going to get killed or worse on this quest, at least he was getting one hell of a ride first. He looked over to see Eric helping Matt get seated in the rear spot of Sebast's saddle, the two of them arguing a little. Jolian shifted beneath him the way horses do, the motions stronger because of her size, and he suddenly wondered if the others might get sick. That would be very un-champion like, puking from the back of a dragon, especially if Eric did it and Matt caught a face full as they flew. At the last minute, he untied his helmet and put it on for some protection from the wind. Or maybe it was for Anna behind him.

Jolian's neck twisted as she turned her enormous head back to him. "Are you ready, Pride of Andor?" Her voice boomed but sounded similar to when she was in human form.

"I was born ready," he said.

"Good."

With no other warning, Jolian took several giant steps forward, smote her wings once, and lifted off just enough to get past the cliff edge. And then they dove over it, the feeling like the first incredible drop of a rollercoaster. He heard Anna scream behind him like girls always did at the amusement park, but then Jolian straightened out and turned into the crevasse to soar just below its top. Wind buffeted Ryan's chest in a steady rush. The great snap of leathery wings was intermittent as they glided. Trees roared by on either side of them, above the canyon, and white water splashed hundreds of feet below among rocks, more trees, and a brief shoreline beside the river, the occasional four-legged animal startled into fleeing at the sight of them hurtling by. Jolian's head lifted a bit and the amount of wind striking Ryan suddenly dropped. Was she doing it on purpose, creating a pocket of calmer air?

After the initial exhilaration, Ryan took stock of himself and realized he was gripping the reins hard but not pulling on them, probably from many years of good horseback riding habits. He jammed his feet into the stirrups, his body tight. But he made himself relax and start gazing around. Turning in the saddle revealed Anna looking a little tense, but she smiled. Not far behind and gaining was Novir on the blue dragon, and just behind, the green one with Matt and Eric. He really wanted a GoPro to capture this experience for forever.

Moments later, the crevasse ended, the cliffs disappearing as they emerged from it, a shimming blue lake below, more forest all around it, snow-capped mountains in the distance. The sun streamed out in places, lighting up a fleet of fishing boats to one side. Suddenly a shadow appeared on Ryan and he looked up as Brazin overtook them, four enormous legs closer than comfortable, especially when he dove toward the water, the tail coming perilously close. Jolian followed him down, both dragons skimming their feet across the calm waters. The spray from Brazin struck Ryan, who stayed dry inside his armor. He laughed as they climbed again, the powerful wing strokes propelling them up faster than he would have believed. The ground fell away, and he wondered just how many thousands of feet in the air they were now. It became quieter, more peaceful, colder, and even boring as they disappeared into the clouds.

And then suddenly they were above them, bright sunlight all around, nothing visible but the sky above, the white moody clouds below, eddies from Brazin ahead of them whisking up. Nearer now than before, the tallest mountains poked above the serene view. Wanting to share it more, he reached behind him with one hand and after a moment, felt Anna's hand grip his. They rode this way for a long time, and as they went, Ryan considered the task before them, reminding himself of what training he had received in swordsmanship and battle tactics.

The batlike kirii at the cave, and the unknown leviathan, concerned him less than the Lords of Fear. But right now, something bothered him about Brazin that he couldn't quite identify. He sensed his own distrust and that the friendliness of Jolian was the only reason he didn't outright dislike her brother. Novir seemed to think nothing of it, so he wasn't sure what to believe. He felt certain that Brazin was only doing this for Jolian, and that if the red dragon somehow fell, Brazin would leave them behind. He didn't want to be alone with Brazin, or give him a chance to abandon them. He decided that as long as someone monitored the blue dragon, maybe everything would be fine. Not being able to trust those who've summoned him away from his life and into danger made these quests even more troubling.

Ryan wasn't sure how long they were above the clouds, but it seemed like over an hour. They passed between the nearest mountains, and when they dove beneath the clouds, he saw they were quite a distance into the range. He realized their flight had made it harder to mentally follow the map he'd memorized. But then he saw a town off to one side and wondered if it was the one he'd noted. Were they getting near? The green dragon came up beside them with Eric and Matt giving them a thumbs up and huge grins. Ryan didn't really have anything he wanted to say, but he realized knowing more sign language as those two did could help in situations like this. The idea of riding dragons so often that he needed that made him laugh.

Brazin banked sharply, which was the only warning Jolian was about to, and now it became concerning as they tilted wildly to the left, a dragon no longer directly below them, but the ground far below, just like when a rollercoaster takes a sharp turn. They glided in circles, the earth rushing up. Ryan began visually searching the area for threats and the cave they needed to enter, but he saw neither, just a cleared area barely big enough for three dragons to land one-by-one, moving aside so another could arrive. Jolian dropped last, powerful wing blasts sending loose leaves and dust into the air. The landing was surprisingly smooth for a creature this size. Ryan exchanged looks with the others, noticing as he did that the dragons appeared on alert but relaxed as if they sensed nothing amiss. He took a long drink of water from a flask in the saddle, seeing Eric doing the same.

Novir was already grabbing a crossbow and quiver of bolts from the saddle pack, then a cloth sack before dismounting. Ryan got himself unbuckled, then helped Anna. He took the quiver and crossbow from his saddle despite not being sure how to use them. Then he climbed down the rope ladder to the ground, almost sorry to be standing on his own two feet again after that ride. Everyone soon gathered in one place, near the heads of the dragons. Even Jolian, with her benevolent attitude, was simply frightening this close to that gigantic mouth. Ryan could have walked straight into it and been swallowed whole.

"Where's the cave?" Eric asked of Novir, looking around. Ryan didn't see it either, just pine-covered, snow-capped mountains all around, the foothills covered in thicker foliage, boulders of every size gathered in old rock falls. They stood on uneven earth with more stone jutting up, most of it smooth from weathering. He had seen a trail leading past this spot and a way to climb down to it, and it made him wonder what had made it. Whatever it was wouldn't be much of a threat to dragons, and likely wasn't dumb enough to try something. They were taking a chance trusting the dragons, because if they left while they were underground, they would be lost without adequate supplies with who knows what nearby and a town a few hours away. He at least felt confident which direction it was from here, the trail leaving only two options.

"That way," Novir replied, pointing past some trees. But when Ryan looked, he saw nothing. "I think it could be best for Brazin and Sebast to remain here. Jolian can change form and come with us? Good. I think one dragon might be helpful inside, just in case we run into more trouble than expected. When we come back, only having to put one saddle back on is better than three."

Ryan was about to ask if they needed to at least loosen the saddle on Jolian when she whispered a few words he didn't catch and morphed into the leather clad vixen he'd first seen. For a second, she had appeared as both, the humanoid form where the dragon head was like an illusion, close to the ground. She dropped a few feet to land nimbly and straightened. The saddle, reins, and halter fell to the earth, the bulky saddle landing with a thud and rolling sideways. He assumed they were designed for such impacts and for the first time, wondered how they got it up there, as he hadn't been watching Sebast get saddled, and the others had already been prepared.

"Is there any chance of Sebast and Brazin being seen while we're inside?" Eric asked.

"Some," Sebast responded, his rumbling voice deep, "but boredom is our greatest threat."

Novir added, "There are trolls and ogres in these mountains, but they are smart enough to stay far from dragons. It's a long walk to the nearest town, and a deadly one. There's a reason few come to this cave." He gestured toward the faint trail leading up into the peaks for what seemed like an arduous climb.

Ryan scanned around them but saw no signs of movement. "What should we expect inside?"

Novir pulled a cloth sack off his shoulder and pulled two torches from it, tossing one to the knight. "A walk down a narrow tunnel. We can talk about the cave itself as we go. Let's move."

He started toward some trees and the others followed, Ryan and Jolian in the rear as they stepped around boulders and over the random fallen trees always lying in the wilderness. Ryan had no tracking skills to speak of, really, though he had learned some from Lorian, but he saw no signs of recent passage, including near the ten-foot-wide cave opening that was low so that he had to duck into it. After another few feet, it rose just high enough to straighten.

And part of a humanoid skeleton was the first thing Ryan saw. A glance around showed another set of bones from something bigger, then a pair of skeletal wings with some of the leathery part still on it. Most of the remains were partial, and he wondered if animals had gotten to the rest, as something had moved various bones around. The bodies not being fresh gave him some comfort that a threat was not imminent, but they left no doubt that danger lay here.

Novir lit his torch and then Ryan's. Matt made the top of his wizard's staff glow with a spoken word.

"I assume we should keep our voices down as we descend," Eric said.

"Yes." Novir stepped deeper into the tunnel, Eric right behind, then Anna, Matt, and finally Ryan and the dragon. "There is little to concern us until the cave at the end, but sound travels here and we want to silently do this so as not to disturb anything."

As they followed on what looked like a natural passage, every surface rough and uneven, Eric asked in a low voice, "What is at the end, and is it really the end or just our destination?"

"The Kirii Cave is at least a hundred yards high, less wide and deep. And it is not the end. There are several passages deeper into the mountains, or in other directions. Some of these are above in the ceiling, and that is how the kirii fly out into the sky to hunt. They are nocturnal, which means they will be sleeping, hanging from the ceiling above the water. They should not disturb us. The leviathan is our concern."

"What is it, exactly?" Eric asked.

"No one is really sure. Hard to get a good look at in the darkness, and partly because it has long tentacles and can pull you from the shore without showing its body. These appear to grow back, so wounds do not easily deter it."

"Do normal weapons hurt it?"

"Yes. It is not supernatural. Our best tactic, aside from not waking it, is to retreat into the tunnel, or near it, and fight from there if we haven't gotten what we need."

Ryan had a thought and asked, "Disturbing it means disturbing the kirii, doesn't it?"

"Yes, it does. One will awaken the others."

They stepped around loose rock that had fallen from a wall. "And what will they do?"

"Attack."

"Us or the leviathan?"

"Everything that isn't them."

They entered a natural cave with the ground falling away to one side. As they skirted around, Eric asked, "How dangerous are they?"

"Very, especially because we are where they live. They do have young to protect and will see us as a threat. Expect a vicious, nasty battle if one happens."

"Are they animals or smarter?"

The passage continued, tightly closed on all sides so that they had to turn sideways to continue, but it didn't last long. Ryan wasn't feeling quite claustrophobic, but a little uncomfortable when the passage got too tight.

Novir answered, "Oh, they're smarter. They have weapons. Small crossbows, slings. They understand tactics. One of them is two or more of them grabbing you and carrying you away. You are as good as dead if this happens, whether they tear you to pieces in the sky, drop you to your death, or save you for food. It is more reason to retreat if needed."

Ryan asked, "Will they follow us through this tunnel? I saw the one skeleton outside."

"Not sure, but they know where the tunnel leads. The one we saw probably flew out and came around to the opening."

"So they could trap us inside."

"Yes, they could, but they don't fight well in small spaces. And they aren't likely to enter the tunnels very far."

"Still leaves you trapped. They can wait you out."

Novir said, "Let's not worry about it. We have a wizard and a dragon in here with us and two more dragons outside. The kirii would see Brazin and Sebast and turn around at once."

They descended in silence from there, the tunnel sometimes getting wider or taller but seldom much smaller. They passed through several small caves and a cave-in, which made Ryan wonder how stable all of this was. The possibility of getting trapped or lost underground wasn't something he had considered until now, and the number of natural tunnels branching out from caves made him want to concentrate and memorize the way. Only a few looked to have been created manually, as evidenced by chisel marks and scattered debris, but they sometimes came upon multiple openings of different sizes and leading up, down, level, or in other directions. It was not obvious which way to go, and their reliance on Novir bothered him. What if something killed him? Ryan had been making a point of always looking behind him when they reached a cave, to visually identify whether other openings were there and which one they had just exited. He couldn't see Eric up ahead until then, but his friend was doing the same. They finally stopped, gathering close.

"We are near," Novir whispered. "Around the next turn. It is best to ready ourselves here."

He wound the crossbow he had been carrying, as Ryan did after watching to see how he did it. He needed to learn these things back on Earth and practice everything related to it. He hadn't opened the weapons that had arrived. He'd been loading them into the house when he was summoned. Confidence that he was an excellent shot would have eased his nerves, and maybe those of his friends. Eric had already drawn a throwing knife, and Ryan knew his friend was deadly accurate. He wanted the others to rely on him the same way he did on Eric right now. As he stood thinking about this, Matt was fumbling in his robes for what turned out to be a vial he held up, nodding that he was ready.

Ryan turned to Anna, asking, "Have you been able to reach a god?"

She nodded. "Yes, on the way here."

"Then I guess we're ready."

Seeing agreement, Novir quietly led them another ten paces and around a curve. A bit farther and it appeared to end in blackness. They continued forward, Novir the first to step out a few paces and then aside as the rest joined him. Ryan exited last and looked around, but there wasn't much to see in the dark. Seeing Novir put a torch on a wall sconce someone had fastened beside the opening, he looked for a second on his side and put his there. The light being in his hand wasn't helping his eyes adjust, but now they all stepped forward on the stone, which extended twenty feet out and to the sides as the cavern opened around them. While most of the lake appeared to be directly ahead, some of it lay to either side of their position.

Two dim shafts of light above revealed two openings to the outside. Against them, they could see dark shapes hanging from the cavern roof, scores of them by one shaft and more by another. Given the room's size, Ryan guessed that well over a hundred kirii were here, most out of sight, and he knew that the number could be far higher. They seemed small from here, but he knew they were four feet tall. None appeared to be moving.

One small, somewhat flat island lay off to one side, but a large, rockier, and taller one stood farther away, jagged spires of rock straining upward. Both seemed to have various shiny items laying on them, and he wondered if they were "treasure" to lure people out there. A rowboat lay on the shore. Another rested off to one side of where he stood, available to them if needed. A third floated aimlessly on the still waters, and the wreck of a fourth jutted up from beneath the dark surface nearer to them. He saw no bodies, but from what Novir had said, maybe the leviathan or kirii carried away anything left here. Nearby, he saw a rusting sword, broken arrows, and loose stones that might have been fired from a sling.

"You're up, Soli," Eric whispered.

Matt sighed and moved carefully on the dark, slick stones, stopping at the water's edge and resting the crook of his staff in one arm. Ryan moved toward him in case Matt needed physical protection, but his eyes were on the kirii, not his footing, and he stepped on a loose rock that slid out from underfoot. He nearly fell with what would have been a loud clatter, but caught himself. The rock wasn't so fortunate, rattling over the other stones and into the water with a small splash. He cringed and watched helplessly as ripples of water spread out and away. He knew Eric's incredulous eyes were boring into the back of his head without bothering to turn around to confirm it.

Ryan asked in a whisper, "Any chance you can direct a focused beam of light from the staff? I'd like to know what is out there."

"What if I wake something up?

"Good point. Maybe right before we leave. Or maybe not."

"Hold the staff, please."

Ryan took it as Matt crouched to the water, opened the vial in one hand, and emptied it into the waters as he spoke words of magic, which Ryan only understood thanks to the spell Lorian had cast on all of them on Honyn.

Into the waters you seek and find
All the creatures, make them mine
Bring them here, all of one mind
Caught like a fish on hook and line

Matt made a gesture as if to spread the liquid out, and then another toward himself, as if bringing back fish. Only now did the knight realize he hadn't noticed Matt getting the fishing cantrip, as he thought of it, from Denir. Matt straightened and took the staff back.

"How long does it take?" Ryan asked.

The wizard shrugged. "Not sure. A couple minutes?"

They waited in silence, Ryan casting a look behind. Eric and Anna stood together as far from the water's edge on three sides as they could, and the opening behind them, as if concerned something might come from there. Or at least, that's what Ryan suddenly thought of. But Novir stood just before the torches, as if expecting it, too, so he had their back. Jolian had walked to the water's edge and crouched, eyes staring off into the dark as if she could see things they could not. She sniffed the air several times, making Ryan wonder what she smelled.

His thoughts were broken when a surge of water a few inches high moved toward them from out in the lake. It came in waves, something under the surface clearly moving closer to them, as if undecided about doing so and starting and stopping, each time causing a new rush of water. Ryan gripped his crossbow and loaded a bolt into it. Another surge started to one side, closer to Jolian, who turned toward it. The first surge came again, this time larger and with an audible sound of moving water. Ryan's eyes darted up to the cavern roof, and he thought several red glowing eyes were visible, but maybe it was his imagination. The earliest waves reached their feet, lapping at the stone shore, but so far there was no sign of the cause.

"I wonder what else is in these waters," he whispered to Matt, watching the source draw nearer. "What if it's not just the one type of fish and this monster?"

The wizard looked back at Novir, who was too far away to ask. "Wish we had thought of that earlier."

"Let's get away from the edge."

"Brilliant idea."

They cautiously backed up, and as they did so, more waves came from the side near Jolian, one being noticeably deeper than the shallower ripples. He couldn't see her face, but Ryan had the impression she was watching intensely.

"Soliander," began Eric, who had approached them silently and startled Ryan, "how exactly does this spell work?"

"It brings nearby sea life to—" He stopped, a look of alarm on his face.

Seeing that, Ryan asked, "What is it?"

Eric asked, "Does the spell specify fish?" Matt's wide eyes turned to him and Eric swore.

Ryan began, "Why does that... oh shit."

"What?" asked Anna.

Eric answered, "The spell summons sea life. That might include the leviathan."

Suddenly splashes came from the first source of movement and a few silvery fish broke the surface as they approached chaotically. Ryan relaxed at the sight. The rush of water grew louder and more intense, which made him look up again. For a moment, he thought one of the kirii that had been a silhouette against the dim ceiling lights had disappeared, but then he realized he was the one who had moved. A quick step to one side to change his angle and he confirmed it was still there.

But now the noise grew uncomfortably loud as a swarm of fish surged toward them, the shallow water causing waves to crash and echo in the cavern. And it only got worse when the hundreds of silver fish reached the shore and began flopping both in the water and on land. Each was about as long as his hand and narrow, but together they were making Ryan nervous with the noise. He saw other fish among them, red and smaller, and large black ones. Something that looked like a turtle was hard to see with the other fish flopping around on top of it. No leviathan, at least.

"Which ones do we want?" he asked Matt, who was pulling out a pouch. A glance at Jolian showed her still watching the other, unseen source of movement, which had come closer, too.

"The silver ones. Just grab a bunch and throw them in here."

The sound of rushing water near Jolian made them turn. A two-foot wave surged forward, and she stood up, her wary posture showing alarm. To the left and right of the surge, two thick, black tentacles broke the surface, one lashing out at Novir near the exit, but missing. The other swung at Jolian, who did a backflip over it, and when she landed, long nails had sprung from her fingertips. Novir fired his crossbow at the place where Ryan suspected the body of the leviathan was, the bolt slicing into the water to vanish. And then several more tentacles sprang from the water.

Ryan hefted his crossbow and wondered where to aim. The tentacles were moving too fast, but then Jolian spoke a word and they slowed to half their speed as if stunned. He fired into one and it recoiled. Novir did the same, but Ryan shook his head. Crossbows would not deter this thing.

"Ryan, back away from Matt and get your sword out," said Eric, coming closer. The knight turned and saw him leading Anna to the wizard, telling her to scoop up some fish into the bag and quickly get to the exit and wait there. Eric was right. She had to get out of harm's way and wasn't much help in a fight, as far as he knew. Just then a tentacle flew toward him and he swung the sword, cutting deep into it as black blood splattered around him and on his armor. The wounded limb came back, and this time he cut it clean. And then a horrible screeching sound erupted from the roof of the cavern, and Ryan turned in realization. The kirii were coming, dozens of flying silhouettes against the rays of dim light from above.

"Matt!" he yelled. "Light this place up!"

The wizard gripped the staff and turned toward the flying menace. "Oonurarki!" he yelled. From the top of his staff, the dim light became blinding and hurtled outward with such force that a shock wave struck everyone and hurled back the kirii. Scores of them had been flying toward them and were so disoriented that several fell all the way to the water and splashed around. Suddenly the jaws of something rose to clamp around one and drag it under. There was another lifeform down there. And above them, the kirii seemed in chaos, but it was hard to tell.

Ryan yelled, "Matt! We can't see."

"Sorry!" The wizard laughed and dimmed the light. Ryan got the impression he loved the power.

Jolian dodged more tentacles, swiping at them with her nails and drawing more blood. But only his sword looked like it was going to help, unless Matt did something. Anna had filled the sack and now scampered toward the entrance.

"Time to go!" Eric yelled.

But then everything seemed to happen at once. The kirii closed in, stones fired from slings clattering on the ground and cavern walls behind them. Eric threw one knife, then another, two kirii dropping to the water with a splash. Matt sent a jet of flames at others, setting a dozen of them on fire, before retreating. A tentacle flew toward Jolian, but she dodged it only to be grabbed by another and hauled high over the water upside down. The leviathan finally rose to the surface, a huge, black, oblong head appearing with a mouth opened wide, multiple rows of teeth as big as a person ready to clamp on Jolian. It dropped her toward its gaping maw, clearly expecting a meal but not the transformation that came. The dragon assumed her true form as she fell, wings snapping out as her mouth stretched wide and a torrent of flames roared down on the leviathan. Deafening screeches filled the air as Jolian landed atop the beast, which tried to submerge only to have Jolian dig claws into its head and beat the air furiously, lifting it from the water more and more.

Ryan stood transfixed until a stone struck his helmet with a loud bang, dazing him. Hearing little flapping wings near him, he swung upward without looking and felt his sword bite into something. He turned, swinging again, slicing through a kirii that he saw up close this time as it hovered before him. A snout like a dog jutted between yellow eyes, a drooling mouth of fangs snapping at him even though it was much too far away to matter. A knife from Eric struck that one in the face and it fell, another kirii replacing it, brown leathery wings pounding the air as clawed arms reached for him. He cut into one of them and retreated as more kirii closed in. They smelled of rot and seemed intent on grabbing him, to fly away with him as Novir had suggested. An energy pulse hurled them back, and he looked back to Matt and nodded.

Suddenly a thundering roar of rumbling stone and earth came from the exit behind Anna and they looked over in new alarm, not seeing a cause, but Ryan sensed it was farther up. Had the passage out crumbled? They gathered at the opening.

Still holding the bag of writhing fish, Anna asked, "Where's Novir? I just realized he wasn't here when I got here with the fish."

Eric looked around. "The leviathan didn't get him, did it?"

"Pretty sure it didn't," said Ryan. "We need to get out of here. We just need Jolian."

They turned to see the dragon biting into the leviathan's head repeatedly, yanking giant hunks of it off and spitting them out. The tentacles had all stopped moving, and the creature seemed dead. Some kirii actually went for Jolian, who jumped off the leviathan and with one stroke of her wings, landed in the shallow water near them, being unable to get closer in that form because of the cavern walls. She turned toward the kirii, and Ryan thought she smiled before blasting them with fire. The smell of burned hair and flesh filled the cavern as bodies hit the water. The dragon changed form again and sauntered over to them.

"Ready?" she asked with a smile. She stopped before Ryan and looked him up and down, then wiped one finger across his armor. It came away thick with black blood, which she licked off her finger.

"Let's go," said Eric, grabbing the remaining torch. No-vir had taken the other. "I have a bad feeling about this."

They hurried into the tunnel and jogged as fast as they could while not banging their heads or risking a twisted ankle. Whether Matt had summoned the leviathan by acci-dent or not, they would likely never know, and Ryan put it from his mind. The thought of being trapped inside a mountain or having to find their way out through some other path, and then make it down to the dragons, worried him. And with good reason. They soon stopped at a rock-fall that had blocked the path.

Eric said, "Unless Soliander or Jolian can do a spell, I don't see getting through this."

"Is going back easier?" Anna asked, frowning. "I don't like either option."

Jolian turned to Matt. "We may need two spells. One to move the rocks, another to hold up the tunnel until we pass so that it doesn't collapse more. My magic is limited and is for dragon-related elements."

That surprised Ryan. "You can't do other things?"

"We can but rarely learn them. The other races mostly use magic. My brother is an exception, spending enough time with humans, elves, and others to have learned. So we can. We just don't."

Seeing Matt thinking, they waited, Ryan feeling impa-tient. But finally, the wizard had an idea and coordinated with the dragon. The rest of them stood back as Jolian cast a spell to bolster the ceiling, and Matt cast a spell that va-porized ten feet of rock. He had to do this three times as they advanced and finally made it to the other side. Once everyone was out, Jolian let her spell end and another cas-cade of debris filled much of the tunnel, though not as much as before. As the others left, the dragon and wizard looked back at the collapse, Jolian studying the ceiling.

"This was no accident," said Jolian, turning around with a glare and striding toward the exit. "Novir did this."

"How?" Matt asked, coming behind.

"I'll find out when I strangle him."

They ran through the tunnels with Matt's staff casting light far ahead of them, Jolian taking the lead as she expressed confidence about their path. After another few minutes, they heard a faint roar ahead, then another. Ryan assumed it was Sebast and Brazin. Jolian picked up her pace, exuding rage. The roars grew louder amid the sound of ice shattering with a loud crack. Then it went quiet for a minute until they burst from the tunnel and paused. All except Jolian, who continued past the line of trees separating them from her kin. The others followed and came into view of a battle just as Jolian yelled her brother's name in disbelieving surprise or anger.

The green dragon, Sebast, lay on his side, one wing visibly broken, shards of ice embedded all along that side of his body, including his neck and head. Gashes that appeared to be from another dragon's claws punctured the body, and several evenly spaced holes that looked like bite marks were on his neck. A green liquid oozed from his nostrils, dripping on the ground and hissing as leaves emitted smoke from its touch. From the lolling head, gaping mouth, and unmoving, open eyes, he seemed dead.

Brazin reared up on two hind legs, his blue body showing burn marks from the green liquid that dripped off of him. Two gashes in his belly oozed red blood, and Ryan saw the body expanding as the dragon sucked in a large breath that heralded trouble. Two baleful eyes fixed them. On his back sat Novir, who lifted his crossbow and fired at the group just before a blast of frost from Brazin's throat flew toward them. Matt put up a shield, and the bolt bounced harmlessly away, but the ice struck the barrier and stuck to it, forming a dome over the invisible protection. As the blast continued, Eric stepped back and then ran away through the trees as Ryan watched, wondering what he was doing.

CHAPTER SIX

FLIGHT OF THE DRAGONS

Eric sprinted through the trees, using them to hide his intentions. Once out of sight, he chose another path and began creeping back toward the blue dragon, hoping to emerge where they neither expected him nor saw him.

"Brazin!" Ryan yelled, "you have a coward on your back."

Eric looked over at them but couldn't see the knight's position. Maybe it didn't matter as long as he kept up a banter, but then another dragon joined the distraction.

"Brother!" Jolian called out, voice anguished. "What have you done?"

"I have done what I am commanded, dear sister. Do not follow or your death is next."

In reply, Jolian transformed into a dragon, and in that moment, Eric threw a knife at Novir. The blade was half-way there as he took off at a run. It did not surprise him that his throw missed, partly because Brazin moved. Seeing the blade go by, Novir turned and fired the crossbow at him but didn't come close. Eric hurled another knife as he ran, then another as he adjusted the aim. The last blade struck Novir in the side.

"Fly!" the guardsman yelled in pain, pulling the blade out and dropping it.

Brazin leaped up and beat his wings furiously, lifting into the sky. Jolian looked ready to follow when Eric called out.

"Wait! Not without me!" He ran for the dragon, who turned with impassioned eyes. He thought she would refuse, but she lowered a wing as her brother continued a climb.

"Climb up the wing, Andier. My magic will keep you on."

He raced up the wing, the footing bouncy until he ran along the bone at the front, wondering why they didn't just use magic all the time instead of using saddles, which there was no time to put on. Reaching the spine, he straddled it and grabbed a handful of red dragon's mane, the insanity of what he was about to do filling him with adrenaline and fear.

"Eric!" Ryan called. "We shouldn't separate!"

"No choice!" he yelled down. "Wait for us!"

He nearly bit his tongue as Jolian leaped up, wings beating the air. The time for talk had passed. She climbed effortlessly, Eric hanging on with effort. The idea of letting go to find out how well she was keeping him there with magic made him laugh, but he knew that if she failed for even a second, he was plummeting to his death. He didn't need to look down to know his knuckles were white. He squeezed her enormous body with both legs, but as he did so, he had the sense that they were almost attached to her back, as if it and him were magnetic. He tried to lift one knee away and found he couldn't.

"You will feel better if you trust me," Jolian said, and he wondered if she felt him struggling despite what he assumed was a preoccupation with gaining altitude. Brazin had turned away, high enough above the peaks to soar for escape to the west and Ortham, but Jolian needed a few more seconds to pursue. Eric looked down and saw that his friends were growing smaller beneath him, a half dome of ice still standing behind them, since they had come out from behind it. With a pang, he sensed he might never see them again.

He yelled to the dragon, "Just tell me why people normally use a saddle and I will relax."

"Because they are as terrified as you if they do not. It is not actually necessary and is frankly a nuisance."

He laughed despite himself. If that wasn't a believable answer, nothing was. He first relaxed his legs and found himself secure there despite the wind tearing at him. He tried to lift his butt but learned he was unable, as if strapped into an invisible saddle. He finally took a deep breath as she turned for pursuit, and he relaxed his grip bit by bit. By the time they were soaring away, he had almost let go but remained leaning forward to shield himself from the wind.

Jolian was bigger and more powerful than Sebast, whom he had last ridden. She was also larger than her wounded brother. As they flew, it felt like they would inevitably gain on the blue dragon. It was just a matter of time, which was wasting. But what would they do? He had no real say in this, he knew, but would Jolian attack her own family? Nothing could answer that, and he realized worrying about it was senseless. He could better use his time to assess what had happened.

Novir was a traitor. Had the Orb of Dominion compromised him? It seemed plausible. But then why had he taken part in the summoning of the Ellorian Champions? If he wasn't enthralled, then he was doing this for another reason. Was he in league with the Lords of Fear? Or the one who had the master orb? Was that why he was not enthralled? It wouldn't be necessary if the orb had already gotten him.

But what of Brazin? The dragon said that he had done as commanded. Who had ordered him? It seemed unlikely that he gave a damn what Novir said. That coward giving orders to a majestic dragon seemed implausible. Had Brazin come under the orb's spell? Eric didn't know how that could have happened and cursed his ignorance. Everything he knew had come from Novir and the wizard.

Could they trust Derin? How much of what they'd been told had been a lie? He wondered if the Orbs of Dominion even existed, or worked as described. Was there even a king enthralled, not to mention a dwarven queen? Maybe there wasn't, and this was why the summoning happened out of sight. What about these Lords of Fear? How could he and the others prepare for a fight against an enemy they have only heard of and when they aren't even sure about the identities or capabilities? He couldn't remember how much of that information had come from Novir, or who said what, but no one in the room had contradicted anything. The only person he trusted right now, aside from his friends, was Jolian.

He remembered the spell Soliander had cast on Matt to read his mind. It was horribly invasive, beyond unethical, but it seemed almost like a good idea. A single lie could get them all killed. How else could they know who they could trust? Supposedly the Quest Rings had an oracle-like quality that validated some of a quest before bringing them, but how much did it really know? And there was no way to know how well was it working. After all, the rings weren't bringing the real champions, just them, by mistake. What else were they wrong about?

Eric had never been the trusting type. That was Ryan, maybe even Matt, for different reasons. Ryan wanted to believe the best of others as his faith in God guided him.

But Matt was just a little naïve and didn't see bullshit coming.

Eric had neither. Juvenile delinquency, some time on the streets, and a few poor foster parents had given him street smarts. He needed to rely on them more now. He had gone soft, his last foster parents being good to him, his dark past behind him, a steady job and brighter future ahead. He hadn't needed his suspicion or calculating mindset in years. But now it was crucial, and he vowed to ask far more questions from now on. Never mind if someone felt offended by an improper question. He imagined Anna frowning at him. He would have a talk with all of them about it. No one was supposed to admire or like Andier of Roir anyway, and Eric would take being feared and alive over being liked but dead any day of the week and twice on Sunday.

And the first person he would try out his new probing mindset on was Novir once he caught up to the little shit.

They hadn't thought to ask when the dragons had come into the situation. Where had the orb been then? Was it long gone before the dragons arrived? How could only one of them have been taken over by it? He sighed in frustration. Maybe the dragon had been compromised some other way. The only way to know was to capture both of them.

Jolian was gaining ground with every mile, the plains beyond the mountains visible in the distance. Novir frequently looked back, Brazin less so. Eric smiled. They had to know it was inevitable. Then he realized his disadvantage. Neither of their quarry would think twice about hurting Jolian, who likely didn't want to hurt her brother if she could avoid it. And Brazin had some magic, more than Jolian. Maybe Matt should have been here instead of him. Too late now.

Not sure if she would hear him, he yelled, "Do you have a plan?"

"I know my brother."

"Are you sure?"

"We used to play this game as children. He will not triumph. I know better than to teach even family all of my tricks."

He had to take her word for that. Suddenly there was no more time to worry about it. With only fifty yards separating them now, Brazin dove. Jolian continued forward instead of following, banking sharply just as her brother rolled sideways onto his back, already spewing shards of ice upward at where he clearly expected his sister to be. The shards flew past into the sky, striking nothing. Had she seen it coming? Jolian banked again and hurtled downward as Brazin rolled onto his stomach, snapping out his wings to continue, but he'd lost forward momentum and Jolian gained with terrifying speed. Eric felt certain she could kill Brazin with little trouble as they neared. What was she going to do? Driving him to the ground had to be the plan.

With Brazin ahead and below them, Jolian soared down and blasted fire into her brother's path, but slightly to his right. It came as no surprise that Brazin banked left, right into his sister's trajectory. She was clever. Eric braced for the collision as Jolian kicked downward with what felt like all four legs, striking Brazin's body with a jarring thud so deep that she knocked the breath from the dragon's body with an audible grunt from him. Eric heard the cough-like whoosh of air from him, a mist of frost expelled as if by accident. Now Brazin fell as if knocked off balance or struggling to regain control, his legs kicking wildly, wings jerked by the wind instead of used skillfully. He pulled himself into a ball as he plummeted, then spread his wings again, once more in control as he looked around for his sister. Eric thought he saw fear.

And it was too late. The trees and a lake weren't far below now and Brazin looked helpless as he beat the air to gain speed and altitude. Jolian closed in from above again. This time she breathed fire directly at Brazin, who heard the flames and rolled once more, countering them with ice, but again the red dragon saw it coming and had already banked left, then right, reaching Brazin just as he completed the roll. At the last moment, Jolian slowed herself and grabbed her brother's neck with her front claws, one back leg clubbing down at his body so that Eric wondered if she had just knocked off Novir. But he had no time to care. The lake rushed up at them until both dragons spread their wings to slow the impending crash near the shoreline. A huge fountain of water hurtled into the air, their momentum making them career onto the short sandy beach, a line of trees near.

When they came to rest, it amazed Eric that he was still alive. Jolian was turning to stand on the ground more firmly, her front claws still around her brother's neck, and it gave Eric a clear sight of Novir having unfastened himself and sliding down the blue dragon's side to splash into the water. The sound of footsteps plunging through the shallows told the rogue that his quarry meant to flee.

"Jolian," called Eric, "let me go."

"Done."

Eric felt the spell holding him to the dragon's back release, and he smoothly pulled a throwing knife out as he raced down the wing that the red dragon lowered like a ramp to the sand. He kept a running count of lost throwing knives and still had roughly half of the dozen. He turned after Novir, who had a thirty-yard head start on him, heading along the beach instead of into the trees. Behind him, Eric heard Jolian take a deeper breath and wondered what she was doing until something crackling went over his head. He barely saw the man-sized fireball that landed in the sand a few strides ahead of Novir, who stopped in visible surprise, then turned and ran toward the woods.

Eric smirked and changed course to intercept him. He took a chance and slowed to throw a knife at his prey. He had already resumed course when the blade sank into Novir's hip to create a second wound. The King's Guardsman staggered a few paces toward the trees, pulling out the blade and throwing it down as he turned to Eric, ripped a sword from its sheath. The rogue stopped ten feet away, certain he wouldn't win that way. Instead, he threw another knife that Novir deflected.

"Coward!" he shouted. "Pull your sword and fight me!"

Eric threw two in quick succession, the first intended to distract and then second going for the sword arm. It worked, Novir wincing, his sword lowering as he tried to remove the blade with the other hand. Eric charged to make Novir think they would land in a heap, but at the last moment he leaped up, delivering a kick to the jaw that sent Novir on his back, the sword falling. And Eric was on top of him in an instant, another knife to his throat, Novir's arms pinned between his body and Eric's legs. The trees were just strides away, and he briefly scanned them for danger he didn't see before returning attention to his captive.

"Why?" Eric demanded.

Novir spat at him, but the rogue saw him getting ready to do it and leaned to dodge it. "I'll tell you nothing."

Eric punched him in the face, not bothering to wipe the spit from his ear. He sometimes forgot that one hand had a magic ring that did far more damage than might be expected of a blow, but Novir's broken lip and shattered teeth reminded him. He almost felt bad for the damage but said, "Normally I'd say I can do that all day, but I don't have time for this. Are you under control of the orb?"

Snidely, his mouth bloody, Novir asked, "Would it make you be civil if I said yes?"

Eric hit him again, but not as hard. "Answer and you'll find out."

A glare of anger appeared, and Eric felt Novir's arms struggling to slip free. Novir said, "I am going to kill you."

"Not likely. Why did you betray your king?"

Novir smiled, bloody teeth making him sinister. "My allegiance is not to him. I betrayed no one." A hint of pride surfaced, and Eric used it.

"For what? Money? Whores? A pint of ale?"

Sneering, Novir jerked his arms more and snarled, "Your petty pleasures are not mine."

"You betray a kingdom for a night with a slut you'll just get another disease from."

Novir shouted, "I betray no one! My master is more powerful than any of you! Even your Majestic Magus."

Mocking him, Eric asked, "Then why does he need the Orbs of Dominion? True power means not needing a magic item to control others."

Laughing bitterly, "Oh, he knows how to control people without it, trust me."

"Trust a man who can be so easily bought? You will live your life in chains if I don't kill you first, beneath Castle Arking in the dungeon."

"I will sit on the throne of Minari! It is you and your friends that will rot beneath *my* castle!" He again tried to move his arms and while he'd succeeded some by now, he wasn't getting them free.

"You betray your king for nothing more than a *promise* to take his place? What a fool you are."

Smirking with condescension, Novir asked, "Am I, Silver-Tongued Rogue? If I am such a fool, then why am I the one who cannot see?"

Eric scowled, not understanding.

Novir spoke a word and Eric's sight went black.

CHAPTER SEVEN

VALEGIS

Novir violently bucked a startled Eric, twisted, and yanked both of his arms free. Eric swung but had his blow blocked, a fist finding his jaw as he fell back into the sand onto something long, flat, and hard.

His sword, Eric thought, rolling off and grabbing it, the edge slicing his finger until he found the hilt. Using his other hand, he swung fast twice, just hoping to ward off Novir, whose movements he heard. He advanced, swinging wildly, feeling disoriented. His own sword was on his hip, which meant he didn't need to see to keep the man away or save himself. That gave him an idea and he pulled out a knife. Novir cursed and ran toward the trees. Eric listened intently, trying to gauge distance and the path. Then he threw the knife, which sounded like it struck a tree. Novir continued crashing through the foliage as he escaped.

Eric turned toward the lake, or the direction he thought it was in, stumbling. He first needed to get the sand off his hands. And the blood. He wished Anna was here to heal him so he could see. All he saw was blackness, and having his eyes open but seeing nothing disturbed him. Hearing his booted feet splash, he dropped the sword, crouched, and cleaned his hands, rubbing one over the other, which is how he felt the Trinity Ring on one finger. He cursed himself for a fool. It had three healing spells. Surely one was strong enough to restore his sight. He didn't really know how much strength was needed but saved the strongest spell for something more serious.

"Enurarki," he said. Blackness lifted as light crept in, his sight blurry before slowly clearing. He sighed and picked up Novir's sword, glancing toward Jolian as he straightened. For a moment, he thought both dragons had left, but both had shifted to human form. He turned back toward the trees, which were quiet now. Either Novir was hiding or he was far enough away to be unheard. Eric wasn't sure if he should go after him, but the surprise spell made him decide against it. There was no telling what the man was capable of. Eric didn't like surprises. He was lucky to be alive.

He went to collect his knives, since he had thrown pretty much all of them. He kept an eye out for danger. Seeing some fruit made him realize his hunger, but there was no way to know what was safe to eat on this planet. There had been rations in their gear. Had Novir put it there? It no longer mattered because Eric wasn't eating it in case it had been poisoned. His face fell. What if the others were snacking on it now? He found several of the knives and hurried back to Jolian, noticing as he neared that Brazin seemed unconscious.

Eric asked, "He changed form?"

"Yes, trying to get out of my grip, but I just knocked him out after he did it."

The rogue looked back toward where Novir had disappeared. "I don't know if I should go after him."

"What did you learn? Was it enough?"

"No, only that he was promised the throne of Minari. He didn't say how he would earn it."

"That's a hefty reward for trapping us in a cave, however briefly. There must be more to him."

Eric nodded. "Maybe he was responsible for the king being enthralled. If so, he has delivered Minari to whoever has the master orb."

"That might be enough, assuming that person doesn't want the throne for himself, which seems likely only because he has already ensnared two rulers. Why stop there?"

Eric agreed. These Orbs of Dominion were far too much power in one person's hands. Part of him wondered if a James Bond-like villain was behind it all, believing he would create peace across an entire world, or multiple worlds, by enslaving minds so that everyone just agreed with everything. The problem with that was the adage that absolute power corrupts absolutely. The sort of person who would use "evil" means to reach a "good" end could not be benevolent, because that required ethics they clearly didn't have.

Jolian looked out over the forest and mountains. "We needn't worry about Novir. He has no escape that will occur in time to interfere with us again. There are many things in between here and civilization. He is unlikely to survive, especially wounded and with no sword. His scent and that of the blood will bring trolls."

"Good for him. Maybe he can be *their* king."

"Their next meal is more likely."

Eric hadn't seen a troll and wondered how big they were. Did they really eat people? Though cannibalism was about eating your own kind, sentient species consuming each other was nearly as disturbing. On Earth, only animals ate people, and usually by accident or in desperation, but then there weren't any other sentient species. Only a few animals like crocodiles ate humans on purpose. He supposed it didn't matter if you were already dead, but the truly awful thing about crocs was the way they twisted a limb rapidly until yanking it off while you were still alive and going into shock. It had to be one of the worst and most terrifying ways to die.

Just today he'd seen a leviathan try to eat Jolian. Being reduced to food felt ignoble and wasn't something he'd ever considered as a likely end to his life before these quests began. Had he entered a new food chain where he was a few notches down from the top of it? How did one go about making themselves unappetizing? The thought made him want to laugh, but maybe he really did need to look into it. How do you convince a predator that eating you in particular will be disgusting or make them sick? Did he just have to run faster than his friends? He smiled at the realization that he was already the fastest.

As for Novir, he felt some sympathy at the idea of being eaten. Traitor or not, it wasn't a good way to go. Hopefully, he'd be dead instead of boiled alive in a stew or something. The thought made Eric realize how dependent on Jolian he was to get out of here. He turned to her.

"I don't suppose you knew he could do magic?"

She frowned. "I did not, but that may explain the cave in. I saw nothing that looked like physical force had been used to cause it, but I thought perhaps such evidence had fallen with the rocks. He appears to only know simple spells, which is not a surprise. He would do more with his life with more power."

Eric sensed she was taking some responsibility for not realizing Novir could do magic, but he had something else on his mind. "What if he can do a spell that could help him contact someone he's working with? That would still interfere with us."

Jolian considered that. "The spell he cast on you was simple, as would be the one for the cave in. It might mean he cannot do much more."

"What if he has a device we don't know about?"

"I think the only one that could matter would be one that allows him to communicate our plans to reach Ortham." She looked down at her brother, frowning. It seemed clear that they had been trying for the city and the Lords of Fear.

Eric observed, "True, but if he had that, he presumably would have already used it. Otherwise, why bother fleeing at all when we came out of the Kirii Cave? He could have just contacted them and remained a hidden traitor among us."

"I think we can safely ignore him." She looked at Eric, eyes on his hips. "We must bind my brother. The spell will keep him in human form until I release him, but he is still dangerous when he awakens."

Eric nodded and began removing the black rope he always had around his waist. When neatly placed, it looked like a belt so that he hadn't actually realized its nature the first time he found himself changed into Andier's clothes. He'd seen Jolian eyeing it.

He had little experience binding people but knew how to tie various knots from his rock climbing days. Apparently, tying people up was another skill he needed to gain, but no bind would matter if Brazin woke and cast a spell. "What about his magic?"

"I have suppressed that with a spell that is normally forbidden among our kind, but it will only last so long."

"Long enough to complete the quest?"

"Unlikely. We will need to think of something."

Maybe this was a problem Matt could help with. That was one of several reasons he said, "We have to get back to the others. What about Brazin? I assume you don't want to leave him, but did he say anything about what he did, like why he did it? Do you think the orb has compromised him?"

She sighed. "He said nothing I care to repeat before I silenced him. His behavior and the way he looked at me left no doubt the orb has enthralled him. This must have been before the orb left Castle Arking."

"I was wondering about that. How do you think that happened? How did the dragons get involved? And when?"

"My brother was already at Castle Arking because he spends time among the races, unlike most of our kind. He must have become enthralled. It wasn't until after Bolin Hill and the Lords of Fear became involved that Brazin asked me and Sebast for help. I am not sure how Brazin encountered the orb and yet did not go with those taking it. He would have been the fastest way to Ortham. It is something to think on. We must go." Jolian gazed at her brother. "You can ride upon my back. I will carry him in my talons."

"Where are you going to take him? I assume you don't plan to leave him at the cave entrance."

"The town, the one we passed on the way there. Valegis is the only safe place for him. He will remain bound, but trolls and others would get to him if left without a guard. He is still my brother and I do not want harm to come to him."

"You think he'll be safe in the town in human form? Will they know the truth? What do they think of dragons?"

She appraised him. "All good questions. I think we must return to your friends, leaving my brother there for now, under their guard. Then you and I will go to the town, landing out of sight and walking the rest of the way. If I fly in, they will almost certainly attack us. Dragons don't appear often among such places, and people fear us. That we mean them no harm would mean nothing. The best way to gain their trust is for us to make our way to the town's leader and convince him of our quest."

Eric smirked. "That should be an interesting conversation."

She smiled. "I'm sure you'll think of something."

That would be a lot easier if he knew more about this world. He would need to think quickly. And he wondered why she thought it was all on him. Should he take it as a compliment? "What then? We admit to the guy that you're a dragon?"

"Yes, once we convince him we're no threat. I hope that you and I can arrange for him to keep my brother under guard and to ease the town's fears so that I retake my true form outside without causing a panic. I can fly back to the cave, and take my brother back to town, no one afraid of my return."

"What about if he awakens and regains magic?"

"The town should have wizards. Everywhere does. Magic is common here. Hopefully, they will subdue him. Several wizards working together could handle him. We will have to ask these questions."

Eric thought was a good idea so far, assuming it went according to plan. "What then? Can you carry all four of us to Ortham?"

"Yes, but two of you would not be in a saddle. You would need to choose one other who handled it as gracefully as yourself."

Eric started laughing and Jolian smiled. "Oh no, I'm not making that decision. We'll let them choose. Anyway, how long do you think it will take to do this whole thing with Brazin and be on our way?"

"Hours. I know we must move quickly."

"Can you hear me well enough while we fly? I must ask you something."

"Yes. Let us proceed."

Jolian stepped away from him and Eric made sure to not get slapped by a suddenly appearing dragon wing as she transformed, both the process and the result once again filling him with awe. She was always more massive than he remembered. That so much bulk could be reduced and then expanded like that made him assume magic made it possible. He wondered if a dragon ever spontaneously returned to their true form unexpectedly. That could be interesting.

He tucked Novir's sword into his belt in case they needed it, since the current plan meant Jolian and him walking into a town, and she might need a weapon that would not reveal her nature. Then he climbed up one offered wing to her back and felt more relaxed this time as she stepped toward Brazin, gently folding a front foot around him. She took to the sky with powerful strokes. Eric hoped the others were safe outside the Kirii Cave entrance, but Ryan and Matt were good enough at their new roles by now, he thought, that he wasn't too worried. They could fend off whatever came for them. Hopefully, they hadn't eaten any of the food, which they could replace in Valegis.

"What is your question?" Jolian asked, her voice rumbling like thunder.

Eric looked out over the forest-covered mountains as they soared between the peaks. He hadn't exactly been paying attention earlier. "After Novir's actions, I am not sure who to trust."

"I am also questioning what we thought to be true."

"Is there any part of the story that you are certain about? Like these Lords of Fear? Or even the Orbs Dominion? Do they exist?"

"Yes, the lords are well known. Whether they are involved or not, I do not know. Preparing to face such dangerous people will have us prepared for many lesser threats. And the orbs are legendary. Enough people saw an item matching the description, both in Hamarven and Minari, that I do not disbelieve this. I am more concerned about the destination."

"Ortham?"

"Yes. It seems unlikely that Novir would lead us to where the orb is truly headed."

She was right. Only a fool would have done so. Still, Novir had to make the orb's destination plausible. He said as much and asked, "Where might they be going that is in the same direction? And is there any proof that they are headed this way?"

"From what I learned, all proof about the orb's location was from reports they came to Novir. There is no way of knowing what they truly contained, and we must assume that they were not entirely accurate."

"Great. So he could have lied."

"Yes, but this may be another reason to visit the town. They are presumably not under his influence of that of the orb, which would not have come this way. Perhaps they are aware of its movement. I heard nothing that led me to believe the orb is not headed north, so it may be headed this way, just not to Ortham."

"It's a long shot, but we will ask the town, assuming they cooperate."

"Yes. As for other destinations, I know of nothing as plausible as the portal at Ortham. Novir did not strike me as a clever man, and he may not have thought of a compelling lie."

"Maybe he expected that leviathan or the cave-in to stop us."

"Unlikely, given your reputations and my presence. It seems clear that he wanted Brazin and Sebast alone, as it was his idea that I accompany you to the cave, which made it easier to defeat the leviathan."

"Do you think he just wanted to injure or delay us? He seemed in a hurry to flee."

"Possibly. I noticed his haste, but I thought it was fear. Perhaps not."

"Maybe the Lords of Fear don't know we're coming, and he hoped to warn them. He knew our plans at least."

"This is likely."

"Do you think we can trust Denir?"

"I think so, but perhaps he is compromised. Let us get to the town and see what they know. From there we visit Ortham and possibly gather more information along the way."

Eric sighed. It was as good a plan as any. He and the others were bound to the quest, and if the orb was going in a completely different direction, they would have to track it down. That would take considerably longer. And that meant more time away from home. The possibility of never returning always hung in the air. The price of failure was steep, even if they lived.

That mind reading spell of Soliander's seemed more and more like a good idea. He knew Matt better than the others and wondered if they should discuss doing it. The techie was as pragmatic as himself and could be persuaded with a good line of logic. Neither was as principled as Anna or Ryan. If they ever used it on someone, it would have to be when the other two weren't around or Eric would never hear the end of it. Matt would likely admit it was Eric's idea, sparing himself the judgment. Or at least some of it.

Besides, everyone knew Eric was the calculating one who would bend ethics when required. It came with his former life and he didn't mind his friends knowing it. He sometimes felt they needed to accept the situations they were now in with these quests and that being honorable was great and all, but not if you ended up dead over it. He was the first to ditch such ethics and didn't feel bad about it in the least. No one knew they were unwilling imposters ripped away from their lives without warning, and while the summoning wasn't unethical by intent, it kind of was for the result. Being ignorant of a crime doesn't make you not guilty of it, and while a summoning wasn't a crime, it was still a great wrong done to them. If they had to bend ethics to survive, then so be it. They didn't ask for this. Didn't want it. Weren't qualified. They just wanted to go home and back to their lives.

There was no sense in worrying about that, so he turned his mind to Novir. Why didn't Novir just take the orb and fly to Ortham on Brazin's back? Instead, he had taken part in summoning the Ellorian Champions. Eric went cold. Was Novir trying to bring them to the orb so they would get enthralled? They would be an enormous prize, one that might warrant being awarded a kingdom for it.

But then why would Novir help them get the fish eyes they needed for the spell that would prevent it? Because that spell didn't exist on Rovell, so he hadn't known about it when they were summoned. He must have been improvising, taking them to the dangerous Kirii Cave, hoping something happened to them. He got Sebast killed, but he must have known that Jolian could carry all four champions if necessary and it would only slow her. That must have been the intention. If he had gotten out of sight in time, they would not have known where to track him. The cave in and flight would have given him a head start to reach Ortham and tell the Lords of Fear that the plan to enthrall the Ellorian Champions would not work. This meant Eric and the others now had an advantage. They could pretend to be ensnared long enough to get close to the orb. It all made sense but was conjecture. He sighed but felt he had made sense of it, but he knew that he may have just been fooling himself.

Jolian soon banked to begin her landing, the tilt helping Eric see the ground. Sebast's green dead body still lay where it had been among the trees and bushes. Nothing seemed to move. He saw no sign of the others and hoped this meant they were just staying out of sight. He looked for signs of fighting and saw none. Jolian landed smoothly despite carrying her brother in a front foot. She laid him down as Eric scanned for danger and saw his friends emerging from the tunnel entrance, unscathed. He climbed down to meet them and quickly filled them in.

"Did anyone eat the food they gave us? It may be poisoned," he concluded, taking a few of the throwing knives that Ryan had collected for him. He had a half-dozen.

Ryan grunted and replied, "No. Didn't think of it. We arrived a little before noon and the Quest Ring always makes us feel like we just ate a solid meal an hour earlier."

Matt said, "If Novir knew that, he would have known we wouldn't eat soon. Poisoning our water would have made more sense, but we all drank some before entering the cave before."

"Nothing since?" He looked over at the saddle for Jolian, which sat upright on the ground. The one for Sebast was still on the dead dragon, half of it under the giant corpse. They wouldn't be reaching anything they needed from that side unless Jolian moved the body. He wondered what was where. "Okay, listen, we'll just replace everything in town."

Looking at the unconscious Brazin, Ryan asked, "You're sure he won't wake up while you're gone?"

Jolian responded, "He may but is well bound and cannot do magic for now. Keep a close eye on him. I suggest Soliander be ready with a binding spell if needed."

Matt nodded, but Anna frowned at Eric and said, "I thought we agreed not to separate. Now you want to again."

Eric assured her, "You guys should be safe here like before, just a little while longer."

She persisted, "And what about you? I mean, sure, I understand that you have a dragon to protect you, but we know nothing about this town."

Jolian, still in her natural form, interjected, "I am familiar with its reputation and we should have no trouble. There are far worse that we could visit, and they would be cause for concern."

Anna didn't look convinced. "What can you tell us? I really dislike not knowing about the places we go."

"Yeah, I know," Matt agreed. "I wish I had a spell that would help with that sort of thing."

To Anna, the dragon replied, "Humans built Valegis before knowing the dwarves were here underground, but the dwarves knew of the town and kept an eye on them. Valegis exists to mine these peaks for metals and gems, and the dwarves weren't interested in sharing what they might find. They believe the mountains belong to them."

Ryan asked, "Are these the same dwarves of Hamarven?"

"No. We are too far north, and if their territory spread all this way, Harmarven could claim the entire mountain range. But the dwarves in one place are much the same as another for not sharing. They are good-natured and came to the rescue of Valegis during a troll attack long ago. There has been an alliance ever since, with agreements on where the town can mine, and how deep, in exchange for dwarven help with safety, gem cutting, even tunneling. Valegis is where the dwarves barter with much of the outside world, so it is a trading town. We will find many dwarves there. This may reassure you we have little to fear. Still, the guards will be surprised to see Andier and I approaching on foot."

Matt asked, "Do you need a good story to get into town? Or to see the leader? Do we know his attitude?"

"I do not know who it is. I am trusting our Silver-Tongued Rogue to get us where we need to be."

Everyone looked at Eric and he admitted, "I will have to improvise. The big question we need an answer for is where did we come from? Why are two apparent humans walking around in the mountains?"

"Speaking of that," began Anna, turning to the dragon, "your appearance when you look like a human is pretty striking. Do you have control over that? I knew when I first saw you that you probably weren't human despite your shape."

Jolian nodded. "Yes. That is how I choose to look, but I will choose something more appropriate."

Eric gave Anna an approving look and turned his thoughts to what to tell the guards. If he and Jolian lied to get past them, and that became obvious while talking to the mayor, or whatever his title was, that could prevent cooperation. But what of the truth could they say? Talking about the Orbs of Dominion might not work if people didn't believe they were real. Remote mountain town guards might not have heard of them at all. But being on a mission from King Orin of Minari would get their attention and likely get them an audience quickly. But what mission could they admit? Maybe he refused to say it to anyone but the mayor. That might work.

But why would anyone believe them? He couldn't even claim to be Andier of Roir, one of the Ellorian Champions. For all he knew, this town thought the champions were still missing, and no announcement of a quest went out because King Orin was enthralled and would have interfered, so no one would expect this. That truth would not pass the smell test. Besides, with only himself present, being one of the champions was hardly convincing. How often did the real champions go around alone? He imagined saying his title and getting a snide response that the guard was really the King of Gisla.

And Andier was a known smooth talker not known for honesty. Admitting to their identities didn't seem like a good move, or at least, not to some guard at the gates. Jolian could prove she was a dragon and impress upon them that something serious was afoot as a result, but that would just get them shot with arrows.

But he had an idea the others agreed to, and with time precious, he helped Ryan carry Brazin into the mouth of the tunnel to Kirii Cave so everyone could stay out of sight while he and Jolian were gone. Eric walked up the dragon's red wing and sat on her spine again. Scattered leaves and dirt filled the air as she lifted off. He felt like he was getting used to this, but he didn't have long for this ride.

Valegis was hours away by foot, partly due to steep and challenging terrain, but they were near within a few minutes, Jolian flying low so that no one from the town saw them. She also didn't fly directly at it, but toward a wilderness area suspected to have fewer witnesses. For their story to hold up, they could only approach on foot from one direction—that of Kirii Cave—and this limited their landing options to that side of town. She glided between the peaks, just above the trees, and finally touched down with surprisingly little sound halfway up a mountain. Then she crouched down behind the trees and transformed to humanoid to get out of sight, hopefully no one witnessing the change.

Jolian looked more human this time, her red hair in a tight ponytail and less fiery. Looser, black leather that seemed functional, worn, and used had replaced the sleek, form-fitting red, her boots appearing scuffed. She gave the impression of a well-paid and skilled warrior who could pass for someone on a mission from a king. She took Novir's sword from him to complete her disguise.

"There isn't much of a path from Valegis toward Kirii Cave," Jolian observed, "but it is there. The town is around the next mountain over. I did not think getting closer in the air was wise. We should move quickly."

"At a run."

"Agreed."

They carefully ran across the bare earth, where small stones and boulders jutted up. The pine trees were sparse enough that they did not need a trail. Eric kept alert for signs of trouble, which could have just been animals, not ogres, trolls, and similar threats, but the way became more dangerous once they reached the way toward Valegis simply because traffic, however rare, might be expected there. It was just wide enough for one person. As they went, they sometimes had to walk because a rising cliff wall or boulder obscured the sight of any trouble ahead. Even when they could see for fifty yards because only smaller boulders dotted the landscape, the stray tree or bush near, they knew a traveled path invited scrutiny. Was anything waiting to ambush travelers? It seemed unlikely only because, as Jolian observed, few went toward the Kirii Cave. But just because they didn't go all the way there didn't mean the path wasn't used at all. An abandoned guard tower suggested the area was largely deserted.

They descended from their landing spot into a valley and took a brief break before resuming. When able to, they left the trail to stay near a line of trees, or even a cliff wall that was away from the trail. Anything to minimize being in plain view of something watching. But they faced no trouble as late afternoon began casting darker shadows. Danger would increase before long, so few breaks preceded them ascending again on widening path, the trees of a valley dropping below them on one side as they climbed toward a pass between two mountains. A pair of guard towers with black flags snapping in the breeze lay ahead. Eric assumed that the town lay beyond.

"They have seen us," Jolian observed, her eyes keener.

Eric had suspected as much and badly wanted some water and to catch his breath, sweat creasing his brow despite the air cooling. Once back on Earth, it was time to resume the jogging they had only just started. Anna and Matt would complain, but their lives could depend on it.

They continued jogging up the path until they saw a group of warriors doing the same in their direction. Giving a sense of urgency would just get the guard's tension up, so they slowed to a walk. Jolian tucked the spare sword into her own belt, having carried it because it had no scabbard, and running increased the odds of hurting herself with it. Now they did their best to seem non-threatening as the dozen warriors came to a halt ten feet away, most wearing studded leather and carrying a rectangular shield, swords of various lengths on their hips in scabbards. Only a few had a helm at all, each of steel. A tall, black-haired man in front was the obvious leader because of his chainmail shirt and finer tunic atop it. It bore the same insignia that seemed to adorn the flutter of black flags—a mountain with a sword and hammer crossed before it. Eric thought he had seen it before on a corpse in the entrance to Kirii Cave.

"Ho there!" said the one wearing chainmail, taking two steps toward them. "What business have you with Valegis?"

"We seek the town's aid. I am Eric of Arking in Minara. This is Jolian. Are you important?"

The man cocked an eyebrow, seeming amused but disdainful. "I am Talis, Captain of the Watch. And I am more important than you at this moment." His men laughed.

Eric smirked, feeling he had a handle on them. "Letting you think that amuses me, so I will allow it. Who runs the town?"

Talis scratched his stubble beard. "That would be Ogren, not that you'll be meeting him, except in chains."

Eric offered his wrists. "Would you like to try putting them on me? I'll tie one hand behind my back to make the fight fairer."

Talis smiled. "Well, I haven't had an offer that tempting in about two hours."

Jolian stepped forward. "If you boys are through playing, we urgently need to see Ogren. Will you take us to him?"

Talis appraised her with an obvious appreciation for her beauty, which did not appear to sway him. As if he meant no offence, he pleasantly remarked, "If I took every mongrel that wandered in from the mountains to see Ogren just because they asked, I wouldn't be Captain of the Watch."

Eric drawled, "And if you don't take us, you won't be Captain of the Watch much longer when he finds out too late why we're here."

Talis's green eyes hardened, and he stepped forward, one hand on his sword hilt. "I am not accustomed to threats."

Eric took a step forward so that they were within arm's reach. "Yes, you are, or you wouldn't be Captain of the Watch."

Talis looked flatly at them. "Enough games. What do you want? Why are you walking around out here with no supplies? Where did you come from?"

Eric felt like this had gone as far as it could. Time for his story. "Our supplies are back at the Kirii Cave. Maybe you can go back and ask the leviathan to return them."

Cocking an eyebrow, Talis frowned. "I don't believe you."

Eric pulled a dead fish from a pocket, having brought one from Matt's bag. "Well, do you know anywhere else I can get a fresh one of these? It would have been handy to know before going there."

Talis appraised him with new respect, and Eric saw that he'd gotten the captain's attention. "What were you doing at the Kirii Cave?"

"The King of Minari sent us to get these fish for a spell we need."

"You are not wizards and do not wear an insignia of any kind, not to mention one of Minari."

"Our wizard is still at the cave. Listen, a force of men left Castle Arking some days ago and is headed for Ortham in Gisla. We mean to stop them, but as you noticed, we are short on supplies."

Talis's eyes looked away for a moment and Eric thought the man knew something about this, but the captain only smiled at him next. "You plan to purchase our falcons to get there sooner? With what? Dead sparis?"

"No, that was for you." Eric tossed him the fish, but the captain let it strike his chest and fall to the rocky trail between them.

"Just two of you are going to stop a force of men over one thousand strong? Oh right. You have a wizard. Why is he still at the cave? Fishing, you said?"

Eric adopted a more conciliatory expression and tone. "Look, if you really want to know the answers to your questions, then escort us to Ogren and convince him to let you listen. Otherwise, and I mean this nicely, please get out of our way. We do not have time for this."

Turning toward his men, Talis mused, "The King of Minari, hmm? If we can't confirm your story, we can always feed you to the leviathan."

"Not after we killed it."

Talis stopped and turned back in visible surprise, eyes intently locked on Eric's. The rogue stared calmly into the captain's eyes and saw his matter-of-fact gaze register. The next question did not surprise him. "*Who* are you?"

Eric gestured up the trail. "Ogren?"

Talis sighed and turned toward Valegis, Eric and Jolian following as the warriors stood back to let them pass, then encircling them. As they continued up the path, the captain barked at one of his men, indicating the fish with a jerk of his head, "Pick that up!"

Eric eyed the forty-foot gray towers as they neared, archers clearly visible but relaxed. He saw little damage to show attacks had ever taken place. A wall extended out and partially up into the mountains. Torches and lanterns were already burning as dusk came early in the mountains, making Eric feel the need to send Jolian back as soon as possible. He didn't like the idea of the others waiting in the dark. They had cleared the area before this gate of brush, and from this vantage point he confirmed an impression he'd had—another path approached from a different direction so that one could continue that way by the gate instead of going in. But now they passed between two wide doors made of vertical wood beams, the gates closing behind them.

To either side as they continued were small barracks and more guards, who eyed them with either indifference or curiosity. A few were dwarves, who paid them no attention. Talis led them forward with only four of the guards accompanying them now, the rest remaining behind. Ahead were trees and a widening path of natural stone that had been chiseled and carved to be smooth. Two mountains loomed beside them, a host of archery towers there. Anything that made it through that gate would get slaughtered. The new road led between various small buildings that seemed disposable, as if necessary, but expected to be destroyed in an assault. As they ventured farther across this pass between mountains, the people increased in number. An archway of stone awaited, two more doors opened wide until they passed through.

And now Eric saw the valley where they had built Valegis. A thirty-foot tall, black stone wall enclosed it in a rough oval, uneven in various places, as if going around obstacles no one had been able to remove. It was wide enough, like the Great Wall of China in places, for wagons to be pulled along the top, as he saw several there now. Towers periodically rose from it for another twenty feet, each with an open top for archers. The wall stood back from the mountains and all trees had been cleared from around it up the slopes. He expected a castle or other fortification but didn't see one. From here, Eric could only see part of what looked like a wide moat that he assumed surrounded it, and from the snow still atop the peaks, he suspected it served as a defense against flooding during spring as much as against an attack.

Inside the wall, the land appeared to have been left alone, buildings alternating with trees and a few boulders so big that he could see them from here. Several very wide towers were inside and didn't seem defensive. Each had several long, horizontal beams sticking out at least thirty feet from the sides from large holes. Beyond it all was another mountain pass that seemed similar from here, except that the sun was shining through it and into their eyes. And for that reason, Eric did not immediately see the giant falcon flying toward Valegis. It bore a rider and circled one tower before landing on what he now realized was a perch. He couldn't see what happened to the rider after that, partly because he and the others began descending a narrow stone staircase. It reached the moat and a wooden drawbridge they walked over to enter the town.

Eric tried to take in the sights. It occurred to him that this was the first time he'd been in such a place without the others, but he was the most street smart and felt comfortable. Jolian had been right. The place didn't have an unsavory feel. He could hear children playing nearby, the smell of fresh breads and meats hung in the air, and the humans and few dwarves he saw watched them curiously but without malice. He guessed the town held about five-thousand people.

They marched straight to the center, past a strolling flautist he'd been hearing for several minutes, a fountain, and men who were skinning something that looked like boar, more of the animals roasting over a fire. A wide lawn that he guessed was used for gatherings stood near the mayor's manor as they neared, and with any luck, Jolian would leave from there as a dragon in under thirty minutes, with the mayor's blessing. He felt urgency. And the town seemed safe, not like some den of thieves.

When they reached a mansion in the town's center, Talis made them wait outside as he ascended the gray stone steps and disappeared inside for several minutes before returning and gesturing for them to follow, the guards still with them. They soon entered a dining room with a long mahogany table and eight high-backed chairs with green velvet cushions. At the table's head and looking unimpressed stood a tall, red-bearded man who calmly appraised his visitors. Eric felt there would be little fooling this man, but he didn't intend to anyway. They placed two mugs of ale on the table as the man gestured to sit. He joined them, Talis and the guards remaining in the room as the door closed. A fireplace cast flickering shadows around the room.

"I am Ogren," the man began in a deep voice, "mayor of Valegis. I understand you are in something of a hurry, and I have no interest in kirii dung, so speak plainly and we can see how we may assist each other."

Eric already liked him. "Forgive me for not being more forthcoming with Talis and your guards, but there are things we mean not everyone to hear. You trust those in this room to not speak of what we discuss?"

Ogren looked at them one by one, and Eric had the impression he was silencing them by doing so before turning his eyes back to the rogue. "Yes."

Eric held his gaze. "I am Andier of Roir, one of the Ellorian Champions. My companions, Soliander, the Lady Eriana, and Lord Korrin, are nearby and awaiting help. You know that there is a Quest Ring at Castle Arking? They summoned us to help this world and now we need some help from you if we are to succeed."

Ogren stared silently at him for several moments and then leaned back in his chair. "I heard the champions have been missing."

"No longer."

"I heard this as well. What proof have you?"

"None. And it doesn't matter. You know that a force of men recently left Castle Arking for Ortham in Gisla. We are here to stop them."

Ogren studied him. "And you believe sparis from the Kirii Cave will help this? How?"

"Do you know what this force of men carries with them?"

"Perhaps."

"One orb of Dominion. They have already enthralled the dwarven queen and King Orin of Minari. We require the fish for a spell that will prevent us from being similarly affected by the orb."

"And yet you are on a mission from that king to stop this orb from reaching Ortham?"

"Not exactly. His wizard Denir still thinks for himself and summoned us without the king's awareness."

"So then you are *not* on a mission from the king, as you told Talis. Why should I believe a man who lies?"

That was a fair question, and Eric thought quickly. "We are here on behalf of the Kingdom of Minari, and the rest of Rovell and other worlds, *despite* the Minarin king being compromised. It is at my discretion what to reveal to a man of Talis' authority as compared to your own."

Ogren seemed to appreciate that answer and looked at Jolian. "And who is she?"

"A dragon."

A murmur from the guards caused Ogren to hold up a hand to silence them. "Will you honor me by proving *that*?"

Eric turned to Jolian, who slowly rose from her seat to stand near the fireplace and a window that was partially open to the darkening sky outside.

"Listen for the sound," she began, "of your falcons screaming. I have done what I can to prevent them from sensing my presence, but know that they have no predators save my kind, and they will react when I let them know I am here."

She whispered something Eric didn't hear and morphed from her current appearance into the red leather-clad vixen he had become accustomed to. At the same moment, a horrible screeching of many birds erupted outside along with the shouts of men that Eric assumed were trying to control suddenly terrified giant birds. And Jolian's shadow on the wall stopped looking humanoid, the silhouette of a dragon replacing it. Several of the guardsmen put their hands on swords' hilts until Talis told them to stand down. Eric turned to Ogren and saw a sobered expression on his face. He gestured for her to sit, a glance at the window suggesting he wanted the reaction to stop. Jolian nodded as she resumed her seat, the disturbance outside ending.

Eric said, "We knew we would terrify the town, so we stopped nearby and hiked the rest of the way here."

Ogren asked, "Why is a dragon involved?"

Eric answered, "It speaks to the seriousness of what is happening. The Orbs of Dominion are real and are a threat to the world order on Rovell and other planets. It is being taken to Ortham to the portal in the Hall of Worlds. Once it leaves, we may not be able to find and destroy it. Many kingdoms would end up under the control of whoever has the other orb. We need to prevent this and you can help."

"How?"

"First, we need you to let Jolian transform into a dragon outside and fly back to the Kirii Cave entrance, and bring the rest of our group here without your people getting upset, or the guards attacking her."

"How many are we talking about?"

"Just three, and another dragon that is in human form and bound."

Ogren cocked an eyebrow. "Explain that."

"It is my brother," answered Jolian. She revealed how the orb compromised Brazin and the measures they had taken to ensure he was not a threat for now.

"And you would leave him here?" Ogren's frown left little doubt as to his feelings about it.

"Listen," began Eric, "it is getting late. My priority is to arrange for Jolian to go get the others before dark, which is any minute now. We can decide what to do with Brazin after. Will you let us do this? What can you do to calm everyone as she comes and goes?"

Ogren sighed but ultimately agreed to this much. He sent Talis out to spread the word and getting people to gather at the town square, where he soon stood before them as Eric and Jolian listened to him answer questions and concerns as darkness quickly descended. Eric wasn't sure how well all of it was going, but it no longer mattered. He watched with a mixture of apprehension and amusement as Jolian walked through the throng to a clear area on the great lawn, where she assumed her true form. The wave of audible fear that swept through the crowd had hardly begun when she took to the sky with powerful thrusts of her wings. Several people hastily left as she rose and flew out of view.

"First time I've seen a dragon," Ogren remarked, watching her go.

Eric commiserated. "It takes some getting used to. Thank you for helping us."

The big man turned to him. "Just be mindful that people here have simple lives. All of this will easily overwhelm them. I would like you and your friends to keep clear of everyone, for their peace of mind and yours."

"But not you?"

He chuckled. "I've seen a few things in my time. I am not given to fanciful thoughts. Listen, it is getting late. I think you will need to stay here overnight, unless you're really determined to go."

"Let me see what they think once they return."

"Sure." He nodded at the mansion. "This is the best we have. I'll be here, and we can have the place surrounded to keep the curious away. I'll get some food brought over. I assume there's more to discuss, including what help we can provide."

"Yes. And thank you again."

Ogren waved him off. "If you're right about all of this..."

He didn't finish, and they waited in silence. It didn't take long for Jolian to return, the saddle attached and Anna riding her back, a struggling and awake Brazin clutched in Jolian's front claws. Those who hadn't cleared the lawn by now scampered aside. Eric helped Anna to the ground and learned everything was fine back at the tunnel entrance, though the sounds of something moving in the growing darkness had alarmed them. Jolian left again as Eric and Talis carried Brazin up to the mansion's steps, where they waited again. Jolian had squashed his magic powers a second time, and the dragon remained bound.

Even less time passed before Jolian returned with Matt and Ryan, morphing into a human again and leaving the saddle on the lawn as they gathered inside with Ogren. They had laid a meal out for the five of them, Ogren, and Talis, the guards told to leave, Brazin lying in the corner. But a knock on the door preceded Talis letting someone in. A guard appeared, quietly reporting something to him as Eric wondered if something was amiss. Then Talis sent him out and closed the door again.

CHAPTER EIGHT

THE LORDS OF FEAR

Matt's stomach growled at the smell of fresh bread, brown rice, and something that looked like pork, the raw vegetables attracting less of his attention. The bitter ale he'd already sampled made him want more, but the danger of intoxication in unfamiliar surroundings had him wishing for water that wasn't there. Did these people know about staying hydrated while drinking alcohol? The room seemed pleasant and even cozy with the warm fire and torches, the scent of burning wood reminding him of the few camping trips he had endured growing up. Sometimes all of this just seemed like one big adventure, and moments like this were pleasant compared to the terror of the Kirii Cave, the fear of Eric not returning, or the awful bellows and screeches he'd been hearing in the mountains while awaiting Jolian's return with Ryan and Anna. Something had been out there and getting closer. Now it didn't matter, and he wanted to relax as much as that was possible, given the circumstances.

"What did he want?" Ogren asked his captain of the guard.

Taking his seat, Talis replied, "He followed their trail as per protocol. He found it began away from the path at Mount Dorun. Several large footprints and claw marks were present. It suggests that their story is true."

"I think we're past that," the mayor admitted. "Now that you're all here, what else do you need? Let me start by saying that we're aware of this force of men moving toward Ortham. You know who leads them?"

Eric helped himself to bread and answered, "The Lords of Fear. You know of them?"

"Yes. We are a trading town and so news reaches us daily. They are north of Durba and should arrive in Ortham tomorrow midday."

Matt remembered the town from the map. Having more time relieved him. He wasn't normally afraid of the dark, but flying through the night on a dragon to a strange city on an alien planet wasn't appealing. Who knew what else flew at night and might suddenly attack? What if they ended up on the ground camping overnight? The security of Valegis made him grateful, and he hoped future quests had far less traveling, though he doubted they would be so lucky. He had seen teleportation spells in Soliander's spell books but wasn't sure he could do them. He really needed time to memorize these things and find out if they could work on Earth. He intended to study tonight once this meeting was over.

What if they were on a quest somewhere and, instead of risking danger while journeying over land, sea, or air, he just cast them to where they needed to be? Fear of camping suddenly seemed a genuine issue because of being exposed in the dark wilderness, vulnerable sleeping, and trusting your equally inexperienced friends to stay awake when it was their turn to stay on guard. Or trusting strangers to do it. Trust was becoming an issue, but the normalcy of their dinner and a secure town had him dreading their departure the next day.

As Matt ate and listened, Eric recounted what had happened with Novir and Brazin, getting reassurance that they would replace any food supplies. He offered some coins

Denir had given them, Ogren waving that off. With Jolian able to carry them all, replacement food and a place to stay tonight was all they really needed. Talk turned to how the Lords of Fear could be defeated, even with the group using the *Mind Shield* spell on themselves.

"Our plan," began Ryan, "was to get close and then pretend the orb has ensnared us. That will hopefully let us get close enough to take it."

Putting down a mug, Talis asked, "What if the orb isn't on?"

Ryan sighed and lifted his own drink. "We'll have to keep fighting our way to it."

"I think it will be on," said Matt, fingering some bread. "Whoever is controlling the master orb can check in with the lords and may expect trouble as they get near the portal, so they would have it on to both watch and assist by ensnaring more people and making everyone compliant."

His eyes on Brazin, who lay glaring at all of them, Talis asked, "How close does someone have to be to this orb for it to work on them?"

"We don't know," Matt admitted, having wondered the same. "My impression is it works up to a hundred yards away. I base this on what Novir told us about what happened at Bolin Hill, but he could have been lying."

"From the reports of what has happened near Durba," began Ogren, "that seems correct. The number of people with them has grown to over a thousand."

"Great."

"Even if you get the orb," began Ogren, "then what? They won't let you just walk away with it."

Eric said, "I am hoping we can do this near the portal and then convince them with violence that they had better leave through it."

Ogren laughed and refilled his mug from a decanter. "Convince them with violence. I do not disapprove! But it would be easier if you outnumber them. Right now, they badly outnumber you."

"I think we need to separate them from the enthralled," suggested Eric.

"How?"

The rogue looked at Jolian. "Sustained blasts of dragon fire."

The dragon smiled. "Without hurting them, yes, but this would mean getting in between the lords and the enthralled first. That may not be possible."

Anna asked, "Why do we think they have all these enthralled people with them? Are they planning to take them through the portal? I don't see why they would. They can enthrall people on other worlds."

"Good question," said Matt, but he thought he knew. "Maybe they are just using them to get to the portal. Save their energy for any trouble there."

Anna asked the mayor, "Do you know where the portal is? Knowing that might help us. Maybe we can get their first and be waiting for them."

Ogren put down his ale. "The Hall of Worlds. They heavily guard it because of its nature, letting people from other planets reach Rovell, and this is the likely reason they have the enthralled, as you say, to save their strength. The lords could probably get inside and to the portal without it, but why take the chance? And this also suggests that the orb may not be on when they arrive. If it was, they could simply walk up and do what they want."

Matt said, "Then maybe the enthralled are a backup in case the wizard controlling the orbs is not paying attention." That seemed reasonable.

Ryan asked, "So how do we get into this hall? If we told the city why we're there, I assume they would let us?"

Talis exchanged a look with Ogren. "Yes, but that may take some convincing, and from someone they know. This would take time. I am thinking I might need to head there tonight."

The mayor nodded. "I will draw up something and seal it with the town's seal. You will take two others with you, each with a copy."

"Is that dangerous," Anna asked, "traveling at night, even with those giant birds?"

Talis said, "Yes, but it is a risk we should take. The kirii are actually one of the bigger dangers, but we can head away from them for a few miles."

"You will not land until you reach Ortham?"

"They can make it without stopping. If we evade the kirii, we should have no troubles the rest of the way."

Ogren said, "I will send more men with you until you are clear of their territory, and then they will return."

Anna asked, "So if we're successful in getting the orb and driving the Lords of Fear through the portal, what is to stop them from returning?"

Talis said, "They can turn the portal off. The city doesn't like to do it because opening it again is difficult, but this is a good reason. You would have time to get away with the orb before the lords could return."

She asked, "Does it make sense to turn off the portal before they arrive there so they can't leave?"

Talis smiled. "Do we really want them to stay on Rovell?"

Matt didn't much care which planet they were on as long as it wasn't Earth, but that made him see Talis' point. "When trapped, people are more dangerous. I'd rather convince them to leave."

"I have a concern about letting them get that close to the portal," began Anna, her brow creased. "What if we're too late or they get through? Then we have to follow."

"Yeah," Eric said, "that is a big risk, and I don't want to go to another world. How fast can they turn the portal off?"

Talis frowned. "I do not know."

Matt had an idea and said, "A few seconds, I would think, but it depends on how they are keeping it open. Are wizards actively casting a spell, or is a spell just in effect and needs to end? That was rhetorical."

Eric asked, "Would Ortham provide some wizards who can help?"

Talis suggested, "I will try to persuade them. They certainly have wizards. More so than us."

Eric said, "It sounds like we have a basic plan."

Matt agreed and raised an idea he'd been thinking of, and when they thought it sounded like a good idea, he asked for some parchment and began copying one spell from Soliander's books. The four of them cut a small lock of hair from themselves, put each in a sealed envelope, and gave those and the spell to Talis to take with him to Ortham. The Lords of Fear had a surprise awaiting them.

"By the way," the wizard began, "while we were waiting for you at the cave, I grabbed get a few things that might be useful, like the green stuff that Sebast had spit on Brazin. I'm not sure but if seems like acid. Never know when that could be useful. Had to be careful about getting it. The other big one is dragon ice."

Eric asked, "What's that good for? Won't it melt?"

"Yes, but I can reform it as dragon ice, which differs from regular ice. I don't know how, but some spells call specifically for it, and that's where it gets interesting. Dragon ice killed this Lord Voth. I may be able to use one of several spells on him because I now have this. I had some time to choose spells, based on what we know of the Lords of Fear."

The rogue asked, "Like what?"

"Something to slow poison if the assassin strikes with a blade. And this sorcerer might freak out if I make him covered in boils or something. I might need something better than that for him."

"Yeah. Keep looking."

Anna cleared her throat. "I used my time as well to reach Aryll, the Goddess of Life. She understands we are facing a necromancer and an undead knight, neither of them from this world, and she is not pleased. We can expect her help."

Ryan asked, "Any idea what form it will take? More than healing?"

"Yes. I sense I can be a, uh, weapon this time, if I see something and call on her and she doesn't like it."

Eric smiled at her. "Time to get your hands dirty."

Anna rolled her eyes and quoted an old line. "I'm a healer, not a fighter."

Ryan turned to Ogren and asked, "What about Brazin? Are you okay with him being here?"

The mayor looked to Jolian, who said, "He cannot shift back to dragon form and his magic is suppressed. He should be no trouble, but I would keep the truth about him known to only those who must know. One of your wizards may need to suppress his magic again. I will show them how."

Looking doubtful, Ogren agreed, and the conversation drifted to less important matters, the mayor drafting a few letters for Talis, who left to get ready and tell others to prepare. Knowing that the *Mind Shield* spell did not exist on Rovell, Matt made a copy of it and felt glad that they had captured far more of the sparis fish than they needed for themselves. Back outside the Kirii Cave, while they had been waiting for Eric and Jolian, Ryan had removed the eyes from all the fish and put them in vials. Matt hated handling them, prompting some good-natured ribbing from Ryan. He now had multiple small jars of fish eyes and had them and the spell brought to Talis, who would convince wizards of Ortham to use the spell as needed. This could significantly improve their chances of impeding the Lords of Fear and their approach to the Hall of Worlds.

"That's great," said Eric, looking him in the eye.

Matt flushed a little at the approval. Part of him wished he was as good at planning as the martial artist. He suddenly realized he loved his friends and would do anything for them. Maybe he should admit to how much he appreciated Eric's plans. What if his friend felt unappreciated and taken for granted?

As the night wore on, with another day of unknowns looming, Matt just wanted to be left alone to study. The four agreed to share one large room for safety reasons, extra cots being brought in, Jolian taking the next room over after some brief flirting with Ryan to see if he wanted to join her, but he looked both intrigued and intimidated and had demurred, to the amused smiles of his friends. That only prompted him to ruefully tell them all to shut up. He settled for cleaning the leviathan blood from his armor.

Matt went in early so he could memorize more spells either for use before returning to Earth or so he could write them down once home. This business of not being able to take the spell books back was an irritant. Sometimes he felt like every minute away from home, he needed to be doing this. He'd been tempted to pull out a book on the flight to the Kirii Cave but had known that was ridiculous and he might drop the precious book. But now he stayed up longer than he should have, the others going to sleep one by one until he finally blew out the lamp. He drifted off to thoughts of how to cause dread in the Lords of Fear. He and Eric especially needed to surprise these bastards.

In the morning, they ate a quick breakfast of porridge and bread with little fanfare and ensured they were ready. The *Mind Shield* spell only lasted a few hours, so they had already agreed to stop southeast of Ortham so Matt could cast it on all of them, including the dragon. They soon took to the sky, Matt feeling secure in the saddle behind Anna. Ahead of her was Eric, who made a show of being comfortable without a saddle. Matt suspected he did this to mock Ryan, who was behind the saddle and holding on to it for dear life even though Jolian's magic would keep him on. The big guy had looked suitably nervous, no assurances from Eric able to relieve his concerns.

With the morning sun behind them, they rose over Valegis and quickly left it and a crowd that had gathered to see a dragon behind, soaring over the mountains until the foothills and plains replaced them. The trip was quiet, a calm before the storm, and Matt spent his time mentally reviewing every spell he had memorized, the words, gestures, and which pocket a needed ingredient was in. Before Ortham came into view, they landed on an open plain and had a quick snack of fruit. He couldn't help wondering if it might be their last meal. They consulted one last time about the plan before taking to the sky again, and what they soon saw threw their plans into disarray.

Ortham stood just north of a river that flowed from the Galla Mountains, and they had been following this for some time before the walled city came into view on a plain. Towers jutted up from the battlements and among the stone buildings, a limestone castle south east of town looking over the rushing river. This attracted Matt's attention, for Talis should have already arrived and hopefully persuaded city leaders to clear the way to the Hall of Worlds or risk the population becoming enthralled. As the dragon banked overhead, he saw few warriors by the river crossing, but hundreds of horses milling around. Something seemed amiss.

They soared over the city, Jolian appearing to track the primary avenue across the river, past the southern gate and castle, and toward the center of town, where they knew the Hall of Worlds stood. And that's when they saw it—a force of warriors a thousand strong marched up the road inside Ortham unmolested. At their front strode four figures, one in a cloak that flapped in the breeze and holding a staff with a golden orb held high aloft. From this distance, they could not tell if it was on, but the Lords of Fear were already here. And they saw the dragon with its riders, the one with the Orb of Dominion pointing toward them. Jolian banked wildly just before a blast of lightning lashed the sky near them, but missed.

"Jolian!" Eric yelled. "Can you land near the Hall of Worlds?"

"Yes." She dove then, twisting and turning in case anything else struck at them, but nothing came as they plummeted toward the buildings farther north. Matt saw a large rectangular structure standing by an open square where Jolian touched down. They might have normally expected crowds, but the place was empty. It took several minutes for all four to climb down to the stone plaza one by one.

"How are they here already?" Anna asked, scowling in worry, her eyes going to the road from where the Lords of Fear were likely coming.

Eric replied, "They must have ridden through the night."

Still in dragon formed, Jolian rumbled, "It is the most likely explanation."

"That means they will be tired," Ryan suggested. "Hopefully. I'll take any advantage we can get."

"Yeah." Eric's gaze made Matt turn to see the familiar figure of Talis running toward them, from what he assumed was the Hall of Worlds. A dozen men followed, some wearing the insignia of Valegis, while others wore the red and black banner of either Gisla or Ortham. This was what might sometimes be helpful to know, but it didn't matter this time.

"Ellorians," Talis called as he stopped, "they arrived recently. But we are ready."

"Someone cast the *Mind Shield* spell?" Matt asked. "On how many?"

"Yes, on those few left in the hall. As many as we could."

"What about the illusion of us?" Matt asked. It wasn't hugely important, but the distraction of it might be the difference between success and failure. This was the reason they had given locks of their hair to Talis, as an ingredient for the spell.

"The wizards stand ready," Talis replied. "There are many more wizards than we could shield, so we couldn't risk others being enthralled by being here. They could just turn against us. We have a hundred and could only bring a handful."

Eric sighed. "Planning around this orb is getting irritating, not that we have a choice."

Matt had to agree. The orb could turn friend to foe in seconds. A few shielded wizards would have to do instead of a hundred that might become a problem for themselves rather than the enemy. He felt a moment of fear that the shielding spell might not work. The memory of Soliander mentally probing his thoughts would never fade. The orb wasn't much better. Anger strengthened his determination, and he turned to face the approaching threat.

"Is the orb already on?" he asked. "I couldn't tell."

Talis shook his head. "No. They haven't used it, maybe because they didn't need to. Like you had suggested, we cleared the streets to prevent their numbers from getting even larger."

Eric said, "Talis, head back to the Hall of Worlds. I assume that is it behind us? Okay. Jolian, any chance you can duck behind that big building over there as you are? If the lords are far enough in front of the enthralled, maybe a blast of fire in between will keep the mob back. They are innocent and should not be hurt, but feel free to singe the lords."

The dragon lumbered over that way, the ground shaking with every step, and the four Earth friends stood alone, silently looking at each other. Ryan loosened his sword and placed the golden helmet over his head, the act triggering the others to make similar movements. Eric checked his knife supply, finding nearly a half dozen left. Anna put one hand to Eriana's amulet at her neck, closing her eyes and whispering. Only Matt stood as he was, as ready as he'd ever be. The sound of footsteps approaching en masse became clearer, but there were no shouts that one might expect from a force of warriors. Instead, they marched silently, the crowd finally appearing around a corner between two-story buildings of stone.

In front strode the Lords of Fear, the undead knight Lord Voth on the left, black mail plate seeming to devour the light instead of reflecting it like Ryan's golden armor. He looked human from here, not something risen from the grave. Beside him strode a blond man with a waist-length cloak, trimmed in white, the underside of it royal purple. It swirled and flapped with the brisk steps of his booted feet, and even from here, his attire seemed elegant. He held a half-staff with the orb atop it, and the device did not appear to be on. Next to him walked a woman clad in black leather, with a ponytail of bright red hair, one hand on a short sword at her hip. She moved nimbly and efficiently, with sleek, dangerous confidence oozing from her. And beside her walked the black-skinned necromancer, in black pants and a matching tunic that appeared covered in silver symbols Matt couldn't see from here. He wondered if they should adopt intimidating stances, but the time had passed. No one on Rovell knew they weren't the real Ellorian Champions; maybe they could intimidate from borrowed reputation.

The enemy continued to advance until they reached the plaza, and by now the lords were twenty paces ahead of the enthralled warriors behind them, most wearing studded leather or chainmail. They bore an insignia of Minari, if anything, but a few showed signs of being from Gisla, a mixed mob of threats. Matt flicked a glance at Jolian, her massive red bulk crouched down by a building and wall out of view to one side. The lords reached her position and strode into the plaza and past the wall she hid behind. A few seconds later, just as the warriors came near, she rose, a blast of flames roaring toward the Lords of Fear, who whirled at the sound. The sorcerer Garian raised one hand and Matt saw the flames strike an invisible wall. Jolian seemed to sense it, too, for she turned to aim the blast at the ground between them and the warriors, who stopped and pushed back into the crowd, the sheer mass of them inhibiting their escape. The dragon could have roasted all of them alive if she had wanted to, but she let the flames die.

"Welcome to Ortham!" shouted Eric, and the lords half-turned to them. "Your fight lies with us."

The sorcerer, Lord Garian, seemed to consider that and Jolian, who glared down at him but made no move to attack again. When Matt saw the sorcerer move toward them first and the others follow, he knew which one led them. They advanced until twenty paces away. Behind them, the warriors appeared to advance again until another spout of flames changed their minds, but one ran forward before slowing to a walk, Jolian letting him go but glaring at the others not to try it. So far, this was working as intended. He noticed the necromancer's lips moving and wondered what he was doing. He could now get a much better look at them.

Lord Garion was young and wore a haughty sneer that ruined his otherwise handsome face, a neatly trimmed blond mustache and goatee adding refinement to his oval face. Green eyes glittered with intelligence and power lust, maybe a kind of eagerness that made him seem a little un-hinged, dangerous, and unpredictable. Until the sorcerer smiled at him, Matt hadn't realized a grin could be so ma-levolent. Instinct told him to look away as if bored and unimpressed, so he did.

Matt's eyes fell on Lord Voth, who didn't look the least bit like undead, but then he had died by being encased in dragon ice that preserved him until the necromancer awoke him. If someone hadn't told Matt that Lord Voth was undead, he might never have known, and yet a sense of foreboding lurked in that direction. The knight's eyes were black and flat as if truly devoid of life, and he stood coldly surveying those before him without the passion Garian showed. He had trimmed close a black beard on his square jaw. Someone had broken his nose, which poorly healed judging by the crook in it. Only now did Matt notice the frost along the edges of Lord Voth's armor near his white skin. The symbol of Aranor, Soliander's home world, adorned the chest plate.

Movement drew his eye to the assassin Kori, whose beauty would make any man stare. Did she use it to kill them? Many a man might stare helplessly until she plunged a knife into them. Large hazel eyes, an upturned nose, and full lips would mesmerize, the depth of her gaze riveting for the mystery it promised within. It might even draw attention away from a sexy figure that her attire only ac-

centuated. For someone dressed to kill, she had still painted her fingernails blood red, neatly bound her hair with a
lace tie, and applied makeup. He wondered if she poisoned
her ruby lips for a kiss of death, and he knew that he only
saw the menace of her because she wanted him to, not
because she couldn't hide it with ease. This was the most
dangerous woman he had ever seen.

And beside her stood a man who spoke with the dead,
raised them, and had their allegiance. Aeron's deep set,
pale blue eyes shone from a black face that he had ritually
scarred using something circular and hot and the size of a
pencil, curving patterns of welts on his face and hands and
rising over his bald head. They stole any charisma that his
round face might have given, and when he blinked, Matt
saw his eyelids had eyes drawn on them in white and blue.
Did it help him see into the underworld? What role did the
scars play? Similar designs on the tunic were now close
enough to be seen but still not understood. And Matt didn't
want to know.

"Are you wondering what happened to Novir?" Eric
taunted them, breaking Matt's thoughts.

For an answer, Kori threw a knife toward him with a
flick of her wrist and the rogue barely dodged it. She was
as fast as him, Matt saw, remembering her blades were
poisoned. She cast a brief glance at the lone enthralled
warrior who had reached them, hanging back.

"I'll tell you anyway," offered Eric. "We fed him to
trolls, just like we're going to feed you to the dragon."

The sorcerer remarked, "I see you are short two dragons from when you started. Pity. But no more of you shall
fall, by our lord's order. We will ensnare your feeble minds
for him after we amuse ourselves with you."

Matt nodded to himself. So it *was* a trap to ensnare the
Ellorian Champions. As if they didn't have enough to worry about, now people were trying to capture them. But at

least they did not face death. Garian was a fool to admit that, but anger at the threat grew. Matt began gathering magical energy.

Eric continued baiting the lords, for reasons Matt didn't really understand, but he trusted the rogue. "Like he ensnared yours?"

Garian smirked. "He already has our allegiance and needed no orb to gain it."

"Was it like Novir? Did you sell your soul for a pint of ale, or maybe a petty fiefdom somewhere?"

The smirk deepened. "We're already lords, fool. And we will take what kingdoms we want."

"Yes, but if you or he were so powerful, you wouldn't need the Orbs of Dominion to do it, now would you?"

Lord Voth pointed an imperious finger at Matt. "Bow before your king, Soliander of Aranor."

Matt tried to stay in character, amazed he was about to have a conversation with an undead knight. "You are no King of Aranor. You bow to another. Care to share who has enslaved you?" Lord Voth ripped his sword from its scabbard in one smooth motion. Maybe pissing them off wasn't a good idea after all.

The rogue asked, "Are you sure you don't want to rest a minute before we kick your butts through the portal? You must have traveled all night to get here. You look like you need a nap."

Kori answered in a rich alto. "We have ways to get our energy back. Show him, Aeron."

The necromancer gestured for the nearby enthralled warrior approach, and once the man did so, he put one hand on the man's shoulder and began whispering words Matt couldn't hear but which made his skin crawl. Rather than light appearing as when Anna channeled a god's touch, a darkness gathered around the necromancer's black hand and spread over the warrior, whose face registered horror. He moaned, soiling himself as his hair turned white, his skin wrinkled and became spotty, and his posture stooped. His life's energy drained away into a ball of shimmering darkness in Aeron's hand. The warrior fell face first to the stones, dead. Glittering blue eyes turned toward them as the necromancer made a thrusting gesture with that hand. The ball of blackness separated into three, one absorbing into him and the other two racing toward Lord Garian and Kori, striking both and disappearing inside them. The assassin looked at them with a renewed blaze of energy.

"That's fucked up," Ryan muttered, scowling.

Matt had to agree and thought Aeron needed to be destroyed. He decided the time for chatter had ended. According to lore on Earth, ice had no effect on undead, but fire was another matter. Given that dragon's ice had killed and encased Lord Voth, and Matt had melted ice in a vial from Brazin, he wanted to test a theory. He opened a vial of ordinary water and poured some as he spoke.

With ice and frost I bind your flesh,
May time stand still, in peace you rest

He thrust the vial toward the target and watched as the water soared toward Lord Voth, growing expanding in volume. That it chilled in flight became apparent from the tinkling of ice shards that dropped on the stones as it flew on, finally striking Lord Voth, who hadn't bothered to move. Would arrogance be his downfall? Matt saw the water freeze around the undead knight's entire body, encasing him in inches of ice like he was a sculpture.

"Fool!" said Lord Garian, chuckling. "So much for the Majestic Magus."

Matt responded by putting the vial back in his pocket and retrieving the one with dragon's ice water. He wasn't surprised by what happened next. A crack in the ice appeared, then another bigger one. The knight was flexing his limbs inside it, and a third crack made a huge chunk fall to the stones and slide away. With a final wrench, the undead knight freed himself, sending ice pieces scattering.

Far behind the lords, Jolian breathed another round of flames to keep the enthralled away, and Matt's glance revealed their numbers had greatly reduced. Where had they gone? The obvious answer was to find another way to the plaza. Countless other entry points existed, but he had more pressing concerns. He repeated the spell, this time more hopeful of the result. Once again, the undead knight had been encased in ice as Garian and Kori stood smirking at him like he was an idiot. They waited. And waited. And waited. But Lord Voth did not appear to be moving. Not until he yelled with his mouth frozen shut did anyone realize he wasn't getting out this time.

Matt returned their smirk until a sudden gesture from Kori toward him made his breath catch. He barely saw the blade flying, instinctively raising his hands, words of magic struggling to form as the twirling knife reached him—and fell with a clatter at his feet. Kori screamed and doubled over, a splash of blood already leaking between her fingers at one shoulder. She staggered and fell to one knee, reaching for the necromancer and calling his name as she tumbled to the pavement, body going limp. Matt had forgotten one benefit of Soliander's staff—any physical blow intended for him caused the wound to appear on the victim instead. It only worked so many times, but sometimes once was enough. Whatever poison Kori was using didn't give one long to live, apparently. Aeron kneeled over her.

A roar of flame attracted Matt's attention, but Garian directed at Lord Voth, his Dragon's Fire Wand rapidly melting the dragon ice. Matt hadn't thought of that. Were the flames truly like that of a dragon and therefore an effective counter to his spell, or would regular fire melt the ice, too? Once Lord Voth had been thawed enough to crack the ice on his own, Garion turned the wand toward Jolian despite the distance. She didn't move as the flames reached and struck her, giving Matt the impression that she knew nothing would happen to her. And it didn't. When flames stopped, she bared her teeth at him as if smiling.

Having healed Kori, who rose with fury on her face, Aeron again seemed to whisper, one hand rising to the sky. That surprised Matt. A necromancer would reach for the earth to get dead things to rise from it. What was up there to care about? He found out when a loud screech split the air and a green dragon flew over the courtyard, barely above the buildings, a rider upon its back. Both were close enough to see that they were dead, large puncture wounds in the dragon's neck, ghastly ones in its body, and a broken wing hampering its flight. Just as Matt recognized Sebast and the missing Novir, they turned toward Jolian and spat a fountain of green liquid at her. The red dragon ducked behind a building as steaming acid began melting everything around her. She seemed unscathed and leaped into the sky to pursue the undead dragon.

"Holy shit," said Ryan, turning to them. "Did you see that?"

"More like unholy shit," said Eric, reaching into a pocket. Matt saw one vial of green acid he'd collected from Sebast's corpse hidden in the rogue's reappearing hand, so he turned and sent a blinding flash of light from his staff at the Lords of Fear, who shielded their eyes. Eric threw the vial, which smashed on Garian's leg. Horrible screaming erupted as it ate away the sorcerer's flesh so quickly that the bone had already appeared. Lord Garian staggered and fell, Aeron running for him even as the sorcerer's blazing eyes turned toward Eric, the Dragon's Fire Wand raising. Matt ran to Eric and put up an invisible wall just as sustained blasts of lightning struck, crackling the air amid thunder that deafened him. From the corner of his eye, Matt saw movement, as did Eric, but neither were fast enough to dodge the knives that Kori threw at Eric, one hitting his shoulder, the other his leg. The lightning cut off from Garian cut off. Anna ran to Eric. Matt swung the top of his staff in anger, causing a half circle of fire to roar up from the ground in between the combatants.

He glanced down at Eric, relieved to see Anna succeeding at healing the rogue, but there was no time to feel satisfaction. The sound of heavy footsteps preceded Lord Voth running through the wall of flames directly toward Ryan, who advanced.

"Matt," yelled Eric, "drop the flames. We can't see what they're doing."

"Right." He killed the spell and swore. With Jolian gone, the enthralled warriors had advanced, and the ones that had gone around were now entering the plaza from the sides. Undead would soon surround them except from behind. Aeron had healed a livid Garian, who now strode toward them, the dark Orb of Dominion in one hand and the wand in the other. To one side, Kori had drawn her sword and ran at Eric, who quickly drew his.

"Fall back!" shouted the rogue. "To the hall! Anna! Matt! Keep the enthralled away."

The loud clang of Ryan's sword blocking Lord Voth's split the air as they traded blows, Ryan steadily backing up and risking glances at the others to as if to measure the pace of their retreat. A flurry of more frequent and lighter clangs sounded on Matt's other side as Kori and Eric fought. Garian raised his wand at Ryan and Matt threw a brief shield up, so close to the sorcerer that the energy wave meant to strike the knight rebounded and knocked Garian into Aeron so that they fell in a heap. Matt smiled despite the tension in the air. Somehow, Eric and Kori were now fighting without swords or knives, each spinning, kicking, punching and sometimes throwing the other, still moving steadily toward the Hall of Worlds. Matt thought to get Eric's dropped sword for him, but there was no time.

A scream of warning from Jolian made him look up as Sebast bore down on them, a blast of Jolian's fire into his path making Sebast bank to avoid it, his spray of green acid missing the champions and striking the stone behind them. The green dragon had fresh burn marks on his head and one wing, but Jolian seemed unhurt. On his back, Novir was too small to see much of from here.

As Garian and Aeron tried to rise, green grass rose from between the stones beneath them, wrapping around their arms and legs, pulling them down. Startled, Matt turned and saw Anna with her arm extended toward them, fist closed and surrounded by white light. He moved toward her to protect the priestess as the grass grew longer, blades encircling Aeron's throat but not Garian's. This suggested that the necromancer was the true source of ire for the goddess of life Anna was channeling. But Aeron shouted a word he didn't understand before being strangled into silence. Some of the enthralled who were approaching ran at them, and Matt realized that each was undead.

Anna saw it, too, her eyes wide. Matt thought maybe she could just make more grass spring up and grab each of them, but she dropped her hand before turning it on the undead to one side. Those undead staggered as white light suddenly shone from their eyes, mouths, and ears. They stumbled and fell face first, unmoving. Anna whirled around and did it again to those on the other side, and then the ones running up behind Garian and Aeron, who had freed themselves and began to rise.

"*Thank* you," said Matt, reaching into his pocket for the vial of dragon ice water. Then he saw Sebast circling back toward them, Jolian once again in pursuit. "Anna, do you think you could hit the dragon with that?" To one side, Ryan appeared to be holding his own against Lord Voth, retreating steadily.

With a gleam in her eye, Anna said, "Let's see."

She made the same gesture at Sebast as he neared. The white light appeared in his eyes for a moment and caused him to turn sharply just overhead, but it seemed Anna wasn't strong enough to take him down. Something fell from his back and Matt recognized Novir's corpse as it plummeted, white lights shining from within his orifices until he smashed into the pavement yards from them, bounced once, and stopped moving.

Matt turned toward Garian and cast another spell of dragon ice, this time foot-long shards of ice hurtling at the sorcerer, who waved his Dragon's Fire Wand and melted them. But one struck a glancing blow off his shoulder and made him drop the wand. Matt struggled for a spell to levitate the wand to himself, but couldn't think of one as the sorcerer picked it up and looked at the sky. Matt followed his gaze, and this time only Jolian was coming, a jet of flames whirling in her mouth. He was about to run for the Hall of Worlds when Garian shouted behind him.

"Enough games, Ellorians! Meet your new master!"

Matt turned and saw that the Orb of Dominion now glowed with a golden sheen along its edges, a darker image within and moving but too hard to make out from here. Then a voice spoke from within it, far louder than he expected.

"Obey and serve," the voice commanded, and Matt wondered if those words acted like a spell to ensnare minds. "Fight no more. My will be yours. Follow the Lords Garian, Voth, Aeron, and Kori as your masters after me."

"Thank you, my Lord," said Garian, gazing at them in triumph.

Jolian flew past without breathing fire, and Matt saw that his friends had stopped fighting. Had the *Mind Shield* spell worked? He didn't feel any different. How should they behave? He looked at the enthralled to see what they did, as he was supposed to be one of them now, but they had just stopped advancing and stood idly by. For a moment, he wondered if the others were ensnared or safe like him, but then Eric caught his eye and the knowing look in them calmed him. Neither Anna nor Ryan was looking at him, and he sensed he should stop looking around like that or risk attracting attention.

"Ellorians," began Garian, glaring as he advanced, "stand together."

Since Matt stood in the middle of everyone, he didn't move as his friends moved toward him. He tried to seem complacent and just hoped they quickly went to the portal so he didn't have to pretend for long. The others stopped beside him and turned to face the Lords of Fear, who came within arm's reach before halting. Waves of cold from Lord Voth made him shiver, the hand closest to the undead knight feeling numb, but the sorcerer directly before him got his attention. Garian handed the Orb of Dominion staff to Kori without looking, his gaze fixed on Matt's staff.

"The famous staff of Soliander," he said, eyes alight despite the anger still on his face. "I have always wondered." He reached for it.

"Do not touch that," said a calm, menacing voice from within the orb.

Garian's hand instantly stopped as a look of fear took hold. He retracted his hand. "Yes, my lord."

"Bring them and the orb to me without delay."

"Yes, my lord." He raised his voice for all and said, "To the Hall of Worlds. Follow." He pushed past them, leaving the orb with Kori, who slipped her hand into Eric's. As Matt turned, he caught Ryan's eye and saw the big guy wink at him, sword still in his hand. The other enthralled all waited until the eight of them passed by, then fell in behind, a growing legion of warriors approaching the nearby hall. He listened for Jolian and thought he heard a distant whoosh of flames, but that was all.

"I think I'm going to make you my consort," purred Kori to Eric. "You disappointed with your sword skills, but the rest was great fun. Maybe you'll do better at poking me with something else."

"It is the Lady Eriana who should be a consort," said Aeron, his voice deep.

"Yes," agreed Lord Voth, in smooth tones. "Aranor needs a queen."

"I will raise one from the dead for you," suggested Aeron, "but she is mine."

Sounding amused, Lord Garian said, "You will wait in line. I understand our master has a special interest in her."

Despite the risk, Matt took Anna's hand to lend a supportive squeeze and found his hand being crushed by the strength of hers. The lords were in front and couldn't see, but he disengaged as they stepped into the shadow of the Hall of Worlds, a white building painted with planets of blues, yellows, and greens all along it except the tall wooden doors. These now swung open slowly, as if heavy, pulled by more enthralled. Matt suspected the lords knew that the path before them had been cleared so that they couldn't use the orb on more people, but were they surprised to meet no other resistance to accessing the portal? Garian commanded all but two dozen enthralled to wait outside. As they entered, Matt looked around. Where was Talis hiding?

The Hall of Worlds reminded Matt of an airport lounge stretching before them. They had entered one end of the long, two-story rectangle. Lining the walls were various supplies travelers might need, such as blankets and torches. A few weapons and light armor were also for sale, but much of it was food and drink. A six-foot high wall separated one from the next, each having an open storefront. They all stood empty of people. The hall's center stood bare except for murals of fanciful beasts on the floor and a stage in the center, a lute and several handheld drums lying discarded. Behind it all against the far wall, dancing golden light shimmered from the nearly two-story portal, its surface rippling as if made of a standing wall of liquid gold. Tall and wide enough for wagons to pass through, it stood unprotected, the guard stations to either side of it empty of life. Or so it seemed. They marched unmolested toward it, stopping twenty paces away when Lord Garian held up one hand as he and the other lords continued forward a few strides before turning to face them.

Garian looked at the enthralled. "You are to remain here on Rovell. Live your lives until word comes that we need you and then obey. Tell the same to those outside." He looked at Matt and the others and smirked. "It was not hard to defeat the famed Ellorian Champions after all."

"Maybe that's because that isn't them," said a voice to one side. Another Andier and Korrin stepped from inside a guard station to one side as the Lords of Fear turned sharply. A second Soliander and Eriana walked out of the other station on the other side, the wizard beginning to cast a spell. As he yanked the Dragon's Fire Wand from up his sleeve, Garian's piercing gaze swept over Matt and the others, none of them having moved.

"What is this?" he asked of no one in particular.

"A trick," said a dismissive voice from the Orb of Dominion. "It is no matter. Obey and serve!"

Eric yelled, "Now, Ryan!"

Chaos erupted.

The knight ran toward the assassin as the lords turned in surprise. Kori was too slow to stop Ryan's blade from cleanly slicing through the staff just below the Orb of Dominion, which dropped as she reached to catch it. Ryan swung again and cut her arm off at the elbow. She screamed and dropped the useless staff from her other hand to clutch at the wound as blood spurted from it. The orb struck the stones with a whack but didn't break.

"Kick it away!" yelled Eric as he backed up, throwing a knife at Garian and striking him in the chest. The knight complied, sending the orb tumbling at the rogue, who stopped it with one foot. Kori staggered toward Aeron and Ryan backed away. The second Soliander completed a spell that sent a hail of fist-sized stones pummeling the lords. Lord Voth leaped at the wizard, sword slicing the man in half and leaving a trail of frost along the wound.

"Rise," said Aeron, gesturing toward the now dead wizard.

"Burn!" yelled Anna, and pointed at the corpse, which burst into flames instead.

As if they had standing orders to protect the lords, the enthralled warriors moved to attack them. Anna turned and held up one hand, palm outward, as if to stop them. And it worked, to Matt's surprise. Had she suddenly become a partner in battle, more than just for the undead? If so, she was a welcome addition. Matt saw Lord Garian's eyes on them and knew something was coming. He struggled for another spell he could cast first.

"Try hitting it with your sword," Eric suggested to Ryan.

"Worth a shot," the knight said. He swung the blade high above his hand and brought it slamming down onto the orb with a clang. A shock wave knocked all of them back and onto the ground, Matt striking his head on the stones. He sat up, trying to ignore the pain, eyes on the Lords of Fear, who had also been felled. He followed Garian's shocked and angry gaze to the orb. It has split into the three pieces, two of them rocking on the floor on their spherical part, the other face down on the broken side.

"No!" said Garian, rising. A glance around the room revealed the enthralled men starting to sit up, their faces no longer intense and enraged, but calm and bewildered. "Attack them!" Garian commanded. But no one moved to comply.

Matt saw his chance and gripped Soliander's staff in both hands, willing as much power as he dared and not bothering to waste precious moments getting to his feet. "Enuminsar!"

A fountain of flame roared from the staff's crystal toward the lords, the scorching heat making Matt's lungs hurt and his eyes sting as if it would incinerate anything in its path.

Just before the wall of flames reached them, he saw both the wizard and necromancer raise their hands and speak words he couldn't hear over the roaring. The flames shot upward and out as if hitting a wall. With a swirling gesture, Matt directed the fire to the right, left, and up to go around any barrier there, and as the flames complied, they cleared his view of the enemy. Both Garian and Aeron stood with hands forward to protect themselves. Matt watched in satisfaction as their horrified eyes watched three tongues of fire rush around the invisible barrier toward them. Aeron turned to block one and succeeded, Garian did the same with the one above, but the other one engulfed Lord Voth and soared past for Kori, who dove out of the way toward escape.

Suddenly a knife flew at Garian and struck him in the arm. He gasped and stumbled toward the portal, the flames above diving closer at him, as if his barrier had nearly fallen, one hand still raised to keep it there. He shot a look of hatred toward Eric, his eyes then widening. From the corner of Matt's eye, he saw the rogue pulling back his arm to throw again. Garian turned and ran through the portal, Kori close behind. Eric's knife flew at Aeron instead, and the necromancer barely dodged it before running for escape, too. A thunderous crash outside suggested one dragon had plummeted to the ground.

Lord Voth stood alone before them, seemingly unfazed by one spout of flames engulfing him, only his legs visible. Wondering if three would be worse, Matt directed the others spouts into one unified blast, now that no magic shield stood in the way. No sooner did all three converge on the undead knight than a scream of pain split the air from the burning creature. Matt kept the flames going for another minute as the knight tried to get away from them. Matt made the torrent follow him, the smell of burned flesh growing. He finally wanted to see what had happened and not kill the fire in case he needed it again, so he made the flames form a low ring around the knight's lower body.

The knight stopped screaming, two blue pinpoints of light gleaming from where his eyes had been burned out in a bone-white skull. All visible flesh had melted away except for what still dripped off, steaming, hissing, and popping. Any cloth had burned off, and parts of him were still on fire. He now looked every bit the undead knight he was. A skeletal hand gripped his sword, the other pointing at Matt.

"You will die by my hand," he said in a voice shaking with fury or pain.

A moment of fear struck Matt before anger took hold and he engulfed the knight in flames again. He heard the metal boots take several steps before the portal gave a pulse and the sound stopped. He let the flames die. As expected, Lord Voth was gone. He turned back to his friends.

Eric flashed a smile. "I don't think he likes you."

Trying to sound unfazed, the wizard said, "He was dead already. Not sure what he's so upset about."

The rogue joked, "Maybe attracting an undead bride is harder now that he's not so handsome."

"Oh, I don't know, I think he looks better now. He should thank me for the makeover. The flaming flesh has a nice, romantic quality to it. Wouldn't even need to light candles on a hot date."

They all laughed and Ryan came forward, giving him a surprise hug. "Remind me not to piss you off. That's some spell you have."

"It's mostly the staff," Matt admitted.

They turned to take in their surroundings, and Matt saw that a pair of wizards that had emerged from hiding had shut the portal off. In human form again, Jolian strode up behind them, looking grim, determined, and irritated but unharmed. The formerly enthralled people had risen and seemed to be no threat, many having put away their swords. He wondered how much they remembered. Did they have any idea where they were or how they had gotten here? Part of him didn't care, but he thought that, as the Ellorian Champions, they should address it. He was about to say something when the pieces of the broken Orb of Dominion began to tremble, then vibrate. He gestured for the others to stand back as the pieces slid toward each other on the stone. Eric took a step toward them as if to stop one.

"Wait," cautioned Matt.

"Are you sure?" the rogue asked, stopping.

"No, but I think we need to see what happens."

Eric didn't look convinced. The three pieces came together on the floor and turned toward the others, each rising on one edge. Matt knew they were reforming before the three put themselves together as if someone were holding them. Was the wizard who controlled the master doing this? It seemed unlikely with the portal closed. He glanced around the room to see if anyone appeared to be doing magic to cause this, but no one was, and half weren't paying attention. His eyes returned to the orb just as the three pieces fused together, a brief burst of golden light shining from the cracks that disappeared. The Orb of Dominion appeared to have healed itself.

"Great," muttered Ryan. "Now what?"

Anna sighed. "Well, the good part is that everyone has been released. Now we just have to prevent it from being used again."

Matt asked, "Yeah, but where do we put it?"

Eric looked at him with a gleam in his eye. "I have an idea."

———— • • • ————

Night had fallen and Anna felt slightly tipsy from the wine, the gait of her white horse doing little to ease the feeling. Behind her rode the others in single file, the Quest Ring on a hill in the distance, Castle Arking behind them. The time had come to return to Earth, assuming no one summoned them in the few minutes remaining here. The idea of going from quest to quest without respite bothered her, but the moment they completed this one, they had become available to anyone else summoning them to solve their problems.

And what of their own? How were they supposed to live their own lives when they had to keep saving someone else's? It wasn't fair, but it wasn't like they could complain about it to anyone but each other. No one on Rovell knew they weren't the real Ellorian Champions. At least on Honyn, the elf Lorian and many of his closest friends, like Morven, had known. They could be themselves. Not pretend. Admit that they were scared and confused. That they didn't know how to do one thing or another that they would be expected to know. Somehow, they had succeeded at another quest. But it seemed like only a matter of time before they failed or got themselves killed.

The thought reminded her of home. Fear about what had happened to her friends when she had vanished from behind the wheel of her car had receded with their more direct concerns, but now that everything had been re-solved, there was no escaping learning their fate soon. Even if everyone was fine and escaped serious injury, she would have some explaining to do. They had all seen her disappear. How does one explain such a thing when telling the truth is likely to get you locked in a padded psych ward? She would worry about that later. Her immediate concern was her own safety.

They now knew that they returned to exactly where they had been before the summoning. Matt would end up on a sidewalk where his interview had been taking place. Ryan would reappear in the guest house at his parent's estate. Eric had been at his job. But Anna had been in the middle of I-270, south of Gaithersburg. They all assumed she would arrive in that exact spot. With no car around her. No air bags. No seat belt. And possibly cars hurtling toward her. They had left Earth in late afternoon but arrived on Rovell before lunch. Based on this, they had agreed to leave Rovell a few hours before midnight. Hope-fully, Anna reappearing on a major interstate in the middle of the night would dramatically lessen the chances of a car hitting her before she ran off the road. It certainly beat appearing in rush hour traffic. She knew that even with this plan, nothing was guaranteed. It was going to be pure luck. Either a car struck and likely killed her, or she got out of the way before one could. Maybe she should have had even more wine. It was the reason she had drunk so much.

They had also talked of the likelihood that they were famous again. Matt had disappeared on camera, so they expected significant attention. By arriving so late, they might sneak home before anyone knew. If reporters were camped out at their homes, which seemed likely, this was a problem. They had been gone three weeks the first time, but now it had been three days and that wasn't enough for people to stop watching, they assumed. For now, the plan was for Ryan to get his car and go get Anna. Matt and Eric suspected that their own vehicles might have been towed by now. Their priority was assessing their situation and then calling each other. Anna sighed, not wanting to deal with it.

Before and behind the supposed Ellorian Champions, a train of other riders accompanied them on their way to the Quest Ring. This included King Orin of Minari, his wizard Derin, the dwarven Queen of Morcanon and her retinue, and a host of revelers they had just partied at a banquet in their honor at Castle Arking behind them. Enjoying such an affair was hard when she knew, at any second, they could suddenly vanish to another quest, but she had pushed it from her mind as best as she was able. It seemed she had to do a lot of that these days. The thought made her sigh.

Just in front of her rode Jolian and her brother Brazin, both in human form and in their preferred tight leather of red or blue. The group had told no one of Brazin's mental capture by the Orb of Dominion, to spare any humiliation or damage to his reputation. Once free of it, he had shown a level of humility and sorrow she didn't expect from a dragon, not that she knew much about that. They had collected him at Valegis and rode him and his red sister back to the castle, leaving all others behind at Ortham. Farewells to Talis and anyone from the city had been brief, but they had earned more friends that they would likely never see again, as much good as that did them.

It had taken hours to implement Eric's plan. First, he had Ryan try to break the Orb of Dominion into three pieces again with a different sword, which had shattered the blade instead. Only Ryan's weapon, made of soclarin ore, could do it. Once broken, Eric, Ryan, and Matt had each taken a piece and walked away from each other in the Hall of Worlds. Twenty steps apart hadn't been enough, because the shards tried to pull together once more, but doubling the distance prevented it from happening again. Eric had wondered if that was true, and with it proven, he told them his idea.

Leaving Anna and Ryan to heal people, and provide leadership, he and Matt had climbed aboard Jolian with one piece and been gone for two hours before returning without it. Then they experimented with bringing the two remaining pieces close together. The parts showed no attempt to merge, so they turned their attention to other matters. This had included a meeting with the rulers of Ortham to inform them of developments. They also arranged for those who had been enthralled to be sent home with necessary supplies for their journeys, whether to the town of Durba, Castle Arking, or wherever they lived. They offered Ortham some gems from King Orin for this, but in a show of appreciation, he had refused it.

And so they returned to Valegis for Brazin, who had proven to Jolian's satisfaction that he was of his own mind again, not that they doubted this. They had questioned various enthralled victims before and knew most had only been dimly aware of having been compromised. Most spoke of feeling an agreement with orders given to them, as if they had long thought of doing the very thing they were commanded to do and now felt certain of its rightness. When the orb had shattered, they had suddenly come to their senses and been disturbed by what they had done.

And for this reason, Brazin seemed genuinely ashamed that he had killed his friend Sebast. Anna had felt bad for him, having seldom seen such troubled eyes in her life.

Brazin was haunted, and she wondered if the same thing would befall her on returning to Earth and learning the fate of her friends. Inspired by a dread that this would be so, she had spent most of the night with the blue dragon, trying to help him and gain some understanding of what this might be like. In doing so, she admitted to some fear of what had happened in her absence without going into details, and he seemed to understand that they had this in common. The kiss he had given her had surprised and delighted her, the tingling feeling of a dragon's kiss not something she'd soon forget. Had he just ruined her for regular guys? She laughed and looked fondly at his back as he rode before her.

That night in Valegis, with Brazin recovered, they had filled in Ogren and spent another evening in town. That had been the first celebration, where a small feast had been done in their honor, there not being much time to anticipate a bigger one. She didn't really mind, and the others had clearly enjoyed the attention. Eric had not returned to their rooms that night, and the smirk on his face the next day erased any doubt he'd been in a woman's room overnight. Ryan had returned late with something of a sloppy grin that had irritated her. She'd had half a mind to go find Brazin and get another kiss, but she wasn't really sure what that would do to her.

Instead, she had spent the night with Matt, memorizing spells with him. She had noticed women intrigued by the wizard, but also intimidated by Soliander's reputation. Matt had seemed little interested in them, but she suspected it was his new obsession with learning magic. She agreed with his desire to commit these spells to memory and write them down on Earth if magic became available to them.

In the morning, they had flown on Brazin and Jolian to the Kirii Cave. Eric seemed fine without a saddle, the crazy boy that he was, but Ryan had seemed concerned by the experience. Once there, they found another way into the cave itself and hid a second of the orbs' three pieces in the bottom of the underground lake. In doing so, they discovered that the leviathan wasn't entirely dead, though it didn't attack, and they returned to Valegis to ensure Ogren and the townspeople knew. This would prevent anyone from seeking the orb shard. Before leaving the cave, they had removed the saddle from the dead Sebast and placed it on Brazin, who had paid his respects while the others were below. His own saddle had been left behind at the lake where Novir had disappeared.

After this, they flew to Morcanon, the dwarven kingdom. It had taken some convincing to get to the queen, mostly by using the remaining piece of the Orb of Dominion to convince anyone of their identities. She had been freed of her enthrallment and been in contact with King Orin, and thus were they given an audience. It was here that they wanted to leave the other piece, figuring the dwarves had learned a hard lesson. This had resulted in their second feast, this time for lunch and once again haphazardly arranged. The dwarves had reminded her of Rognir, her Honyn friend and mentor, but their offered tours of their underground world seemed too much of the Kirii Cave, an apprehension that vanished before long. Their stonework skill had her and the others in awe, but there was little time to enjoy it. They soon departed for a short flight to Castle Arking.

They told King Orin a riddle that Eric and Matt devised. No one was to know where the three pieces of the slave Orb of Dominion lay in case someone brought them together again. But since it was possible that they might need this and the four Ellorian Champions were no more, they decided on leaving a clue. The result was a quest they devised for someone else to complete. Even Ryan and Anna didn't know where the first piece lay and found the clues to be suitably cryptic.

> *In ruins lies the first of three*
> *Where once stood man but nothing be*
> *Entombed in stone for none to see*
> *In high noon's light it can be free*
> *Where monsters swim and darkness lies*
> *The second piece it does reside*
> *All arms and wings, two deadly foes*
> *Beneath the waves that one must row*
> *The third lies in the tunnels of stone*
> *Among those who were once overthrown*
> *Now free again they have all sworn*
> *To hide the shard and keep it torn*

Anna wasn't sure which of the two came up with text because they looked equally proud of it when reciting it the first time, and they had cared little for her suggested edits. The thought made her smile. With danger over, they had returned to being like two boys playing *Dungeons and Dragons*. She wasn't one to stifle someone's entertainment anyway, and certainly not after everything they just went through. On the first quest, they had thought they would just go back to their lives after some initial attention, but this time they knew better.

Now Eric and Matt had created a quest instead of solving one. Maybe one day someone else might go on the quest to recover the slave Orb of Dominion, but hopefully it wouldn't be the Lords of Fear, or anyone else during their lifetime. The orb pieces would not be unable to come together on their own, and only someone who knew the location of each piece could find them. Only Eric, Matt, and Jolian knew. They trusted the dragon.

Anna grew nervous as they neared the Quest Ring, the path to it lined by torches, an honor guard lining the way. The ring itself had been lit with more flames that illuminated those standing near it. Despite efforts to keep the crowd at bay, they were getting a hero's send off, and she got the impression the guards had given up on keeping people away. The mood was positive but quiet, as if the night sky hushed everyone, kids jostling for position. She had learned that the champions had never been here before and with their summoning happening in secret, no one had seen the spectacle. They weren't going to be denied this time.

The group dismounted and said their farewells, accepting some gifts despite knowing they wouldn't arrive with them. What happened to them they didn't know. Did they just fall to the ground here on Rovell? They would likely never get an answer. This was the first time they were supposedly bringing something they hadn't arrived with back. Before going, Anna asked Jolian to please come find them if she heard that they had arrived on Rovell again. They could use a friend.

Then they mounted the dais as people cheered, Ryan turning to them and assuming the role of a heroic knight that he played at RenFest. Who knew he would ever get to do it for real? He might have been the only one who truly enjoyed the pomp and ceremony of it all. And his wealthy upbringing had sort of prepared him for it, with the fancy balls and other stuff his parents had made him go to. Anna couldn't relate, but she could admire the way he worked the crowd. Better him than her. They hadn't really talked about it, but they knew Eric was their actual leader, the man with a plan, but that Ryan was the public face of the group. It seemed to work for all of them. The shy Matt could hang back as the intimidating Soliander while Anna could smile and try to soften their fearsome reputation.

Taking the edge off boys and their sometimes-unruly leanings was something girls did anyway.

But she was faking it this time. It wasn't until they had said last goodbyes that everyone but them stepped off the dais. King Orin made a final brief speech, the dwarven queen did the same, and a shout went up from the King's Guard. Then everyone fell silent, Matt having decided to use Soliander's staff to trigger the return spell. He did the deed as people watched, then resumed position, the floor beneath them lighting up just as the pillars did. The crowd cheered and for the first time, Anna felt the weight on her lift. She hadn't let herself feel the gratitude or happiness until now and tried to cut herself some slack. Maybe Raven, Heather, and Jade were fine, and all this anxiety wasn't worth it. Then the Quest Ring and those outside it disappeared.

The familiar vortex of light and sound roared around her. This time she remembered to cover herself as Eriana's robe vanished, making her nude before her Earth clothes returned. She felt the lump of her smartphone in one pocket and briefly wondered what would happen if she tried to make a call. How soon would it get a signal to let her know how many texts, calls, and emails she hadn't seen? Across from her, the others looked excited, if tense. Whatever happened to feeling safe now that they were going home? The three of them disappeared before her along with the noise, but the bright light remained, blinding even more, the sound of a car horn blaring, followed by the screech of skidding tires.

Then the darkness took her.

CHAPTER NINE

IN THE DEAD OF NIGHT

Soliander held up a plastic card with numbers embossed on it. "What's this?"

A credit card, he suddenly realized, knowledge from his previous mental contact with Matt surfacing. Pieces were falling into place, but many of them weren't particularly useful. Still, he needed to know how to get around in this world. No magic portals existed, not that he couldn't cast him and his apprentice somewhere. But he grew eager to experience this place he'd only seen in Matt's memories before arriving on Earth himself. And then there was the question of seeming like they belonged here while avoiding suspicion. He had admonished Darron not to gawk, but part of him knew he was doing it, too. It was one reason they were in a Gaithersburg, Maryland hotel room now, gathering intel out of sight, with fewer bright lights and fantastic sights to make them stare.

"My credit card," answered Joe, a middle-aged, portly man who seemed typical of those encountered so far. He sat before them on the lone chair, tan slacks and a white button-up shirt at odds with their jeans and t-shirts. Darron had asked about the differing clothes, but Soliander wasn't inclined to explain trivial details, which he only sensed the significance of from Matt's memories. The fourth-floor hotel room had two queen beds and furnishings that the wizard suspected were normal. Joe's bag, or suitcase, lay open on one bed, the contents already rifled through.

"How does it work?" Soliander asked, images of using it to pay for goods flashing in his head. "You purchase things with it?"

"Yes."

"What sorts of items?"

"Almost anything. Food, hotel rooms, merchandise."

"Homes?"

"No, that requires a mortgage, a home loan."

"Explain."

Soliander and his apprentice listened as Joe explained about credit, banks, and the housing market. They had been at this for ten minutes, the spell Soliander had cast on Joe making him compliant and honest to a fault. This world was unlike anything he'd known. By morning, they'd likely know everything they needed. The information was overwhelming, and Soliander was growing impatient, because there was so much that was so different. He finally made Joe stop talking, grabbed his apprentice's hand, and cast the *Mind Trust* spell on Joe. It allowed both of them to sift through Joe's memories, which they did for hours, gorging on intel. They had previously done this to a hotel maid, then made her forget the encounter.

It had not taken long for Darron to contact him via the orb from a local park, then cast a cantrip to make a ball of light appear. Soliander had arrived moments later, but as strong as he was, magic was not without a cost and he felt a little weakened by the exertion. He recognized the sight of Matt's house, or that of his parents, technically, but he didn't go in. The lights and movement inside had not deterred him so much as the recollection, courtesy of Matt, of what lay inside. The memories returned more concretely now that he was here, his eyes going to one house or another, to places where Matt had experienced pain or pleasure, or where childhood friends had lived. And that's how he realized the parents of Anna lived next door. That could also be useful.

It was partly for this reason that the pair had spent hours walking around town and sometimes sitting on a bench, watching people, and quietly remarking on observed details great and small. Everything became more distinct for Soliander, as if the disjointed nature of his *Mind Trust* spell with Matt was undone by being in the places where those broken memories had originated. It was all more fantastic than Soliander had envisioned. Darron had been less prepared for it and so wide-eyed that Soliander had finally cast a spell to calm the dark elf.

Arriving at night had been helpful, as fewer people had been around to encounter, and they had spent until morning getting a feel for life on Earth. The need for sleep and a quiet base for further exploring had led to this hotel and Joe, who was in town for business. The right spell had resulted in Joe going about his day job while the wizards slept in his room with the "do not disturb" sign on, with breaks for exploring, then Joe dutifully returning to them for the night. Tomorrow would include trips to Anna's condo, Eric's place, and the home of Ryan's family, with much information falling into place. But one subject Soliander most wanted to know, he found nothing on, so he returned to the inquisition to ask directly.

"What do you know of Merlin?" he asked.

"Merlin?" Joe asked with a frown.

"The wizard."

Hesitating, Joe asked, "You mean the legend guy? From Arthur's Court? Knights of the Round Table? That's just a myth."

Soliander scowled in frustration, for his spells had rendered Joe helpful, and yet here he was not being so. It suggested the information was beyond his reach. "From what year is this myth?"

"I'm not sure. The 11th century maybe."

"And it's... the 21st century?"

"Yeah. It's after 2000."

Soliander stepped back. "A thousand years."

He had half-expected something of this sort, but not nearly that long. It explained the weathering at Stonehenge, which he was curious to visit, but it could wait. Matt's memories were quite clear on that one, being so recent. He asked Joe about the myth but learned little until Joe offered to look it up on his laptop, so they did. But for all the legends, there was nothing about Stonehenge in them, or Quest Rings, and no mention of himself, Eriana, Korrin, or Andier. And while Morgana appeared in quite a few of the tales, he found nothing about the Ellorian Champions. Or Merlin's Pendant. Or faerie creatures vanishing along with magic to their own world. It was as if none of it had ever happened.

Soliander sighed in frustration. No answer would come soon, he realized, so he turned his mind to practical matters. He wasn't sure how to go about acquiring his own credit card or smartphone to pay for things, and with cash still acceptable, he soon magically robbed a nearby bank by turning himself invisible, casting himself inside, and removing a small fortune in bills before leaving. Similar stunts helped prepare himself and Darron for further escapades, but with the Stonehenge Four, as he had learned they were called, gone on a quest, he had time.

He had seen news reports of Matt vanishing on camera, and the stories about Anna's disappearance, the others reportedly missing as well. The footage of Matt had been important for understanding one thing—they weren't going voluntarily. The expression of surprise on Matt's face had made it plain. This came as no real surprise. After

Everon's betrayal, he and the others hadn't been doing it willingly either. The real question now was how the four Earth friends had been substituted for them. He had wondered if Korrin, Andier, or Eriana had somehow done this, despite it being improbable, but now he knew they had not.

Like him, they had railed against the forced quests and having to pretend they were happy to solve someone else's problem for them when no one could solve theirs—how to escape the quest cycle that only Everon and Diara knew was undesired. His friends would never have forced others to take their place even if they had known how, and if Soliander didn't know, they couldn't. He was the wizard who had invented everything about the Quest Rings—with a little help from Eriana for the healing elements—until Everon altered them.

His curiosity about them had only increased on learning of the quest on Rovell. They had somehow defeated the Lords of Fear, who had earned their nickname. The victory was impressive and unexpected. They seemed a threat to anyone up to no good and had surprised him twice now. This warranted respect and caution, maybe a little more reconnaissance. Had his old friends somehow trained them, or were they just getting lucky? It took more than good fortune to defeat the lords.

Aeron had suffered a loss of pride, and Garian had recovered from his wounds. Kori's severed arm had grown back with supernatural help, but there was no way to restore Lord Voth's previously handsome appearance. Soliander liked him better this way anyway. An undead knight who looked like a normal man wasn't nearly as frightening as one with bones and bits of charred flesh hanging from him.

The quartet had been suitably concerned about their future well-being after the failure, but they didn't have to explain what happened. He had seen their collapse himself, right until the moment "Lord Korrin" had slammed his sword down at the orb. After that, he lost contact, but he knew what must have happened, and the Lords of Fear had confirmed it. The slave Orb of Dominion had broken, leaving only the master. And now the subservience that had ensnared two kingdoms of the many to come had been lost. He frowned as he gazed over at a black velvet cloth atop a round object. When he caught up with these supposed Ellorian Champions, he would make them reveal what they had done with the other orb's pieces.

———— • • • ————

The moment he sensed he had returned to Earth, Eric dropped into a defensive crouch and scanned around him. Then he relaxed and straightened. He was alone. And he had arrived where he'd expected—back at work, which was predictably deserted. He once again wore his karategi, its white pants and jacket too bright for his comfort as he stood there in the dark. A glance at the clock showed just after two in the morning, so their guess at the time had been close. He turned to where his clothes should have been but weren't. His shoes, car keys, wallet, and phone were all gone. He searched for them, thinking his boss might have moved them, but then he went to window and looked for his car. Gone.

"Damn it," he said, not surprised. Someone might have called the police. He had a bad feeling they were about to be famous all over again. He went into the office and dialed Matt from the landline. To his relief, the techie picked up.

"Hey, it's Eric. I'm stuck inside at work because the alarm is on and I don't know the code."

"Just let yourself out anyway. Who cares if it goes off?"

Eric laughed. "Good point, but there is a problem. A couple. I don't have my regular clothes, or my wallet, and that stuff. And my car is gone."

"Yeah, so is mine. Is that why you're calling from another phone? I almost didn't pick up but figured it was you or Ryan."

"Yeah. My parents likely have it all. Listen, I forgot I was wearing karate stuff, which is what I'm in now. If I set off that alarm, and I'm walking the streets in this because I don't have a car, I'm going to draw attention."

"Yeah, you'd get picked up for sure, though I'm not sure how quickly they'd know a guy in a karate outfit is the one who set the alarm off there."

"Me either." But an alarm at a karate place going off and a guy walking around in a karate outfit would be too much coincidence for the police to not quickly put it together, then confirm it, all after arresting him. Technically, he had done nothing wrong, but that wouldn't stop the arrest or cause problems he wanted to avoid. It seemed obvious that his disappearance was known, so he might not get out of custody easily if apprehended. He felt like he didn't have time for that anyway.

"Why don't I come get you?" Matt asked.

"Still risky. I was just going to spend the next few hours here and try to sneak out in the morning or something. Hopefully, the owner won't notice. You could pick me up then, assuming you find your car." Eric sighed. This was getting irritating.

"Yeah. What time does the place open? I'll try to be there with clothes."

"Good idea. I need shoes, maybe sandals as they'll fit better since they aren't mine. Anyway, I think my boss gets in by 6:30."

"Then I'll be there by 6. It'll give me time to go by my house for some stuff."

"Okay. Listen, try Anna next. I will call Ryan. It's important none of you try to call my cell. If it's at my parent's house, they might see you calling and if everyone knows we all disappeared, they'll know you guys are back, and me."

"Why does that matter?"

"Just don't do it. I have to call Ryan before he calls my phone. Bye."

He wasted no time, dialing Ryan and having it go to voicemail, where he left a long message and a number to call back on until 6:30, anyway. Then he settled in. He wanted to hide their arrival as long as possible and control the narrative of when they returned. They had to lie, of course, but they had to know what people were thinking in order to do that well, so keeping quiet about their return was a good idea for now. He settled in for a few hours, being refreshed as usual by the spell and not needing sleep. He suspected a long day awaited him.

———— • • ————

Matt wished there was no flash of light when he returned to Earth. It was especially troubling at night, not only for attracting attention, but momentarily blinding him. Despite his impaired night vision, he quickly glanced around and didn't see anyone near him as he stood on a sidewalk. He wasted no time dawdling and began walking away just in case he'd been seen, pulling the hood of his hoodie over his head, though doing this at night might have made him look suspicious. He sighed and pulled it down. The roads had been empty, but the first car headlights appeared up the street as he took his bearings.

He was still outside the office building where he worked, as expected. The longer they could keep people from realizing they always returned to where they'd been, the better. He wasn't sure what would happen then but imagined being tasered by police or something. That would be an entirely different blinding light and hardly a warm welcome after having saved another planet, kingdom, or whatever. He laughed.

But the sound died in his chest as he rounded the corner of his employer's building to see his car was gone. Then his phone rang from an unfamiliar number, but he assumed it had to be one of his friends at this hour. He found Eric on the other end and had their talk while walking away from the building to create more distance. He would need an Uber, and after he hung up, devised a plan, his ride appearing minutes later. Before entering the car, he put the hood up again and tried to disguise his voice a little, while keeping his face averted. Then he just put his head down and pretended to be tired.

"What brings you out so late?" the twenty-something Indian driver asked.

Matt drew a blank and then said, "Fight with the girl-friend. She threw me out."

"Oh! That's terrible! The woman is always right. That's all I know about dating. It's so hard."

"Tell me about it." Matt recognized a talkative guy and hid behind someone else's wall of words, but within minutes, talk turned to his own disappearance days earlier because he'd just been picked up near there.

"Yeah," the driver said, "now the police and even FBI, the CIA, are looking for this guy."

"What? Why?"

"There's a rumor that he can just come and go whenever or wherever he wants, so what's stopping him from showing up in the White House and killing the president?"

"Holy shit."

"I know! It's crazy."

"But why would I... uh, he do that?"

"Oh, I don't know. People are all over his Twitter feed and all that, Facebook, but there's no report of him being like that, so I don't know."

"Do people think he's dangerous?"

"No. I don't think so. But I don't know. I guess they'll catch him at some point, I mean if they can. How do you catch a guy who can disappear when he wants to?"

Holy fucking shit, Matt thought, mind racing. He couldn't go home. Not like this, pulling up in an Uber to be arrested? And of course people thought he had vanished on purpose. That was great. Nothing like a misunderstanding to make this even worse. He couldn't go back, or at least not pull up in a car.

"Hey, there's a Denny's on the way. Can you drop me there instead? Kinda hungry."

"Yeah, sure thing."

"Great. Thanks."

Within minutes he had gotten out and left a tip for the guy via his phone app. He went inside and straight to the bathroom, trying to get a minute to himself. Then he studied his phone, wondering if it was being tracked even now. He furiously looked up how to turn off any tracking features. Not for the first time, he wondered what happened to anything he was holding or wearing when summoned. Did it go into some sort of suspended animation between worlds until he returned? Maybe he'd ask Jack what he saw in a tracking app when they went away. For now, he didn't feel comfortable bringing it but needed it, so he turned it completely off and left the nearly empty restaurant, trying not to look suspicious as he glanced repeatedly over his shoulder. He was a mile from home and ducked into a neighborhood to get out of sight.

Hugging tree lines and bushes while trying to act like he wasn't, Matt approached his parent's two-story, single-family house from the next street over, cutting through a back yard to reach it. In the deeper shadows of a maple tree he stopped, carefully eyeballing every hiding place he'd ever used as a boy, not for himself to go into now so much as to see if anyone was in one. While Anna had moved out to her own apartment, Matt had not, and her parents still lived next to his. They had been friends most of their lives, she being among those who had played those games with him. Who knew those childhood adventures would turn all too real?

He saw nothing suspicious and entered the property, mindful of the motion-detecting light he knew was above the backdoor. He had a plan for that and was staying clear for now, but first he wanted to check the front yard and cautiously reached the corner behind a tall evergreen shrub. He scooted into the opening between it and the house and looked out.

The first thing he noticed was his own car in the driveway, so at least it wasn't impounded or something. His mother's was beside it, which meant his father's was somewhere else. His parents were pack rats, the two-car garage full of boxes and other crap. Across the street were townhomes, which prevented on-the-street parking and resulted in two sets of parking spaces, on one either side of the town row, and his father's Prius sat in one of them, sandwiched between two SUVs.

No one seemed to be out there, and his eyes went to each car in a driveway or in the parking spots. All were familiar, but one that sat in the set of spaces that did not include his father's car. It immediately drew his attention because he saw the orange glow of a cigarette inside as someone took a drag from it. The dark silhouette of two heads were visible. The house was being watched. His Mazda 3 was out of the question. So was the front door. Thank God for that Uber driver or he'd be face down in handcuffs right now.

He leaned against the house for a minute. Did people really think he was a danger to national security? He was suddenly glad that he had never gotten involved in any political commentary online. What would he say if apprehended? If he told the truth, they'd put him in a psych ward somewhere, and lying would not work. Even Eric, who was pretty good at that sort of thing, probably wouldn't acquit himself well. He realized he needed an attorney—like he could afford that. Life as a software developer could be lucrative, but he was at the start of his career, not yet raking in six figures. He sighed. One problem at a time.

He went to the back corner of the building and looked around, then scooted toward the rear door with his back against the house. Stopping at the first window, he tried to peer inside, wondering if his parents knew the place was being watched. Would they cooperate with the FBI or whoever was out there? Would they let someone stay inside to grab him? Would they let him be arrested? He wasn't a criminal, had done nothing wrong. His mom and dad would be worried about him, just like when the Stonehenge disappearance happened, but he doubted they would help someone other than him.

Suddenly he realized that his credit card, which was associated with his phone and Uber account, and which he had just used to pay for the ride, had likely triggered an alert that was probably set up.

"Fuck," he whispered. "No time for this."

He moved past the window quickly without worrying about it, making it to the door just under the security light. He had argued with his parents about its positioning when his dad set it up, pointing out this exact flaw, but his father hadn't listened or cared because they really had no reason to worry about it. Of all the times his mom and dad didn't listen, now Matt was suddenly glad for it. He unlocked the door, which swung inward, and stepped inside. He didn't wait to see if anything happened and instead went straight for his room upstairs, moving as quietly as he could in the dark. Sneaking into your own home has the advantage of knowing exactly where everything is, despite the blackness. Thinking quickly, he grabbed a phone charger, clothes for Eric, sandals, and an extra change of clothes for himself, stuffing them into his backpack. He also stripped and donned darker clothing, then grabbed two baseball hats and some sunglasses. It suddenly occurred to him that it didn't look like they had searched his room. They would have needed a warrant and a reason.

He was about to leave when the sight of his big remote-controlled car gave him an idea. He took it and the remote with him, stole his father's car keys from where they hung downstairs, and wrote a brief note to his parents.

I'm okay. Sorry for worrying you. I had to take Dad's car. Don't report it stolen. If an unknown number calls, it might be me. Pick up. Talk soon, I swear. Matt. P.S. Destroy this.

He put it inside the microwave and then exited the rear door carefully. Then he put the remote-controlled car on the ground, facing away from the house, and carefully exited the area the way he'd arrived. He went down two blocks, crossed the street, and then returned near his father's car so that those watching the house wouldn't see his approach. Once beside it, he fired up the remote and made the car move a few feet. From the house's front, he could still see the white glow of the security light's beam as the car triggered it. As Matt crouched down, the guys in the car got out and jogged toward the house, both holding up a gun that made Matt go cold. He waited until they were out of sight, got into his father's car, turned it on, and backed up without the lights on. Electric cars had a significant advantage of being quiet and the men never seemed to hear it as he put the car in drive and crept away, turning on the headlights once far enough out of sight.

⸻ ◆ ◆ ⸻

Ryan's eyes adjusted to the dark night as he stood outside the family guest house, beside his car. Someone had shut both the trunk and door, which didn't surprise him. They had been here. The house door was also closed. He went up to it, finding it locked. All the gear had been seen. The question was by whom. Daniel would likely have not said anything to anyone. Gardeners would have, especially given that he had been missing for days. Patting his pockets, he found his wallet and phone, but no car keys, which he'd been holding when he vanished.

He tried Anna, knowing she was at risk, but the phone just kept ringing and then went to voicemail. As he prepared to try for the third time, getting worried, the phone rang with an unfamiliar number, but he answered it.

"Yeah."

"It's Eric."

After being filled in, Ryan said, "I can't get Anna. Just keeps going to voicemail."

"Can you get to her location?"

"I'm not sure. No car keys. I have to see if I can get into the house for the spares."

"Okay. On the off chance that your car is known to police, maybe grab another."

"Not sure it's worth it, but sure. I mean, someone knows it's here and may have told the police, so I don't think they'd be looking for it, but maybe they are."

"Call me back on this number when you find her."

Ryan agreed and hung up. Then he went for his car just to see what was still inside it from the supplies he'd been unloading. The door was unlocked and a piece of paper sat on the front seat along with a house key. He picked them up.

Alarm is set for delay. Beware pigs.

Daniel, he realized, recognizing the handwriting. He owed his brother one. Now he knew who had been back here to see the gear.

He ran for the main house. His family always set the alarm overnight, but with it set for the 30-second delay, he could get inside and turn it off before it called the police. This was the usual approach when no one was home, but overnight, his family used the no-delay setting. Whether or not his parents were doing it, Daniel was making sure it was that way. Arriving at the door, he let himself in, turned off the alarm, and went for his room, quickly changing clothes before heading to the garage but being intercepted by his brother.

"Glad you're back," Daniel whispered from his wheelchair, pajamas bottoms below his bare torso. "Had a motion detection camera on, in case you're wondering."

Ryan felt relief to see him again, but no time for, well, anything. And Daniel was a little too smart sometimes, so the days of keeping him in the dark were not meant to last. "Yeah, listen. I owe you a huge favor, but I need you to trust me. I have to leave right now, and no one can know that I'm back. Cover for me and I swear I'll tell you everything."

Daniel's eyes grew intense. "Okay. Do you need anything?"

"To find Anna." He started for the garage again, Daniel following.

"Is she hurt?"

"I really hope not."

They entered the six-car garage, Daniel rolling down a ramp, and Ryan went for the rack of car keys. He ignored the vehicles that would attract attention, like the red Lamborghini Countach, a silver Aston Martin convertible, and a yellow Ferrari 308 GTS.

"Take a bike?" Daniel suggested. "Faster and she's been on the back if you are planning to pick her up. The cops are looking for you. Easier to lose–"

"Yeah, got it." Ryan went for the Ducati motorcycle and quickly grabbed a spare jacket for her, cramming it into a saddlebag, putting on his and zipping it, then attaching a helmet for her to the back seat and pulling his on.

"Your intensity is starting to worry me."

"I'm just worried," Ryan said, getting on and starting it, as his brother hit the garage door opener. He decided to stop hiding things because his brother had probably put together a lot already. Everyone had to know Matt had vanished, and the rest of them, too, so he admitted, "Look, she disappeared on the highway, which means she reappeared on it, but without a car, and that means she might have just been hit by a car."

"Jesus. Call me if anything has happened. I'll stay up."

"Love you, brother."

"Yeah. Be careful."

Once the door was high enough, Ryan hit the gas and flew out of the garage. As he neared the estate gates, they were already opening courtesy of Daniel and he blew past them long before they completed opening. Gratitude for his brother's help mixed with fear for Anna. He had a bad feeling about this.

River Road was empty as he hurtled onto the two-lane road, heading away from the Capital Beltway. He expected ten minutes to reach Anna's general location, but there was more than one way to get there, and if Daniel was right that the police were watching him, the back way offered many ways to lose them. And as it turned out, his brother was right. Within moments of hitting the road, red and blue flashing lights appeared behind him. He gunned it and turned up one road, rolling on the throttle and hoping they didn't follow.

But they did, and he sped up more, going over several hills at 90 mph before slowing and veering off another way and gunning it again. He could not turn the lights on a motorcycle off, unlike a car, and he roared over two hills before dropping out of sight. The flashing lights didn't follow, and he slowed, opting for several more twists and turns that made it unlikely he'd be found. He finally turned back toward I-270 and reached an overpass that made his heart sink.

More lights appeared, but this time they were below on the interstate. Police, a firetruck, and an ambulance. And a lone car with significant damage to the front. Heart in his throat, he made his way down to the partially blocked highway and used the mobile bike to get around snarled traffic. He also went around the first few cops who tried to stop him before he slowed to get off, other police rushing toward him.

"Sir," an officer began, running up as he pulled off his helmet, "Back behind the cones!"

Ryan was hardly listening, his eyes seeing a stretcher that lifted up as EMTs wheeled the person on it toward an ambulance. It was a young woman, long blonde hair in disarray and bloody, a torn shirt dangling from one limp hand, her neck in a brace. He couldn't see her face. The cop grabbed his arm and Ryan yanked it free.

"I know her!" he shouted, anguished and trying to get past him. "I think I know her."

"Well, you need to stay here and let the EMTs handle this. We can get your name and—"

"Stand back!" demanded another officer. "Hey wait a minute." His eyes scrutinized Ryan's face and went to the bike before one hand moved to the gun at one hip. "Are you Ryan LaRue?"

"What? Yeah. How–"

"Down on the ground!" he yelled, and the first officer shoved Ryan while tripping him, several pairs of hands forcing him down, painfully yanking his arms behind his back. Before he knew it, cuffs were on him and he struggled to glimpse the stretcher again from his stomach, the pavement inches from his face.

"Is it her?" he asked frantically as hands began searching him, removing his wallet, phone, and more. "Is it Anna? Let me up. Let me see!"

"The only thing you're seeing it the back of a patrol car."

"He's clean," announced another officer.

As they hauled him upright, he fought to turn and look for the ambulance, but the doors had been closed and it began to drive away. His eyes scoured the highway nearby for any sign of any other blonde woman in the vicinity, desperate for this to be a coincidence. But the search ended when they shoved him into the back of a patrol car and slammed the door, ignoring his questions about who the victim was.

CHAPTER TEN

THE PRICE

Matt sat behind the wheel of his father's Prius as it sat parked on the upper, empty level of a public garage. "I feel sick."

Eric looked over to make sure he didn't mean it literally, seeing his own worry mirrored on the techie's face. Both of them had changed their clothes and wore hats and sunglasses. He left his job without his boss realizing he was even there, mostly because the business had several rooms and setting up for the day meant going into more than one, leaving the foyer. The front door had beeped when he opened it, but a quick jog to a stairwell had gotten him out of sight before being seen.

Now, a handful of tall hotels loomed overhead in two directions, shorter buildings closer and across the I-270 highway. Few people were out yet, so they didn't have to worry about anyone finding it weird that they were just sitting there in the car and never getting out.

The radio was tuned to WTOP and gave yet another update on the accident investigation on I-270, noting that a man on a motorcycle had been taken into custody hours earlier. Neither knew how that related to anything. All that really mattered is that neither Anna nor Ryan were answering their phones. Every time they tried, Matt drove around while Eric turned Matt's phone back on, dialed,

206 | RANDY ELLEFSON

failed to connect with them, and then turned the phone back off. They didn't know how cell phone tracking worked, but after what Matt had told him, Eric wasn't taking any chances and made sure they weren't sitting still to be tracked to an exact location. Then they returned here to park again. Now the sun was up.

"You're sure that your parents will find that note in the microwave before realizing the car is gone?"

"Yeah. My mom likes to know how warm her morning tea is, so she uses that, not the stove."

"I have a plan."

Matt sighed. "That took longer than I expected. You usually think faster."

Eric smirked. "Since neither of us can go home or risk using a credit card for a hotel, we need somewhere to stay tonight, assuming we don't hear from Ryan. Even if we don't, I think I know how to get onto his parent's property and to the guest house. Ryan was showing me the grounds. The security is okay, but it's not like they're really expecting intruders. They aren't a drug cartel or something, with armed guards and all of that. I can scale one wall away from the road, in case the cops are watching the house, as I assume they are."

"I likely can't climb a wall. You can do that with sandals on?"

"No, barefoot. We need to add rock climbing to our list of skills to train on." Eric had been doing it for years along with parkour, so getting into the LaRue estate wasn't an issue for him. His feet would get scraped doing it, but rock climbing shoes that let your toes grip were a help anyway.

"What then?"

"For food today, you have enough cash for us, and maybe we'll get some for tomorrow just in case. And we've got the car with a half tank of gas. Once we're at the guest house—I'm thinking after midnight we do this—then tomorrow, I'll see if I can get Daniel's attention at the main house, by going to the back door or something. We'd just keep an eye out for his parents, making sure they already left."

"You think we can trust him?"

Eric watched a red Toyota Camry pull into the lot ahead of them. "To not tell the police we're there? Yeah, I do. We might have to tell him more. He already saw the gear. He doesn't believe Ryan about the Stonehenge disappearance, and he's too smart. He would be a good ally."

"Okay. Are we ready to try the phone again?"

"Yeah. This time let's go near Ryan's house. I want to see what's around there and find a good place for you to drop me off tonight."

Matt started the car, and they drove off. This time, when Eric turned on the phone, he found a voicemail from someone named Quincy King.

———— ••• ————

The metal door opened, and the rarely seen Quincy, one of the LaRue family attorneys, stepped inside. A former football player, he was tall, muscled, black, and had a direct, piercing gaze from brown eyes that now looked grim. With it being before sunrise, he didn't have an expected suit and tie, just a hastily thrown on button-up shirt and jacket and jeans, and a shoulder-slung tote.

On seeing him, Ryan jumped to his feet from behind the small table in the police station holding room, knocking over the metal chair he'd been sitting on. It fell with a clatter.

"Anything on Anna? They won't tell me shit because I won't tell them anything."

Quincy closed the door and the sober look on his face made Ryan's heart sink. "Have a seat."

"Just tell me." The lawyer gestured for him to sit again, and Ryan irritably picked up the chair and sat down, the table before them, Quincy's bag on top as the attorney sat and looked him in the eye.

"There's no simple way to say it," began Quincy, his face resigned. "A car hit her. From the look of it, she wasn't in one herself. She's in terrible shape. Both legs are broken, one arm. Her spine."

Ryan felt a horrible pain in his chest and could feel the blood draining from his face. Knowing all about spinal injuries from Daniel, he just stared, too horrified to speak.

"She has a skull fracture, punctured lung. She's in surgery and will be for a while longer. She's stable, but there's no telling how well she will recover, though they do not believe she is at risk of passing."

Ryan held still, as if to make any motion, including breathing, would be to accept what he had just heard. All this time, they thought that being on a quest was such terrible peril and getting home meant safety. They could relax. Not worry. Be ordinary. This illusion had just shattered, just like Anna's body. The image of her on the stretcher stuck in his mind, as if refusing to get out of the way to make room for another picture with that list of injuries. He didn't realize he had stopped breathing until Quincy shook his arm and his eyes refocused on the attorney.

"Are you alright? Hold on."

Quincy got up, opened the door, and yelled for some orange juice, coffee, or something else sugary or caffeinated, saying something about Ryan being in shock. Ryan supposed that was true. He felt dazed, his head foggy. Not until the bottle of OJ sat before him and Quincy made him drink it did that start to clear. He gulped the drink until it was gone, coming back to the world a little more.

"Okay," began Quincy, "some color back in your face. Listen, I know you've just had a big jolt. We're not in a rush. Just listen a minute. The police, FBI, CIA, and probably a couple other acronyms have been looking for you, Anna, Matt, and Eric, because Matt disappeared on camera. They slowly figured out Anna did the same from the car she was driving on 270. They assume you and Eric can do this, too. They think you guys can go anywhere at any time, including into the Oval Office to kill the President of the United States."

Already in shock, Ryan reacted with confusion, the absurdity bouncing off him. "Why would we kill the president?"

"I assume you wouldn't, but they aren't certain. I've been on this a couple of days now, since your family called me, so I've looked into things like your social media presence, and there's nothing that would raise suspicions. We're already fighting with these agencies, who are trying to say you guys are a national security threat, but we've shot that down. I ended up coordinating with the parents of the others a little, and their attorneys, taking point on this."

Ryan had a thousand questions, but urgency to get away from here led him to ask, "Can you get me out of here?"

"Yes, but it's going to take a while. They think you evaded them on a motorcycle, and this gave them enough reason to arrest you. They also say you went around cones to get to the accident scene, then tried to push past them."

"That last one, at the crash, isn't illegal, is it? I was just worried. With good reason."

"Depends. They can spin it. It's mostly stuff like moving violations, so they can't really hold you over that. Did you flee from them, though? They are saying you did."

"Sort of. I saw cop lights far behind me and sped up, but if Daniel hadn't told me the police were looking for me, I never would have known from the lights that it had anything to do with me. I lost them immediately. It wasn't like some prolonged chase or something."

Quincy let out a breath. "Okay, that's something I can work with. You'll have some stuff to explain at some point, but I should be able to get you out. The police aren't the real issue here. NSA and all that shit is. They're outside and they're being difficult, but your family has clout. And you haven't actually threatened the president or U.S. or something, so they really have nothing. Besides, no one saw you personally disappear, so what they think they have is thin. They are calling you a person of interest and known associate."

"Of Matt?"

"Yeah. And Anna."

Ryan frowned. "Are they going to arrest her or something?"

"I don't know, but they're over there now, waiting for after surgery, like she'll be in any.... Look, don't worry. I won't let them pull any bullshit there. When you talk to your friends, you need to tell them not to tell anybody anything without talking to me first. And on that note, I need you to tell me what is going on." Quincy's gaze hardened. "And don't tell me I won't believe it. I saw the footage. I also saw the stuff you guys bought and which is at the guest house. Daniel told me in private. Your parents know nothing about it. I'm already covering for you, you understand? You're my client. Never mind that your parents hired me. And from where I'm sitting, I suspect you have far bigger problems than car accidents, the media hounding you, or even these agencies coming after you. Your friend Matt looked surprised and afraid when he disappeared. You aren't doing it on purpose, are you?"

Startled that the attorney figured this out, Ryan met his eyes and saw certainty. He relaxed, wanting to get a load off his chest. "We have no control over it. We have no idea until it happens, and we can't control where we return to."

"You just go back to the same spot?" To Ryan's startled gaze, Quincy added, "Daniel told me you were at the guest house when you disappeared and again hours ago. Anna obviously reappeared where she was. Look, you need to tell me what the fuck is going on. That includes whether I am in danger, because while I'm determined to help you and your friends, I'm not getting killed, not to mention over some shit I don't even understand."

"You're not in–" The statement died on realizing Soliander might come to Earth for all of them. Quincy saw the look, and Ryan knew the attorney was sharper than he'd realized. He would rather have someone like this on his side than against him, certainly. Having decided, he almost laughed in relief. "Okay. I'll tell you, but you have got to get me out of here first. They would lock me up if they heard, and I don't trust that this room isn't bugged or some shit."

"They can't do that. It's illegal."

"Don't care. If they are that worried, they would do illegal shit and worry about the lawsuits later."

Quincy sat back and looked around. "Okay, fair enough. You're gonna need to hang tight a bit."

"I need you to do something. Call Matt and Eric. Tell them where I am and that we'll meet up soon. Don't tell them about Anna. Let me do it."

"Sure. Do you know where they might be? I know where they were when they disappeared, but where would they be now?"

Ryan shook his head. "Honestly, I don't know. I think the better question is where do we go once I'm out? Where can I meet them?"

Quincy thought for a moment. "Your parents' place is the best option, at that guest house, but you can't stay there. The media are already going berserk now that it's known that Anna returned on the highway like that. Let me think of something."

He stepped out and Ryan put his forehead on the cool metal tabletop, thoughts on Anna. How were they going to get in to see her with media and worse hounding her? He needed to visit her for his own peace of mind, and to let her know they were around. They had thought the situation with summoning was serious on learning she'd left while driving the car, but now it had skyrocketed, their worst fears about her return realized. It suddenly occurred to him that he hadn't learned what happened to her friends when she vanished.

— ● · ● —

Jack wasn't sure what expression he was supposed to be wearing, a concern so trivial compared to the day's other worries that he might have laughed if he'd had the heart. And that was the issue, really. Should he show the fear consuming him or project an optimism that everything would be fine? Anna's parents slowly paced back and forth nearby in the Intensive Care Unit of Shady Grove Hospital. Maybe they could have used some faith from him, as theirs was clearly rattled. But then he would have been faking it. Was he supposed to do it anyway? Would reflecting their worry on his own face make theirs boil over into tears so that his presence wasn't helpful?

They had known him for years. And since the accident—well, the first one on I-270 with their daughter—he had talked to them several times. He had tried to find the exact spot where the crash happened and hang out somewhere nearby with a view of it, waiting for the moment

Anna reappeared, but the police were sometimes called, making him leave. It was unfeasible anyway. He couldn't just stay there all day, and being on the road was impossible. Crazy ideas like getting a jackhammer and destroying the pavement so that cones were up for a week and blocking the lane had gone through his head, but he didn't even know which lane she'd been in. Now it didn't seem so crazy after all. He'd woken this morning to the news on TV.

Anna was out of surgery, but the ICU staff hadn't let them see her yet. She was still unconscious. Jack wasn't sure what was more devastating—the concern about when she might wake up, or that she was paralyzed. Her mother had asked how they could know that if Anna wasn't awake to try moving, but they knew from the spinal damage and the way her body failed to react to stimuli. Bleakness threatened to consume Jack except that his mind kept going to those reports that had been going on around the world, of people having the ability to heal. There had to be a way to get her in front of someone like that. Whatever it took. Ryan would pay for it, he was sure, if he had to.

Suddenly he wondered if those people were being hounded with requests for healing by the rich and famous, whether to cure their cancer or something else. Were they as sought after as the Stonehenge Four? The media crush outside had been easy for him to dodge with a side door because no one knew who he was. Not until getting to the ICU did he have any trouble, with police and stern-looking agents from one agency or another trying to bar his way until Anna's parents let him through. The FBI had briefly interviewed him days earlier as a kind of character witness and friend of Anna's, asking about her politics, and he assumed that's who these people were.

Now he sat out of sight from them, overhearing Anna's father suggest to his wife that they go downstairs to the chapel. As they departed, Jack wondered what Anna would think of her parents praying for her. Was she still an atheist after her new ability to call on gods on other worlds? Would she be pleased or annoyed with her parent's decision? He knew she hadn't been able to heal here on Earth, but would it work now? What if she could finally call on God and just heal herself, then walk out of here? These thoughts gave Jack hope, and he wished he could tell her parents something to give them the same, and so he sat in turmoil in the waiting area, lost in thought and wondering where the others were. He hadn't had a chance to call without being overheard. He knew he would have to tell them what was happening because they'd never make it past the media or authorities.

An Asian nurse stopped before him and said, "I'm sorry, I forgot your name?"

"Jack," he said, rising. "Is there news?"

The woman smiled. "Yes. Anna is awake. She has been for a few minutes and the doctors are talking to her now. I know you're a friend of the family, so you should be able to see her shortly. Are her parents still here?"

"Yeah, they went to the chapel."

"Okay. I can call down for them." She turned to go as relief consumed Jack, but then he saw several doctors and nurses exit a room, and the woman turned back. "Oh, I think they're done. Come on over and let me check."

Before he really collected himself, she showed Jack into Anna's room. Light streamed in from outside to fall on a yellow, upholstered chair, causing a mild golden hue to light the white walls. White and blue cabinets and closets lined one wall, an open door to the bathroom off to one side. In the center lay her wide bed, the curtain pulled back to reveal the occupant and all the outlets for wall attachments, many plugged into a machine on either side of the bed. A sheet and yellow blanket were pulled up to Anna's chest as she lay nearly flat, her upper body raised a little.

An IV was in the one arm not in a cast, an ID badge around the wrist.

For a moment, he hesitated at the door, but then he saw her open eyes blink and a sudden desire to rush over brought him to her bedside. This time a smile came naturally because he was so happy that she was at least awake. With an effort, he tried to ignore the bandages around her head, the cuts on her face, the casts on her legs and one arm, and the noises of machines beside the bed.

"Hey," he whispered, leaning over her partially swollen and bruised face. Her eyes seemed clouded, but maybe it was just the result of waking from anesthesia and a concussion. "Can you talk? You don't have to say anything."

Anna licked her lips and nodded a little. It was hard to tell, but she seemed pleased to see him. "Jack. Yeah. Just weak. Confused."

"Okay. Let me just give you some updates before your parents get back." He glanced back at the door for signs of her parents, seeing nurses walked by. "They went downstairs for a few minutes."

"What happened?"

He took a deep breath, unsure what to say. "You don't remember?"

"No. Last thing was being in the Quest Ring."

"Okay. You came back around 2am and it's now about 8 in the morning, the same day. You arrived on 270 and were hit by a car. The media are all over this because they know it was you, and Matt was caught on camera when he vanished before, so it's been crazy with media attention. I don't want you to worry about that, though. They can't get in here, okay?"

"I can't feel my legs."

Jack didn't have the heart to tell her the truth, partly because he was hoping they were wrong despite the gravity of her injuries being impressed upon him now that he saw them. "Well, they have you pretty heavily sedated, and you just came out of a lot of surgery, so that might be normal. I don't know. Don't worry, okay? You know Ryan's loaded and he'll do anything to help you. The best care anywhere, I swear."

"What about my friends?"

Apologetically, he said, "I'll keep trying to reach them."

"Not the boys. The ones in the car. When I disappeared."

"Oh." Jack's face fell. He didn't want to tell her the news. Not when she was like this. But he knew it had been days, and she had almost certainly been wondering the whole time.

"Please," she whispered. "I see it in your face. You have to tell me. The waiting...."

Their eyes met again, and resignation settled on him. She had a right to know, and wondering wasn't going to help. He whispered, "I'm so sorry, Anna."

"What is it?" she said. "Please."

He licked dry lips. "Jade lost both legs. Raven also survived, but she's paralyzed." He paused and felt awful as he admitted, "Heather didn't make it."

Tears welled up in her clouded eyes and spilled down the sides of her head as she blinked furiously. Jack wiped them away, whispering that he was sorry over and over, that it wasn't her fault. This was all too much for anyone to deal with her investigator had and sudden anger struck him. He hid it by closing his eyes and putting his head on her shoulder, whispering for her to remain calm because of her punctured lung. She seemed to hear him, for her breathing became shallower.

He straightened and looked her in the eye, "You know I am here for you. Whatever you need."

Anna looked at him calmly, eyes clearing, and after a few moments, said something he wasn't expecting.

"Get me a priest."

———— ⁕ ‧ ⁕ ————

If there was anyone Daniel trusted, it was Ryan, and yet part of him thought that his brother, Matt, Eric, and even Jack were bullshitting him and Quincy, with whom he had just shared more than one dubious look. And yet their demeanor suggested they were telling the truth about these Ellorian Champions and their disappearances. And of course, he knew about the various vanishings and footage. And reports of healing or magic working around Earth. That they were having this talk in the family guest house, surrounded by the swords, shields, crossbows and more that his brother had purchased, added a welcome, tangible sign that this outlandish stuff was real. Or at least, they certainly believed it. If he had only just seen this stuff now, he might have still thought it was an elaborate put-on, even though Ryan had never done anything even remotely like that. Accepting it was still an adjustment.

Quincy had gotten Ryan out of the police station, then picked up Matt and Eric somewhere. Someone grabbed Jack away from the hospital, and it was from him that they had learned of Anna's situation. Arriving at the LaRue estate, they had avoided the media mob outside the main gate, but Quincy's SUV with its darkened windows was seen entering the grounds, though too late to be intercepted, at least this time. They finally reached the guest house where they were now, calling Daniel down to it without his nurse, Susan.

Daniel felt a weird kinship with Anna on hearing she was paralyzed. It was one that he didn't want. He had also never felt it for another person destined to live their life in a wheelchair like him, maybe because he didn't know them, and he resisted much of the sentiment about this because too much pity had come his way over it long ago. Never before had he understood—not really—the depth of Ryan's concern for him, having just assumed guilt at causing Daniel's paralysis was behind it. Now he knew that personally caring for someone so grievously wounded was enough to make one want to hover. His heart ached for Anna and he already knew he would give her all the emotional support and encouragement he could muster, whether or not she wanted it. Resisting that seemed to come with the territory, at least for him, but he wouldn't let her get away with it for long any more than his physical therapists had let him.

Daniel's thoughts returned to the silent men awaiting his reaction and Quincy's to their story. He sighed. "Okay, I believe you. I think. But don't push your luck. No fucking with me."

Ryan sighed from where he sat on the pile of rugs in between Matt and Jack, Eric comfortable on the floor. "Fair enough."

"So what now?" Quincy asked, leaning against a wall. "We need some priorities."

"We?" Eric asked with a small smirk. He sat barefoot, sandals near.

Quincy nodded. "Yeah. No one but the people in this room, and Anna, know what's going on. *We* need to keep it that way. On one hand, I'm representing the Stonehenge Four, and this is something that only you guys are going through, but it's clear you need a team helping you, both while you're here and while you're gone." He paused. "I'm pledging you this help, more than as your lead attorney. Let me be your coordinator. You need continuity here and can't do it when you're gone. No offense, Jack, but you're not enough."

"Yeah, none taken. I'm glad for the help at least."

Quincy continued. "You guys are all pretty young and out of your depth, like anyone would be with all of this going on, just the stuff on Earth. You have enough to worry about when you get summoned. Let me take care of shit here. You need someone covering for you. I'm already doing it with the police and all of that, but you need a person who knows the truth directing a spokesperson who *doesn't* know the truth, at least not yet. I will get someone to handle the media on your behalf. I also know all of your parents to some extent from these last few days and can run point on that as well. Speaking of, officially I'm only Ryan's attorney. Technically I'm working for your folks, but we need to change that, too. You all need to make it officially me."

"Why?" Matt asked.

Daniel answered. "Attorney-client privilege."

"Right. The police, FBI, whoever. They can't make me say shit."

"What about me?" Jack asked. "Should I do this?"

Quincy nodded slowly. "I'll have something drawn up for both you and Daniel, ready to be signed. You may not really need it now. Technically none of you have committed a crime, but there are reckless driving charges and a few others pending against Anna."

"Great," muttered Ryan.

Daniel felt himself glowering. She didn't need more problems. They needed to make that shit go away, even if it meant an expensive settlement he and Ryan paid for. His eyes went to his brother, Matt, and Eric, seeing a seriousness and muted strain in their eyes, faces, and body language. This was all real. He suddenly felt like an unsupportive asshole and vowed to drop every last thing to help them. How that would manifest, he wasn't sure, but the surrounding gear caught his eye. Research. Buying stuff. Planning. It was a start.

Eric asked, "What about civil stuff for her? Are the families suing?"

"They haven't yet," Quincy said, "but I expect them to. Wrongful death. That sort of thing."

Daniel frowned. "She can't afford that kind of shit."

"She won't have to," said Ryan. "I think this is where you come in, Daniel. If mom and dad put up any resistance to anything, I need you to get them to back down. We are paying for all of this. We have all this money we don't need and I never use. That's changing."

"Yeah, totally agree. I can do that."

Quincy warned, "This is going to get expensive."

After a pause, Eric said, "Not nearly as pricey as not doing it."

"So I have a question," Matt started, looking at the attorney. "Can they track our phones and all of that? I've been leaving mine off."

Quincy said, "They don't have a reason, as much as the government people were trying to claim they do, but they may still do it."

Daniel knew how to solve this one. "New phones. I'll buy them and new numbers today."

Eric nodded and said, "Yeah, I was about to ask if you can get my phone from my parents. I assume they're the ones who have it."

"They do," Quincy replied. "They got all of your stuff when it became apparent you were missing with the others, and your boss cooperated with police, who initially took it, but I made them give it back after they checked it for evidence."

Jack asked, "Evidence of what?"

"Exactly. There's nothing, so they couldn't hold it all despite trying. Maybe they figured you'd want it so bad that you'd walk into the police station and they could interrogate you."

Daniel interjected. "Clothes, other stuff. You need all of that." He turned to Jack. "Can you go to each of their places to get whatever they want from home?"

"Yeah, of course."

Eric shook his head. "Jack, I think I'd like to keep you a silent, unseen partner. We don't want anyone thinking they should follow you because you'll lead them to us. You need freedom to move." He paused and then joked, "What I'm trying to say is that I don't want to be seen with you."

This met with muted laughter, and Daniel had an idea. "Listen, you guys need a break. Take a couple hours off from this bullshit. I hooked up the TV and other stuff while you were gone. Well, Susan did. I can bring the Nintendo Switch down from the house and set it up in a few minutes. Later, I think each of you needs to call your parents, preferably on video, but it can wait. Mom and Dad are at the house, Ryan, but they don't know you're here yet, I don't think. I'll keep it that way for a bit. I'll order pizza for lunch in a few hours. Quincy can set some shit in motion. Me, too. Let me think of some ideas on what you can tell the parents so you can just forget about it for a while, and we'll take it over later. I think we need to be on the same page, keep the story the same, as simple as possible. I think the lie you were telling before, that for you no time passes at all while you're gone, is the easiest."

The claim would be that one minute everything was normal. Then a white light surrounded them, and when it faded, they were in the same place. But sometimes the time of day had changed. Or the weather. Or the people who had been there were all gone. And if they were holding something in a hand, it was missing. They subsequently learned from someone else how much time had passed and were shocked. That was it.

The others agreed and split up. Quincy got in the van and left the property. Daniel went to the main house, having Jack come along to grab some chairs for himself, Matt, Ryan, and Eric, who stayed in the guest house. It took a bit of time and multiple trips for Jack, but the four of them soon sat playing Minecraft Dungeons, a game that bore some resemblance to their quests. Each player had a character, armor, weapons, special items, a bunch of zombies and other "mobs" to kill, and needed to work together to survive, get treasure, and complete a level. The similarly caused a brief conversation about whether they should play a game father removed from reality, but all expressed interest, remarking that it might give them ideas. "Splitting the difference," Eric called it, between all playing and all thinking about their situation.

Hours later, Daniel returned with pizza and new cell phones and numbers, having raided two local stores to get them all set up ASAP. They finished connecting the devices, adding emails and each other as phone contacts. They had a spare for Anna, and Daniel had gotten another for himself and Jack.

Then it was time to deal with their parents. By then, Quincy had already contacted all of them except Anna's, leaving her folks out of it for now. They aimed for brevity and even doing parts of the call together, Jack and Daniel staying silent and off camera. They didn't mention quests or other worlds, and they purposely kept the swords and other gear around them out of sight.

Matt's call went first, Eric and Ryan making a show of agreeing with his account and being supportive so that the parents didn't think their kid was going through this alone, with the police, media, and other stuff. Matt apologized again for taking the car, but his father was fine with it. His older brother and sister lived in Charlottesville, Virginia and Manhattan, and weren't on the call, but had been asking about him. He promised to call them but wouldn't anytime soon. The fewer people he had to lie to, the better.

Eric went second, and his was easier, shorter, and done alone, the others again off camera but in the room, no one opting for privacy. He knew nothing about his birth parents, had no siblings, and had been raised by foster parents he kept in touch with, albeit infrequently. As a result, they didn't really know who his friends were until the Stonehenge disappearance. Now they knew their names, so when Matt and Anna vanished, they once again suspected Eric had, too. And then the police had arrived with his car and belongings after this last quest, as he still listed them as an emergency contact. They offered to help him in any way they could, but he just told them not to talk to the media.

Ryan was up next, but they handled it differently. He and Daniel went to the main house alone, because they wanted to hide the others and the use of the guest house. Their parents argued at length for him to use the GPS tracking features of one thing or another so they could help when this happened or he returned, but he said the FBI and others would just follow him, even with Quincy running interference. They didn't agree, as Ryan evaded the subject with his brother's help. He told them Jack was helping Quincy with anything they needed, like using his car so the media wouldn't know to follow, and asked them to cooperate with him. They didn't want him to leave, however, and he realized there was no going back to the guest house for now.

But then Quincy did a conference call with all the boys at once, Ryan and Daniel in their rooms to escape from parental hovering. They reached a decision. The guys wanted to be free to move around the world, at least incognito with hats and sunglasses, rather than feeling imprisoned at the guest house. And Ryan's parents were already smothering him, worse than the media presence outside. Quincy arranged for a hotel suite on his corporate credit card for Ryan, Eric, and Matt. He would get Matt's father's car brought there for them to use. Jack would help as needed, and Daniel would assist from afar, not tagging along. The wheelchair just made him too conspicuous. Things like clothes would await them there, though Ryan was bringing a stuffed duffel bag. They would take things one day at a time.

In late afternoon, Daniel distracted the parents while Ryan and Jack carried a ladder from the garage down past the guest house and to a distant corner of the property, Eric and Matt joining them. Both houses were far enough back from the road, and enough trees stood in between that the media did not know. Leaning it against the wall, they climbed up and over, dropping onto the neighbor's yard before tipping the ladder back onto the grass out of sight. Daniel would get a gardener or someone else to deal with it later. Some estates in Potomac, Maryland had decent acreage, and they could stick to the distant rear of properties, most of which were not as walled off. A half mile passed before they turned in between two houses and headed for the street, where Quincy picked them up and soon dropped them at the hotel, giving them the room keys. Jack left to get his car, visit Anna once more, and return later with Chinese food and beer.

For only the second time since returning to Earth, the boys felt like they could relax a little. Matt had wisely brought the Nintendo Switch, controllers, and the box and cables to hook it to the TV, and they intended to amuse themselves later. They sat around a round kitchen table now, having settled into the rooms where they meant to spend at least this night, if not quite a few more. Talk quickly turned to Anna.

"How is she?" Eric asked, dripping soy sauce on his white rice. He really wanted to see Anna, but neither he, Matt, or Ryan could get there yet. Maybe tomorrow. Jack had scouted the hospital and learned just how many entrances there were and that most of the reporters were at one of them. But it also seemed like the police were keeping them back so that other patients and their families could come and go without a media circus in the way. But if the boys got inside to see Anna, they needed permission from Anna's parents, who Quincy and Jack would try to convince, but they worried this would cause a conversation with them about what was going on. They owed her parents that, but one reason Jack had just gone there was to bring Anna up to speed.

"No real change," Jack replied.

"What did she want with the priest?" Ryan asked. He had asked earlier but got the same answer as now—she wouldn't say.

Matt asked, "Do you think she's going through a religious experience or something?"

"Hard to say," Eric asked. "It's certainly enough to cause that sort of thing, from what I know, which isn't much. Ryan is our expert on trauma making you religious."

Ryan grimaced, spearing a piece of orange chicken. "Yeah. I mean, her guilt has to be astronomically worse than mine. I only paralyzed Daniel. I really wish I could be there for her."

"I know you will be," Eric assured him. "We'll get to her soon, hopefully on Earth before we get summoned–" He paused, eyes lighting up. "Jesus! We forgot about something. When that happens, the summoning spell is supposed to heal us."

He watched their faces as realization sank in, which was obvious from the smiles and Ryan jumping to his feet.

"Holy shit!" the big guy said. "It should heal her!"

"Oh my God," said Jack, as Ryan paced in excitement. "Are you guys serious? You all forgot this?"

They all looked caught between relief and feeling stupid, this being a minor detail they may not have told Jack. Eric put down his chopsticks and said, "Well, we've never tested it. I mean, we only went three times, and we were already fine. We only know this because Lorian told us."

"Do you think it would really heal her all the way?" Jack asked.

"It almost has to," said Ryan, turning toward them, eyes bright. "I mean, what would be the point of summoning a paralyzed healer?"

Eric observed, "Even if it doesn't do it, she should be able to heal herself once there, if she can reach a god."

"Right!" agreed Ryan. He picked his beer for a celebratory drink.

"I have to get to the hospital to tell Anna this," said Jack, looking like he meant to do it now.

Eric shook his head. "Well, I agree, but let's not get ahead of ourselves. I don't want to give her false hope. We should not be too excited to tell her in case we're wrong. I think right now we're all a little too keyed up about it."

Jack laughed. "Yeah, sure. I hear you. I wouldn't be able to say it calmly and her parents might ask questions."

"Exactly."

Matt said, "And here all this time I've been worried about being summoned again, and now I *want* to do it." He let out an enormous sigh that mirrored the room's mood. "Do you guys get nervous when we get into a car now? I mean, what happened to her could happen to any of us."

"Yeah," said Eric, having thought the same thing all day, since he'd spent far too much time in one. He had kept thinking to stay off a highway, but even the back roads were at least 35 mph and being hit at that speed was still enough to kill anyone. Driving through neighborhoods meant less traffic, but it could certainly take forever to get anywhere that way, though it was worth it. They were

THE LIGHT BRINGER | 227

lucky Anna was not dead, as no healing would change that. "I think we need to limit our travel."

"Imagine being in a plane at thirty-five-thousand feet," started the techie, "and you get summoned. When you come back, this time there's no plane."

"Geez," said Jack, opening a beer. "I should think through more of this."

"Yes," said Eric, taking a beer for himself. "Speaking of summoning, the next time it happens, Anna will return to the hospital room she's in at the time. Jack, that means you may need to hang around the hospital for a sign of her."

"Sure, whatever you need. How am I going to know she's back?"

"Keep your phone on and charged. We all need to make a point of having our phone in a pocket. When we get back, our first action aside from getting out of sight and safe is to call or text Jack."

"Good plan," said Ryan, coming back to the table and sitting down. He grabbed a fork and dove into a dumpling.

Eric turned to Jack. "You can be in the hospital lobby, or cafeteria. Just keep changing places so no one sees you hanging around too much for too long, and when you get a message from one of us, you head straight for her room to help her. I would have a change of clothes for her, a hat to hide her hair in, that sort of thing. She might need shoes."

Jack nodded. "Yeah, I still have the key to her place and will head over there, keep a bag ready." He pursed his lips.

"What?" Eric asked, sensing another problem he would need to solve. Fortunately, he enjoyed being analytical and creating plans, especially when they worked, but there seemed to be an awful lot of issues coming up all the time now.

Jack let out a breath and looked apologetic. "You know, today is a day off, but sometimes I kind of need to be at work."

"No, forget Starbucks," said Ryan, shaking his head. "They have other managers. I'm hiring you as my personal assistant at four times your current wages, maybe more." To Jack's raised eyebrows, the big guy softened his tone. "I know it's a good job, but we need you, desperately, and you're the only one qualified for what we need, you know."

"Sure."

Eric saw that Jack wasn't too happy, but was willing to do it anyway. He also knew the job wasn't supposed to be forever anyway, as Jack was still trying to figure out what to do with his life, but it was a good gig in the meantime.

"You know," he said, "we really appreciate everything you've already helped with, and this might be the most important thing of your life, just like with us. Many things are happening in the world now that weren't before, and you'd be on the front lines, so to speak."

Jack nodded. "Yeah, I know. I get it. Sorry if I don't seem excited. I just hadn't thought about it before. It's just a piece of my life I'm giving up, but you guys are losing so much more."

Ryan added, "Financially, you will not have to worry about anything in return for your help. I'm thinking to get you a credit card for you to use, so you can buy things we need. We seriously need you for so many things."

Ryan called his attorney, letting Quincy know he needed a discreet way to access his money. He also told him to set up something to pay Jack a salary, a large "signing bonus," and creating an expense account and credit card for his use. He made a point of all of it being as untraceable as possible.

Eric had been thinking of something else that usually took a while to arrange, so they needed it to start immediately. "I think we're going to need somewhere to stay long term. We have to assume these quests are indefinite. I'm talking a house."

Ryan offered, "I'll pay for somewhere."

"I want to focus on a home base to set up," began Eric. "This is a priority. We can use this hotel room for a few days, but we need a long-term location, one we never have to leave, with Jack getting things for us, or delivery service. Jack can live there, too."

"So we need five bedrooms," mused Matt.

"We're thinking too small," said Ryan. "We need an estate, somewhere up on Route 28 near Sugarloaf Mountain, where all those large farms are. They have a bunch of land. Some have multiple buildings, like a guest house, or an older house before a new one was built. We need a barn where all of you can practice your riding. We need a martial arts training room like what we were setting up at the guest house. We need an archery range no one can see from the road. We can do swordsmanship in an indoor riding ring. We need a place where Matt can do magic, where no one sees it, if it's really working here. Maybe we need a set of locks we all learn to pick, or a rock-climbing wall so we can get experience with that, too. We need to cross train each other and get private lessons when we can, though doing that with no one knowing it's us might be an issue."

Eric's intense gaze fixated on him. "That was good. You are right. How much are those estates?"

Ryan shrugged. "Don't worry about it."

"How much?"

The big guy smirked at the insistence. "Two to four million."

"How do we get your parents to do that without asking questions?"

Ryan lifted a beer bottle wryly. "That is a great question."

"I think he's right, though," added Matt. "That would be ideal. We need good security but not so good that it looks like we're fugitives or something."

"Too late for that," Jack joked. "But seriously, if no one knows about it, you'd be freer. Not looking over your shoulder all the time."

"Right," admitted Eric, "and it's exactly why we need it all done discreetly, which is another problem. If your parents buy an estate up there, people will wonder why. Places like the FBI would know."

A moment of silence followed that before Matt suggested, "Maybe there's some sort of shell corporation your attorney can set up and they buy the estate. I don't know how that works, though."

The others seemed to agree, but no one said anything for a few minutes.

Ryan suggested, "Maybe in a few minutes, you can show me more sign language."

Matt agreed and opened his mouth to respond, when a knock on the door stopped further conversation. They exchanged a look.

"Does anyone know we're here?" Eric whispered.

"Shouldn't," said Jack. "Quincy?"

Ryan nodded. "I'll check."

"Peephole," Eric suggested.

Ryan went up to the door and peered through the hole. Then he turned back with a scowl and motioned for Eric to come over. The others followed. "It's a woman, about forty years old."

Eric looked and stepped back. "I don't know her." Matt and Jack looked, too, but they didn't either, so he thought a moment and then asked loudly, "Who is it?"

The woman answered, "Eriana of Coreth."

CHAPTER ELEVEN

A NEW FRIEND

Erin waited in the hall for a sound from beyond the door, her long skirt swaying with her fidgeting. She smoothed her blouse and tried to calm herself. She had good ears and heard furious whispering. She had to play this right or it might quickly go south, and she had a lot riding on the next several minutes. Many years of facing horrific danger had made her serene in the face of just about anything, but she was nervous for the first time in forever. All for a conversation.

But the information it might reveal was so devastatingly important to her that it had literally kept her up at night since the moment she'd seen that pretty girl—Anna was her name—playing with that pendant... *that* pendant... and talking about her reappearance at Stonehenge after three weeks of being missing with the young men on the other side of this door.

Erin had been following the news before they returned this week, and she knew about the three girls in the car accident, one maimed, one dead, and the other paralyzed. She knew the police had been looking for Anna and now patrolled the hospital where she lay. And she'd certainly heard about Anna then reappearing on the highway and being struck by a car. That wasn't supposed to happen. Something was terribly wrong for several reasons, mainly because no one on Earth should have been trying to summon the Ellorian Champions a thousand years since the last time they did. All of them would have been long dead by now. But the Ellorians had also never just returned to where they had been before a summoning. They had always gone to their Home Rings from a Quest Ring. This modern world offered a horrible danger that all of them had just realized with Anna's fate now caught in it.

After the recent events, the private investigator she used had grilled her a little about her persistent interest in the Stonehenge Four. He had helped her collect supposed magic items from around the world for years, making inquiries about a purchase on her behalf. Now he had asked her to explain about the pendant the girl Anna wore. She only said that it might have once been magical. This was true, except that she—and likely she alone—already knew what it was and what it did. Or had done. If she remembered right, the pendant's power should be spent by now. She couldn't tell this to her investigator because he would never understand.

Before now, she had only asked him to find addresses and biographical information of the Stonehenge Four, not hack into financial records to figure out where people might be staying. So Erin wove the truth through a story that the girl's pendant was partly responsible for the four disappearing. It was dangerous to them and she had to warn them, but with reporters and now people after them, she couldn't find them and needed his help. All of this was true, except that the pendant itself posed no danger. They had already set the effect of returning it to Stonehenge after a thousand years in motion.

He had grudgingly accepted the explanation, wanting to know what she was looking for. Trying to think like an old friend of hers, who was far better at this, she had reasoned that the rich one, Ryan, was likely paying for lodging somewhere but under another name. None of their parents could lend support because if they opened an investigation into Anna or the others, the same financial records Erin wanted to use would track their whereabouts. It had to be someone else.

Her hunch had been correct, but it wasn't until Ryan's attorney bailed him out, revealing his identity, that they got another name to check and learned of the hotel room reserved under the lawyer's name. She had to promise her investigator that she would pay every legal bill if anyone ever found out, arrested him, and destroyed his business. That had only made him more suspicious, but there was a good reason she had spent considerable time with him over the years, earning his trust, even having a long affair with him to bewitch him as much as she could. And it had worked. She could tell he still loved her. She wondered if that would remain true once he found out who she really was.

Now she waited for that hotel room door to open, trying to look unthreatening and pleasant, which on one hand was easy because she was both. But her mind raced, for the reaction to her true name had told her something. She just wasn't entirely sure what it meant.

Then a voice she recognized from the TV interview spoke from beyond the door. "Can you repeat that?"

"Eriana of Coreth, one of the Ellorian Champions."

After a pause, the same voice asked, "How do we know it's you? Eriana is in her mid to late twenties, from what we understand."

That brought her up short and her mind raced. "Honestly, Eric, I do not know how to answer that. I have lived here for twenty years, but by my reckoning, you should not expect me to be alive at all, or I would be a thousand years old." After a pause, she added, "I would very much like to discuss this with you, and learn what you know of me, Andier, Korrin, and Soliander, and how you came to be substituted for us. It appears clear that this has happened from the news reports, and your friend Anna in the hospital, and—"

"Open the door," said another voice from inside.

Eriana thought it sounded like the techie, Matt. Andier had long ago taught her to memorize faces, voices, and more to aid in dealing with the considerable intrigue that had sometimes dogged them. She heard some arguing before the door suddenly opened to reveal four young men, three that she recognized. Her eyes moved between and stopped on Matt because of the intense way he was scrutinizing her face. This went on for several seconds of tense silence as she waited, eyes drifting to Eric and Ryan, then lingering on the other man, who expression spoke of attraction to her more than curiosity. Matt finally broke the silence.

"It's her. She's older, like you said, maybe twenty years, but it's her. We found her. We found Eriana!"

She smiled, comforted because they were looking for her, and they seemed excited, not the least bit threatening. She relaxed a little. "It's more like I found you," she observed.

Eric turned to Matt. "How can you know that it's her?"

"Soliander's spell, remember? I recognize—"

"You've seen Soli?" Eriana interrupted, stepping forward. "How is he? *Where* is he? When did you see him?"

More questions surged in her mind as relief and excitement filled her. It had been twenty years with no sign of them. She stopped looking long ago, convinced they were dead or possibly flung to another planet, like their home, Elloria. With magic no longer working here, had they been looking for her and unable to reach her, like the Earth was a phone giving a perpetually busy signal? And now there was an answer. Or maybe Soliander somehow was here all this time. Had they given up the search for her? She had to know if it was only him or the others, too.

Eric held up one hand to stop her and then gestured for her to enter. "I think you had better come inside."

She followed them as they moved toward the table where leftover food remained, the unknown guy locking the door. Being in a hotel room with four young men she didn't know might have given many women pause, but Andier had taught her a thing or two about self-defense long ago, and enough of her healing power had returned in the last month that she knew a quick word would render all of them unconscious. Well, normally it would. In her weakened state, it might only weaken *them*, but it would be enough to escape.

As Eric gestured to an upholstered chair, the guy she didn't recognize said, "I'm Jack, by the way. You seem to know everyone else."

"Yes," Eric began as they sat, "how is that? News reports?"

"Yes," she admitted, deciding not to admit that her investigator had turned up everything he could find on them. It would cause distrust, and she had to gain their trust first. As if reading her mind, Eric spoke again.

"Well, we've exchanged some names, and Matt thinks he recognizes you, but is there anything you can do to prove you are Eriana?" After a moment, he asked a similar question in elvish.

She smiled at that, thinking he was clever and quick. Eric picked up a sharp knife, holding it over his hand. She sensed his intent and replied in elvish, "My healing powers have begun to return, but you needn't do it to yourself, and don't do too much."

He returned to English. "A small demonstration is fine with me, and I can't let a lady cut herself for my sake."

He sliced the top of his hand, a line of blood rising but not dripping. It wasn't deep and would hardly need a band aid, but it was enough for her to get the point across. She placed two fingers on either side of the wound. "Please heal this man, Almighty One."

A soft light filled the wound, which closed, though it wasn't apparent until Eric used a white napkin to wipe away the blood, leaving smooth skin. His eyes met hers then.

"I also have this," Eriana began, reaching into her bag. She pulled out something in a soft jewelry bag, laid it on the table, and unwrapped the item. It was a gold amulet depicting one figure kneeling beside another that was rising from a supine position. From their expressions, she saw they recognized it. She had been wondering if they would and asked, "Do you know what this is?"

"The Amulet of Corethian," Ryan replied, looking a little confused. "It belongs to Eriana of Coreth."

So they did recognize it. She wasn't sure how that could be, given that she'd had it since arriving in New Zealand two decades ago. She had never let it be captured on film. The technology for photos or video didn't exist on the other planets she had worn it to before that, so if they were journeying to them, they wouldn't see images of it there unless someone had drawn it. But she had shown it on a hunch. And while it seemed to confirm her identity to them, it only raised more questions for her. How could they know what it looked like?

Eric had been smiling since she revealed it and laughed. "Well, it's extremely nice to meet you, my lady. We have tons of questions for you, and I think I speak for everyone when I say we are elated that you're here."

"Wow," said Jack, still looking at Eric's hand. "That's the first time I've seen any of you do something like that, the healing or magic."

Eriana raised an eyebrow at the others. "You've been trying?"

"Yes," admitted Matt, fingering an uneaten spring roll. "I have gotten little to work. Neither has Anna. In my case, it's partly difficulty remembering the spells, and maybe having none of the ingredients if those are needed. But for Anna and the healing, well, she's an atheist, so calling on God is a stretch for her. It's a bit of a sore point, really." He hesitated. "You know, you're already a legend to us. Sorry if we're all staring a bit. Part of me can't believe you're here."

It had been a long time since anyone knew the truth of her identity, or that anyone looked at her with awe, though their gazes weren't quite that fascinated. They had likely seen amazing things already. She saw respect and maybe some intimidation, though not from Eric. He seemed pragmatic and less impressed. She reassured the techie, "It's okay."

Matt continued, "You should know that when we get summoned, everyone thinks we are the four of you."

She had been wondering about this, even though she did not know how it could have happened. She had seen the surprise on Matt's face when being summoned. They had clearly been taken more than once, just like her and the others. She knew they had returned the pendant to Stonehenge, unlocking the Earth. But she also knew something had gone wrong long ago and the side effects might be unpredictable. Now she had to confirm the details.

"So you are arriving in a Quest Ring?" she asked, seeing them nod. "The ring is lit up with magic words that fade? And someone has cast the summoning spell. They welcome you as the Ellorian Champions, meaning that this is what they expect, four people."

Eric said, "All correct."

"Are you wearing all our clothes? The armor?" She paused. "My amulet?"

"Yes."

"And it happens each time? That's interesting."

"Why?"

"The summoning spell is supposed to outfit us, as it appears to be doing for each of you, but it takes the original item, like my amulet, and makes it disappear from its current location before putting it on me, for example. I arrive with it on even if I was not wearing it before the spell summoned me."

"That's what we're experiencing."

"Yes, but I have kept the amulet with me since your return to Stonehenge. You have disappeared at least once since then."

"Twice," Eric corrected. "No one but us knows about the second one, partly because it was very short. A few minutes."

She frowned. In their years of quests, she and the others had seldom experienced a quest nearly that short. It usually took hours, if not days, sometimes a week or more. If a quest was so easy that it could be accomplished quickly, the summoning spell would not bring them because others could likely handle it. After all, the Ellorian Champions were the heroes of last resort, brought in when no one else could handle the challenge. Still, a quick quest had happened, and she wanted to know how their second one proved to be that kind.

"Why only a few minutes?" she asked.

Eric said, "Goblins and ogres killed the wizard who summoned us before he could tell us the quest, so we could come back without doing it."

"Hmm. That happened to us once. They have to tell you within an hour. Less, I think. Anyway, the point I'm trying to make is that you've been summoned two more times, with one of you having the amulet on your quest, and yet it has not left my side during this time. The Quest Rings appear to have somehow created a duplicate."

"That *is* interesting," commented Matt, looking intrigued, "but I think we already know this, as I have a copy of Soliander's staff when I'm on a quest. Just to clarify our roles, they think Eric is Andier, and he is wearing his gear. Anna is you. Ryan is Korrin."

"And you're Soliander," she finished. Unable to resist her curiosity any longer, she asked, "You said you've seen him. I assume he is twenty years older like me? What of Andier and Korrin?"

Eric interjected, "We haven't seen or heard a word about the others."

"As for Soliander," said Matt, "I don't think he is twenty years older. I didn't get a good look, really, but I have some of his memories in me and they include his face in a mirror. No images are past mid to late twenties. I think it's only been a few years for him, though I'm not sure that makes any sense."

"Not much does," Ryan said sourly.

Eriana leaned forward, wondering if far more substitution had occurred than she would have imagined possible. Did they all have shared memories? That could be rather invasive and unsettling. What did Anna know of her life since before arriving in New Zealand? Her thoughts drifted to the troublesome parts of her past that she had never shared with anyone.

She asked, "How could you have his memories?"

Matt looked unsure how to explain and Eric interjected. "I think we need to exchange some history for the answer to make sense, because it's just going to cause more questions. It will get confusing out of order like that."

"Yes," she reluctantly agreed, then offered, "and as much as you have questions about me, I think your situation is more urgent."

"Do you have a situation going on?" Ryan asked. His eyes went to the hotel room door, beyond which they could sometimes hear people passing by, unaware that three of the famous Stonehenge Four were hiding on its other side. His thoughts went to Anna.

Eriana shook her blonde head, leaning back into the chair again. "No. Only to find out what is happening with all of you and how I can help."

"No one is after you?" Eric asked.

She cocked an eyebrow. "Not that I know of. I suppose it is possible now, but it wouldn't be someone from Earth, I don't think, only one of the many enemies we earned during our quests. You've given me something to consider, but no one knows that Erin Jennings of Florida is Eriana of Coreth from the planet Elloria. You are the ones everyone is after right now. And this is partly my fault."

"What do you mean?"

Eriana sighed, unsure where to begin. Too much history existed, so she focused on what would be useful to them at once, especially if this somehow proved to be their only conversation for a while—or maybe ever. "You went to Stonehenge while Anna had the pendant with her, right?"

"Yes," answered Ryan, playing with his fork. "We figured that's involved but only after the first quest, because we saw the poem inside it, the one written in magic words. Matt can read them now. Well, all of us can. Someone cast a spell allowing us to read various languages."

Jack looked at them jealously. "Kinda wish someone would cast that on me," he remarked.

Matt smirked. "If you're nice, and I learn it, maybe I will."

Eriana knew the lines, even though she had only heard them once. They had become a critical part of her life's course. She said now to make sure everyone was familiar. They were part of an explanation she sensed she had to give.

Within the jewel magic resides
Creatures, too, and all abide
To keep Earth safe from she who lies
The prison here keeps hope alive
The henge of stone shall set them free
Good and evil, equal be
Undo what's done and come what may
Risk the price all life could pay

"What does it mean?" Matt asked, leaning forward on the table, eyes intense. "Who is 'she who lies'?"

Looking concerned, Jack said, "Better question. What is the 'price all life could pay'?"

Eriana looked away, collecting her thoughts as they waited with naked eagerness. "One thing at a time. You might find this hard to believe... okay, well, maybe not anymore."

"There's a lot we'd believe today that we would've laughed off a month ago," observed Eric.

She sighed and helped herself to one beer. It was that kind of tale. "Magic is real on Earth. It is always has been. What you would call fantasy creatures like elves, dwarves, dragons, and more are also real."

"Then why don't we see them?" Jack asked. "Are they still here?"

"The quest that brought us to Earth has hidden them from view, you might say."

"All four of you, right?" Eric asked. "Soliander, Andier, Korrin, and yourself were all here?"

"Yes. We were always summoned as a group and this was no exception."

"Who summoned you?"

Eriana paused, wondering if they would recognize the name. "Morgana."

She saw Matt cock an eyebrow before he asked, "As in Merlin and Morgana?"

"That's the one," she admitted, pleased that they knew some history.

Matt asked, "You're saying they were real? That was a thousand years ago, I think."

"Yes. Historical records are a little thin and people think they are a myth, but they were both real. We met them." She paused, letting them absorb that. Too much too fast wouldn't go well.

"So Morgana summoned you. What for?" Matt asked. "She was supposedly a, uh, good character, not evil, though modern TV shows make her out to be evil."

Pleased with his remarks, she observed, "You seem to know some of this."

"Yeah, I watch and read a lot of fantasy, even tried to write a book once. Sometimes I get curious about whether someone was real or not and google them. Now I'm really curious what's real and what isn't."

She said, "Well, these modern shows may have been more accurate. We only know what she and Merlin told us. Morgana summoned us to get that pendant and return it to Stonehenge. She is the one 'who lies' from Merlin's poem, the words inside the jewel."

"I'm guessing there's some backstory to the quest, like usual," mused Ryan. He took a swig.

"Yes, and hopefully it isn't too much to absorb." She took a sip and dove into it. "The faerie world is where dragons, elves, dwarves, goblins, and more are from on Earth. Magic exists in that world more than on Earth. That world intersects this one at key points, like doorways, and it is at these locations that faerie beings can cross over into this world, and the people of Earth can sometimes, pass into the faerie world."

"Are these doorways just opened all the time?" Eric asked.

"No. And they are sometimes guarded, and the character of the guardians can differ, of course, meaning obey laws, others not so much. The guards may exist on either side, Earth or there. There are times during the year when the openings are easier to pass through, as if the barriers between worlds are thinner. At other times, it is reversed. We celebrate some of these occasions as holidays, like May Day and Halloween."

She took another sip, gauging their reactions, which didn't seem skeptical, so that was good. Eriana continued.

"As you're likely aware from stories, dwarves and elves are benevolent, despite any personality quirks, and trolls, dark elves, and others are more nefarious. Dragons can be either. There are many more. What the so-called evil ones have in common is that they are often aimless and with little purpose unless they have a leader who encourages cooperation. This is where Morgana comes in.

"Both she and Merlin were half-human, one parent being fae. It is the reason both were so strong in magic, the strongest among humans, anyway. Some saw them as belonging to both worlds. Others to neither. Most humans did not know the truth about them, but fae can tell. From what Merlin told us, he did not approve of Morgana's growing influence among the so-called evil fae. They were like her, being interested in creating trouble for fun, some turning deadly. That turned humans against the fae world more."

Matt remarked, "I guess all of it being real is where these stories have come from, and somehow it turned to myth."

Eriana nodded. "Humans have always been fearful of what they do not understand, and making everything a myth might have eased fears. There were countless stories of humans attacking faerie folk of whatever kind, which caused some like goblins to decide humans are evil. Humans sometimes found these doorways between worlds and built barriers to keep anyone from entering Earth through one, or if the fae did, they would just find themselves imprisoned underground. This is what various mounds found around the world, especially in England, are really for. Each is over a known opening between the worlds. At other times, bolder humans would do a raid into the fae world, killing and even capturing those they found, bringing them back for evil purposes. This included making magic items from the remains after they killed the captured. A war was brewing."

"I have a question," began Eric. "You're saying that faerie folk are from this alternate world, or whatever. Is this true on other worlds?"

"Sort of," she answered. "It once was, but it appears that on other planets, integrating them was much more complete so that they effectively merged into one. There are sometimes what we think of as leftover magic doorways to supernatural places, or even between non-magical ones."

"That's incredible," said Matt, eyes bright.

Eriana continued, "I'm not sure why, but this merging hadn't taken place much on Earth when we were brought here, and the quest from our summoning ended it altogether, forcing near total separation of what appears like a natural process everywhere else. I guess that this separation is unnatural."

Jack asked, "Why did it happen? Was that the quest? To cause this?"

"Basically, yes. At some point, Merlin aligned himself with the more benevolent faerie folk, but some among the elves, dwarves, and others who supported Merlin did not believe the lengths to which Morgana might go until it was too late. Ultimately, as matters escalated, Merlin decided there was only one solution to protect everyone on Earth—a spell to banish all faerie back to their world, drain all magic from the Earth back into the Land of Fae, and seal the doorways."

Eric remarked ruefully, "That's one hell of a spell."

Eriana nodded, amused. "I imagine it was, but Merlin cast it, with the help of other fae, from what he told us. And yet there was a problem with such enormous forces at work. It takes time. And after he cast it, in the week that it would take for all magic to flow from Earth into the fae world, and all the creatures to be pulled there, too, Morgana learned of what Merlin had done. She also learned that there was a key to undoing the spell should that ever need to happen."

After a moment, Matt guessed, "The pendant."

Eriana confirmed, "Merlin's Pendant. It just had to be returned to Stonehenge, the most powerful doorway between the worlds. With that done, magic would resume working on Earth, albeit slowly, the same way it faded slowly, though there's no telling how quickly it will fully return. It has already been a month since Anna unwittingly brought Merlin's Pendant to Stonehenge and the spell was undone. Now, the doorways between worlds are opening."

Eyes intense, Eric asked, "Does that mean we will begin to see fantasy creatures here?"

"Yes, for two reasons. The first is that the ones associated with Earth should arrive once they know the spell is undone. The second is that, with magic not functioning, this world could not be reached by magical means, and all other planets that I'm aware of, like Elloria, could not reach us here. Now they likely can, assuming they know to do so. I don't know how long it might take for any alien fantasy creatures to arrive here. Or what they might think of this place, with its technology."

She paused again, giving them time to absorb this. For weeks, she had been running through all of this, rehearsing it in her head and trying to figure out what to reveal when, not because she really wanted to hide things so much as not overwhelm them. They had already seen much themselves, but learning some truths about your world like this could be unsettling. Life was not what they had thought it was.

Ryan turned to Eric. "I think we only told Lorian, on the first quest, where we were from."

Eriana's eyebrows rose. She recognized the name, though more than one such elf existed, she was sure. "Lorian from Honyn, near Olliana?"

"Yes," Eric answered. "That was the first quest. We can get to that in a minute, but we trusted him. He was the one who filled us in on you guys. In fact, almost everything we know is from him."

That relieved her. They had spent significant time with him, and she liked the elf. "Unless he has changed, and elves seldom do, we can trust him. However, he may not have known to hide your origins."

"Yeah, why is it important?" Ryan asked, concern on his face.

Not sure she should admit it for fear of worrying them, she said, "I'm only speculating, but if people think you guys are the Ellorian Champions and have been on Earth for years, it may cause visits from both good and bad people. We had a lot of friends. Enemies, too."

"Like Soliander," said Matt, frowning. "He knows we are from here. I'm sure of it."

Eric observed, "But he also knows we aren't them."

"True. Not sure how much that will stop him from coming here."

"Neither do I," Eriana agreed, keen to see her old friend, but before she lost her train of thought from earlier, she added, "Before I forget, another effect of Merlin's spell being undone is that the connection to the gods of this world has been restored."

Ryan leaned forward. "Wait, are you saying that God has not answered prayers in a thousand years because of this, and now He will?"

"Yes, all the gods that people did not invent. There's no telling which is which, really. Not yet, anyway."

Looking dubious, Ryan said, "It seems unlikely that Merlin would have the power to stop God like that. It's a little hard to believe."

"He's got a point," agreed Eric, who then smirked at his friend, "unless, of course, God isn't real."

Ryan rolled his eyes. "I should have known you'd say something like that."

"In fairness," Eric continued, smiling, "maybe God agreed to go silent. He could have been like some of the fae, feeling that humans couldn't handle the supernatural wisely. Look what we do with nuclear weapons."

Eriana asked, kindness in her eyes, "I assume you are religious, Ryan?"

"Very," he proudly answered.

"Well, I don't have a real answer for you. Merlin only had time to explain so many things to us." The big man rose, pacing back and forth. "This is interesting." He pointed a finger at Eric, grinning. "You had better believe now, my friend, or it's the lake of fire for you!"

The rogue replied, "I have more pressing concerns right now, but for the record, my atheism has everything to do with there being no proof of God. If He gives proof, I'll be happy to acknowledge He is real. And maybe now we know why there has been no evidence, not for a long time, anyway."

Eriana patted his healed hand. "You already felt the proof now. Who do you think I channeled earlier?"

As Ryan grinned at him, Eric conceded, "I can't really argue that."

"Let's get back to the quest that brought you to Earth," Matt interrupted, not seeming interested in any of the religious subjects. "So Merlin cast the spell to get rid of magic, and Morgana summoned you four to get the pendant and return it to Stonehenge, but you didn't."

"Right," Eriana confirmed, wondering what else to tell them, but so far everything had gone well. "There is what I think of as a morality matrix in the Quest Rings. It prevents us from being summoned to do evil, but Morgana could bypass it."

"How?"

"Well, the separation of the worlds might be considered unnatural, and we were summoned to stop it, so this could be seen as a good quest. Morgana certainly seemed to think so. But according to Merlin, Morgana had done many bad things and had plans for new ones, which was the whole reason he cast the spell."

Matt noted, "So her summoning should have failed. Any guesses why it did not?"

"Yes. I think part of it was the ambiguity of this, but the principal reason is that Stonehenge is not a real Quest Ring. Merlin implied that the builders were both humans and fae during an earlier period of cooperation, and that the goal was to establish a stronger foothold for fae here on Earth.

They built Stonehenge at a doorway between the Earth and fae worlds."

Looking at her intently, as if fascinated, Jack asked, "It's not a proper ring, but she still summoned you to it?"

"Yes. Morgana turned it into a kind of makeshift Quest Ring. It bears some resemblance to one. But Earth had no genuine rings. Still doesn't. I don't think we had ever heard of the world."

Eric asked, "How did Morgana know to do this with Stonehenge, or the summoning spell, or even who you guys are?"

She had wondered the same thing and only had partial answers and some educated guesswork. "According to Merlin, both he and Morgana had the power of prophecy, and we don't know what they saw or how it has played out, but Morgana could learn the summoning spell this way. After we arrived and had a moment alone, Soliander revealed having seen Morgana's face in his dreams days earlier. He thought nothing of it until after we came to Earth, when he recognized her. We surmised she had gotten the spell from his mind during the dream and turned Stonehenge into a Quest Ring, one that is missing certain aspects."

The rogue said, "Like the morality matrix that would have prevented her from summoning you."

"Yes. And the keystone."

"Keystone?" Eric asked.

Matt's eyes suddenly lit up. "The keystone! Of course. It is made from soclarin ore." He turned to the others. "Remember when I stuck the end of Soliander's staff into that hole in the Quest Rings? That's the keystone I'm inserting it into. Only Soliander's staff works on that. The rest of the ring is not of soclarin."

Eriana nodded. "Yes. Morgana summoned us, and in theory, they bound us to the quest just like any other. That part of the summoning spell worked. She told us the quest was to return the pendant to Stonehenge, because if we didn't, Merlin's spell, already cast, would remove magic and fae creatures from Earth. The way she said it, it certainly seemed compelling that Merlin was the bad guy. We went to confront Merlin and get the pendant, but he told us what was really going on, all the stuff I just told you. We sensed he was right.

"And we realized we had a problem. We couldn't return home unless we did the quest, as this is always true. And magic was about to stop working, trapping us here for good. But Soliander realized that there would come a moment when the magic had drained from Earth. And at that moment, we might theoretically be free of the quests. Not just that one, but any further ones."

She noticed Eric's shrewd eyes on her. "You weren't doing them voluntarily, were you?"

"No," she admitted, not at all surprised he knew this. "This isn't something you can tell anyone except Anna. It was a closely guarded secret. Many worlds looked up to us. We gave them hope. It would not have looked good if anyone knew. We never really had a choice, forced to go on a dangerous quest to solve their problems. I would ask that you maintain this ruse."

"Sure," he agreed. "It isn't really ours to reveal. Please continue."

Eriana sipped at the beer again. "We were trapped and had no way to get out. But now we had our chance. But it would leave us trapped on Earth, and none of us wanted that. We have friends and families back home. Merlin and Soliander had an idea. They would pool their remaining magic energy to combine their strength, which was fading. They would time Soliander's return spell to the same moment that magic stopped working and released us. In theory, either it would work and we'd all go home, or it wouldn't and we would just remain here forever."

Eric observed, "But neither really happened. You're here, and Soliander isn't."

She sighed, knowing she didn't have a good explanation for this. "I don't know what happened. I remember Soliander looked alarmed, right before the spell completed. And moments later I found myself in New Zealand. That was twenty years ago. I have seen no sign of the others since."

A long silence followed this. Finally, Jack turned to his friends and asked, "Twenty years? I thought you guys said that when you get summoned, everyone thinks you've only been gone three years? And Merlin was a thousand years ago. Something isn't right about all of this."

That caught Eriana's attention. "Three years? Are you saying only three years has passed on the worlds you've been to, since we went missing?"

"Yes," said Matt. "They were saying they've been trying to summon us for that long. And my impression from Soliander's memories is that this is how much time has passed. By the way, as you were talking, I could suddenly remember some of your quest here, from his memories in my head."

Eriana felt confused by much of that but smiled, then laughed. Sudden tears filled her eyes as relief washed over her, an old grief vanishing. The tears flowed down her cheeks. She had lost all hope long ago and resigned herself to an awful possibility that had just gone away. The others watched her curiously, smiling at her reaction without understanding it, so she took a moment to calm herself enough to explain.

"I thought everyone was dead," she admitted, wiping her tears as Jack handed her a tissue box. "I thought everyone that I have ever known was dead. My family..." More tears came and she stopped, her lungs heaving. New questions needed answering, but the boys had just given her something she hadn't felt in a long time—genuine hope of seeing those she loved again. She had been nursing some hopes since realizing the Stonehenge Four were being summoned repeatedly, but nothing like this. She wanted to just sit and laugh. She needed it.

"Well," began Ryan gently, "we don't know what is happening with your family, but it's only been three years everywhere but here. So there's hope. They're probably not all dead, certainly."

She patted his hand. "I have wondered before about the role of time travel in all of this, because when we were summoned, this world was like the Medieval Ages, and yet when I arrived in New Zealand two decades ago, it had changed so much. I thought Morgana had summoned us in the same time frame to Earth, and that I had been thrown a thousand years into the future. I didn't know that at first, only after researching about Merlin and Morgana and learning how long ago they had lived, according to what we now see as myths.

"Now it appears Morgana summoned us to a thousand years in Earth's past, and in all the worlds. And when the quest ended, and Soliander's return spell completed, something went wrong. It seems like I didn't quite make it back to the present, just close, the same way that I didn't make it home, but ended up somewhere else on Earth."

Matt nodded, eyes far away as if struggling to remember. "He sensed it. He felt something was wrong. His last look..." He looked at her knowingly, and she suddenly wondered how much the techie knew.

Eric observed, "So it seems like he was sent back to the right timeline, and the right planet, or close enough, but you were left here, and you arrived maybe seventeen years short of the right time. Another three have passed since then."

She nodded slowly, calming herself. "That seems accurate."

He asked, "And there's no sign of Andier or Korrin on Earth?"

"No. No sign of Soliander either, except for what you say. I have some questions about that, but I assume from our talk that you did not know what Merlin's Pendant really was until now."

Matt shook his head. "None. Sometimes info pops into my head, but there's no controlling it. Now I'm curious to know how Anna ended up with it."

Eric pursed his lips. "Yeah, and where it's been all these years."

Eriana remarked, "I have a private investigator that I use to track down supposedly magical items, and this was the first one I had him look for. But we have never seen or heard a word about it in all this time. Maybe when she is feeling better, she can say more about where she got it and we can track its history, but I'm not sure it's that important."

"You never know," said the rogue. "I wonder if it was a coincidence that she ended up with it. You said something about a prophecy. Was there anyone left on Earth who knew any of this and ensured she would end up with it?"

Intrigued expressions mirrored Eriana's own. "An interesting scenario. Merlin had a few Earth friends who knew what he'd done. It is possible one of them took possession of it when the spell completed."

"Any ideas what happened to Merlin and Morgana?" Matt asked.

Eriana frowned. "No, only what was supposed to happen. Both were to return to the fae world because any creature with that much fae in them would have died when the spell completed, if they were still here. Because magic is part of them, and they can't live without it."

Eric stood up. "Well, this is all beyond fascinating, but I have to hit the bathroom. Let's take a quick break. Eriana, if you need anything, please help yourself."

She nodded thanks and rose to stretch her legs, finding herself at the window, looking out over suburban sprawl as night gathered, lights twinkling on to brighten the dark. They mirrored how she felt, like a light had been lit inside her. Soliander was alive. And only three years older than she last saw him. This meant everyone else likely was, and a real possibility of seeing her friends and family again existed. She smiled as Jack came up beside her.

CHAPTER TWELVE

THE LADY HOPE

Jack remarked to Eriana, "Seems like an enormous weight off your shoulders. I'm happy to hear that you may see your friends soon, and that your family is alive."

He bit his lip. How much of one did she have back on Elloria before all the quests began? His curiosity about her was strong, and it wasn't just that she was physically attractive; she was old enough to be his mother. There was something charismatic about her. Comforting. Radiant. Sweet. And wise. Whatever was causing it, he wanted to know more, and to have her look at him. He sensed she knew he was attracted to her, and he didn't care that she knew, but not because he was a fool. He just felt a compassionate sincerity in her eyes and felt drawn to it. He'd seen the others, especially Eric, smirk about his interest and ignored it. This wasn't about sex. He didn't know what it was. He just felt good when she looked at him, somehow comforted, like everything would be alright, even though he wasn't the one who had any actual problems right now.

He added, "That must have been hard all this time, thinking they were gone a thousand years. They must have wondered if they'll ever see you again, too. That could be some reunion."

Eriana smiled at him and he blushed, then tried to make himself stop it. "Thank you. I don't even know what to think about it yet. Soliander, at least, would be shocked by how I've aged. The others could be even older for all I know."

"Hopefully, the guys and Anna will find some information on Andier and Korrin soon, on one of their quests. Like Soliander, they've probably heard the champions are back but know that can't be right, so I assume they'd be curious and investigate."

"That's an understatement," she agreed ruefully. "I want to get a message to my family, that I'm okay, but I'm not sure if we should keep my whereabouts and situation hidden for a while."

"Why? What kind of trouble do you expect?"

"I really don't know, but with these guys the apparent Ellorian Champions, news of another champion being elsewhere and doing other things will confuse people, and possibly cause problems when these guys are summoned. We have no way of knowing how people will react, but it's something to think about, maybe planning for."

"Gotcha. Well listen, if you need anything, let me know. I'm now like a full-time helper to them when they're gone, and that includes you. Ryan's literally paying me." He grinned. "I apparently just quit my job and got a new one working for them."

She laid a hand on his arm. "Thank you. I appreciate that, especially you stepping up to help them. They really need it. It's really important. We had many people who knew the truth and were helping. Right now, they just have you."

"I have some help now." He related his role so far, concluding, "We told the attorney the truth earlier, and Ryan's brother, so it's been nice to not be alone with this. And now I have you here, too."

"I can relate. I haven't told a soul the truth in nearly two decades."

He frowned, unable to imagine being that isolated with such a huge truth for so long. As secrets go, hers was beyond epic. No one knew anything about why God stopped answering people, so many believing He never had and wasn't real, and yet she knew. And everyone thought magic wasn't real, but she knew. Fae weren't real, but she knew. Her ability to keep quiet impressed him. She likely understood the padded walls awaiting her for admitting it. What a relief it must be now. He felt a mixture of regret for her and happy she wasn't so alone anymore.

"I'm sorry. That must've been awful, but now you can at least talk to us. I'm more than happy to listen." He was going to say more when the other boys gathered at the table and she gave him that warm smile of hers, laying a hand on his arm again before she joined the group to resume their talks.

"Okay," began Eric, who resumed his seat, "it's our turn to tell you what has been happening."

"Please."

As Eriana listened and held her questions, Ryan, Matt, and Eric related the quest to Honyn to close the Dragon Gate, and that Soliander had opened it, apparently not caring that the dragons might return and destroy the planet. Jack saw that the revelations, including Soliander's attack on both Lorian and Matt, concerned her. She said that this was not the noble, self-sacrificing man she had known. Had he, like her, believed that the rest of the Ellorian Champions were dead? She revealed that Soliander had always blamed himself for their being trapped in the quest cycle, but that had really been Everon's fault. To this, Soliander had replied that Everon was his apprentice, and it was therefore still his fault. They had endured countless arguments about it. And if the wizard believed they were dead, then he undoubtedly blamed himself.

Jack asked, "Do you think this was enough to turn his heart? It seems like he isn't doing, uh, pleasant things."

Eriana pursed her lips. "Yes, I think so. He was always troubled, and I knew he sometimes struggled to not give in to his demons. I helped him with that as I could. I'm afraid that what happened could have easily pushed him into the darkness he fought against. There's something else I wanted to ask about. When you guys arrive, you are fully healed and rested?"

"Each time, yes," confirmed Eric.

"And you are dressed in our clothes, and they fit?"

"Perfectly."

Eriana eyed them. "You three are about the right size. From a distance, you can easily pass for us. It may have been luck that, so far, no one who knew us well, besides Lorian, has been present at your quests."

"What do you think would happen if the truth were known?" Matt asked.

"I honestly do not know. It would really depend on the individual person's reaction."

The techie elaborated, "I guess what I'm getting at is that we haven't known how to react to the assumption that we're you guys, so we've been playing along. I think I can speak for all of us that we don't want to offend you by doing so."

Eriana smiled. "It's fine. I'm not offended and I agree with the decision, honestly. It's probably for the best. The reaction to learning you aren't us might not be a good one. It would cause disillusion with your ability to do the quest, for one. How has that been going?"

Eric smiled ruefully and replied, "It's been a little rough. We badly need training. We were just talking about that before you knocked. Some of it is easy enough, like horseback riding or swordsmanship, but for Matt and Anna..."

Eriana offered, "I can help Anna, certainly."

"Are you able to heal her now?" Jack asked, the images of Anna in the hospital hard to get out of his head. He didn't want to wait until she was summoned, and he really wanted her here with the rest of them. She all alone over there, kind of like Eriana had been for two decades with her unknown truth. Maybe they had more in common than he had realized. "She really needs it."

"I know. I can help, but not all the way. I'm not that strong yet."

Jack offered, "I can take you to the hospital anytime. Her parents let me go in and I can get you in. The minute you're ready."

"Sure, I would be happy to. I would really like to meet her. One thing I wanted to assure all of you about, especially her, is that I don't think you need to worry about her health long term. Once you are summoned again, the summoning spell will fully heal her."

"We were talking about that earlier," admitted Ryan. "Are you positive? There isn't a limit on that? It even fixes paralysis?"

"Yes. As long as you're still alive, it will completely heal you. The spells in the Quest Ring are powerful. I put the healing ones in there myself."

Looking visibly relieved, Eric said, "*Thank* you. This is beyond great to know. We've all been so worried. What questions do you have for us that we haven't answered?"

Eriana looked away for a few moments and then admitted, "I'm not sure you can answer some, but together we might figure out a few things, either now or as this continues." She pursed her lips again. "I assume you know by now that your substitution appears to be consistent, possibly permanent. Ours was until a uniquely powerful spell and situation ended the cycle. I don't know how you can get out of it. We didn't know for a long time, and it wasn't for lack of trying. Soliander was very determined and is the smartest, most resourceful person I've ever known, and even he couldn't figure it out until the end. I'm sorry."

"The worst part," Ryan started, "is that based on what you've told us, we would need a spell to stop magic from working on Earth again, to once again break the cycle. I don't suppose it's in Soliander's spell books?"

Matt shook his head. "Saw nothing like that, and it was Merlin's spell, anyway. I don't have Soliander's spell books either. That raises a question for you, Eriana."

"Sure."

"We can never bring anything back with us, so I have been trying to memorize spells, then write them down here. We also never keep the items we're wearing or using. Is that supposed to happen?"

She shook her head. "No. We could bring things back whether the Quest Ring's spell sent us home or if Soliander personally brought us back. I don't know why that is happening, but it might be related to the other, more pressing issue, the one that resulted in Anna's hospitalization. You don't have Home Rings, I'm assuming."

"Home Rings?" Eric looked surprised, but Matt's face registered sudden awareness.

Seeing his expression, Eriana offered, "Each of us had one at our home. The Quest Ring sent us back to our individual Home Ring every time. Since the four of you don't have them, it appears to be returning you to where you were before being summoned."

Groans of realization came from all but Matt, who said, "We need to figure out how to create these immediately. Otherwise, this is a consistent, huge problem. It almost got Anna killed and certainly isn't great for the rest of us. We were just realizing we can never go anywhere in a car for fear of this happening."

"Or a plane," Ryan interjected.

Jack asked, "Was *that* spell in Soliander's books? How to create a Home Ring?"

Matt sighed. "Don't think so, but I feel like I understand parts of it. We need soclarin ore to make them."

"Yes," Eriana acknowledged. "You said Lorian took some on Honyn on your behalf. You should contact him when able and see if he can come here."

"Still don't know the spell really," observed a nodding Eric.

Eriana said, "Listen, I have a private investigator I trust, and he is the one who was able to find out you might be staying here. Ryan, when your attorney got you out of jail, we got his name and used it to look for credit card purchases, which led to this hotel. I'm sorry for snooping, but I had to find you guys, and you have been missing, whether you've been hiding from the police or press."

Ryan waved her off. "It's fine. But if you found us, someone else could."

"Yes," she admitted, "that's what I'm getting at. Now, my guy did some illegal things to achieve this and the police wouldn't be able to without a good reason, but you guys cannot stay here indefinitely. Check out sooner, even tonight. I could get a room for all of you within walking distance. It would not be traceable to any of you."

She saw encouraged expressions and Eric said, "That's an excellent idea."

"I can repay you," Ryan began, but she waved him off.

"Don't worry about it. I purposely married a wealthy banker who lets me do what I want, more or less."

"You're married?" Jack asked in disappointment. He hadn't meant to react that way, and her broad smile made him blush. "I just assumed... well, I don't know what. I guess you've been here long enough with little hope of your old life returning that you moved on? Settled down."

She conceded he was right. "No one wants to be alone forever."

Eric asked, "I assume your husband doesn't know the truth about you?"

"No. Not yet. Will cross that bridge when I come to it, probably relatively soon."

"Before you got here," Ryan began, "we were talking about setting up a long-term base where we can train, and not be bothered. Is this something you can help with? I mean, we don't know about buying estates and we were thinking my attorney can help. My family has the money, but I can't really arrange it if I'm disappearing all the time."

She nodded. "Absolutely. It's another thing that can be done in my name. If you like, you can always be a kind of silent partner where you name is not recorded on the deed or a mortgage, and no funds from you are involved in any way that can be traced, but you are an owner."

"Yes, something like that."

"There's always my apartment in the meantime," Jack offered. "It's not really big enough, but it can work before we get somewhere bigger. That way you're not in a hotel, which is kind of busy. Lots of traffic."

"I think that is a good idea," agreed Eriana. "Why don't you switch rooms tonight, and tomorrow you'll all go to his apartment. We can start planning a base for you. And I can go visit Anna with Jack."

No one disagreed with this and they set things in motion, their minds too full for more revelations. Eriana got them a hotel suite across the road and, with Jack's help, took over all of their suitcases so that they could essentially sneak in a side door, climb the stairs, and head inside while drawing fewer eyes. They walked over to do this to minimize the risk of being in a moving car when summoned, so Jack moved their cars. Then Eriana left for her own hotel.

In the morning, Jack loaded their bags into his trunk, Eriana arrived to check them out, and then she followed Jack as he drove the guys to his apartment. The twenty-minute trip made everyone nervous, but they weren't summoned along the way and finally relaxed once inside. They spent some time hooking up Eriana's phones to their new numbers and otherwise making some plans on what to do when they all disappeared again.

Now it was time to see what Eriana could do for Anna. She wouldn't predict the amount of healing that would come, remarking that her strength with it seemed to ebb and flow like a tide as magic slowly returned to Earth. The hope was to get Anna out of any remaining danger, but it relieved them to discover on arrival that she had improved overnight, enough that the hospital began considering if they should remove her from ICU. Jack hoped Eriana would ensure this happened today. He felt grateful even before they reached Anna's room, her parents not having arrived yet, which Jack knew because he'd talked to them this morning. He purposely made it here first to minimize explanations about who Eriana was. They planned to do their thing and then the priestess, at least, would leave so that Jack could talk with Anna's parents. For now, he intended to claim ignorance about where Matt, Eric, and Ryan were. There were just too many things to explain.

"Let me go in first," Jack whispered to Eriana, who was peeking around the door at Anna. She nodded and Jack slipped inside the familiar room, with its whirring and beeping machines, various wires and tubes like an IV attached to the patient. A TV high on one wall, and which he hadn't noticed before, quietly played a movie that Anna didn't appear to be watching, her gaze far away until she noticed Jack, when she smiled a moment. He knew concern likely shone from his face but, with an effort, he forced it away, because the woman he'd brought with him had brought hope with her.

"Hey," Jack began gently, gripping her hand, the one that wasn't part of a broken arm. Her fingers didn't react, and he wondered if she even felt it. "How are you doing?"

"Not great," she admitted, eyes going to their hands together. She met his gaze with a sad resignation, and he knew she didn't feel it.

"Well, I'm not going to waste any time with my announcement, because it's very important to me and the others that you feel hopeful about your future."

"I could use some good news," she admitted. "How are the boys?"

"Great, except they're worried about you, but we have reason to be excited. There's someone very special I want you to meet. We met her last night, and she's a game changer." He looked back to see Eriana coming in to the other side of the bed. With any luck, that benevolent radiance exuding from her would work on his friend like it did on him, even before a healing spell. "Remember when you asked me to bring you a priest? Well, I found a better one."

"Hello Anna." Eriana gripped her other hand, smiling fondly at her. "It's so very nice to meet you."

"Who are you?"

"On this world, I'm known as Erin Jennings. But on my own and many others, I go by many names. The Lady Hope. The Blessed One. The Light Bringer. I am Eriana of Coreth, one of the Ellorian Champions that you and your friends have been impersonating without meaning to." As Anna stared up at her in a mixture of disbelief and curiosity, Eriana pulled the gold scarf from around her neck to reveal the Amulet of Corethian. "I understand you wear a copy of my amulet when you are summoned. And I'm sure you wear it well. I know you must have many questions, but your parents will have more if they see me in here, and so Jack and I have come before they arrive in a short while."

Anna's eyes went to Jack, who grinned at her and answered the question he assumed she wanted to ask. "Yes, it's really her. We've learned a ton last night, but right now, it's important for her to heal you before your parents get here." He saw sudden hope appear in her eyes, which went to Eriana with a desperation that hurt to see.

"Can you really heal me?"

"Yes," Eriana replied, "enough to get you out of ICU, anyway. For the rest of your injuries, you will need to wait until you are summoned again. I want to assure you, as I did your friends, that the Quest Rings will fully heal you. Anna, you will not be paralyzed for long."

Tears sprang into Anna's eyes and down her cheeks.

"We all forgot about that," Jack confessed. "And I think you might have, too." She nodded wordlessly, still crying, Eriana wiping her tears away.

"Thank you," Anna whispered, overcome. "Thank you. It is so nice to meet you."

"Rest a moment and I will do what I can to improve your health. Just close your eyes, sweet one."

Anna did as she was told, her breathing deep from emotion. They heard whispered words to a God Anna had never believed in, longer than what Eriana had said to heal Eric's hand the night before. The soft glow surrounded her as Jack watched in amazement, thinking he'd never tire of seeing this. The superficial wounds on Anna's face slowly faded, her complexion bore more color, and the fingers Jack held onto flinched, then curled around his. He squeezed in excitement and looked at Eriana, full of wonder. She had healed at least some of the paralysis, despite her earlier cautions. He wanted to ask Anna to wiggle her toes, but as he looked back at her, it was apparent that she had fallen asleep.

"Rest, Anna," whispered Eriana. "We will meet again soon. You are not alone and have much help."

Jack beamed at the healer and mouthed a thank you. She smiled in return and excused herself, leaving him alone with Anna, whose parents arrived ten minutes later to find him still standing there. They noticed the missing cuts on her forehead, but he quickly distracted them by observing that she had squeezed his hand. Her mother didn't seem to believe it until Jack replaced his hand with hers, and a sleeping Anna closed her fingers around it. Her parents hugged each other in relief and he gave them privacy and quit while he was ahead, so he left. He'd return later to fill her in on everything they'd learned.

In the meantime, he went home, where Eriana and the boys were jointly looking up real estate listings on a laptop hooked to his TV as a big monitor. They found several estates for sale north of Darnestown in a rural area that was still only minutes away from shopping centers. Some were better suited to their needs than others. One was especially nice, with an old house, a newer one, and a large indoor riding ring attached to a barn that had several apartments. There were riding trails and several open fields, one of which was out of sight behind a line of trees. That would make for a good archery range. The land had some forest on it, as well.

With Eric, Matt, and Ryan leery of going anywhere in case they were summoned or seen, Eriana and Jack called the realtor to see up a visit while they brainstormed things they needed to consider in a property. They also video-called Quincy and Daniel to introduce Eriana to get their "Earth team," as Eric called them, working together more. They made rough plans for a moving truck to grab all the gear at the guest house.

Just when it seemed like everything was moving in the right direction, Matt excused himself to the bathroom, and no sooner did the toilet flush than Eric and Ryan, who were seated neck to Jack, began to softly glow and then vanish. Jack sighed, then remembered that Anna should have just been healed all the way. He went to the bathroom to find the sink running and a soap bottle knocked over. As expected, Matt was gone, the toilet still refilling. He returned to the couch and sat.

Jack looked at Eriana and joked, "Does the summoning spell wash your hands, too?"

———— • · • ————

Darron felt uneasy. He had watched enough TV since arriving that he understood this world treated children with a far softer touch than anywhere else. Not being the fatherly type, he had no kids of his own and never intended to change this. Sure, he might father a brat or two, and probably already had, but they would be on their own, unless their mothers looked after them. He had no sense of how to handle a child and could not have cared less about it.

And so he stood on the edge of the park where children were playing on various metal bars, plastic slides, and a wide lawn, their parents standing idly by or slouched on benches, chatting together. He counted two dozen of the little monsters and amused himself with thoughts of which spells he could cast on them. The sleep spell was the more benevolent and therefore only brought a frown to his dark face, but fiery darts, a wall of flames, or making the Earth swallow them whole all cheered him. The thought of summoning creatures to chase and devour them made him laugh, the sinister sound chilling even a few adults nearby.

They were watching him, he knew. There seemed to be no help for that. Unless he had a child of his own to watch, he seemed to attract attention. Observation suggested no adults were here without one, and this had resulted in him being singled out. Why did these parents care? Something called an Amber Alert had been issued that morning, raising his awareness of kidnapping and worse. Where he came from, a missing child had typically been eaten by something. A missing kid on Earth hardly seemed worth getting upset over.

Maybe these parents could tell he wanted to do something to their brats. People were too sensitive. He wasn't going to actually *do* anything, of course. Zoran would've killed him for attracting any attention. And yet he was somehow doing that, anyway.

But he wasn't leaving. He had a job to do, and overprotective parents ranked last on any list of dangers he had faced over the years. The thought made him laugh again. They were like arrogant children if they thought they posed a threat to anyone, least of all him or those with whom he kept company. They knew nothing of being in genuine danger, and yet they had enough sense to be afraid of him. Exuding menace was a trait he had used to keep people in line before, but now it seemed likely to cause problems and he resented having to stifle his natural inclination for these people.

Darron turned his attention back to the apartment building across the two-lane street from the park. He and Zoran had now visited the homes of Ryan, Anna, Eric, and Matt, but not gone inside. Each time Zoran arrived at a location, the memories of Matt in his head coalesced into something more understandable, making entering unnecessary. From news reports, Darron now knew what the four looked like. His time lurking at the hospital had resulted in seeing a young man and middle-aged blonde woman exiting Anna's room separately. Not knowing their identities, he had followed the man for a time, turning himself into a raven once outside to more easily track his car from above. On describing the man to Zoran, his master unceremoniously cast the *Mind Trust* spell on him long enough to see for himself, announcing the identity of Jack.

"What of the woman?" Darron had asked.

Zoran waved him off. "I didn't look. A middle-aged woman is of no importance to me."

"It's probably his mother," Darron had mused, but he hadn't cared then or now. Still, Jack and the woman had gone into the apartment he stood watching, so perhaps Darron was right. Zoran's order to follow Jack had proven fruitful, but that came as no surprise, as his master was wiser than anyone he knew. Anna's location at the hospital since returning to Earth had been known, but there had been little sign of the others, though the news confirmed that Ryan had been arrested and released. They hadn't been able to locate him since, and Matt and Eric had also disappeared...

Until Darron's spying on Jack had revealed all but Anna were at Jack's apartment. Zoran would be pleased, once Darron informed him. The master had cast himself to England to visit some place called Stonehenge, the significance of which Darron did not know. But he had googled it when Zoran was otherwise preoccupied and noticed that pictures of it bore a resemblance to the infamous Quest Rings the Ellorian Champions had used. Since then, he'd been wondering if that's what all of this was about. But he knew better than to ask. Zoran didn't appreciate questions. Not for the first time, Darron wished he had the nerve to immobile his master and cast the *Mind Trust* spell on *him*. What extraordinary knowledge must be inside that man.

Like everyone, he had heard that the Ellorian Champions had returned, but that they never went home, unless this place was a new home after their long absence. He had never heard of Earth, nor seen anywhere anything like it. He wondered how Zoran knew of it, but it was clear his master had never been here before either. These four they were following didn't seem like any sort of champions. They didn't dress like them, or act like them. And the police were always after them, so they seemed more like fugitives than renowned heroes. Was that the problem? Had they been imprisoned on Earth all this time?

The bigger question was why Zoran cared about them at all. His master had seemed preoccupied since returning from Honyn with burn marks on him and a singed robe. It had taken an effort not to ask what had happened. He had never seen the master wounded before, however briefly. A healing potion had taken care of it. Surely these feeble Earth humans hadn't been involved in that, or had they? Like everyone else here, they didn't even seem to have magic, but then maybe it was just diminished. Zoran had said as much when cautioning him to never be seen using it on Earth, but the master seemed unaffected. Or maybe he was just so prodigiously strong that he could do things Darron could not. Not here anyway. Turning himself into that raven had been surprisingly challenging when it normally came easily, and yet Zoran could cast himself far away with little trouble. Perhaps the master held an enormous advantage over everyone else here. But then that was true, regardless of what planet they were on.

As he stood musing, trying and failing to not look conspicuous in his shorts, t-shirt, and Washington Nationals baseball hat, a pink, round, plastic disc some children had been throwing to each other landed near him. A little girl about eight-years-old ran toward him to get it but stopped short on seeing him turn to her. Darron smirked at her wariness. She was right to be afraid, but he stepped up his charade of civility. He stepped to the disc and bent to pick it up, the motion causing his hat to tip forward. He repositioned it with one hand while extending the disc to the girl, who did not try to take it. Instead, she was staring wide-eyed at him.

The girl excitedly noted, "Hey, you have pointed ears! Are you a Vulcan?"

Moving the hat must have made his ears emerge from under his hair, he realized. He didn't know what a Vulcan was and wasn't inclined to answer, anyway. Instead, he leaned forward, dropped the disc, and pulled the sunglasses away from his red eyes.

"Run away," he snarled.

The girl screamed and took a step back so suddenly that she fell on her butt. For a moment, Darron wanted to laugh. But then a man yelled something and began approaching aggressively, followed by other men. Kids stopped what they were doing, and women began holding up their phones, pointing them at him. Making videos, he knew. Zoran would not be pleased. Darron sighed, stifling the desire to just kill everyone as a crowd began to form. One man in a *Star Trek* shirt lifted the crying girl to her feet as another stepped closer to Darron than was wise.

"Did you push her?" he demanded.

"No," Darron answered, but then couldn't help adding, "but I wish I had."

"Well, why don't you pick on someone your own size, asshole?"

"Are you volunteering yourself?"

"Yeah! What the hell is wrong with your eyes? You some kind of freak?"

Darron put the glassed back on. "By the laws of this country, if you attack me, I get to–"

The man slapped the glasses from his hand and a jolt of anger tore through Darron. "Not if I'm defending a little girl."

The dark elf couldn't really argue the specifics, having only learned so much, but he didn't much care. It was obviously time to go. There would be no additional scrutiny of Jack's apartment today. He was dying to teach this man a lesson and struggling to contain the power in him.

He asked, "Are you hoping to impress this girl so you can do what you want with her, or perhaps her mother?" It was a fair question. He'd seen humans do that very thing, and goblins, ogres, and even his own kind, but from the fury that appeared on the man's face, he immediately knew that was not as neutral a question as he had intended it to be.

And then the man swung a fist.

"Kunia," Darron said instinctively, magic power filling him stronger than he had done on Earth so far. And the man flew backwards ten feet, colliding with several other people, including little kids, before they landed in a heap together. Cries of pain, fear, shock, and anger suddenly surrounded him. Darron dropped all pretenses and warily glanced around, quickly seeing the very thing he now worried about. He spoke another word and the gun in a man's hand burst into flames. No one else seemed to have another one as people backed away, but he had another problem. He cast a spell to emit an energy burst in all directions and heard the shattering of glass as the phones pointed at him overloaded and fried all footage of this encounter. Zoran would not be pleased any of this had happened, but at least Darron could destroy the evidence.

He strode farther onto the lawn as people scrambled to get out of his way. A line of trees beckoned and was the place from where he had emerged before. Now it offered escape as he left the mob. To his surprise, they followed, and he thought seriously about just killing all of them. Instead, he took off at a run, swallowing pride at the implication that they were a threat to him. They quickened their pace as well, but it would not matter. He disappeared into the trees, which was a thin line of them, and once out of sight spoke another word to turn himself into a raven that was already flying away. He circled above for a minute, watching everyone milling about in confusion as they tried to figure out where he had gone. One little boy seemed to know from the way he pointed at Darron, but maybe no one took him seriously.

Before long, the wizard landed on the balcony of a hotel room, changed back into a dark elf, and went inside. Fear of Zoran's reaction dominated his thoughts. By now he'd learned that news of such events spread quickly here, far faster than on any other world, and so he turned on the TV and sat waiting. Within an hour, the first reports of it were broadcast, with people he recognized claiming that he had struck the little girl. Humans were cunning with lies to cover their own destructive behavior. It was true on every world he had visited. Then security camera footage from a nearby eatery contradicted that account as they broadcast it. Darron frowned. He hadn't thought of that. The distance between him and the camera wasn't enough to hide that three separate moments happened, each best explained by magic. Reports of similar incidents from around the world were growing common. Would that make this incident less noteworthy to people? Would Zoran agree with that?

Darron didn't have long to find out. With a brief flicker of white light, his master appeared before him, the severed head of a dwarf dangling upside down from its beard in one hand. The dark elf rose and bowed.

"I hope your trip was fruitful, master. More than for just a head."

Zoran chuckled, the evil laugh pleasing Darron when it would have chilled any other. "This head confirms a door is open."

The apprentice did not know the significance. "I have news."

"Some of it I know," replied Zoran, voice hard.

Darron knew better than to ever play dumb with this man, who always seemed to already know what he wanted to say. It was a wonder he ever used the *Mind Trust* spell at all. He hardly seemed to need it. "Yes, I attempted to destroy the gathered footage but–"

"You did not think of the security cameras."

"Yes. Forgive me. There are fortunately many reports from around the world of similar moments and–"

"This may be considered one, yes. Why were you there? What have you learned?"

"The Stonehenge Four are dwelling with Jack and the middle-aged woman in Jack's apartment. The girl is of course still with the healers." He quickly related the success of his following Jack, hoping to bolster any punishment coming his way, but Zoran's next words crushed his hopes.

"So this incident happened across the street from the people we are hoping to ambush."

Darron went cold. Before he could reply, Zoran asked for the address. The elf gave it. Then one hand gripped his shoulder and words of magic he recognized paralyzed his mind. Horror. Desperation. Anger. Futility. Resignation. There was no besting the master wizard whose familiar words caused an expected burning sensation to rise from within. Darron had cast the spell before, never really imagining he would one day learn what it felt like.

"You have left enough evidence."

These were the last words Darron heard before he turned to black ash.

CHAPTER THIRTEEN

A TALE OF THREE KINGS

As the priest left, Anna watched him go and still felt unsure what to think. She hadn't really expected solid answers, and yet she was still disappointed that she was no closer to knowing how to reach out to God and get an answer. Each of the priest's replies about interacting with God had suggested that he had never actually done it. Never had a prayer answered. Never heard a voice in his head. Saw a vision. Had his faith confirmed. He certainly hadn't been a vessel for God's power to flow through to heal the wounded.

And that was what she really wanted to know. How did God choose someone? Had he ever? She had wanted to ask if any stories about that were true, but suspected she wouldn't get a straight answer, just something about having faith. Or seeing that this guy believed it. That just reminded her why she had always been so cynical about religion. If it was real, you didn't tell people to just believe like it wasn't. Faith in something that had no proof was not the ultimate test of whether you were worthy. It just sounded manipulative.

She sighed, not wanting to rehash all the reasons for her atheism. She had accepted the gods on other worlds were real. She had heard reports of people healing others on Earth. And of course, Eriana had just healed her. An energy she knew to be the touch of a god had coursed through her. There could be no denying that He was real, but what concerned her now was what was true and what was not. Because it seemed like until that first quest from Stonehenge, it was all baloney. Why was God suddenly back? And how did Eriana reach out to him? She wanted to ask but would have to wait.

She had met with a different priest before, the first time Jack had fetched one. She had hoped for better answers from this, but no luck. Healing herself was certainly on her mind, but she needed to get out of here so she could heal her friends and undo what she had done to them. The fate of Heather, who had died, hung on her mind because she seriously doubted ever having the power to raise someone from the dead. She was no Aeron, the Lord of Fear necromancer. It seemed that even he could not raise his dead wife in satisfactory condition. Despite all the extraordinary things that had turned out to be real, even that one was pure bullshit. Raise the dead and they were still dead. Unless they were Jesus Christ? That was something to think about. But if he had been real, he still wasn't like the rest of people, being half god.

Her mind drifted often to her girlfriends and what had become of them. The grief loomed so large that she sometimes didn't feel it, but the drugs might have contributed to that. She should have known better than to drive—the source of her guilt. And she imagined her friends thought the same. Blaming questions likely awaited her when they met again, for those still alive. Would they even agree to see her? She felt a renewed interest in learning to heal so she could undo as much as she could, and this thought helped motivate her to not fall apart in tears. She had a solution, if she could only achieve it.

As she lay there pondering, a tingling in her belly made her catch her breath in anticipation. Never had she felt excited by a possible summoning, as they filled her with dread. But if everyone was right, a Quest Ring was about to fully heal her. As the room disappeared around her, the now familiar of vortex of swirling light and sound replacing it, she began to smile.

Ryan, Matt, and Eric were now before her in their usual positions. And she was facing them, standing in a hospital gown. She looked down and saw her bare feet. She was never really sure what she felt beneath them while being summoned, but she felt *something* solid. And that was all that mattered because she hadn't felt her feet in days. She wiggled her toes, the gown suddenly vanishing. With a yelp, she covered herself and started laughing that she could, and a moment later the now familiar robe of Eriana, the Lady Hope, draped from her shoulders, down to her white-booted feet. She looked at the others, similarly attired in their adventuring gear of golden armor, black leather, and a dark robe. All smiling eyes were on her as the commotion stopped. She was so taken with her miraculous healing that she forgot to immediately scan for danger. Anna was quietly giggling, tears springing to her eyes and one hand reaching absently for the nearest of them, which was Eric, because he had stepped closer.

"Are you okay?" he asked.

"Yes!" she whispered, more because her voice was choked with emotion than because she was trying to be quiet.

"My Lords," began Ryan in his knightly voice, addressing the summoners, "thank you so much for inviting us. We are honored to be here. We would appreciate just a moment to confer among ourselves before giving you our full attention."

"Certainly, Lord Korrin," said someone.

Then her friends were all before her, asking how she felt and hardly letting her answer. That they were so genuinely concerned touched her and she felt grateful for them, suddenly realizing how desperately she had missed them when she most needed them, trapped in a hospital. Trapped in her own body. She threw her arms around each, not caring who was watching, though a quick glance past them showed a wide castle hall, the Quest Ring around them off to one side in an alcove. Scores of nobles, guards, and attendants waited, but the place was nearly empty, as if no one had expected them to appear, or few people were caught up in the possibility. Maybe there wasn't much riding on their success. That would be a welcome change.

She assured her friends that she felt fine, could feel her entire body. Indeed, as always happened when summoned, she felt fantastic, the thrill inside her adding to the sense of physical well-being. She finally insisted they get on with the quest business and everyone turned back to their summoners.

A lean middle-aged man came forward, putting one hand on the shoulder of the wizard who appeared to have summoned them, gently pushing him aside. Calm brown eyes shone with unexcited politeness, his thin lips curled in a smile that brought no life to his gaunt cheeks. Feathered brown hair covered his ears and touched the upturned collar of a cloak of purple and gold hanging to his waist. A boar had been emblazoned on it. A brown tunic covered his torso, tan, tight leggings disappearing into darker shoes. That this was a seasoned politician seemed clear.

"Ellorian Champions," he began in a smooth voice, "I am Prime Minister Othor of Kingdom Thiat, on the world of Eridos. We are pleased to host you. If you will follow me, some introductions are required."

"Thank you," replied Ryan.

As Anna walked out of the alcove with her friends, and into the two-story throne room, she sensed their overall mood was the best it had been so far at the start of a quest. Normally, being snatched from Earth upset them. She made a note of her own grin so she could at least fake it the next time. This is what it feels like to be thrilled with a quest. She doubted she would ever be so happy to start one again. The others seemed similarly affected, and their jovial mood may have inspired the men and women they passed as they followed Othor. Most bowed or made similar displays of respect, and she surmised that the boar silhouette several wore was the symbol of Thiat. Polished tile floors had inlays of fanciful beasts beneath their feet, while tapestries and giant, gilded mirrors hung from the walls, two unlit chandeliers evenly spaced. Enough light came in from the windows to not light them.

Ahead were several steps leading to a pair of golden thrones, one empty, the other occupied by a lounging, overweight, bored looking man in his fifties, with multiple jowls that were visible through his scruffy gray beard. A tall, gold, jewel-encrusted crown sat atop his round, balding head. A long purple cloak covered most of his wide body, gold fasteners keeping it closed. The King of Thiat sat frowning at them, watery-blue eyes unimpressed. The idea of summoning them clearly hadn't been his. Could they count on his support? It didn't seem like it. The two dozen others who had assembled remained standing like the champions, for no seats were here as they stopped before the steps, Anna wondering how many of them were royalty. Most were men.

"King Varrun," Prime Minister Othor began, "may I present the Ellorian Champions, Lord Korrin of Andor, Soliander of Aranor, Andier of Roir, and of course the Lady Eriana of Coreth."

"So, where have you been?" the king demanded, surprising Anna. At least he could be honest, and that was something. King Varrun waved a hand toward one group of standing nobles. "We could have done this years ago and gotten this lot out from underfoot."

Ryan bowed his head. "Our apologies, Your Majesty. We hope we are not too late to help."

"No, just too late to restore the peace of my home these last few years, but I suppose I should be grateful. You are about to do me a service worthy of earning a fiefdom. I should re-knight you just for giving me hope."

"I would be honored," replied Ryan.

"Yes, everyone is always *honored*."

Looking caught between amusement and embarrassment, the Prime Minister said in a conciliatory tone, "As you can likely tell, our matter is not urgent, though needed all the same. We will make preparations for a banquet in your honor this evening and a more proper welcome. We were not entirely sure you would arrive, given the number of kingdoms whose needs have waited while you were absent. We are thrilled that you have returned, both for our small matter and all the great ones in your future."

"Fine speech," King Varrun said with sarcasm. "If that's what it takes to earn power, then I'm glad I was born into mine and am spared the humiliation." He turned to a fidgeting man who was dressed in blue and green, the symbol of a bird of prey on his breast. He snapped, "Oh, stop shuffling your feet. It's like you have to pee or something. Show some dignity. And do it elsewhere. Othor take our guests and our restless friend away to tell them what is expected."

Prime Minister Othor bowed. "Yes, Your Majesty."

The fidgeting man bowed and said, "Forgive me, Your Majesty. I merely share your excitement."

The king snorted. "Well, *Your Majesty*," he sneered, "one day you'll learn that being king means not being so polite about everything. Now get out. Of my castle, and my kingdom. I have long looked forward to your departure from both."

Anna cocked an eyebrow. Was King Varrun just being snide or was this other man another king? He didn't wear a crown, but then she wasn't sure how that worked. It wasn't like royalty always wore one. She was glad to be leaving the curmudgeon's presence and didn't want to speak with him personally.

"Lords and ladies," began a smiling Othor, "please accompany me."

They filed out of the room behind him, several of the nobles coming along but the rest remaining behind. Passing through a short hall, they turned into a meeting room with a large oval table surrounded by high-cushioned chairs, a large map spread across it. Several youths were hastily laying out plates and goblets. Another stood ready to help beside a small table filled with pastries and crystal decanters, each filled with different color liquids. Anna wondered what time of day it was, but saw the sunlight coming in at an angle that suggested either mid-morning or late afternoon. They needed a list of things to ask about every time they arrived somewhere. As if expecting that, one young girl curtsied and handed her a scroll, presumably with gods in it.

They were shown to their places as the door closed, and everyone remained standing as Prime Minister Othor looked at them apologetically from across the table. "The king is used to speaking his mind, as is his right. Ironically, it is here without him that we can do the same. He is a good man but still smarting from our change decades ago into a constitutional monarchy where he no longer has the power he once held. And he quite chafes at all displays of ceremony. It is all worsened because he has been host for some years now to an absolute monarch, as he was once, but he enjoys pointing out that he, at least, still has a kingdom to rule over."

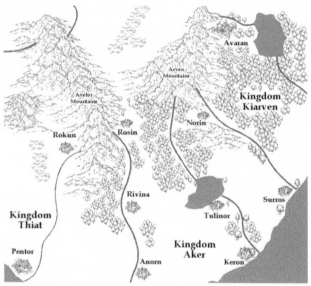

Map of Kingdom of Aker, on Planet Rovell

Othor turned to the man who had been fidgeting earlier. He was no older than them, tall, well-built, and confident. He wore a waist-length cloak similar to Othor but of different colors and style, being more ostentatious. His tailored tunic was embroidered, and he wore multiple rings on each hand along with a ceremonial dagger on one hip. Something about his brows and intelligent black eyes reminded Anna of a hawk, like the symbol on his breast. The pointed jaw and thin nose helped, as did the air of proud regality that shone from his bearing and mannerisms. And yet he seemed somehow uncomfortable, as if out of place or unsure what level of authority he held.

"Ellorians," began the Prime Minister, "this is His Majesty, King Sondin of Kingdom Aker. It is at his behest that we have summoned you, and as the quest is his, I will leave to him to lead our discussion."

King Sondin smiled graciously and with more genuineness than anyone so far. "I am so very grateful that you have come. Please be seated and be comfortable." Everyone did as he asked before he gestured to the young woman in the seat beside him. "This is my sister, Princess Miara. We have other members of our family here in Thiat, which has been gracious enough to host us for several years, but we're hoping you can put an end to the need for this."

As a servant put a plate of pastries before him, Eric asked, "What do you need us to do? Your Majesty."

The king waved that off. "We can be informal here in this room. I need you to restore us to our rightful place in Aker. I must assume the throne."

The champions exchanged a glance and Anna asked, "May I ask, why are you not there now?"

He gestured for goblets to be filled and indicated the map on the table. "This explanation will be thirsty work, but let us begin. Here we are in Thiat, across the Pumian River to the west. Beyond it, all this land you see is the Kingdom of Aker, a human power, though we have fair numbers of halfings, some elves, and a few dwarves. The river is our western border with Thiat, down to the ocean in the south, north to the mountains, and to near the eastern forests. That is where the dark elf Kingdom of Kiarven stands to our northeast. Years ago, the dark elf king broke a longstanding peace treaty and attacked Aker. I am sad to say we lost the unexpected war, and now all of Aker stands under dark elf control. However, we are still considered sovereign. No one recognizes Kiarven's claim to our lands."

Anna wasn't sure what that meant but suspected Eriana would be expected to, so she chose her words carefully. "This can be different across worlds, so we want to be sure we understand. Are you saying you are still seen as the King of Aker?"

King Sondin nodded. "I was a prince. My father, the king, died a month ago here in Thiat, and I have since become king."

"I am sorry for your loss. May I ask how it happened?"

"A tragic accident."

A petulant Princess Miara added, "He never should've been on a horse at his age, but I, for one, am glad it happened. Now perhaps we can go home." She had sorrowful brown eyes and a dreamy quality about her, as if she entertained romantic fantasies that had recently suffered a blow. Her freckles accentuated her youth, as did the braided hairstyle that exposed her round face and its remaining baby fat. She might have barely been twenty and gave the impression of impetuous emotion, whether born of immaturity, status, or frustration. Anna sensed the princess was restraining herself while silent, but then she spoke and said things she should not have, which she seemed to realize and then find herself caught between embarrassment and defiance about it.

"To an answer your question," began the king, laying a gentle hand on his sister's arm, which she pulled away, "other kingdoms must recognize sovereignty. While Kiarven is long recognized, their possession of Aker is not. We have found our kingdom to be contested territory, but there are no kingdoms who recognize Kiarven's claimed right to Aker. It is still seen as Aker, and I am the rightful king, living here in absentia and unable to return to my people, or to free them. As for my sister's remarks, our father wanted us to return but did not see it as possible. He has been content to wait for an opportunity, but my sister and I were more adamant about creating such a chance, which is why we have summoned you now that I am king. We should not wait longer to restore peace due to the conditions in which our people continue to suffer."

Fingering the food, Eric asked, "The dark elves are not peaceful rulers, I assume."

"Not to humans, no. They have plundered what they can of Aker. Our people have been enslaved. Terror rules them. It is not safe for any but dark elves to live there. Other powers have pledged their aid, including Thiat, in exchange for the peace and stability that comes with the restoration. There are trading and other issues that have arisen since the dark elf incursion. Others would also like this to stop."

Anna sipped at her drink to be polite. It was a little early for wine. Or maybe it wasn't. What time was it? "Does that mean you have an army?"

"No longer does Aker have one. But a force of others will drive the dark elves back. They await word from me and have recently begun more serious preparations now that I am king. I intend to invade."

Ryan asked, "What do these other powers get in return? What is to stop them from assuming control?"

King Sondin sighed. "I have conceded power. Kingdom Aker will no longer be an absolute monarchy, but a constitutional one with a Prime Minister as head of state. This is believed to give more governance to the people. I must admit that they have earned it after what they have been through."

"Why do these other powers want this?" Ryan asked before biting into a cream-filled treat.

Anna wasn't sure if they should munch on things to be polite or avoid it, since their hosts weren't eating, but once Ryan had done this, the princess nibbled on something. Were they waiting? She really wanted to understand protocol to avoid mistakes. Did Ryan know, or was he just clueless?

"Thiat has such a government. Nearby lands are similar or a democracy. We have been the remaining absolute monarchy, aside from Kiarven. Call it political vision. They would like to share one with us. Absolute monarchies are a dying breed in this region of Eridos."

The knight asked, "Are you waiting for us to do something before your invasion?"

King Sondin nodded. "I would prefer you to succeed first, but the assault happens regardless. When Kiarven conquered our lands, they put to death many of our royal family. Others fled here, but the rest were captured and remain prisoners. We are not sure of their whereabouts. I believe this to be on purpose. The dark elves use them to keep us from acting. We have long suspected this and recent events have proven it true."

"What do you mean?"

"A previous attempt at summoning you from the Quest Ring, that time in Aker, failed. We received the head of the Duke of Surros, my uncle, shortly thereafter."

Anna's heart had been sinking on hearing all of this because it sounded like they could be here for weeks, if not months. How do you restore an exiled king quickly? You didn't. She leaned forward. "You will risk the lives of the royal family?"

"No more than necessary. That is why you are here."

Eric asked, "What exactly is it you want us to do?"

"The quest is to restore us to power. How you achieve this is your decision. But my desire is for you to destroy the dark elf leadership so that they are more easily defeated. This would be one of two things, preferably both. Prince Kammer of the dark elves must be removed from power in Aker. He is the eldest son of King Erods and a ruthless tyrant like his father, who we would also like re-moved from power in Kiarven."

Trying to find a middle ground between being disap-proving—of a king!—and polite, Anna asked, "Do you mean killing them?"

King Sondin pursed his lips. "As a king, I would not lightly condone the assassination of another sovereign."

"And we are not assassins," Eric observed coolly, and Anna tried not to look too approvingly at him. She would thank him for that later. Eric as Andier was the one who could get away with saying things like that to a king. Odd-ly, it was Eric's personality to do that very thing.

"Of course. But you have a long history of, well, stop-ping hateful regimes from continuing to inflict harm on a large scale. And from my understanding, this is often done by removing the leadership responsible. You need not kill King Erods or the prince. We would settle for capturing them, and a trial in either Akers or Thiat, where they can be made to answer for their war crimes. If the penalty is death, then so be it, but we do not seek their death."

"Speak for yourself," interrupted Miara.

"Sister..."

"No! They must hear this." Impassioned, she leaned toward Anna, appealing to the only other woman present. "My Gian was the one who tried to summon you. He did it for me. For us. We were to be... He went to Aker, to the Quest Ring. He was a wizard, a skilled one, and brave. We don't know what happened. All we know..." She turned angry eyes on her brother. "All we know is that it was not only our uncle's head that was returned to us!"

A moment of tense silence followed, Anna watching the princess with genuine sympathy. The girl's accusing glare at her brother hardly softened when looking else-where around the room. She clearly wanted a reaction from someone else, so Anna gave her one meant to calm her as her brother hid behind his goblet.

"I'm so sorry. That was very brave of him."

The Prime Minister spoke with some compassion as he observed, "Gian was a wizard of Thiat. He did not have the blessing of either king to reach the other Quest Ring and summon you. His action took place days after King Sondin was crowned. Discussions about the invasion and the need to somehow recover the royal family were underway when Gian took matters into his own hands. We assume for love. That can account for his... foolishness."

"Speak no evil of the dead!" Princess Miara demanded, eyes ablaze.

"I meant no disrespect."

Hoping to change the subject away from ones that upset the princess, Anna asked, "Why does Kiarven claim a right to Aker? Simply because they now occupy it?"

King Sondin lowered his goblet. "No. Many thousands of years ago, the forest spread to the river that borders Aker and Thiat, and that land belonged to them, so they say. We do not doubt it. There are still sometimes ancient buildings or relics of dark elf origin discovered within our borders. Kiarven extended beyond the river into Thiat, possibly all the way to the sea, and they are believed to want this territory back as well. King Varrun is unconcerned about this threat, however, as the dark elves have made no further moves. I suspect that they realize they will meet greater resistance now that multiple lands are on heightened alert regarding their activities. Also, while Aker still has forest, Thiat is less suited to their liking. I understand that not all dark elves have an interest in these lands anymore, and in fact, we are hoping a defeat will further sour them on the idea."

Eric asked put his own goblet down and asked, "These dark elves prefer the trees like all elves, I assume. How widespread are they?

"Not very. Before the war, they were in their lands, occasionally seen elsewhere in tiny groups. They cause distrust. Since the attack, they have largely withdrawn from all such places, so the conquest of Aker has increased their territory and yet shrunk how welcome they are elsewhere. We believe many among them are not happy about this and do not support further expansion or even holding on to Aker."

"And you believe removing the king and his son will cause a retreat?"

"That is our hope. If we are wrong, your quest is still done and you can return."

"The dark elf king is in Kiarven?"

The king replied, "We are not sure, as his whereabouts change, but yes. He is the lesser priority. You must eliminate Prince Kammer. He is in Aker at the capitol, Rivina."

Dreading the answer, Anna asked, "How far is that?"

"From here it is nearly a week by horseback, but with Soliander's powers, you should be able to cast yourselves there."

Anna stifled a frown. Matt didn't know how to do that. How were they to explain that? The idea frightened her anyway, unless he had a lot of practice. What if they showed up inside a wall? Instant death. Were there any safeguards against that? She had to admit, if Matt could master that spell, it would save them all sorts of time. Maybe it was time to practice, like casting himself ten feet away. Or did the distance not change how hard it was?

Eric asked, "Do you have a plan in mind for how we can reach and deal with the prince?"

The king nodded and talked turned to details on city layouts and suspected locations of royal prisoners. What stood out to Anna was the guesswork. They had few solid leads on where anyone might be, and she knew her friends were thinking the same thing. So did their hosts. Princess Miara excused herself in irritation early on, and the champions tried to be polite with King Sondin and Prime Minister Othor, who finally admitted that they only had rough ideas because they had felt certain that the champions would need to devise their own plans based on the information provided. This was true and Eric more than Ryan took the lead in assuring them they were right and not to worry. But he did say they really need to gather more information first. They agreed to provide various maps or anything or anyone else who could help give ideas. After several hours of this, they were shown to a suite of rooms and told what time they would be escorted to dinner.

Finally, they were alone together, ornate white couches and divans embroidered in elegant finery, numerous mirrors on the walls, thick curtains open to let the sunlight in onto the hardwood floors. The place reminded her of pictures of palaces in France. The sitting room had three suites adjoining them. But they would look it all over later. Right now, they all converged on Anna.

Eric asked her, "Okay, you seem fine, but are you absolutely sure?"

She put a hand on his shoulder. "Yes. I feel normal. Really, it's like a miracle, what the Quest Rings can do. I'm very grateful. Jack could only tell me a little about your talks with Eriana. I really need to get caught up. And read this scroll to find a god. Then we need a plan because these people don't have one."

"I know," he admitted, turning to sit in a chair that he seemed to think was uncomfortable from the way he kept repositioning himself. "One thing Eriana told us that you need to know is about your amulet. You can use it to find a god more easily. We didn't quite get into how. While the scroll and all of that will help, this is how she did it quickly, especially if that kind of info wasn't available."

"Yeah," said Matt, "like the last time we saw a dark elf. As they were talking, I was wondering if by some miracle that was the same guy. You know, that wizard who summoned us and was killed, and we went home with all of those goblins and ogres trying to get to us."

"And there was that dark elf I hit with a knife," he Eric.

"We never learned his name," admitted Anna, "or what the quest was."

Ryan suggested, "Maybe we should get a description. But I don't suppose it matters."

"It could," said Eric, turning to Matt. "Can one Quest Ring teleport us to another?"

The wizard cocked an eyebrow. "Well, that's an interesting idea. We could get to this city quickly if so, and it's the same place, or where we need to reach. It would save time at least."

Eric spread his hands. "Anything pop into your head from Soliander's memories when I said that?"

Matt thought for a second and shook his head. "No."

"Well," began Ryan, taking off his armor, "let's catch up with Anna here, get ready for this banquet, and then meet with whoever else we can talk to for ideas, either tonight or tomorrow morning. As we meet people tonight, grill them for info. You never know what someone might know."

Eric nodded. "I'd kind of like to talk to some regular guardsmen who've been to Aker. They often know stuff, but keep their mouths shut around official people like kings. Maybe you and I can hit some taverns tonight, dressed like normal guys."

"Yeah, I'm up for that."

Anna said, "That will give me and Matt time to prepare in other ways. Spells and gods."

With that decided, they changed into what Eric called "off duty" clothes that were brought to them, and which were more comfortable for everyone but Anna, who needed the help of a maid to get into a gown. It was more that she didn't understand how to do it than that it was too complicated.

She listened with great interest to everything Eriana had told them, but it was overwhelming after the details about the quest. Information overload had her asking for the simple versions, and they covered the highlights just before someone arrived to escort them to dinner. She could hear an orchestra long before they rounded a corner to find a crowd of well-wishers applauding their arrival, parting to let them into a grand hall that stood two stories high, empty balconies, chairs, and golden curtains above. Rows of tables and chairs had been laid out on the hardwood floor, where it didn't seem like any dancing was expected, to her relief. Anna almost wanted to add dancing lessons to her list of items to study on Earth, though she suspected it wouldn't help much. The dances had so far been unfamiliar, but then maybe that was normal. The champions couldn't be expected to know *everything*.

At the far end stood more steps to another pair of thrones that sat empty, and just before it lay what she assumed was the royal table. Prime Minister Othor indicated they would be seated there, two of them on each side of the king, who they had learned was a widower with an eye out for a new bride. Others in the room mingled with them as the group tried to stay close together, fielding questions, turning away amorous advances, and otherwise trying to be cordial. They had arrived before either royal, with King Sondin announced first before King Thiat joined them and the festivities began. Red wines, pheasant, boar, brown rice and steamed vegetables made the rounds along with several pies. Anna wondered if the Quest Ring could reduce the caloric content of what she ate when sending her home again, but she decided that eating sparingly was the elegant approach. Fortunately, their hosts weren't barbarians who expected them to belch to show approval.

During dinner, she listened to the King of Thiat complain about one thing or another, but sensed he wasn't as disagreeable as his first impression. He just seemed to find no real joy in life. She hoped to talk more to Princess Miara, who appeared sullen, whether about the recent death of her wizard lover or something else. Anna thought the girl might be trouble because she just acted intent on throwing a wrench into everything. It might have been better were she not around too much as planning went underway.

After dinner, the tables were cleared but not removed, with so many guests coming around to talk to each of the Ellorian Champions that a line had formed. They mingled as they could, with Anna discussing the gods of Eridos with those who held an interest in them. She hadn't tried to use the Corethian Amulet to contact one yet but planned to after returning to their rooms.

As Anna stood listening to a married couple, her eyes fell on Eric, who stood chatting with two noblemen. He was good at this sort of schmoozing, even if he pretended to not like small talk. Well, he didn't, as he liked to get to the point and for others to do the same, but maybe these alien worlds fascinated him. He certainly enjoyed trying to get information from people, and they sorely needed some. Hopefully, the outing he and Ryan would do tonight would help give them ideas because she really did not know how they were going to do this quest. Sneaking into an entire kingdom overrun with dark elves was far worse than their other adventures because the enemy was everywhere. Eric needed to find a plan.

He saw Eric's eyes go to a balcony and his face become serious. Following his gaze, she saw a curtain moving as if someone had just been behind it. She looked back to Eric to see that he was gone, and her eyes darted around the room, just catching sight of him stepping through the exit. She hurried after him, not liking the idea of getting separated, but when she reached the hall, he was gone. A concerned Ryan joined her, then Matt, but they saw no sign of the rogue.

Eric had disappeared.

CHAPTER FOURTEEN

THE PRINCE OF KIARVEN

Aside from no one having been on the second-floor balcony all night, something hadn't seemed right to Eric about the figure peeking out from behind a curtain. The movement had caught his attention, and then the dark skin and a hint of white hair made the words "dark elf" jump into his mind. The moment he'd seen the man, the guy turned away. Eric had seen stairs to that floor on the way here and left from the ballroom to the steps. He saw no one else as he climbed his way to the top, where he found several doors leading toward the ballroom and a hall that presumably led to the other side. He heard a door close that way and dashed after the sound on light feet. The first door he found led away from the ballroom, the sound of faint footsteps beckoning him to follow. Did the man know he pursued? Maybe Eric should have gotten others to come with him, but it was too late now.

He crept after and regretted that he didn't have Andier's leather armor on for the dozen throwing knives he could hide within it, and the rope belt that might help him bind someone if needed. Feeling exposed made him count on stealth and his hand-to-hand fighting if it arose. He still wore the Trinity Ring if he got hurt, but he always wondered how close to death he could get and it still save him. He just didn't want to find out.

Eric brushed another door open as he listened for sounds within, seeing dancing light from what he assumed was a torch he didn't see yet. He suspected no other escape existed. If he'd trapped someone, this would turn into a fight. He shoved the door wide and crouch, and as he did, he heard nothing fly over his head to strike the wall. But he saw someone standing to one side far against the wall.

"Andier of Roir," said the figure in elvish, "I am glad you came, and I mean you no harm, even after what happened the last time we met."

The room suddenly brightened as the figure touched another torch to the one on the wall. The figure remained still and Eric rose to his full height, casting one look back at the way he'd come. They appeared to be alone, and he stepped into the room for a better look. He had been right about the race, the dark elf before him wearing black plate mail with silver insignias on it. The black skin and white hair made him wonder how this one had gotten so far inside the castle, given that one look at him would have alerted the guards. It gave Eric even more reason to be suspicious. But recognizing the man, partly from the scar on one cheek, was what really put him on alert.

"You're the one who tried to kill us at the Quest Ring with the goblins and ogres."

The dark elf nodded. "Regrettable, but necessary."

Eric wanted to test his opponent before any blows and said, "I could say the same about killing you now."

From his smile, the dark elf seemed genuinely amused. "I did not come here to die or threaten others with death."

"Then why are you here?"

"For peace."

"Explain."

"I would rather do so to both King Sondin and King Varrun as well as you and your companions at once, but I understand you must agree to get me an audience. It is why I sought you out."

That surprised Eric. "You sought–" He cursed himself. This was a trap. He had been lured here. He needed to be smarter about that from now on. "Why don't you give me the short version."

"It is my intention to remove my king," the elf began. "I will take his place, withdrawing elves from Aker to Kiarven and brokering a peace between the kingdoms. In exchange for the help of the Ellorian Champions in achieving this, I will also release the royal prisoners. There is no need for the war that is brewing."

Now the elf had his attention. Maybe this was the guy who had information they needed to complete this quest, but there was at least one problem with this, aside from a serious trust issue, of course. "You do not have the authority to make such a deal."

The elf nodded. "And yet I can make it happen."

"Who are you?"

"Prince Dravo of the House of Alrond, former general of Kiarven. Some recognize my lineage. Others do not, for I am in exile."

Well, that was interesting, Eric thought. "And why are you in exile?"

"There are those who believe the elves should reclaim territory that was once ours. The king is among these. I do not, nor do many of my kin, and they made an example of me for being outspoken about this."

Eric wasn't prepared to take a single comment at face value. If this dark elf was going to lie, he would have to do it extensively and immediately. "Why didn't they just kill you?"

He frowned. "His son Prince Kammer wanted this, but I am royalty, or I was until they stripped me of my titles and land. The king spared me, to humiliate me, I believe."

"And yet you would kill him," Eric interrupted, trying to throw him off balance. He glanced back into the hallway again, since he still stood in the doorway and someone could see him.

Prince Dravo cocked an eyebrow. "I did not say I would kill him, though it is likely necessary. They thought they would suitably demean me to live among others not of my kind, but they underestimated me. I command a considerable force."

"Of goblins and ogres?"

"Among others. I had thought to use them to strike at the king, but then they invaded Aker. Since then I have been waiting for a good opportunity and often working beside the same elven forces I used to command. Many are still secretly loyal to me, I have learned. This does not surprise me."

"You are not exiled from Aker?"

"I was exiled from Kiarven before the conquest of Aker. Now that they claim Aker as theirs, some say my banishment should extend through it as well. Prince Kammer certainly wants this, but the king appears to find it amusing that I lead a band of brutes, as he calls it. He allows me to remain."

Smirking, Eric said, "So you just want to be king? Is that it?"

"No. That is a means to an end. I want the elves to withdraw to Kiarven and be done with these lands. We do not need them. Many of us don't want them, but the king wants to reclaim something lost a thousand years ago. He has done great harm to elven kind, and I want it to end."

Eric suspected something and had to ask, "Is there more to this? You must want your old life back, or family, or something."

"Of course I do. That life is gone, but my family still suffers on my behalf. This, too, must end."

Eric had a question that he expected would get a pre-pared answer, as the dark elf had to know it was coming. He already felt distrustful of an answer he hadn't even sought yet. "You seek my help now, and yet you tried to kill me just a week ago."

Dravo acknowledged this with a nod. "Things have changed."

"How so?"

"I was in Aker, the city Rivina, when we received word of that wizard trying to reach the Quest Ring at Castle Rivina to summon you. Prince Kammer ordered me to find and kill him, so I did. I had no choice but to try the same with you. You would have killed me and nearly did, so you cannot judge me for the attempt on your life."

Eric frowned. The guy had a good point, not that he wanted to admit it. In fact, throwing the knife at Dravo hadn't been necessary. Should he apologize? Instead, he wondered if he could provoke the calm dark elf. "How was the knife in your chest?"

Dravo smirked. "Painful, but I've felt worse. An elixir resolved the matter soon. I do not begrudge you."

Eric doubted that. He suspected something else had changed but wasn't going to suggest it, because it would only help the dark elf lie, if that's what he was doing. "Why didn't we have this conversation then?"

"Goblins and ogres have no patience for such a talk, so it would have gone poorly even had I wanted it. But more has changed. After my king learned I had killed the wizard and undone your summoning, he was pleased. He sum-moned me and my troops to Kiarven, the first time I have been there in the open since my banishment."

Something caught Eric's attention. "You've been there, but not where you could be seen?"

Dravo smiled, red eyes cold. "Several times, usually alone."

"Why did you go?"

"To plan a way to reach the king. To learn who my friends were. To remain aware of changes in the city. Anything to help my eventual return."

Eric couldn't really disagree with those reasons and didn't much care to. That the dark elf could get into somewhere he wasn't welcome was quite apparent, or they would not have been having this conversation. He glanced into the hall and back again. "What did the king want with you?"

"We were discussing how else I might be useful, given the need of more elves with my skills in military leadership. He intends to extend his conquest of Aker to Thiat, though this is not for some time. I soon learned that a new attempt at summoning you would take place, this time here. I came for your help."

"Not revenge?"

"I seek an alliance between kingdoms, brokered with your help."

"Why would we trust you?"

"I would prefer to reveal this to the kings. Have you heard enough to bring me to them? I, of course, will be disarmed, even bound if you like."

"I'm certain they would insist on it."

"We have an agreement?"

Eric sighed. He couldn't see why not, but who knew what the prince might be planning? He didn't like it, but it also wasn't his decision to turn him away. Only the kings should do that. "Yes, I will take you."

The dark elf nodded. "Thank you. One last thing. I am not alone." Dravo didn't pause long, maybe on account of Eric's eyes quickly scanning the room. "I have brought someone I do not want harmed. While you have a reputation for cunning, you also have one for honor. Will you do your part to safeguard her? We will both surrender."

Eric held his gaze for a moment, gauging him and sensing that if he seemed insincere, the opportunity would be lost. He nodded. "Who is she? *Where* is she?"

"My sister." He raised his voice and spoke in elvish, looking to one side. "Liera, please come."

Eric immediately noticed two doors he hadn't seen. One of them opened slowly to reveal another dark elf, this one wearing a dark gray, slender, ankle-length dress fastened with a gold belt. Two clips held straight golden hair back from her heart-shaped face. Her eyes seemed wary but inquisitive as she looked between Andier and Dravo, who gestured for her to step out of the small dressing room she occupied. She came to a stop nearer her brother.

After a moment of silence, Eric bowed his head at her and said, "Your Highness."

She flashed a wary smile. "Lord Andier. We have come at significant risk to ourselves. Our faith in humans is not strong, but you and the Ellorians are unlike most. We are trusting you with our lives."

Eric took a deep breath and let it out. He understood not being able to trust those you were with. "If you both behave, I promise no harm will come to you. Now I need to bind both of you."

Dravo removed his sword and a few knives from where they were hidden on himself. He came forward slowly as Eric took a sash from a drape and used it to bind the elf, who was slightly taller than him. He did the same to Liera. With them walking before him, Eric carrying Dravo's weapons, they made their way toward the balconies and then down the stairs, where they were seen at once, a shout going out and guards rushing in. Eric made them stand back as more important people arrived, including the Prime Minister, King Sondin, and Ryan, Matt, and Anna.

"Everyone remain calm, please," began Eric, doing his best impersonation of the commanding presence Ryan used as Lord Korrin. "This is Prince Dravo and Princess Liera of Kiarven. They voluntarily surrendered and seek an audience with both kings. I suggest that this be granted at once, with only those who must be there present. King Sondin, I would strongly recommend against Princess Miara being there." If the princess learned that the dark elf who had her wizard lover killed was here, this conversation wouldn't go smoothly.

The king nodded and turned an inquisitive eyebrow toward the Prime Minister, who said, "All of you present keep quiet about this. Take them to the throne room, which is to be sealed. Someone get His Majesty."

People began scurrying in various directions as the dark elves followed the Prime Minister with Eric and the others bringing up the rear, his friends giving him looks of frustration, curiosity, and respect. They soon waited for King Varrun, who waddled in looking irritable and slightly drunk. Eric suspected this conversation would go better without him. Princess Miara was fortunately not present. As King Varrun has no real authority, all of it being with Prime Minister Othor, he wasn't really needed, but keeping him informed was wise. He took a seat on the throne and turned to those standing before him as if impatient, when they were the ones who had just spent ten minutes waiting for him. The two dark elves stood in front beside Eric, his friends off to one side to watch the faces of the guests.

Eric summed up the previous conversation with Prince Dravo, and when finished, it prompted King Sondin to remark, "Beware of dark elves who talk of peace."

"We could say the same of humans, Your Majesty," replied Dravo. "I was not part of the forces that conquered your kingdom."

"No, but you are there keeping it under elven control."

"It was that or come to Thiat, and I'm sure you wouldn't want to be responsible for my presence here." He smiled as if trying to show he wasn't serious.

"Enough bickering," snapped King Varrun. "We have an elf who would be king, and king who has no kingdom, and a king who has no power. Why not enter into an agreement? It is as worthless as an empty wine goblet." He belched for emphasis and held out his empty cup for a page boy to refill.

"With apologies, Your Majesty," began Othor, "but I have the authority, as does King Sondin. But any agreement should be invalid until and unless Prince Dravo is successful. This means assuming the throne of Kiarven, releasing the Aker prisoners, and withdrawing troops at once."

Eric didn't particularly like King Varrun, but his bluntness could be useful. The king saw past bullshit with ease. Maybe he was more useful than expected. "There are a few more items we need to discuss. For starters, how did he and the princess get here?"

As if expecting that, Prince Dravo conceded, "There is an old portal deep beneath this city," he began, the statement causing a murmur of alarm from the guards present. "These lands once belonged to my kin, and what you likely do not remember, as your lives are far shorter, is that this city is built over the ruins of several previous cities, most of them human, but the oldest is elven."

"And how do you come to know such a thing, about this portal?" asked a snide King Varrun. "You just happen to know this now?"

"I have been aware for decades, Your Majesty, but I believe few know of it, or remember, or consider the knowledge useful, because the other side of the portal is in an abandoned area of Avaran in Kiarven. There has been little reason to use it, though I have before my banishment, mostly out of curiosity. It is how I knew the layout of this palace and could get in undetected."

"We need to find this portal and destroy it," King Varrun suggested, glaring. He seemed ready to say more when the dark elf spoke.

"On the contrary, Your Majesty," began Prince Dravo, "is it important to this mission. The Ellorians and I can travel to Kiarven and use this to both rescue the hostages and deal with King Erods."

King Varrun snorted. "Fine. *Then* we will destroy it."

"As you wish, but I think it would be more beneficial to guard it on both ends and use it to maintain our peaceful relations."

King Varrun frowned and then took a long draught from his goblet.

"What of your sister?" asked King Sondin, eyeing her with what Eric thought was appreciation. His eyes had returned to her again and again. "Why is Princess Liera here?"

The prince began, "I did not expect you to trust me, so—"

"Wise decision," interrupted King Varrun, leaning forward for emphasis.

"So I have brought her as a hostage."

Liera swiftly turned to him. "Brother!"

Eric heard genuine shock in her voice and wondered what Dravo had told her about the reason for her presence. That he had lied to her was apparent. How were they to trust him? Then he realized that maybe she would have been in danger in Kiarven had he left her and been discovered. He wasn't going to speculate about that aloud again to avoid handing the dark elf lies.

"Fear not, dear sister."

"How can you say that?"

"Andier has promised your safety." His gaze went to Eric, who nodded.

"No harm is to come to Princess Liera," announced Ryan in a commanding voice, taking his cue. Eric met his gaze in approval. People expected more honor from Lord Korrin, the Pride of Andor, than Andier, the Silver-Tongued Rogue. "She is under the protection of the Ellorian Champions."

King Varrun sighed. "Fine. We will accept your *hostage*."

"With respect, Your Majesty," began Prince Dravo, turning to King Sondin, "she is a hostage for Kingdom Aker, not Thiat."

King Sondin arched an eyebrow but nodded. "All disputes are between Aker and Kiarven. We must rebuild that relationship. What do we gain from having this hostage?"

"Hopefully some trust, Your Majesty. My sister is very important to me. I would not risk her safety. I need the Ellorians to accompany me to deal with my king or all of this is for nothing."

Anna spoke up. "He is trying to assure us that this is not a trap."

Dravo nodded to her as Eric frowned about her helping the prince's story be convincing. He might have to have a talk with her about making that sort of remark. Dravo met her gaze and said, "The Lady Eriana is correct."

"I don't feel reassured," Matt remarked, scowling. "You tried to kill us."

The prince looked him in the eye. "And you tried to kill me and killed many of my men. And this has brought us the opportunity we now have."

"What is your plan, exactly?" Eric asked, having already been over Matt's argument with him. "We go with you through this portal to Kiarven. And then what?"

"I do not need your help in reaching King Erods, and I could have killed him before now, but it would have cost me my life and been pointless. I can get to him alone but am then defenseless against all those loyal to him. I cannot possibly fight them off alone. What I need from you is protection until my forces can reach me."

"Where are they?"

"My forces are outside Avaran, where King Erods is. He summoned me to discuss a role I might play in further conquest. Once I am in power and call them to me, and I have their protection, you can leave back through the portal to here."

Eric said, "I assume they will meet resistance getting from where they are to you."

Prince Dravo turned to Matt. "I hope Soliander will resolve this. Perhaps an illusion to make the guards believe it is at the request of King Erods rather than myself."

Matt seemed to consider that. "I might be able to do that."

"All of my men cannot get to me without arousing suspicion, so I will need the most important of them. There are also dark elves loyal to me there, and I can summon them as well."

Eric surmised aloud, "You would have our help to take the throne first, then freeing the hostages?"

"Yes, because once I am king, I can order their freedom. If we free the hostages first, we must break into the prison, free them, get them through the portal, and then return to deal with the king. It will be impossible to reach him by then."

"How many hostages are we talking about?"

"Twenty-three."

"I don't like it," said Anna, her arms crossed. "We would find ourselves surrounded by the dark elves. What's stopping us from becoming four new hostages?"

"Good question," agreed Matt, frowning.

"My sister," Prince Dravo said.

"Sorry, but that's not enough," replied Anna. "We are considered a great prize in many places, and there are many who would think nothing of trading in a hostage for the Ellorian Champions. Dark elves do not have a good reputation for honor. For all we know, you are willing to sacrifice your sister for us."

"She's right," Eric agreed. "I want the hostages freed first. This way, even if we fail in dealing with King Erods, we have allowed the armies who want to reclaim Aker the opportunity to do so without fear of the hostages being killed."

Ryan observed, "Yeah, because getting you the throne only helps you with your goal. Our quest is to restore King Sondin in Aker, not a dark elf to the throne of Kiarven."

Prince Dravo didn't look pleased. "My price for freeing the hostages is helping me take the throne."

Eric stated, "It will have to be in the order we choose. Do you accept?"

The dark elf sighed and considered this. Eric could tell he was thinking, hopefully how it could be achieved, not how to betray them. Not for the first time, he wondered about that *Mind Trust* spell of Soliander's. Maybe now was a good time to use it. Was it wrong considering that being deceived might cost them their lives? Was it better to be honorable and dead or dishonorable and alive? He didn't know and wanted to ask their opinions about it.

Prince Dravo finally said, "I accept your terms. I propose we free the hostages tonight. No one checks on them when they are supposed to be asleep."

He was probably right. Eric observed, "We cannot remain on Eridos indefinitely. We need a faster way to restore King Sondin to Aker than letting troops slowly withdraw. I'm not saying your plan isn't sound, but your control of Kiarven or the army will not happen overnight. Would capturing King Erods, rather than killing him, make the forces capitulate more quickly? He would be a hostage of Aker or Thiat."

Prince Dravo considered and replied, "Yes, but we should do the same with his son, Prince Kammer. He is in control of Aker and the army. With both in custody and to be on trial for war crimes, change happens sooner."

Ryan asked, "So where is Prince Kammer? Somewhere in Aker? And how do we get him to Kiarven?"

After a moment, Prince Dravo smiled. "I think I know how."

CHAPTER FIFTEEN

KINGMAKERS

Anna said, "I don't agree with this. I will not be a part of it." She turned and strode out of the small meeting room.

Matt exchanged a knowing look with Eric but tried to not let on too much that this was what they wanted. Ryan went after her, his golden armor as quiet as ever as his feet thudded across the floor and out the door, which Eric closed behind him. This was a bonus, as the knight wasn't in on the plan either. It had been hours since the meeting with the kings, everyone having rested for their after-midnight mission to Kiarven. Now it was nearly time to go.

Now the wizard and rogue stood alone, the unrestrained Prince Dravo in a chair before them in the room's center, palms on his thighs and feet planted on the floor. The dark elf wore his sword once more. A podium stood near, with one of Soliander's spell books—the one with silver lettering on the black leather cover—spread open on it. Matt had already examined its pages in view of the others.

"Perhaps I erred in thinking you honorable," the dark elf remarked to Eric, who flashed an insincere smile.

"You heard our argument with Eriana, so you know what I think. Soliander, too. And we are asking your permission. There's a difference."

Dravo smirked. "I think that point was lost on the Lady Eriana."

"She also left before you agreed," observed Matt, pretending to look over the spell.

"I still have not agreed. It is not reassuring that the two most known for their honor have left in protest."

Eric observed, "Korrin only left to appeal to Eriana, not to protest."

"Ah, yes. Well, there's little sense in getting technical, I suppose."

"Listen," began Eric calmly, "you know time is short. While we appreciate the steps you've taken to gain our trust, I'm sure you understand it is not quite enough."

"I do not argue this. But what you propose is as invasive as the Lady Hope suggested. I am to be a king and yet you would have access to everything I know."

Eric remarked, "If you don't agree, you may not become a king at all, making your knowledge as useless as it is now."

Prince Dravo laughed. "Your silver tongue needs a little polish, my friend. Is there a way to limit what this spell probes?"

Matt said, "Not really. However, you can assist me by picturing the relevant subjects. The path to the portal below us here, how it works, what is on the other side, the prison where the hostages are, the place where the king is likely to be, and where your forces are outside the city. I will be able to tell if you are hiding something about it."

He wasn't sure if that was technically true. He had never cast the *Mind Trust* spell on anyone before and wasn't even sure how he would control what he saw. It was one reason he just said all of that, to get Dravo to help him without realizing it. A cooperative subject would likely make it easier the first time.

The thought made memories of Soliander doing it to other people besides him suddenly come to mind and he stood still for a moment, sorting through images, impressions, and feelings. The emotions were part of it, he now knew. This was how he could tell the subject was hiding something. Otherwise, getting what he wanted just seemed a question of searching through memories of events or time periods that were likely to produce them. The spell worked like putting a thought into someone's head, as if they were reminded of a subject Matt sought, unwittingly leading him right to it. Matt wondered if this knowledge would make it easier to resist someone doing it to him.

The idea gave him pause. He knew just how wrong this spell was, but that was why they wanted Dravo's cooperation. That, and making it easier on Matt. He and Eric had discussed the plan, which had included convincing Anna and maybe Ryan that they were going to do it whether or not the prince agreed. It was necessary. If Dravo agreed, they would not cast it, because the agreement would strongly suggest he wasn't hiding something. But if he refused, that likely meant the opposite, though there were plenty of reasons to say no. Still, a "yes" spoke volumes. The plan was Eric's, of course. Matt often wished he was half as wily as his friend.

"I have your promise," began Prince Dravo, staring into the wizard's eyes, "that you will seek only this?"

Matt stared back and tried to project reassurance, the dark elf's red eyes creeping him out a little. "You have my word. I seek nothing more. I won't have time for it anyway. The spell can last a long time, but I anticipate being done in just minutes, especially with your cooperation. You know we must do this raid on the prison tonight."

This was especially important because of Dravo himself. His absence might have already been noted, but according to him, he had left guidance for the trusted few who had been allowed into the city with him and were staying in his quarters. If anyone asked, the prince was entertaining a young woman and was not to be disturbed. Like the rest of his family, his sister had been kept close to the Avaran castle in a virtual imprisonment. Her accommodations had not been far from Dravo's. No one would look for her, in theory, but she was to be reported as unwell, if so.

Holding his gaze, Prince Dravo said, "I will accept."

Matt made a show of consulting the spell book one last time and approaching the dark elf, even putting the fingertips of one hand on his forehead. "Closing your eyes will help." Dravo complied and Matt stood still a few moments, looking to Eric, who nodded in satisfaction, so Matt stepped back. The elf opened his eyes in confusion.

"Thank you, Prince Dravo," said Eric. "We didn't need to actually cast it, though it would certainly help us. We only needed to trust you, and now we feel like we can."

Dravo turned to him with a pleased smile and direct gaze. "Well done, Andier. I trust you more for this as well, since you did not go through with it. I imagine the Lady Eriana was not aware of your ruse? I suspect she will forgive but not be as pleased as I."

"Our reputations have their advantages."

"Indeed."

When told of the ploy, Anna alternated between relief, exasperation, and acknowledgment that it was a brilliant idea. She seemed a little grumpy about it as the group made their way to the portal far below the city. They first left the castle with a score of guards accompanying them as an initial force to permanently guard the magic doorway—until or unless it was destroyed later. With over twenty prisoners expected to be coming back through it, several maids and healers were also coming. Dravo had reported that the dark elves kept most of the royals in poor conditions on purpose, and while they were alive, their needs were not exactly attended to. This included poor feeding, which had resulted in two sacks of food also being carried down to give the rescued more energy for the climb back to the surface. Two wizards, one of Thiat and one of Aker, were joining them, both under Matt's direction. The result was nearly forty people in the group.

The darkness provided little opportunity to see anything of the city as they walked across an empty square, where various seemingly temporary shacks stood, each closed up for the night, wooden signs indicating food or drink were sold there. Stone buildings that reminded him of an "old town" in Europe flanked the courtyard. He didn't see a moon. The night air smelled and felt like spring, making Matt wish he knew more about this world, from how many hours in a day there were, or days in a week, to which continent they were on. He knew from the map that they had seen that they were in the southern hemisphere. They needed to start asking about these things, but it was hard when more important details were thrust before them.

Prince Dravo led them a few blocks away through empty, narrow streets, the group moving quietly, but not enough to prevent curious citizens from sticking their heads out of windows to silently watch the procession go. A few saw the dark elf and cursed, one even throwing a piece of bread that missed. The group passed under a stone bridge between two hills, a doorway in the base of one, and this is where the elf led them, two guards remaining behind. Matt brought light forth from the staff, others bringing their burning torches, as they descended steps and into the cellar of a building. From there, a hidden door led into a roughly cut stone stairway leading down through earth and stone. It wasn't the most secure tunnel, but neither did it look like a collapse was imminent. Within minutes they had reached a level floor of dry earth, a puddle to one side of a room too small for all of them. Three hallways disappeared into darkness from it.

"The catacombs," remarked a guard.

"Yes," said Dravo. "The king may want to secure it more now that he knows it leads to a magic portal. This way."

They followed him through various branching corridors, through small empty rooms, and down flights of stairs, the air growing musty and colder than outside. Sometimes they passed a discarded item like broken pottery, an empty scabbard, and part of a skeleton, usually an animal but once a human. Matt suspected they were hundreds of feet below the surface and felt uncomfortable about finding his way back. Had the guards brought enough torches to light the way? Was someone marking the trail? They passed a sinkhole that had collapsed a wide area of earth to create a cavern, and here they had to climb over the fallen stones to reach a partially blocked stairway, which led to the buried dark elf city below it.

"No wonder no one knows it is here," remarked Ryan.

"There is little to see," observed the prince.

They followed him another ten minutes as they moved through crumbling rooms of what was obviously a long buried and abandoned settlement, the elegant designs apparent despite the age. Faded paint remained on walls and floors, carvings revealing they were in the elven city, whatever it had been called. They finally came to a wider room, the ceiling partially caved in to one side. The far wall had a carving of a doorway on it, with various symbols around it like a wide frame or border. Matt saw trees, stars, moons, castles, and a few animals he didn't recognize, but two silhouettes of elves stood out. He read the words carved around the door silently.

Here to the Land of Kiar this pathway leads
For elven kind or those in need.

Prince Dravo moved to stand before it as others kept their distance, but Matt joined him and spent a few moments learning the spell. It wasn't complicated, which was why a dark elf with limited magic talent like Dravo could perform it. The magic worked the same from this side or the other, and to ensure they could return even if something happened to the prince, Matt made sure the other two wizards also knew it before he cast the spell. The letters glowed green as the stone door faded and disappeared. Through it they saw bare earth with tufts of grass, a cascade of vines, and darkness that their torches pierced.

"We should go without light," said Dravo, Matt turned off his staff, others leaving torches behind.

The prince and wizard went first, Ryan, Eriana, and Eric following. A half dozen guards dressed for stealth came with them to assist the freed prisoners so that the Ellorians could fight if necessary and not have to worry about the hostages being led away while they did so.

The night air felt as warm as before when Matt stepped onto the earth. He moved to the thick, leafy vines obscuring anything beyond. He looked back at the portal as Prince Dravo spoke a few words and it closed, the soft green glow fading. They listened in silence but heard nothing, which didn't surprise Matt. The dark elf had explained their location in the cliff-side city of Avaran.

Only the royalty and those who served them likely knew of the ancient portal because it stood near an area reserved for them, which meant few others went there. But even the elves, who lived for hundreds of years on this world, didn't have memories that lasted forever. Overgrown and forgotten near a part of the royal enclave that had suffered a rockfall long ago, the portal hadn't been used in a thousand years. As he had told the champions, Prince Dravo only knew of it because he had long made a point of studying the defenses as one of the most strategic thinking generals of Kiarven. He had stumbled upon it. He had told no one what he'd found or of his explorations of the underground world on the other side under Thiat.

"Which way?" the wizard asked.

"Across the bridge, then left where the trail splits," answered the dark elf. "The prison is inside the mountain and reached via the town. With stealth, you, Andier, and I must lead, then the other wizards. Have your spells and wits about you."

"Yes." Matt had spent the last few hours memorizing them and raiding the local shops that catered to wizards. The two with them were among the more seasoned ones available, neither having any idea that they had far more experience in wizardry than Matt.

With the prince and rogue in the lead, Matt followed them out from behind the vines. The mountain's white stone loomed all around them in the moonless night. A mass of shattered rocks lay strewn to one side where they had fallen, some covered in vegetation, which grew untamed before them in what looked like an abandoned welcome area. An empty, cracked dais stood there, and beyond it, a curving stone bridge with small obelisks jutting from its railings. The earth fell away on either side.

Over the bridge, beyond the tall pines, rose one rear corner of the white-walled castle of Avaran, where King Erods likely slept right now. The castle was mostly below their position so that only the tallest towers were at eye level, but no lights twinkled in them. The odds of being seen were low, which was good, because the bridge was exposed. Beyond the castle, they saw some of the city, but very little. Pointed dark roofs topped white stone buildings, but they could see little else. They built Avaran along terraced cliffs so that it overlooked the forest valley below. Most of the mountain it lay on rose above their position.

As they crossed the bridge, Matt looked down into a rushing river far below. He wondered why they built the portal here where the destruction of the bridge would render reaching it difficult, but then maybe that answered his question. Anyone trying to invade from the portal's location could be more easily stopped. Stepping off the span found them on a stone path with grass overtaking it, trees all around and providing cover as the path quickly descended stone steps so that they were now level with the castle wall visible through the trees ahead. The path split, one heading right toward the royal grounds and another leading left and to the city. They headed that way, the castle on their right.

Matt and the other wizards cast a simple cantrip to mask any sounds they made, and the group crept along the underbrush off the path to keep any guards from looking down and seeing them. It didn't take long to reach the castle's front corner. The castle stood to the right, with more mountain and the river gorge to the left, for they built the structure in one corner of the available space. The settlement itself was ahead and to the right. They heard a waterfall tumbling down out of sight.

The path they weren't using was partially blocked by a crumbling wall, giving the impression that the way to where they stood had been walled off at some point and not maintained. The path curved around toward the front gates, where several buildings flanked a courtyard. Instead of heading there, they climbed over the debris and passed over the road. Then they hugged the rear wall of one such structure, edging their way down the steep rocks along the edge of the settlement. The hostages would never make it up this way, but they had a plan to use the streets by then.

They maneuvered past several buildings to reach the edge of a cliff. Matt gazed down and wished he could see better. Multiple terraces of buildings lay below toward the valley, none uniform in length, width, or vegetation, but even in the dark, a kind of loveliness was apparent.

"It is time," whispered Prince Dravo.

Matt knew what he meant and gestured for the other wizards to join him. He pulled a vial of cold liquid from a pocket in his robe, opened it, and whispered a spell. "Obscure all sound and light, a haze that blinds like night."

Then he began blowing across the bottle top. A mist formed in the air, slowly turning into fog. He made a fanning gesture with one arm and the fog drifted over and down the cliff face to seep into the city streets. He handed the bottle to the guard who would remain behind at this position, instructing him to continue blowing across the opening. The fog would spread on its own, rising and falling up and down the mountainside, growing thicker by the minute and appearing to come from the river gorge they had crossed. By the time the prisoners were in the open, seeing them would be far harder. The other wizards cast the same spell.

"Where exactly is the prison entrance?" Eric whispered.

Prince Dravo pointed to a location down one level from their position and a street over. "The one with the bell tower. The fog should reach it soon. We must be patient. Only the Ellorians and one wizard should come, so the other wizard can remain outside to assist. Once the fog has spread, the guardsmen we have brought should take positions where they can lead the hostages back up this way."

They waited in silence, hearing only the sounds of an alien world at night. Once, they heard footsteps and low voices as two dark elves passed the prison on the other side, heading from the castle to lower in town. The only other sign anyone was awake was the random golden glow from windows, but none were near them. Sounds became more hushed as the fog rose, covering the buildings near them so that couldn't tell what was happening anywhere else, including how far the fog had spread. They had to hope it wasn't localized, or anyone walking by might realize it wasn't natural because it only covered a small area.

Some of the group moved down to wait behind another building on the same level as the prison. Standing beside Ryan, Anna, and the other wizard, Matt watched Eric and Dravo disappear into the fog. He couldn't help looking around repeatedly, as if he would see something, and tried to focus on sound, hearing nothing, which was good. Several tense minutes passed before a short, dark figure began returning. It was Eric, who gestured for them to follow. As they reached the entrance to the prison, Matt stepped inside curiously, finding a small room with no one inside it, a lone hallway extending back into the mountain. To his raised eyebrow, Eric gestured at a closed door to one side and held up two fingers. Apparently, there were two unconscious dark elves over there out of sight.

"Ryan," began Eric, "I'd feel comfortable if you stayed here and guarded the entrance."

"Sure," replied the big man. Matt thought he didn't look comfortable being left behind. Who could blame him?

Dravo motioned Matt over and whispered, "At the end of this hall is a room with as many as ten people. Can you subdue them?"

Matt thought about what spells he had ready for that and made a quick decision, pulling out a pouch and fishing inside for a small marble he finally retrieved. He stepped up to the hallway and put the marble in his palm.

"How far?" he asked. The corridor wasn't lit. Only light from this end and the other filled it, but the flickering glow was faint at the other end and he wasn't sure what he was seeing.

Dravo answered, "Fifty feet."

"Straight?"

"Yes, but the room opens to the left for ten paces. There are several ways to leave that room, and if anyone does, it will be to alert others inside. We control the entrance, but they could reach the hostages before we stop them. They can also ring the bell, and then..."

Feeling like he understood the significance, Matt tried to ignore the pressure. It seemed like a long time ago when doing this or anything in front of others made him nervous. Now he only felt that way because failure meant people getting hurt, a different kind of pressure that made his old fears seem trivial. He shrugged it off, focused his will on the marble, and said the words of magic.

Safely fly through wind and air, burst with force, and strike what's there.

The marble rose above his palm and floated down the hall into growing darkness as he focused on its movement. He only had a general sense of how far it had gone and stared hard for some sign it had emerged into the torchlight at the end. It was too far, and too dark, but he thought it had reached the end. Hoping for the best, he made a hand motion as if to swat something to his left. Someone shouted in elven just as Matt said another word and a percussive blast of air walloped everyone in that room, sending bodies into walls and whatever else was there. While he couldn't see it, he heard the commotion of wooden furniture being overturned and metal falling to the floor. Maybe the noise made that an unwise spell. He nodded at Eric, who sprinted that way with Prince Dravo right behind and Matt following with everyone else.

Nearing the corner, Matt heard struggling and soon saw Eric deliver a kick to a guard's head as Dravo held another dark elf in a headlock that was making the victim lose consciousness. Both scuffles were soon over. Eight bodies lay on the floor, along with two tables and several benches. Anna pushed past him and checked several.

"They're still alive."

"They should be out for a while," Matt remarked, his voice still low. Suddenly he saw movement from a hall to one side. Eric saw his alarm and chased after a dark elf with one of their human guards following. A shout in elven rang out from there, and Dravo grabbed his arm.

"With me." The prince turned toward a stairway leading down and descended with Matt coming as fast as he could, lifting his robe with the hand that didn't hold Soliander's staff. A glance showed Anna coming, too. When they reached the bottom, they saw a dark elf trying to close a metal gate ahead until Dravo threw a knife that struck the bars and bounced off.

"Down!" Matt shouted. He didn't wait for Dravo to dive to the floor as he summoned a torrent of fire that hurtled down the hall from his staff and caused a shriek of pain. He stopped the flames to see two men on fire, the gate still swinging open. Dravo rose as they rushed forward and kicked his way in, their own guards moving to the left and right where other doors led elsewhere. A glance at once showed a water well inside, but then Matt was through the gate ahead, gagging at the burning smell of the two fallen elves. Behind him, Anna stopped to help them. He wondered if that was a good idea, but he also felt bad about what he'd done. The sight of white light surrounding and healing both men made him sigh in relief. As long as they didn't get up again soon and become a problem...

They heard a commotion ahead as the short hall opened into a wide room with several jail cells full of humans, many of whom were rising, sleepy eyed and fearful. The smell told him of their poor condition, the sight of torn clothing, dirty hair, and smudged skin confirming it. No jailers were here, and he counted twenty-two, one short of what they had heard. He wished Ryan was here to do the nice sort of speeches he gave, or even Eric. Fortunately, Anna saved him from having to do it.

"Hello everyone," she said, stepping toward the cells. "We are here to rescue you, but we need you to keep quiet and move quickly but cautiously with us. Do you understand?"

"Yes," said one middle-aged man. "But who are you? Why is a dark elf with you? They cannot be trusted."

"We are the Ellorian Champions, and this is Prince Dravo of Kiarven. He is helping us. We don't really have time to explain more. I need you to trust us."

The man pursed his lips. "You I can trust. Him I cannot."

"Fair enough. You speak for all?"

After a moment, he nodded. "I do."

Steady footsteps behind him made Matt turn to see Eric arriving.

"What's that?" Matt asked.

Eric tossed a thick rope in his hand to the floor. "The rope to the bell. He was about to ring it. I cut off enough to keep anyone from reaching it soon. I checked the other rooms on the way here. We're clear."

"There are more rooms back here," advised Dravo, moving toward them, Eric following. They came back a minute later, indicating that the only dark elf left was the prince. By then, the keys had been found, and the jails opened, the hostages all awakened. Some were just children, but none so small they would have to be carried. Anna crouched down to talk to them as Eric addressed the adults, telling them the basic plan. Anna did a cursory examination of anyone, healing a few of minor issues like dehydration, sores on their feet, and anything else that might inhibit the escape. It seemed they were ready to go.

Matt turned to the rogue. "Eri, um, Andier, why don't you tie up the two I burned?"

"Right."

"Catch up. We'll wait at the exit to the prison."

Within minutes, the group had gathered by Ryan, who looked relieved. He said that no one had come by. Matt and the other wizard, the one from Aker, cast another spell to muffle sounds, and the group left the prison with Eric in the lead. The fog had grown thicker, but the rogue led them right to the awaiting guard, who reported that two more dark elves had walked by minutes ago. Dravo took the lead, because this time they were staying on the streets and not walking behind buildings. They moved with good efficiency and stealth and reached the castle's corner sooner than Matt expected. They went over the crumbling wall back to the path, the wizard belatedly realizing they should have spread the fog here, too. So far, this was going fairly well. But no sooner had he thought it than the prison bell began tolling.

Prince Dravo turned to them and whispered, "Run! Quietly, but run!"

They did as he told them, moving to the path, Eric in the lead, his head turned toward the castle walls. Even if someone saw them there, they likely couldn't be stopped from reaching the portal now. Matt had seen no doors from the castle over here. He stayed at the rear with Ryan, gesturing for others to hurry. They heard shouts inside the castle now, feet charging on the other side of the wall, the bell still ringing. But the group reached the fork back over the gorge and went up the stairs, the healthy helping the women and children. Matt had the impression this was the most exercise they'd had in a long time. Their eyes shone with fear and desperation, but he felt calm as he crossed the bridge with the knight and looked back, everyone else continuing without them.

"I think we made it," he said, feeling excited by the adventure.

"Yeah, but now getting to the king is going to be a bitch."

"Can't argue with that. Go on without me. I need to do something."

"No, staying here to guard you at the least."

"Okay. Thanks." He pulled out the vial from earlier.

"What are you doing?"

"More fog. We need to get back across this bridge in a minute."

"I think we do it now, to be honest. We can do that out of sight at least and the others can catch up."

Matt nodded and glanced back to see Ryan gesturing to Eric where they were going and seeing Eric give a thumbs up. He and the knight went back into the shade of trees and Matt cast the spell from there, trying to speed up the fog's spread by gesturing more often and not sure if that helped any. He made sure it flowed in the other direction that they hadn't been yet—the one Dravo said led to a rear entrance in the castle. The royals who had long ago wanted to use the portal went that way, as did important guests. But any commoners had to go toward the city just like he and the others had just done. Presumably, no one would think to look back here at all.

They waited in silence, correctly assuming the rest of the group would join them once the fog was thick enough, and they did. Now the only ones left were the Ellorians, Prince Dravo, and the other two wizards. At the least, the rescue had been a success, the hostages through the portal and being taken care of in Thiat. But now they had to avert disaster. If they failed, getting King Sondin restored as the quest demanded would take longer.

"What now?" Eric whispered to the dark elf.

"The plan has not changed. We move to where my man waits for me. He may be delayed, however."

Matt frowned at the truth of it. While Dravo had been exiled long ago and many of his men dispersed so they could not operate together in any way, there were still those loyal to him. Some worked in the castle in various positions, and one such dark elf had helped him and his sister leave. They had climbed down a temporary rope ladder near the rear corner tower. Now he and the others would wait for that person to lower it again. He just wouldn't be expecting so many people to climb up. They headed that direction and, to even Dravo's surprise, the ladder was already lowered. He appeared to consider that a moment before ascending alone, pausing near the top to look over the wall. Several minutes passed as they listened to the sounds of activity inside, but virtually all of it was at the castle's front. Lights had appeared in far more windows.

The elf motioned for them to follow and disappeared over the top. Eric went first, then Anna, the other wizards, Matt, and finally Ryan. When Matt reached the top, he found a cart loaded with arrows, bolts, crossbows, and long bows had been left in the way so that he had to get on the wall and move over a few feet before dropping to the walkway. That's when he saw the cart had a broken wheel, preventing it from being moved. He gazed around and saw that the wall was about fifteen feet wide, the walkway they crouched on a few feet below the top. No one could see them unless from above, where his eyes darted to towers, but the fog had risen over the wall to obscure everything.

Dravo turned to them as Ryan finished arriving last. "The broken cart is a ruse, I'm certain. My man put it here so the rope ladder could be here all the time."

"How do you know this?" Eric asked.

"I don't, but it's too coincidental. He is smart. We must go down this tower, now, and head for the king's quarters. He is likely awake, as are far more guards, so we should expect a fight."

"Right. Lead the way."

They made it into the tower and descended the spiral stairs to the ground floor, where they could have stepped out into interior grounds. The fog was nearly absent there, having not seeped over and down the fortifications. Matt hoped they would stay within the castle walls, as they were not solid but hallways full of storage items like barrels and crates, but the prince led them onto the grounds. The castle itself stood not too far away, and they made it to its side wall, creaking open a door to get inside, where it was dark.

"Where do you think the king is now?" Eric asked whispered. "Throne room?"

"No. That's only used for formal moments, on the first floor. He is probably not in bed on the third, given that everyone knows who is in the prison and what the bell means. He will be on the second level, where business is done."

"So up this flight of steps?"

"Yes. There will be two chambers we must get through to reach the main one where he is likely to be. Expect a fight, and we must be quick to prevent them from sealing the other doors, the king inside. Soliander?"

Matt pursed his lips. "I'll be right behind you. See if you can create an opening for me to cast through to the next room."

The prince remarked, "Even if we make into that room, there is a way out the other side."

Eric sighed. "I don't like it. Can we go around and trap him? I feel like we don't have enough people to do that, but we have three wizards."

The prince agreed. "That is my concern as well. However, we have surprise to help us. If you take Soliander around to the other side, and the other wizards come with Korrin and I, this may work, but you risk being discovered."

Eric and Matt exchanged a look, and the wizard shrugged, remarking, "Even if we start fighting over there, and you start doing so over here, they will realize they are surrounded and that can cause confusion. Let's try it."

Dravo measured them with his gaze and then turned to Ryan. "I suggest we purposely make noise to draw them to us."

"Right." The knight didn't look too pleased with the idea.

They agreed to wait a few minutes before ascending, voices being audible above. Eric led the way along the hall that stood against the castle's rear wall, then stopped. Ahead were several guards at the rear exit, the one that likely led to the path toward the portal, though the door appeared to be blocked by more crates and barrels as if no one ever used the rear door. They wouldn't make it past the guards and retreated quickly to the others, telling them the issue.

The prince said, "Go up to the third floor here and use the same hallway there. You will not find the same problem."

Realizing they should have thought of that before, Matt followed Eric up the corner stairs, the same ones the rest would use in a few minutes. They reached the second floor and didn't bother peeking out to see what or who was outside the stairwell, multiple voices chatting idly about the fun they would have hunting the escaped humans if they weren't stuck inside guarding the king. Matt and Eric continued up to the third level, where the royal rooms were. Less noise was here, and they easily made their way to the other side of the castle, and then down the stairs just as the fighting broke out. They heard yelling from there.

"What is going on?" someone bellowed closer to them.

"Your Majesty," said another elf's voice, "we must get you to safety."

"Dravo!" someone yelled farther away.

"Dravo?" King Erods barked. "What is... Did he...? Bring that elf to me now!"

Several men screamed in pain, and Matt assumed one of the other wizards had cast something.

"Your Majesty! They will enter the room any moment!"

Eric peered in, turned back, and smiled. Then he pulled out his short sword and stepped into the room with Matt following, a spell on his lips. In front of them, the king stood facing away, straight white hair down his back from a balding black head, a disheveled red robe covering him. A wide oak table sat before him and on the other side of it stood a tall elf who faced them, sunken cheeks below red eyes that widened, his thin lips parting. He also wore a robe as if having hastily dressed and was apparently some sort of counselor. The rest of the room had chairs along the walls but was empty because whatever guards had been here had rushed to the fight.

"We're already here, King Erods," said Eric, kicking a chair out of the way and raising a sword. The king turned around in outrage that gave way to fear. "Soliander, make sure no one comes behind us."

"Right."

"Who are you?" demanded the king.

"The Ellorian Champions. Two of them, anyway. Don't try anything or I'll stick you with this sword."

The sound of two bodies falling made Matt look across the room, where Ryan and Dravo strode in, followed by Anna and the wizards. He saw Ryan was bleeding from his leg until the knight used his Trinity Ring to heal himself. They could hear yelling beyond them and barred the door against the reinforcements that were on the way. This was the part that the prince had needed them for. Matt knew he and the wizards were the key to keeping a considerable force of dark elves from breaking into this room and killing them all before Dravo's troops could get up here to protect him.

"How did you get in here?" the king demanded of Dravo.

"Why would I tell you that?" the prince asked as he approached. He shoved the table aside, then tore a long piece of cloth off the counselor's robe and ripped it in half. He roughly gagged King Erods and tied his hands behind his back, shoving him into a chair. "I don't have time for pretty speeches. Your hostages are gone. I will be king and I will try you for war crimes."

The counselor said, "But, Dravo, no one will recognize your sovereignty, just as other lands are refusing to acknowledge we control Aker."

The prince turned on him. "I have an arrangement with both Aker and Thiat for exactly that, and enough of our people agree that this war should never have happened that they, too, will support me. We will withdraw from Aker."

The counselor seemed taken aback but accepting of this news. "What of Prince Kammer? He will not agree."

"His opinion won't be needed much longer. Enough of this." He turned to Eric. "The tower bell has spoiled our plan to get my forces up here for protection. We need another plan."

Eric turned to Matt. "How good of an illusion can you do?"

Matt shrugged. "What do you need?"

The rogue smiled, and they got to work so quickly that it made Matt nervous of a mistake being made. The shouts and heavy footsteps of armored dark elves charging up the stairs didn't help. Eric threw open the doors to the room and everyone assumed their positions. It had taken some hair from the dead and living elves and themselves, plus the skills of all three wizards, to create the scene the rogue devised. The dark elves charged into the room to find the bodies of several humans scattered about, King Erods standing with a dagger at the throat of a kneeling and captured Price Dravo, who was the only person whose appearance was not an illusion. A half dozen elven guards appeared to be already in the room, having defeated the intruders and captured others.

"You're a little late!" snapped King Erods. "Next time try not to be asleep when someone is trying to kill me."

The lead elven guard looked aghast and bowed. "Your Majesty, we did not expect–"

"What?" King Erods interrupted. "To be hanged for incompetence? If you want to be useful, bring me every one of those disgusting ogre and goblin leaders from the prince's forces. And bring the biggest and meanest looking of the warriors, too. And their weapons still on them, so they suspect nothing. I'm thinking we'll have a little fun in the courtyard today with these traitors."

The guard nodded and turned on his heel, instructing his men to remain behind until the king barked at him to take them because he had his band of heroes already. He told them to guard the entrance to the castle, and no was allowed up here until the errand was complete. The humiliated guards left and everyone remained in their positions until they heard the sounds of them running across the courtyard.

From his knees, Prince Dravo looked up at the king and rose. "That was a fine performance."

"Thank you," said Ryan, stepping back and pulling the blade away.

"That went better than I expected," said Eric, looking like a dark elf guard. The real guards were all dead on the floor and disguised as humans. The actual king and counselor were among them, bound and gagged, though no one could tell. They talked it over and put into play Dravo's plan to deal with Prince Kammer.

Before leaving Thiat, Dravo had revealed that, while magic portals were rare, the people most likely to have them were royalty, of course, regardless of race. An elven Mirror of Sulinae was on the first floor of the castle and was part of a pair. The Ellorians had used one on Honyn when escaping Castle Darlonon. With King Erods not much interested in travel but recognizing the value of appearing in Aker as its new sovereign, he had made his son bring the other Mirror of Sulinae to Aker. Dravo had suspected they existed but been unsure where they might be.

But he learned the truth after he arrived in Avaran by horseback in the vanguard of his rebel band. The sneering Prince Kammer had made no indications of planning to travel from Aker to Kiarven, as Dravo had just done, and yet Kammer had somehow gotten here before Dravo, who then discovered the Mirror of Sulinae. This meant the other one must be in Aker.

Now the group staged a scene, most of them standing out of sight beside the Mirror of Sulinae. Dravo held a knife to the neck of Ryan, who was still pretending to be King Erods. Matt studied the words on the device. Memories from Soliander helped him understand how ones like this, though the design was slightly different. Everyone indicated they were ready, and he turned it on. The gold frame filled with a dark image that revealed very little. Eric, still looking like a dark elf, snatched a nearby torch from a wall and threw it through, the light from it showing a dark room that still told them little of where the other Mirror of Sulinae stood. They were taking a small gamble that it was near the bedroom of Prince Kammer.

"Kammer!" yelled King Erods in a panic. "Kammer! Help me!"

"Yes!" called Dravo, playing along. "Come watch your father die!"

They kept up the banter a few more moments before the alarmed face of a dark elf appeared in the mirror. He stood barefoot and naked from the waist up. The expression turned to one of outrage and fury.

"Dravo!" the dark elf yelled. "Traitor!"

Dravo pulled the king backwards, trying to create the impression that the king had activated the Mirror of Sulinae before he could be stopped, and now Dravo was dragging him farther away. The real goal was to create room for the expected arrivals.

"Save me!" yelled King Erods, but the face of Kammer disappeared. They heard him hollering for guards, as half-expected. It didn't take long before four armored reinforcements arrived and rushed through the Mirror of Sulinae and into the room, swords swinging. Pretending to be one of Dravo's elves, Eric drew some of them to him, and Dravo let go of King Erods to take on the other two. Matt wondered if Kammer was coming or if they would have to go get him. But then the prince stepped into the room with a wicked sword poised before him, his eyes catching sight of Matt to one side. Even as he turned, Matt spoke a word, and the prince collapsed.

Seeing this, King Erods said, "Stop in the king's name!"

The remaining four intruders hesitated, allowing Eric to slug one of them to the floor and Dravo to disarm another. The last two lowered their swords. It was over.

———— ♦ · ♦ ————

Ryan watched the late afternoon sun fall on the upper half of Castle Rivina with mixed feelings. He was glad to be going home, but the last time they were here, Dravo had tried to kill them. The scene had been among the more unsettling they'd experienced, one that added to a feeling that he and the others needed to make a plan for what to do once summoned. That included the moment of arrival and questions to ask about situations and even details about life. The day here was apparently an hour shorter than on Earth, and they counted the weeks differently. Would they one day arrive somewhere more drastically different?

After capturing Prince Kammer, the group had awaited Dravo's men, a hundred brought into the courtyard in Avaran and soon overtaking the surprised dark elves who had accompanied them. Some fighting had broken out despite Ryan, still pretending to be King Erods, having told the elves to disarm themselves. The order was dubious, and it didn't really surprise anyone that some had disobeyed, but with help from Matt and the other wizards, the castle had come under the command of Dravo, who waited until dawn to crown himself King of Kiarven from the castle walls as much of the city watched. It hadn't been up to the Ellorian Champions to help him secure the city or his kingdom, so they had returned to Thiat with the news.

Even the grumpy King Varrun gave them credit for the mission's success before pointing out that no one from the Kingdom of Thiat had benefitted from any of this so far. The Ellorians still needed to get King Sondin restored to the throne of Aker and out of Thiat. They had ideas on this, but first, they needed rest and slept into early afternoon, when they awoke to learn of various plans made in their absence. To secure peace, King Dravo had agreed to marry a human duchess from Aker. King Sondin was to marry the dark elf Princess Liera, Dravo's sister, who didn't look too pleased.

But her reaction paled to that of Princess Miara. By now, she had learned that the wizard Gian, whom she loved, had reached the Quest Ring at Castle Rivina in Aker a week earlier and summoned the Ellorians, only to be killed by Dravo's forces. Now Dravo's sister was to be Miara's aunt by marriage, and Queen of Aker. The fury had been impressive, and no one had to say aloud that if Miara were to remain in Aker with her brother, no peace would last. King Sondin was to marry his sister to someone in Thiat, to strengthen that bond as well, removing the princess from his kingdom. Miara hadn't exactly calmed with the news.

Prince Kammer was to stand trial in Aker for his war crimes, but Erods was to stay in Kiarven. Ryan wondered how that worked, when someone took over as monarch in a coup and the previous one was still alive, but they didn't have time to question it and it wasn't their problem. He just hoped that the elves didn't rise against King Dravo and do something that required another quest. Once was enough.

None of these marriages had taken place yet when the Ellorians traveled with King Sondin and Princess Liera, plus a few hundred soldiers, to Kiarven via the portal under Thiat. With King Dravo's blessing, all of them then used the Mirror of Sulinae to reach Aker, completing the quest.

As for Ryan and the others, it was time to go home. Rather than returning to Thiat, they would use the other

Quest Ring in Aker, declining any attempt at a banquet or celebration. King Sondin had enough to worry about rebuilding his kingdom anyway, and no real staff set up to do such a thing. He settled for a procession that led them to the half-burned Castle Rivina. He could do nothing to restore it yet, but when they arrived in the room where their battle with Dravo had taken place, there were no bodies. They hadn't been sure what to expect. King Sondin couldn't keep the frown from his face as he surveyed the damage, vowing out loud to have it all restored.

Eric wanted a moment alone with the three of them, so they went to one side of the hall to speak. "The last time we returned to Earth, we aimed for nighttime. But this time, all of us were at Jack's except Anna. It should be midday, and maybe there is enough activity at the hospital that you can lose yourself in it on the way out. It depends on how well that room is being watched."

Ryan said to her, "We know that we always return to where we were, but we aren't sure if anyone else knows that, but I think they do because of you disappearing and reappearing on the highway. Someone may be waiting for you."

Eric looked concerned as he said, "There is probably still a warrant for your arrest. There might be someone in the hospital room you were in, either a patient or police."

Ryan frowned. "Yeah, the *bed* might have someone in it. I hope you don't end up on top of them or something. Not really sure how that works."

Anna asked, "What if something occupies the space we were occupying?"

Matt spoke up. "I know the answer to this from my talks with Lorian. You just get moved over to the nearest space. Most teleport spells have this sort of thing built into them. I think we can assume Soliander was smart enough to do this with the return spell."

"Good point," Eric agreed and turned to Anna. "Listen, regardless of what happens, you need to be ready."

"Yeah, I know," she said irritably.

"I'm not trying to boss you around. Just thinking out loud."

"Yeah, okay. Sorry. It just stresses me out every time we do this."

"I know. I'm sorry, but maybe we can start working on getting those Home Rings set up."

Ryan did not know how they were going to get that done, but it was definitely needed. So was a home base they could stay in and use for training. He wondered if his attorney or Jack had done anything for that in their absence, but it had been just over a day, so probably not. Sometimes it seemed like more time was passing from all the actions they had to take. Quests made for long days.

At least they hadn't been stuck on this planet for weeks, as he'd assumed would happen when he learned of the quest to restore a king to power. He just wanted to feel in control of his life again, but saw no sign of that happening soon. Anna was the more immediate concern this time, just like last time. He thought of something to help her.

"If people are in the room when you arrive," he began, "they will call security. I think you need to run out of there and hide. We can send Jack to get you."

Anna admitted, "Not sure I want to go back."

Eric pursed his lips in commiseration. "It will be okay, Anna."

"Will it?" she asked. "I've killed one of my friends, maimed another, and paralyzed one for life. I hurt several more and destroyed their property. I have all these lawsuits coming. There's an arrest warrant."

Ryan had almost forgotten all of that and put an arm around her, saying he would use his family's lawyers and money to fight everything for her if he could. She did not have to go through this alone or be financially destroyed. There were other problems, of course, but in the back of his mind was the possibility that she could heal those who had been hurt. They hadn't talked about it in a while because he didn't want to pressure her, but he never forgot it.

One day, hopefully soon, she would heal his brother Daniel, who could finally walk again. Anna could heal her friend, and as someone who had been paralyzed herself and knew what it was to walk again because she had been healed, the importance of it had to be apparent to her. Maybe he would talk about it with her soon, but not now. They needed to get home and be safe again, even if for just a little while. Anna, of all people, had felt this taken from her the most.

With the King of Aker waiting for them, along with those gathered to see them leave, the Ellorian Champions gathered inside the Quest Ring, confident it could send them home again even though it wasn't the one that had brought them. That didn't seem to matter, at least according to Matt. If it did, it wouldn't take more than a few hours to get back to Thiat and go home that way. But it worked. The familiar sights and sounds of a quest starting or ending enveloped them as another world disappeared from around them and they found themselves headed for Earth.

CHAPTER SIXTEEN

REUNIONS

Anna braced herself for arrival. She really hated not knowing what awaited her. Leaving Earth was one thing, but being able to relax on the way back would have been nice. At least a car would not hit her this time, although being arrested wasn't great either. Nor was shocking people who might scream and calling all sorts of attention to her. The idea of fleeing in a hospital gown with her butt visible made her smile. She tried to hope for the best as her friends assumed their Earth clothes before her. She felt herself wearing the thin gown, but she had forgotten having both legs and one arm in casts. Then the vortex of light ended.

The hospital room was empty, but the wooden door was wide open. She breathed a sigh of relief but had to grab the wall one with hand to steady herself. How was she supposed to get out of these casts? She felt healed and rested as usual, but walking without bending either leg had her wobbling toward the bathroom to get out of sight. If someone saw her like this, the attention would be immediate. She got inside and closed the door to remain hidden, listening intently. Her familiarity with hospitals meant she knew where to get a cast saw, but she would never make it there, even if she waited until nightfall, because plenty of nurses were still around then.

The guys had to come get her. And find a saw, plus some clothing. It was the only way. She cracked the door, looking for a phone she saw on the wall. A call to them would set that in motion, but they might see her doing it. She wasn't sure where her room was, near a nurse's station or farther away. Anna sighed. She was tiring of this whole thing. The likelihood of getting caught and arrested made her want to just walk out of there and not even bother trying to get away.

Footsteps sounded in the hall and she shrank back as a man and woman began arguing.

"Miss, you can't go in there." A guard. The room was guarded, after all.

"Oh, I'll just be a minute. I wanted to see what the rooms are like." The woman's steps came closer.

"This one is off limits. You'll have to—"

"I'll just be a minute."

More footsteps, this time from both, getting nearer. They had entered the room.

"Miss. Miss!"

"Does this one have a decent view? I so dislike not being able to see out."

"Okay, look, you've seen the—"

"Sleep."

The sound of a body hitting the floor made Anna's eyes widen. Had the woman just cast a spell on the guard? The woman's steps moved away and the room door closed with only a faint sound, but the lock turning made a louder click. Anna backed up as the woman's footsteps approached the bathroom door. There was nowhere to hide if it opened, but the steps stopped just outside it, a shadow visible under the door.

"Anna," said a woman's voice, "it's Eriana."

Relief washed over Anna, and she peeked out to see her smiling savior holding a white plastic bag. An unconscious police officer lay on the floor. She let out a big breath and laughed. "I am so glad to see you right now," she said emphatically.

"The feeling is mutual. Let's get you on the bed and out of that stuff. The officer will be fine and should wake soon, but we'll need to be gone, of course." She helped Anna wobble over to and onto the hospital bed.

"Do you know how to use that thing?" Anna asked on seeing the cast saw in Eriana's purse. She had never felt so happy to see one.

"Sort of. I've been watching videos."

Anna smiled, not reassured by that. "Well, I do. This is the hospital where I work, which means I really need a disguise to get out of here without being recognized."

"I have a hat and sunglasses for you, too."

"Okay."

They slowly cut through the cast on her arm first, and then Anna took over doing the upper part of one leg cast and teaching Eriana how to do the lower part. It took uncomfortably long to get them all off, at which point Anna changed into the undergarments, jeans, and t-shirt. She put her hair in a ponytail and pulled it through a baseball cap, impressed with Eriana's thoughtfulness. Then she donned the glasses she didn't really need and exited the room, which she now learned was toward the end of a hall, making it easier to be undisturbed. The officer was the only one here right now. They went down a stairway just a few steps away.

"You're a real lifesaver," Anna said, her voice full of gratitude, a feeling that was becoming common. That she needed a lot of help wasn't something she was accustomed to, but the devastating nature of her problems blew past any pride she might have felt about going it alone. Self-reliance was great, but she didn't care anymore. Let the help come by the truckloads. She was entirely happy to rely on others and eager to show her appreciation, which made her wonder how to do so for the woman she was so often impersonating now. What was an appropriate thank you gift for healing your paralysis, or knocking out a police officer, or rescuing you from impending jail time? Was a fruit basket not enough? She laughed a little, needing some comic relief even if she had to provide it herself.

Eriana smiled. "That's been the literal truth in my past."

"How did you know I arrived?"

"Hidden camera with motion detection," she said, slipping something tiny into her purse. "They have guarded the room since you disappeared, but I was able to flirt my way inside and plant one. I've been hanging out nearby or in the cafeteria or other waiting rooms since then."

They soon left the hospital by a side door and walked across the parking lot to Eriana's white BMW rental car. As the car started and they buckled up, they saw officers running into the hospital.

"I guess they've seen the guy you put to sleep. Or the casts. Maybe we should've hidden those."

"Maybe." The priestess handed her a red phone. "Why don't you call the others."

"Right." Anna called Eric first, filling him in, then asking her driver, as they headed down the road, "Where are we going?"

"Back to Jack's apartment, as quickly as we dare. I don't want you disappearing from a moving car again."

Anna had no argument against that. Along the way, they discussed the Corethian Amulet, which Eriana had in her purse. She asked Anna to take it out. She did, a weird feeling coming over her at the familiar sight of it. So far, they never saw something on Earth that they had seen on a quest. Though she had just been wearing a copy, seeing it on Earth brought a dose of reality to her. She shuddered, tears springing into her eyes before fading. The strict separation between quests and Earth had just ended for her, and though it had already been obvious that her life had changed forever, something about this brought it crashing in on her. She felt inexplicably lonely, frightened, and like the universe was infinitely bigger than she had known. And she was lost in it.

That reminded her of the trouble awaiting her, but when asked, Eriana said there had been no real developments. The police were obviously looking for her, but no one knew anything, though reports of her disappearance were all over the news despite it not being witnessed.

"Do you know how to create the Home Rings?" she asked. "I know Soliander did most of it, but the guys said you helped with the healing part of the Quest Rings."

Eriana turned off the highway into the even heavier side-street traffic. "I'm afraid I don't know enough, or have the power to make one. I just know what they're supposed to do. I think if we can get the four of you settled somewhere and you don't leave, you will be fine until we can create them. One thing I know is that you need soclarin ore."

That didn't surprise her. "That's interesting. We gave some to Lorian when we were on Honyn." She sighed. "If only we knew how to contact him."

"There are ways to send messages. Matt can look into it and either do it from here or the next time you are on a quest. It would be easier if you're already on Honyn, of course."

Talk soon turned to how to use the amulet, but there wasn't much to it. Anna would need to concentrate her will on it, and her emotions, opening herself to the touch of a god who might help her. The amulet would collect that energy and act as a kind of beacon to the gods of a world, whether she knew their names or anything about them or not. It facilitated an initial contact and all subsequent ones, but that was not all. The amulet helped channel power from that god under certain circumstances, mostly offensive ones, like when she had done things to the undead in Ortham.

For healing, the amulet didn't do that, as Anna's body was the conduit instead. It seemed to make sense to her, and Eriana suggested she try using it here on Earth to contact God for the first time. That seemed like a good idea, but she felt afraid of getting an answer. She still resisted the notion that He was real.

But she needed to get over it. And she wanted to. She had a friend to visit and see about healing because, inadvertently or not, Anna was responsible for what had happened to her. That was a conversation she badly wanted to have but was also afraid to do. And there was the issue of traveling there. There was too much risk to herself. Maybe she could send Eriana to heal Raven, but the real Light Bringer reminded her that even she was not strong enough to do it yet. Anna knew it to be true because Eriana would have healed her. Raven might have to wait.

The same went for Daniel. Ryan hadn't brought up the subject of healing his brother for a while, a fact for which she was grateful. But Anna felt a new appreciation for his guilt in causing the paralysis, a new sympathy and compassion that had made her want to hug him more than once and apologize, not for anything specific, but in case she had ever seemed dismissive or frustrated with his requests to heal Daniel.

She had paralyzed Raven by accident, just like he had done to Daniel. Having been paralyzed, she knew the fear and uncertainty of it. Raven was likely still in that same spiritual place. Daniel was not, having been in a wheelchair most of his life. How would he react to the possibility of being able to walk again? In theory, he would be all for it, but after so much time, there had to be some adjustments he would go through. While she assumed this would be positive, maybe he would resist such a tremendous change to his life.

Jade had lost both legs, and Anna didn't know if she would ever be strong enough with healing to fix damage like that. Even Eriana might not. That Jade would never dance again filled her with a different grief, because all of Jade's ambitions and dreams were about that, and Anna had killed them, probably forever. And even if it wasn't, Jade had no way of knowing that. Anna wasn't sure she could ever face her and the unspeakable loss she had caused.

Worse than all of this was that Heather was dead. She had had little time to come to terms with it, other than those awful hours in the hospital. The strong desire to visit her grave—if she had even been buried yet, and she didn't know—would have to wait. These Home Rings were everything and needed to become top priority. The random summoning was bad enough by itself, but having to be virtually imprisoned in Jack's apartment, or somewhere else, so they would be safe when they returned caused too many problems.

Looking at the phone in her hand as Eriana neared Jack's apartment, she wondered if she should call her parents. Would someone tap the phone? Would an email give away her location? What was happening with any lawsuits or other legal problems? She felt relieved as they parked. Jack hopefully knew these things. She badly needed an update and wasn't even sure where they had left off with any plans to create a home base that wasn't his apartment.

The champions soon reunited with Eriana and Jack being the only other two present. They dialed Ryan's attorney and Daniel for an update and planning session. The first surprise was minor; Eric and Ryan had been on the couch when summoned and had reappeared there, but

Matt had been in the bathroom. Instead of arriving there, he was standing in Jack's kitchen. Anna had also not appeared on the empty hospital bed, but standing a few feet away. She hadn't actually noticed this. They didn't know what it meant, but clearly the return spell wasn't foolproof. Eriana speculated that the blast that had freed the real champions from questing had added some unpredictability to being sent home.

From Quincy, the lawyer, they learned that Heather's parents had filed a wrongful death civil suit against Anna, who just wanted to settle and get it over with. Both Jade and Raven were discussing legal action or their parents were. Ryan and Eriana both pledged to take care of it, financially, so Quincy would represent the matter and make it "go away" as she said. They could handle the other suits for various kinds of other damages the same way. The accidents had involved other cars.

Anna wasn't sure how to feel about all of it, from guilt over what happened to guilt that others were dealing with her problems. And part of her just didn't care, having too many problems as it was. She didn't want to think about it, didn't want to try talking to Heather's parents or anyone else, but she felt she owed it to them and that not doing anything was cowardice. But until they fixed this Home Ring situation, it would have to wait. And if the victims did not understand this, and they likely wouldn't given her inability to tell the truth, there wasn't much she could do about it. More powerlessness made her sigh in frustration and turn her mind to things she could resolve.

Jack and Quincy had moved forward with trying to find a rural estate to set up as a new home base. Jack had visited several for extensive tours with a video camera rolling, knowing they couldn't visit in person without unnecessary risks. One stood out and, while not perfect, would work. The group made a quick decision to gain it, Eriana footing

the three-million-dollar cost and admitting she had to figure out what to tell Paul, but assuring them he would do
what she wanted. Anna couldn't help wondering about that
relationship and what the excuse would be, but Eriana believed it was best to start telling her husband some version
of the truth.

Eriana had been collecting supposed magical items
throughout their marriage, Paul well aware of the collec-
tion that they showed off in their house to wealthy friends.
With the reports of magic and healing working around the
world growing, he would believe that some items were real
after all. With the friends back on Earth now, Eriana was
booking a flight home to have this talk with Paul and, just
as importantly, bring every last one of those items back
here for potential use. She would tell Paul that Ryan and
the others had some items of their own and needed her
help to deal with them, and that the items were causing
them trouble she wanted to help them with. She also intended to bring her private investigator for physical and
digital security at the new estate. Anna felt beyond grateful
for all of it. Maybe soon they would have less to fear while
on Earth.

Daniel revealed that he had purchased tons of additional equipment for them—period appropriate clothes,
crossbows, long and short bows, bolts and arrows, swords
and daggers of every kind, suits of armor, shields, lances
and more, and a small library of books about medieval life
and culture, how kingdoms worked in various parts of
Earth, and a copy of every supposed book about magic,
including ones with spells. Some were about witchcraft,
others about necromancy, and pretty much every variation
on the subject. He had also ordered a ton of ingredients
that were listed as needed for magic, whether or not any of
it was true. They would soon have a lab set up.

On a more mundane level, Daniel was now going to shop for furniture for the estate with Jack. And it was time to buy horses, with Ryan placing an order for the related gear like tack. Eriana knew more about it than anyone but Ryan, who couldn't go, so she would take care of it once she returned, including hiring a barn manager. Ryan already owned the horse he used at RenFest but wanted a few extras, all transported to the new estate once set up. But this was going to take a while. Anna felt relieved to know that everything would progress even in their absence, and the others shared their appreciation aloud. They needed friends like never before.

Despite the return spell refreshing them physically, Anna felt exhausted by the night's end. She needed a mental respite but decided not to join the boys for a streaming movie to get their minds off everything. Eriana left to make preparations, promising to return in the morning and leaving the amulet with Anna, who sat on Jack's bed, where she would spend the night, the guys settling for the floor or couch in the living room. She felt bad about that and wondered which of the three other champions, if not all of them, she should get used to sharing a bed with. She trusted them, so it wasn't like one of them would behave inappropriately sleeping beside her, but she just had too many other things on her mind. And she felt violated, like she had no control or privacy, so she didn't want to give up one minor element of it sooner than she needed to. She knew the guys understood and didn't begrudge the uncomfortable night they would spend, but she felt guilty and was tired of that feeling.

As Anna lay trying to sleep, she had the Corethian Amulet beside her, one hand on it. Closing her eyes, she focused her will and tried to remember the feeling coursing through her when Eriana used the power of God on her. It had felt just like any other deity's touch—firm, gentle, reassuring, powerful, and a little intimidating, as if the god was holding back to avoid hurting the vessel—her. What would the full force of a god's will feel like? She doubted anyone would survive it. Pushing the thought from her mind, she reached out with her senses for long moments, her heart full of a desire to help those she had hurt and the wounded still yet to come. It had always been true of her, since she was a little girl, and led to her interest in medicine. It's just that in the apparent absence of God, she had resorted to other means of helping. Now maybe she had another way.

It took some time, but finally, she felt something, and the first touch of it made her smile. And somehow that made it rush into her so that she chuckled, and then cry at the truth enveloping her. God was out there, and real, and He had answered. A new reality had finally dawned here on Earth, now in Anna, and she let go of the amulet, certain she didn't need it anymore. Not here. The power filling her felt strong enough to do what she needed, and she vowed that in the morning, she would find Raven and undo the damage she had done.

Anna would finally become the Light Bringer.

———◆•◆———

Jack turned away from Eriana to his kitchen sink to resume cutting an apple, having just explained that he'd woken to find the apartment empty of all but him. While they couldn't be certain because he hadn't seen it, both knew that Anna, Ryan, Matt, and Eric were not on Earth, having been summoned once more. Even Jack was feeling frustrated, and it wasn't even happening to him. Eriana had mentioned that the rate of quests was higher than what she and the other real champions had experienced, but their prolonged absence had likely caused a backlog of them to accumulate. Maybe it would slow down after what, a few months? Every time they disappeared, there was a good chance he was never seeing them again.

"Ouch!" Jack yanked his finger away from the knife, expecting the blood that seeped from the wound. Pinching it tight, he ran water over it.

Eriana approached and put a hand on his forearm, her skin warm. "Let me see."

The feel of her hand and motherly instinct made him glad he'd cut himself. There was something very comforting about this woman. A faint hint of perfume added to the feminine air that he sometimes felt was missing from girls his age, most of them wearing jeans or other clothes not far from that of a guy. He knew such attire was more comfortable for them, but he appreciated the way Eriana dressed—long flowing skirts and blouses that bore no resemblance to a man's clothing. Sometimes she had leggings on, like now, but then she had a smaller skirt atop it. He liked her style and had already recognized the signs of his growing interest in her. That they had spent some time alone lately had helped, and she had even seemed receptive to some gentle flirting.

Now Jack pulled his hand from the water and let her take it, the blood flowing more as he stopped squeezing the wound shut. She looked it over a moment and then whispered.

"For a kind soul, please."

Jack's finger tingled and the cut stopping stinging. A soft glow lit the inside as the cut vanished. A slight feeling of bemusement came over him, from the healing touch within him, as small as it was. He wondered how strong that would be if he was more desperately wounded. What had Anna felt? He turned to Erin, their eyes meeting. She pulled her hand from his, but he closed his fingers around it.

"Your touch is wonderful," he confessed.

She smiled. "It's the touch of your god."

"No." He held her gaze. "I felt it long before you did that."

Her smile broadened. "You're sweet."

He bit his lip, recognizing the sound of rejection coming, or so he thought. "I'm sorry. I know that you're married."

She gave his hand a small squeeze. "Where I come from, monogamy is not a thing. Not really." Jack tried to keep a hopeful look from his eyes and opened his mouth, but she laid one finger across his lips. "I honor it here because it is custom and expected, and I have made a promise."

He nodded and pulled his hand away. "Of course. I meant no–"

"A promise my husband made me, and which he has broken more than once."

That surprised him. Her clear eyes showed no sign of pain about her husband's betrayal, but it bothered him and he wanted to say he would not do such a thing. "He should not have."

"And yet he did. And it freed me from honoring the same promise to him, whether he knows that or not."

Startled again, he flushed at the implication, now noticing that her eyes held a smile. Unsure what to say, he murmured, "If you don't mind my saying so, your husband is a fool."

"I know."

Heat rising in his cheeks, he leaned forward when the doorbell rang and she put one hand on his chest, stopping him. "Good things come to those who wait."

Jack inwardly groaned as she turned toward the living room and front door, footsteps moving away. He turned back to the apple and bit into a piece just as he heard her open the front door. Then she gasped.

"Soliander!" Eriana said.

Jack almost choked on the fruit. *Oh my God..* His eyes darted for a way out, even though he knew the wizard stood at the only exit. *What is he doing here? How did he find...? If he hurts her....*

"Eriana?" said a man's voice, sounding confused.

Jack edged toward the kitchen corner, carefully peering around to the front door. Eriana had thrown her arms around a twenty-something year old man in blue jeans and a dark t-shirt, his wavy brown hair touching his shoulders. A pang of jealousy overtook Jack's fear. But neither overpowered his curiosity. He wanted to get out of there, but he wasn't leaving without Eriana, and he had to remain out of sight. Thinking of a security camera he had pointed at the front door from a corner table, he pulled up his phone, brought it online, and set it to start recording, watching via the phone and stepping back without a sound. Eriana had pulled back from Soliander and placed both hands on his cheeks.

"I can't believe it's really you!" she said. "I've been waiting. I've looked. I..." She paused as if to stop herself from gushing.

The wizard repeated, "Eriana? How? You look... older. How could you be...?" They stopped talking and stared silently for several seconds before he asked, "What happened to you?"

She took his hand and pulled him, closing the door, an enormous smile on her face. "It's a long story, but I've been here for about twenty years, Soli. And I just learned in the past few days that only three years have passed on other worlds. That's why you haven't aged nearly as much as me."

"That doesn't make... Wait. Let me think. Morgana. I have suspected that she summoned us to the past."

"I think so, yes."

"So there was already some time period alteration going on."

"I think something about the spell you did with Merlin threw us back to our own time, except I didn't quite make it, it seems."

"Twenty years." He sounded exasperated. "All this time, you've been *here*."

"And now *you* are here. What are you doing here?" Then she seemed to realize something, and the same question in Jack's head came next. "Wait. What *are* you doing here, in this apartment? You didn't know I was here."

He glanced around the room and sighed. "I am looking for these four imposters. Do you know about this? They are pretending to be us."

"Yes. It isn't their fault. They–"

"Are they here?" He stepped past her toward the kitchen but stopped and turned back when she answered.

"No, they were just summoned overnight. Soli, what is going on? Do you know how they became us?"

"They are not *us*," he snapped. She recoiled a bit, and he softened his tone. "They are not the Ellorian Champions. The champions are dead."

Eriana shook her head. "What do you mean? You and I are alive. Have you seen Korrin and Andier?"

"It doesn't matter."

She approached and took his arm in one hand. "Hey, answer me. Have you *seen* them?"

Soliander shook his head. "I have not. No one has."

"Have you looked?"

"I... Yes. You think I would not have looked for all of you? I have searched everywhere that makes any sense, except here, because I couldn't find Earth until recently.

Like it didn't exist. I suppose I should have been searching *when*, too, had I known." He shook his head.

Jack thought that would be impossible, having to research every place at different points in time.

"While I have been here," began Eriana, "where have you been? They tell me no one has seen you either. How can that be? Are you in hiding?"

A moment passed before he asked quietly, "What have they been telling you about me?"

She shook her head. "Things that concern me, frankly. You opened the Dragon Gate and left it that way after all that trouble we went through on Honyn to create and close it. You attacked Lorian and Matt. You cast that mind reading spell on him when it's forbidden."

He turned and stepped away from her. "Nothing is forbidden unless I say it is."

"Soli," she began, but he cut her off, turning back.

"Don't you disapprove of me. No one gets to disapprove of what I do, or how I do it. Not anymore. I will not be *powerless* again like we always were. If I have to cast a supposedly forbidden spell to be free, then so be it. I have done far worse."

She watched him quietly, putting one hand on her heart as he turned away again. "What happened wasn't your fault."

"Are we going to have this argument again?"

"Until I win it, yes," she said lightly, and he shot her a sideways look before sighing. She added, "It's nice to argue with you again, Soli. Really. I'm thrilled to get the chance. But I wish we didn't have things to argue about. I never thought I'd see you again, and I certainly didn't think that if I did, that I would have reasons to believe you've done terrible things. Or that I have reason to be afraid for you. Even afraid *of* you."

He turned toward her, sounded wounded as he replied, "I would never hurt you. You know that."

"The man I knew before would not have."

"He is dead." He said it with no trace of uncertainty.

"Then I have reason to fear you, and to grieve you." When he didn't respond, she asked, "What were you planning to do when I opened that door?"

For an answer, he only said, "I'm a wizard, aren't I?"

Seconds of silence passed before she asked, "Kill or immobilize?"

"I wasn't going to kill them. Not yet, anyway."

Listening, Jack wasn't sure if that was meant to be a joke. The wizard sounded blasé about it, and from what he'd heard from his friends, that seemed like the new Soliander, not the one of the Ellorian Champions. He had changed, and Eriana clearly knew it.

She asked, "What do you want with them?"

"I could ask the same of you."

"You didn't used to be so coy. I liked the direct Soliander."

"No one calls me that anymore."

"What *do* they call you? Are your deeds really so awful that you live under another name?"

"Some would say yes. I would say no. I have killed. I have tortured. I have destroyed entire cities. I have brought kingdoms to ruin. I rule several more and everyone fears me, just as I would have them do. And they do not know me. I do not want them to, out of respect for you." He frowned, and Jack heard bitterness when he spoke again. "I would not drag your memory down with me as Soliander, and there is value in the ruse. None know that the Majestic Magus is now the Arch Wizard Zoran the Devastator, the one who has made everyone afraid to cross him." He seemed caught up in his litany of exploits and hardly noticed Eriana's fallen face until now. Sounding

356 | RANDY ELLEFSON

resigned, he remarked, "You don't really want to know these things."

She sounded angry as she replied, "You might be right. I can't be with a man who does evil things. You know why."

In a low voice, he said, "Do not compare me to your childhood tormentors. I would never... not to you."

"Maybe. Maybe not. You don't seem to realize that you are breaking my heart anyway."

"Eriana," he began as if pained.

"I looked for you. All over this Earth. Anywhere I could think you might be." Her voice grew strained. "You more than the others. I eventually gave up hope, that you were lost and I would never see you again. And now after all this time, I heard there might be hope. I met these replacements for us. And they told me they had seen you, that you had attacked them without justification. I finally found hope again and can hardly believe it. And I just dreaded to find out that it was true, that you had changed in the worst of ways, and here you stand before me confirming all of my fears. I have found you only to find that you are more lost to me than I would have ever imagined you could be."

Imploring Eriana, Soliander said, "I am not *lost* to you."

"Then what were you going to do when I opened that door?"

"I... I was going to capture them. To get information from them. So I could find *you*. I thought them replacing us must have meant something, and there was hope to find you."

"That is the reason?"

"Of course. You have *always* been the only reason for me. You know this. Or have you forgotten in your new life here?"

"Am I the reason you have done terrible things? In the name of finding me? Avenging me?"

"No, that is not what I meant."

"Then what?"

He let out a breath. "Everything I have done since I learned you three were gone, and I was free of those damn quests, has been to make certain that no one ever makes me a prisoner again. I will be free even if I have to destroy a thousand worlds. I have tracked down some of those who helped Everon, and they are dead now. They cannot do anything further to any of us again."

"So it was for all of us?"

"No. No, it was for *me*, Eriana. You have your demons and I have mine. You can tell me as many times as you like that none of this was my fault, that it was just Everon and his band of vengeance seekers who trapped us in the quests, but it will always come back to me. You have never admitted that there is any truth to this."

"I'm sorry for that. I didn't want you to feel responsible. To valida–"

"It was too late!"

"None of us blamed you."

"It doesn't matter. *I* blamed me. If anything, you guys forgiving me just made it worse. Isn't anyone going to hold a grudge?"

"None of us want us to be like the Betrayer. Everon was wrong."

"Yes, I know. All three of you were always more noble than me. We all knew it. And I don't begrudge you for it."

"We were *not* more noble than you. I always knew you felt that way. It's why you always made snide remarks at Korrin. I don't know why you have a hard time admitting that you are a good man."

"Well, I'm not anymore. Isn't that what we're agreeing on here?"

She gestured futility and remarked with a light tone, "I'm mostly hearing us argue, not agree to anything."

He smiled insincerely. "Well, at least we can agree to *that*."

"So what now? The imposters, as you call them, aren't here. They are good people, Soli. They don't deserve what has happened to them any more than we did. Even less."

"Yes, so this is *also* my fault."

She sighed. "That's not where I was going with that. Stop that." He didn't respond, and she continued, "They would answer your questions without an interrogation. They answered mine."

His tone became aggressive. "What did they tell you?"

"That's between me and them."

"I can find out, you know."

She glared at him and softly observed, "If you *ever* cast that spell on me, me never forgiving you will be the least of your problems."

He held still and then laughed under his breath. "You are the only person on a thousand worlds who can get away with threatening me."

"I'm honored. But I think you need to leave."

Soliander shook his head. "Come with me."

"No."

"Eriana, please. I just found you. Do not make me leave this planet without you again. It was an accident last time and I'm certainly not doing it again, especially on purpose."

"I must help them, because you will not."

"They appear to be doing fine from what I've heard."

Eriana shook her head. "They are struggling, especially when they come back. They do not have Home Rings and it is causing very serious problems."

"Well, Matt seems powerful enough to create one. I'm sure they'll solve that problem soon enough."

"I know you are upset about the situation we were in, and yet you are so cold and callous about them being in one that is even worse."

Soliander sighed. "I am tired of ever caring about anyone other than myself, because all it does is cause me pain.
And it is all because I lost you. No matter what you say, it
was my fault. I thought I had *killed* you. Do you understand? Please, at least tell me you understand. All those
years of protecting you, trying to stop this thing, trying to
stop Everon and others from destroying our lives while we
were gone on a quest we didn't want and couldn't protect
anyone we cared about because of it. And at the moment
we're about to finally be free, and we can be together
without fear, I thought I had killed you."

"I'm still alive."

"I didn't know that."

"But now you do."

He made a gesture of futility with one arm. "It's been
years, Eriana. How long was I supposed to keep the hate
from my heart?"

Sounding concerned, she asked, "Is it you that you hate
or everyone else?"

He laughed bitterly. "You always could see right
through me."

"You don't have to hate yourself anymore." She walked
up to him, very close. "I'm not dead, Soli, and it's because
of you that I'm still alive. And free. You deserve credit for
freeing us, not trapping us."

"Are you trying to save me?"

After a pause, Eriana said, "I *am* the Light Bringer."

Soliander put one hand on her arm. "Well, you can't
save me if we're not together, and as you said, I should
leave. Come with me."

"I can't."

"Then I'm sorry."

"For what?"

Somehow, Jack knew the intent and shouted "No!" as
he ran from the kitchen and burst into the living room,

heart pounding, a surge of adrenaline giving him speed. Words of magic reached his ears. Eriana's wide eyes darted from Soliander to him, and she held up one hand to ward off Jack, who suddenly realized his vulnerability. The powerful wizard shot him an icy glare that sent a jolt of fear through him, but he dove for them just as a soft light enveloped the pair. Jack braced for the impact—and passed right through where they were to land hard on the carpet. He turned back frantically, eyes racing over his apartment.

They were gone.

Continue the adventure in *The Silver-Tongued Rogue* (*The Dragon Gate Series, #3*) at https://amzn.to/3ypIWaQ or use the QR code below:

ABOUT THE AUTHOR

Randy Ellefson has written fantasy fiction since his teens and is an avid world builder, having spent three decades creating Llurien, which has its own website. He has a Bachelor of Music in classical guitar but has always been more of a rocker, having released several albums and earned endorsements from music companies. He's a professional software developer and runs a consulting firm in the Washington D.C. suburbs. He loves spending time with his son and daughter when not writing, making music, or playing golf.

Connect with me online

http://www.RandyEllefson.com
http://twitter.com/RandyEllefson
http://facebook.com/RandyEllefsonAuthor

If you like this book, please help others enjoy it.

Lend it. Please share this book with others.
Recommend it. Please recommend it to friends, family, reader groups, and discussion boards
Review it. Please review the book at Goodreads and the vendor where you bought it.

JOIN THE RANDY ELLEFSON NEWSLETTER!

Subscribers receive discounts, exclusive bonus scenes, and the latest promotions and updates! A FREE eBook of *The Ever Fiend (Talon Stormbringer)* is immediately sent to new subscribers!

www.ficiton.randyellefson.com/newsletter

Randy Ellefson Books

Talon Stormbringer

Talon is a sword-wielding adventurer who has been a thief, pirate, knight, king, and more in his far-ranging life.

The Ever Fiend
The Screaming Moragul

www.fiction.randyellefson.com/talonstormbringer

The Dragon Gate Series

Four unqualified Earth friends are magically summoned to complete quests on other worlds, unless they break the cycle – or die trying.

Volume 1: *The Dragon Gate*
Volume 2: *The Light Bringer*
Volume 3: *The Silver-Tongued Rogue*
Volume 4: *The Dragon Slayer*
Volume 5: *The Majestic Magus*

www.fiction.randyellefson.com/dragon-gate-series/

THE ART OF WORLD BUILDING

This is a multi-volume guide for authors, screenwriters, gamers, and hobbyists to build more immersive, believable worlds fans will love.

Volume 1: *Creating Life*
Volume 2: *Creating Places*
Volume 3: *Cultures and Beyond*
Volume 4: *Creating Life: The Podcast Transcripts*
Volume 5: *Creating Places: The Podcast Transcripts*
Volume 6: *Cultures and Beyond: The Podcast Transcripts*
185 Tips on World Building
The Complete Art of World Building
The Art of the World Building Workbook: Fantasy Edition
The Art of the World Building Workbook: Sci-Fi Edition

Visit www.artofworldbuilding.com for details.